PENGUIN CLASSICS

A DOLL'S HOUSE AND OTHER PLAYS

HENRIK IBSEN (1828–1906) is often called 'the Father of Modern Drama'. He was born in the small Norwegian town of Skien and made his debut as a writer with the three-act play *Catilina* (1850). Between 1851 and 1864 he was artistic director and consultant for theatres in Bergen and Christiania (later spelt Kristiania; now Oslo), and contributed strongly to a renewal of Norwegian drama, writing plays such as *The Vikings at Helgeland* (1858), *Love's Comedy* (1862) and *The Pretenders* (1863). In 1864 he left Norway on a state travel stipend and went to Rome with his wife Suzannah. This marked the beginning of what would become a 27-year-long voluntary exile in Italy and Germany. Ibsen experienced a critical and commercial success with the verse drama *Brand* (1866); this was followed by his other great drama in verse, *Peer Gynt* (1867), the prose play *The League of Youth* (1869) and his colossal *Emperor and Galilean* (1873), a 'world-historical play', also in prose. The next decisive turn in Ibsen's career came with *Pillars of the Community* (1877), the beginning of the twelve-play cycle of modern prose plays. Here he turned his attention to contemporary bourgeois life, rejecting verse for good. This cycle would include *A Doll's House* (1879), *Ghosts* (1881), *An Enemy of the People* (1882), *The Wild Duck* (1884), *Rosmersholm* (1886), *The Lady from the Sea* (1888), *Hedda Gabler* (1890), *The Master Builder* (1892), *Little Eyolf* (1894), *John Gabriel Borkman* (1896) and, finally, *When We Dead Awaken* (1899). By the time Ibsen returned to Norway in 1891, he had acquired Europe-wide fame, and his plays soon entered the canons of world literature and drama. Following a series of strokes, he died at home in Kristiania at the age of seventy-eight.

DEBORAH DAWKIN originally trained and worked as an actress and theatre director for ten years. She has worked as a translator from Norwegian to English for ten years in collaboration with Erik Skuggevik and independently, translating novels, short stories, cartoons, poetry and non-fiction. Her translation of Johan Harstad's *Buzz Aldrin, What Happened to You in All the*

Confusion? (2011) was longlisted for the Best Translated Book Award, 2012. With a particular interest in translation history, Deborah currently holds a Collaborative Doctoral Award with University College London and the British Library, researching the life and work of Ibsen translator Michael Meyer.

ERIK SKUGGEVIK has a background in theatre. He has worked as a translator from Norwegian to English for fifteen years. In collaboration with Deborah Dawkin, he has translated novels by Ketil Bjørnstad and Lars Ramslie and, over many years, the cartoon strip *Nemi*, as well as non-fiction works by Ingar Sletten Kolloen and Petter Aaslestad. He has been a lecturer in both Translation Studies and Intercultural Communication at the University of Surrey as well as a Norwegian teacher at University College London and the University of Oslo. He currently lectures in Interpreting Studies at Oslo University College.

TORE REM is Professor of British Literature at the Department of Literature, Area Studies and European Languages, the University of Oslo. He has published extensively on British and Scandinavian nineteenth-century literature and drama, including the books *Dickens, Melodrama and the Parodic Imagination* (2002) and *Henry Gibson/Henrik Ibsen* (2006), as well as on life writing, the history of the book, reception studies and world literature. Rem has been Christensen Visiting Fellow at St Catherine's College, Oxford, was director of the board of the Centre for Ibsen Studies and is a member of the Norwegian Academy of Science and Letters.

HENRIK IBSEN

A Doll's House
and Other Plays

with Pillars of the Community, Ghosts
and An Enemy of the People

Translated by
DEBORAH DAWKIN *and* ERIK SKUGGEVIK

Introduced by
TORE REM

General Editor
TORE REM

PENGUIN BOOKS

PENGUIN CLASSICS

UK | USA | Canada | Ireland | Australia
India | New Zealand | South Africa

Penguin Books is part of the Penguin Random House group of companies
whose addresses can be found at global.penguinrandomhouse.com.

First published in Penguin Classics 2016

020

Published with the support of the Norwegian Ministry of Foreign Affairs.

Set in 10.25/12.25 pt Adobe Sabon
Typeset by Jouve (UK), Milton Keynes
Printed in Great Britain by Clays Ltd, Elcograf S.p.A.

ISBN: 978-0-141-19456-1

www.greenpenguin.co.uk

Contents

Chronology

1828 Henrik Johan Ibsen born to Marichen and Knud Ibsen, a retailer and timber trader, in the town of Skien, 100 km south of Oslo (then Christiania).

1833 Starts school at Skien borgerskole (*borgerskoler* were schools for the bourgeoisie of the towns).

1835 Knud Ibsen is declared bankrupt. The family's property is auctioned off, and they move to the farm Venstøp in the parish of Gjerpen, just east of Skien.

1843 Travels to the coastal town of Grimstad, about 110 km south of Skien, where he is made apprentice in an apothecary's shop.

1846 Hans Jacob Hendrichsen is born to Else Sophie Jensdatter, the apothecary's maid, on 9 October. Ibsen accepts patrimony and is required to pay maintenance for the next fourteen years.

1849 Writes *Catilina*, his first play, as well as poetry, during the winter. Has his first poem, 'I høsten' ('In Autumn'), published in a newspaper at the end of September.

1850 Leaves Grimstad on 12 April, the publication date of *Catilina*. The play is published under the pseudonym Brynjulf Bjarme. Visits his family in Skien for the last time.

Goes to the capital, Christiania, where he sits the national high school exam in the autumn, but fails in arithmetic and Greek.

His first play to be performed, *Kjempehøien* (*The Burial Mound*), is staged at the Christiania Theater on 26 September.

1851 Starts the journal *Manden*, later *Andhrimner*, with friends. The famous violinist Ole Bull hires Ibsen for Det norske

Theater (the Norwegian Theatre), his new venture in Bergen. Ibsen begins as an apprentice, then becomes director and resident playwright. He agrees to write and produce one new play for the theatre every year.

1852 Spends over three months in Copenhagen and Dresden studying Danish and German theatre.

1853 *Sancthansnatten* (*St John's Night*) opens on 2 January, the founding date of Det norske Theater.

1855 *Fru Inger til Østeraad* (*Lady Inger of Ostrat*) performed at Det norske Theater on 2 January.

1856 First real success with *Gildet paa Solhoug* (*The Feast at Solhoug*) at Det norske Theater; the play is subsequently performed at the Christiania Theater and published as a book.

Becomes engaged to Suzannah Daae Thoresen.

1857 *Olaf Liljekrans* premieres at Det norske Theater to a disappointing reception.

Moves to Christiania during the summer and takes up the position of artistic director at the Kristiania Norske Theater (Kristiania Norwegian Theatre) from early September.

First performance outside of Norway when *The Feast at Solhoug* is staged at the Kungliga Dramatiska Theatern (Royal Dramatic Theatre) in Stockholm in November.

1858 Marries Suzannah Thoresen in Bergen on 18 June.

Hærmendene paa Helgeland (*The Vikings at Helgeland*) has its first night at the Kristiania Norske Theater on 24 November and is met with a resoundingly positive response.

1859 A son, Sigurd Ibsen, is born to Suzannah and Henrik Ibsen on 23 December.

Writes the long poem 'Paa Vidderne' ('On the Moors') as a 'New Year's Gift' to the readers of the journal *Illustreret Nyhedsblad*.

1860–61 Ibsen accumulates private debt, owes taxes and is taken to court by creditors. He drinks heavily during this period, and the family has to move a number of times. He is criticized for his choice of repertory at the Kristiania Norske Theater.

His epic poem 'Terje Vigen' appears in *Illustreret Nyhedsblad*.

1862 The theatre goes bankrupt, and Ibsen is without regular employment.

Ethnographic expedition to the West of Norway in summer, collecting fairy tales and stories.

Publishes *Kjærlighedens Komedie* (*Love's Comedy*) in *Illustreret Nyhedsblad*.

1863 Employed as 'artistic consultant' at the Christiania Theater from 1 January and made able to pay off most of his debts. The first, short Ibsen biography published by his friend Paul Botten-Hansen in *Illustreret Nyhedsblad*. Applies for a state stipend in March, but is instead awarded a travel grant of 400 *spesidaler* (in 1870 a male teacher would earn around 250 *spesidaler* a year) for a journey abroad.

Kongs-Emnerne (*The Pretenders*) published in 1,250 copies in October.

1864 *The Pretenders* performed at the Christiania Theater on 17 January. A great success.

Ibsen leaves Norway on 1 April and settles in Rome.

1865 Writes *Brand* in Ariccia.

1866 The verse drama *Brand* is published in 1,250 copies by Ibsen's new publisher Gyldendal in Copenhagen on 15 March, with three more print runs before the end of the year. The play is Ibsen's real breakthrough, helping to secure financial stability.

Given an annual stipend of 400 *spesidaler* by the Norwegian government, plus a new travel grant.

1867 Writes the verse drama *Peer Gynt* on Ischia and in Sorrento. Published in 1,250 copies on 14 November, with a second, larger print run appearing just two weeks later.

1868 At the beginning of October moves to Dresden in Germany, where he lives for the next seven years.

1869 Travels to Stockholm for a Nordic meeting for establishing a common Scandinavian orthography. Publishes *De unges Forbund* (*The League of Youth*) in 2,000 copies on 30 September; the play is performed at the Christiania Theater on 18 October.

Travels from Marseilles to Egypt in October and participates as official guest in the festivities at the opening of the Suez Canal.

1871 *Digte* (*Poems*), his first and only collection of poetry, is published in 4,000 copies on 3 May.

The Danish critic Georg Brandes, the propagator of the so-called 'Modern Breakthrough', comes to Dresden and meets Ibsen for the first time.

1872 Edmund Gosse's article 'Ibsen's New Poems' appears in *The Spectator* in March.

1873 Gosse's 'Henrik Ibsen, the Norwegian Satirist' appears in *The Fortnightly Review* in January.

Travels to Vienna in June, as a member of the jury for fine art at the World Exhibition.

Kejser og Galilæer (*Emperor and Galilean*) published in 4,000 copies on 16 October; there is a new print run of 2,000 copies in December.

Love's Comedy performed at the Christiania Theater on 24 November.

1874 Ibsen and his family in Christiania from July to the end of September, his first visit since leaving Norway in 1864.

1875 *Catilina* published in revised edition to celebrate Ibsen's twenty-fifth anniversary as a writer.

The family moves from Dresden to Munich on 13 April.

1876 *Peer Gynt* receives its first performance at the Christiania Theater, with music composed by Edvard Grieg.

Emperor and Galilean translated by Catherine Ray, Ibsen's first translation into English.

The Vikings at Helgeland premieres at Munich's Hoftheater (Court Theatre) on 10 April, making it the first Ibsen production outside of Scandinavia.

1877 Is made honorary doctor at the University of Uppsala in Sweden in September.

Samfundets støtter (*Pillars of the Community*) is published in 7,000 copies on 11 October and performed at the Danish Odense Teater on 14 November.

1878 Moves to Rome in September.

1879 Travels to Amalfi with his family in July and writes most of his new play, *Et Dukkehjem* (*A Doll's House*), there. Goes on to Sorrento and then Rome in September and moves back to Munich in October.

Edmund Gosse publishes *Studies in the Literature of Northern Europe*, devoting much space to Ibsen.

A Doll's House is published in 8,000 copies on 4 December and receives its premiere at Det Kongelige Theater (the Royal Theatre) in Copenhagen on 21 December.

1880 Ibsen returns to Rome in November.

Quicksands, an adaptation by William Archer of *Pillars of the Community*, at London's Gaiety Theatre, 15 December.

1881 Goes to Sorrento in June and writes most of *Gengangere* (*Ghosts*) there; the play is published in 10,000 copies on 13 December and is met with much harsh criticism, affecting subsequent book sales.

1882 First performance of *Ghosts* takes place in Chicago on 20 May.

Miss Frances Lord translates *A Doll's House* as *Nora*.

En folkefiende (*An Enemy of the People*) published in 10,000 copies on 28 November.

1883 *An Enemy of the People* first staged at the Christiania Theater on 13 January.

1884 *Breaking a Butterfly*, Henry Arthur Jones and Henry Herman's adaptation of *A Doll's House*, premieres at the Prince's Theatre, London, on 3 March.

Vildanden (*The Wild Duck*) is published in 8,000 copies on 11 November.

1885 First performance of *The Wild Duck* at Den Nationale Scene (the National Stage) in Bergen on 9 January.

First performance of *Brand* at the Nya Teatern (New Theatre) in Stockholm on 24 March.

Henrik and Suzannah Ibsen go to Norway in early June. They travel back via Copenhagen at the end of September, and in October settle in Munich again, where they live for the six following years.

Ghosts, translated by Miss Frances Lord, serialized in Britain in the socialist journal *To-Day*.

1886 *Rosmersholm* published in 8,000 copies on 23 November.

1887 A breakthrough in Germany with the production of *Ghosts* at the Residenz-Theater (Residency Theatre) in Berlin on 9 January.

Rosmersholm staged at Den Nationale Scene in Bergen on 17 January.

1888 Ibsen turns sixty. Celebrations in Scandinavia and Germany. Henrik Jæger publishes the first biography in book form.

Fruen fra havet (*The Lady from the Sea*) published in 10,000 copies on 28 November.

Newcastle-based Walter Scott publishes *Pillars of Society, and Other Plays* (it includes *Ghosts* and *An Enemy of the People*) under the editorship of the theatre critic William Archer and with an introduction by Havelock Ellis.

1889 *The Lady from the Sea* premieres both at the Hoftheater in Weimar and at the Christiania Theater on 12 February.

The production of *A Doll's House*, with Janet Achurch as Nora, at the Novelty Theatre in London on 7 June, marks his breakthrough in Britain. This production goes on a world tour.

Pillars of the Community is produced at London's Opera Comique.

1890 André Antoine produces *Ghosts* at the Théâtre Libre (Free Theatre) in Paris, leading to a breakthrough in France.

The Lady from the Sea translated into English by Karl Marx's youngest daughter, Eleanor.

Hedda Gabler published in 10,000 copies in Copenhagen on 16 December, with translations appearing in near-synchronized editions in Berlin, London and Paris.

1891 *Hedda Gabler* receives its first performance at the Residenz-Theater (Residency Theatre) in Munich on 31 January with Ibsen present. Competing English translations by William Archer and Edmund Gosse soon follow.

Several London productions of Ibsen plays, starting with *Rosmersholm* at the Vaudeville Theatre in February. In order to avoid censorship, *Ghosts* is given a private performance by the new Independent Theatre on 13 March, leading to a big public outcry. *Hedda Gabler* is produced under the joint management of Elizabeth Robins and Marion Lea in April, with Robins in the title role, and *The Lady from the Sea* follows in May.

George Bernard Shaw publishes his *The Quintessence of*

Ibsenism, based on his lectures to the Fabian Society in the preceding year.

Henry James publishes 'On the Occasion of *Hedda Gabler*' in *The New Review* in June.

Ibsen returns to Kristiania (as it was now written after the Norwegian spelling review of 1877) on 16 July and settles there for the remainder of his life. This year he befriends the pianist Hildur Andersen, thirty-six years his junior, often considered the model for Hilde Wangel in *The Master Builder*.

1892 *The Vikings at Helgeland* is performed in Moscow on 14 January.

William and Charles Archer translate *Peer Gynt* in a prose version.

Sigurd marries the daughter of Ibsen's colleague and rival Bjørnstjerne Bjørnson.

Bygmester Solness (*The Master Builder*) is published in 10,000 copies on 12 December.

1893 *The Master Builder* is first performed at the Lessing-theater in Berlin on 19 January. It is co-translated by William Archer and Edmund Gosse into English, and premieres at London's Trafalgar Square Theatre on 20 February.

The Opera Comique in London puts on *The Master Builder*, *Hedda Gabler*, *Rosmersholm* and one act from *Brand* between 29 May and 10 June.

An Enemy of the People is produced by Herbert Beerbohm Tree at the Haymarket Theatre on 14 June. Ibsen's first commercial success on the British stage.

F. Anstey (pseudonym for Thomas Anstey Guthrie) writes a series of Ibsen parodies called *Mr Punch's Pocket Ibsen*.

1894 *The Wild Duck* at the Royalty Theatre, London, from 4 May.

Lille Eyolf (*Little Eyolf*) is published in 10,000 copies on 11 December.

Two English verse translations of *Brand*, by C. H. Herford and F. E. Garrett.

1895 *Little Eyolf* is performed at the Deutsches Theater (German Theatre) in Berlin on 12 January.

1896 *Little Eyolf* at the Avenue Theatre in London from 23 November, in a translation by William Archer.

    John Gabriel Borkman is published in 12,000 copies on 15 December.

1897 World premiere of *John Gabriel Borkman* at the Svenska Teatern (Swedish Theatre) and the Suomalainen Teaatteri (Finnish Theatre) on 10 January, both in Helsinki.

1898 Gyldendal in Copenhagen publishes a People's Edition of Ibsen's collected works.

    Ibsen's seventieth birthday is celebrated in Kristiania, Copenhagen and Stockholm, and he receives greetings from all over Europe and North America.

1899 *Når vi døde vågner* (*When We Dead Awaken*), his last play, is published in 12,000 copies on 22 December.

1900 *When We Dead Awaken* is performed at the Hoftheater in Stuttgart on 26 January.

    C. H. Herford translates *Love's Comedy*; William Archer translates *When We Dead Awaken*.

    Ibsen suffers a first stroke in March, and his health deteriorates over the next few years.

    James Joyce's 'Ibsen's New Drama' appears in *The Fortnightly Review* in April.

1903 Imperial Theatre, London, produces *When We Dead Awaken* on 25 January and *The Vikings at Helgeland* on 15 April.

1906 On 23 May Henrik Ibsen dies in his home in Arbins gate 1 in Kristiania.

    The Collected Works of Henrik Ibsen, translated and edited by William Archer, appears in twelve volumes over the next two years.

Introduction

'*The sound of the street door being slammed is heard from below.*'

That famous stage direction, the last words on the last page of a play which in English tends to bear the title of *A Doll's House*, was first read, albeit in Henrik Ibsen's original Dano-Norwegian, in December 1879. Since then it has reverberated throughout the world, from Copenhagen to Canberra, from New York to New Delhi, from Bejing to Bristol.

A Doll's House, in which Nora leaves not only her husband but also her young children, has led to controversial and celebrated productions and received iconic status both as a play and as a central document of female emancipation. It has even been hailed as 'one of the great pages of bourgeois culture: on a par with Kant's word on the Enlightenment, or Mill's on liberty'.[1] And it has, without exaggeration, contributed to change in numerous people's lives and, however directly or indirectly, in societies at large. Ibsen's art somehow continues to affect us, to produce spellbinding and transformative effects, around the world, well over a hundred years since it was first produced.

How did such dramatic innovation occur, and that from Henrik Ibsen, a nineteenth-century Norwegian, someone shaped by a culture and writing for a readership and audience at a great remove from the cultural centres of the world? How did Ibsen end up as 'the Father of Modern Drama'?

The Great Dependant

'Never before has a poet of world-wide fame appealed to his world-wide audience so exclusively in translations.'[2] The theatre critic and translator William Archer's observation, made in 1901, may serve as a reminder of how most readers and spectators encounter Ibsen, whether on page or stage. Coming from a small language culture, Ibsen was to depend on translation from the early point at which his plays began to travel, and he has remained so till this day; his status as world author or world dramatist was from the very beginning aided by the work of others: by translators, critics, publishers, scholars, actors, directors, as well as, inevitably, by new readers and audiences.

Ibsen's plays may thus be seen as poignant examples of one of the most frequently quoted definitions of world literature as 'writing that gains in translation'.[3] Gaining in this respect does not of course mean in every respect or in every instance, and the new meanings created in and through translation are not necessarily better than the first or earlier ones. But since having had his first play translated in 1857, Ibsen has been the recipient of innumerable readings and stagings abroad, often in the form of strong appropriations and radical reuses of the originals, and these have certainly accomplished more than, and different things from, what has been achieved within his native culture. His plays have gained, more generally, simply by reaching audiences to whom he would not otherwise have been available. Translation has been an inescapable part of Ibsen's survival as a classic and has given him his current status of a global phenomenon.

Ibsen, it ought to be added on a general note, reinvented his nation's language; Norwegian (as well as Danish) was not the same after him. And it is impossible, or at least exceedingly difficult, to convey the freshness – including the neologisms and new coinages – the strangeness and poetic qualities of his works. Contrary to widely shared notions of a prosaic realist, Ibsen's plays represent no transparent window to reality or the world; his prose is subtle, complex and self-conscious and has habitually been exposed to a smoothing-out and flattening in English.[4] If we want to confront Ibsen and the 'Ibsenesque' in as much of its richness and complexity as possible, linguistic, aesthetic, historical and cultural, we need at the very least to be conscious of the fact that we are encountering him and it in translation. Starting in a small language, Ibsen is a dependant, always strikingly at the mercy of mediation.

And something is always lost in translation.[5] Take, as a way into this volume of Ibsen's first four so-called modern prose dramas, the titles of the plays. The first one, *Samfundets støtter*, has most often been translated as *The Pillars of Society*. But the key word 'samfund' in Dano-Norwegian (Ibsen's written language was Danish, but he availed himself of many Norwegian words, expressions and constructions) contains the meanings of both 'society' and 'community', with the latter here being more prominent than the former. This is not least so in the play's title, and this edition calls it *Pillars of the Community*. The expression 'et dukkehjem' was a neologism in Dano-Norwegian in Ibsen's time, only, as far as we know, used once before in writing, and it literally means 'a doll home' (the closer equivalent of 'a doll house', 'et dukkehus', was available to Ibsen, and he did not use the genitive form, 'en dukkes hus'; this is not just the doll Nora's house, but a home for dolls). But Ibsen's most famous play is so strongly established as *A Doll's House* in English that we have chosen to retain it here.[6] The next play, *Ghosts*, was called *Gengangere* by Ibsen, and is both more evocative and poetic in the original, literally meaning 'something that or someone who walks again', primarily with reference to a belief in people who return from the dead. It is closer to the French translation *Les Revenants* than to the English *Ghosts*. And, finally, the title of the last of the plays in this volume, *An Enemy of the People*, *En folkefiende*, had a much more novel feel to it when Ibsen first used it in Scandinavia in 1882 than it has today or even than it had when first translated into English. The compound 'folkefiende' had only rarely been used in Danish and Swedish, and then with the more restricted meaning of 'an enemy of democracy'.

The Contemporary Turn

How, then, was Ibsen possible? And why should he be of concern to anyone outside his own country, one which had hardly yet produced a literature of its own when he began writing and publishing in the 1850s? There are, of course, no single or simple answers to such questions. But we may get somewhere by considering where he came from and the contexts in which his art was first created.

When the plays in this volume began to travel through the world from the 1880s onwards, they inevitably triggered questions of relevance. Why should theatre audiences and readers in London, Paris or Berlin feel that these new plays from the continent's periphery applied to them? Why should Americans, Australians and Indians think that this was about them? Many wondered and expressed their puzzlement. A great number of foreign critics began by simply rejecting him as irrelevant, as what they called 'provincial', of no use to the centre and their own understanding of the world.

For quite some time, then, Ibsen was seen as a conspicuously backward writer. 'If Ibsen were an Englishman ... I should say that he was provincial; I should say that he was suburban,' the conservative British critic Frederic Wedmore typically noted.[7] The same critic wondered how such a playwright could claim 'to be a "path-breaker" for our world of Western civilisation if the world he represents lies under conditions from which this Western world has long ago been delivered'.[8] The cosmopolitan American Henry James – who after some initial scepticism became an Ibsen devotee – asked how this 'provincial of provincials' could have produced such captivating art, originating as it did 'too far from Piccadilly and our glorious standards'.[9] To James it was a 'miracle' every time Ibsen produced yet another play of such fascinating quality and attraction. He was struck by the advanced, 'civilized' and 'evolved' form of Ibsen's dramas, seen in relation to the 'bareness and bleakness of his little northern democracy'. Almost every critic or literary mediator who took part in what became a cultural and political battle over Ibsen in Britain in the late 1880s and early

1890s, be he or she what was termed an 'Ibsenite' or an 'Anti-Ibsenite' or something in between, seems to have felt a need to relate to the problem of Ibsen's provincialism, and not just to his foreignness per se.

If we move beyond these inherited narratives and stereotypes, however, Ibsen's Norway was, in certain significant ways, not the backwater imagined by many foreign critics. For one thing, Norway, and Denmark, to which it for cultural purposes still belonged (the union between the two countries had been dissolved in 1814, and Norway had since been in a union with Sweden), were import cultures in literary terms. With an extremely small literary and dramatic output of its own, Norwegian publishing and theatre were dominated by continental impulses. This meant that Ibsen was deeply familiar with the plays and conventions of nineteenth-century European drama. When he entered the profession, Norway had, furthermore, an emerging national theatre movement, one which, through first giving him experience as a theatre director at Det norske Theater (The Norwegian Theatre) in Bergen from the age of twenty-three, gave him an early chance of hands-on experience. Besides this came both a system of state stipends and an extraordinary Scandinavian, or more precisely Dano-Norwegian, book market which developed with Ibsen and helped secure his freedom as a writer. Well before he came to write the plays which appear in this volume, Ibsen was a commercially successful author in his home market, a much-admired writer and poet supported by the state; he had acquired the liberty to focus solely on his drama. In his writing, he redeployed the resources of his culture, which is, of course, not to say that he only operated from within existing norms. His plays were also about responding to a set of contemporary issues which came to be seen as European, if not international, in nature, and they included contestation, conflict and change. In this way Ibsen created something which was to be seen and experienced as new: contemporary tragedies of middle-class life.

An exaggerated emphasis on Ibsen's twenty-seven years of exile from his native country – he left in the spring of 1864, spending his time in Italy and Germany, and only resettled in 1891 – may also have blinded us to the resources available to him at home, resources which must be taken into account if we are to understand his astonishing career. One of these paradoxical resources was the fact that the dominant genre of the nineteenth century, the novel, had not yet come into its own in Norway or Denmark. At the outset of Ibsen's career, the drama was still a respectable option for a Norwegian writer. Contrary to the greatest writing talents in the larger European cultures, Ibsen therefore came to invest his energy and creativity in the renewal of, and, in a European context, the elevation of, the drama.

Over a period of just over twenty years, beginning in 1877 and ending in 1899, Ibsen produced a series of twelve plays which seemed to engage more or less directly with his contemporary world, i.e., with the plight of the middle classes in a capitalist society. His series of modern plays are all written in prose, which was not entirely new for Ibsen. He had tried it on contemporary material already in *The League of Youth* (1869), but then in the form of satire or prose comedy. And in what he intended to be his 'main work' ('hovedværk'),[10] his colossal drama of ideas set in Ancient Rome, *Emperor and Galilean* (1873), he had chosen to reject verse as the appropriate form for contemporary drama. The illusion which he wanted to produce was that of 'the real', Ibsen noted.[11] 'We no longer live in the age of Shakespeare', he added, explaining that he had wanted to portray 'human beings'. It had thus been necessary to reject the 'language of the gods'. *Emperor and Galilean* was to be a new kind of tragedy, the playwright insisted, although he had still concerned himself with an emperor.

The Norwegian context was still crucial to Ibsen's development, in the midst of his self-imposed exile: his fellow Norwegian and long-term rival, Bjørnstjerne Bjørnson, had started writing prose plays with contemporary topics two years earlier (*A Bankruptcy*, 1875), and this is likely to have influenced a change of direction. Georg Brandes, the influential Danish critic associated with the so-called 'Modern Breakthrough' in Scandinavia, had hailed these plays as finally heralding the introduction of a new era, that of 'the now and

reality'.[12] Ibsen must also, more generally, have registered a
'social turn' in contemporary debates, one which meant a new
interest in social issues, not just poverty or 'the labour question', but also the family and the 'the woman question'. But
form was clearly central to his new vision, as was, when he
came to *A Doll's House*, his eye for dramatic potential and
conflict. When the playwright in 1883, ten years after *Emperor
and Galilean*, looked back on his own choice of prose, he
stressed 'the much more *difficult* art of writing a consistently
truthful language of reality'.[13] These statements are also true
of the plays which followed from 1877, but with one important
difference: Ibsen shifts his attention to the here and now.

Ibsen's plays were no longer to treat of topics from his
nation's distant past or of a classical subject matter. Nor do
they concern themselves with the aristocracy or nobility. Not
only does the playwright turn his attention to contemporary
society, while creating his own artistic mythology; he decides
to scrutinize the life of a particular, emerging class. 'No other
writer', Franco Moretti asserts, 'has focused so single-mindedly
on the bourgeois world'.[14] Workers are hardly present in
Ibsen's twenty-year-long experiment, Moretti notes, because
the ambition is to explore conflicts 'internal to the bourgeoisie
itself'. The wrongdoings perpetrated within these plays char-
acteristically inhabit 'an elusive grey area', an area of 'reticence,
disloyalty, slander, negligence, half truths'. It is this grey area
Ibsen explores with such painstaking attention; it is within this
grey area that the characters of his play operate. While a number
of Ibsen's central characters, and perhaps also the playwright
himself, may seem to entertain dreams of absolute freedom
and truth, such ideals are never achieved. Ibsen is one of the
great chroniclers of such greyness, of muddle and untidiness,
of the less than perfect, of everyday life.

Pillars of the Community

The first play in this volume begins by thematizing the back-
wardness of Norway. In the very first scene of *Pillars of the
Community*, Rørlund, the schoolmaster, dismisses all 'these

larger societies and communities' (the original word is 'samfund') as 'whited sepulchres'. 'Out there' is immorality, the
subversion of family values, general rottenness and corruption.
At home the task is to 'close the door' to the outside world.
Rørlund goes on to suggest to his lady friends that they 'shut
ourselves off a little from this', and then draws the curtains.
But already at the end of this act the exiled Lona Hessel has
arrived from America with a declared intention of letting in
'some fresh air'. So she goes on to do, and that in a number of
ways. But it is hard not to think of this line as also representing
Ibsen's poetics, part of what he wants to achieve with the play
and, perhaps, more generally, by opening up the territory of
his chosen art form, the drama. And while he clearly began by
wanting to expose his fellow countrymen's insularity, his
works soon came to appear as acutely relevant to others than
the original audience. Among other things they seemed to
question any kind of self-satisfied position, any contentedness
with the status quo, the lack of ability to adopt other perspectives than one's own. From a two-way movement, then,
between home and abroad, periphery and centre, indoors and
outdoors, smugness and openness, stems much of the dynamic
of *Pillars of the Community*, as well as some of its central concerns. And these are issues that continue to be explored, albeit
in ever new ways, through both radical and subtle changes in
perspective, throughout the remainder of Ibsen's plays.

Samfundets støtter, *Pillars of the Community*, was published in Copenhagen (Ibsen had opted for the Danish publisher
Gyldendal since the publication of *Brand* (1866), and had,
from this point onwards, reached a substantially larger readership and obtained greater financial security) on 11 October
1877. By this time, Ibsen had already made something of a
name for himself in Germany. An authorized German edition
was rushed out in November 1877, but – the playwright's
copyright not being protected – it was followed by two un-
authorized translations within the next two months. The sales
at home also exceeded expectations, and the first edition of
7,000 copies sold out within days. From about this time
onwards, Ibsen insisted that book publication would precede

first performances, and these followed in Denmark, Norway and Sweden in November and December. In Germany, the play's success in the theatres was phenomenal; in early February 1878 it was played in five different Berlin theatres at the same time, and had been produced by twenty-six other German theatres by the end of the year.

Ibsen should, in other words, not be thought of as a marginalized or avant-garde writer at this point. He was established as one of the leading writers in Norway as well as in Denmark, and was a commercial success in both Scandinavia and Germany.[15] In Britain the play's fate was somewhat different. The critic who later went on to become Ibsen's main translator and most important mediator, William Archer, managed to have it produced in adapted form in December 1880 in London, under the title *Quicksands*, but without success. The play did not appear in book form in English until 1888, but then as the lead play in Ibsen's first English-language publishing success, *The Pillars of Society, and Other Plays* (which included *Ghosts* and *An Enemy of the People*), edited by Archer and with an introduction by the social reformer, physician and psychologist Havelock Ellis. The year after, the theatre columnist of *The Sunday Times* ironically admitted that the play 'may excite Scandinavian audiences', while noting the absolute need of adaption to 'English theatrical conditions', unless *The Pillars of Society* become 'the pillows of society'.[16]

The play's proper title is a metaphor and, it becomes clear, a delusion. The pillars of society, and not least this society's main pillar, Consul Bernick, are, by the end, shown to be less than solid, not least as 'moral support'. The action takes place in Bernick's house in 'a moderately small Norwegian coastal town', and it is from this place that the movement between 'out there' and 'at home' is activated. What sets the plot in this well-made and fairly conventional four-act play in motion is the return from 'out there', that is America, of Lona Hessel and her half-brother Johan Tønnesen. These two arrive back in a small community which is just on the verge of radical change, through the arrival of the railway. The consul's behaviour in relation to his community, as well as an episode from his and Johan's shared past, drive the plot on. Slowly, as much through action as through talk, the murky past and the morally dubious behaviour of Bernick are revealed, and his and his class's questionable, paternalistic concern for their local community is exposed.

Ibsen's satire in *Pillars* is fierce, and it may be interpreted as the exile's perspective on his native Norway, the writer at this point having lived abroad, in Italy and Germany, for thirteen years. But it is also, and perhaps more interestingly, critical of simple oppositions between us and them. In the end, the world at home is not quite so ideal, nor the world out there perhaps quite so corrupt, as Rørlund would have us believe. The issue of provincialism, then, was being explored by Ibsen in his art; quite apart from being an important and perhaps inescapable feature of his own early reception abroad.

In the play Ibsen explores the function of lying and the costs of truth in bourgeois society, as well as showing how many may have reasons to long for a different social contract, one based on truth, freedom and equality. 'And you call yourselves the pillars of the community', a shocked Lona Hessel exclaims. But the play should not be reduced to a simple or symmetrical opposition of truth against lies; it is rather, as Inga-Stina Ewbank has suggested, a more 'arabesque-like enquiry into why we say what we say'.[17] In spite of the play's conciliatory ending, with the consul's response to the wonderfully ironic procession in his honour, it is hardly clear that he has passed the moral tests he has been exposed to through the plot's various twists and turns. While there is a real leap between this and Ibsen's next play in terms of its radicalism, we may nevertheless ask whether we should trust the reformist conclusion of this play or consider it ironic.[18] Long before we get to this point, something more fundamental than an individual consul's conversion has in any case been shown to be at stake, and it is worth noting that Bernick's final declaration echoes Rørlund's parodic speech in which he proclaims the coming of 'a new age', one of truth. It is far from clear how far Bernick's transformation goes.[19]

The title's term 'samfund' comes up in a great number of

different contexts throughout the play, and is contested from the very beginning. 'My community is not the consul's community', pronounces Aune, the shipwright, in the play's first scene. Nor is this community, importantly, a community for women. Hilmar Tønnesen scoffs at the conservative Rørlund's reading matter, *Woman as Servant to the Community*, and Lona Hessel not only articulates a demand for change, she embodies it by simply behaving as men's equal. She does not understand the notions of 'duty' which are being imposed on her, and claims that she lives in a society in which women are invisible: 'you don't see women'. In a number of respects, Lona prefigures 'The New Woman', the controversial ideal of the educated, fiercely self-sufficient woman that emerged in the 1880s and '90s. With her it is as if we are hearing a new voice, the voice of a woman speaking up for herself and rejecting the roles imposed upon her by society. That is a voice that famously comes into its own in Ibsen's next play.

A Doll's House

Ibsen's earliest notes for *Pillars of the Community* indicate that he had planned to make the position of woman in a man's world of business the central concern, even if other themes in the end became more prominent. In his working notes for his next play, he went further, observing that 'a woman cannot be herself in today's society', since this was exclusively male.[20] 'There are two kinds of moral law, two kinds of conscience,' he added, drawing on essentialist notions of the relationship between the genders, 'one in man and a completely different one in woman'.[21] Men not only wrote the laws, Ibsen remarked, but they acted as both prosecutors and judges.

In addition to these early ideas there is, more specifically, no doubt that Ibsen had been inspired by the example of the author Laura Petersen Kieler, an acquaintance whom he may be said to have mentored, even calling her his 'skylark'.[22] Hoping to help heal her husband's tuberculosis, Kieler had secretly borrowed money in order to finance a trip to Italy and, while not in the end committing it, later entered into forgery when she struggled to repay the loan. Importantly, however, the similarities between Laura and Nora stop there. While Kieler's husband had her locked up in a mental hospital and managed to gain custody over their children, before, two years later, letting her back into the family, Ibsen's Nora has recourse to another solution: she rebels.

While not his greatest play in aesthetic terms, *A Doll's House* is Ibsen's greatest international achievement. Nora can, moreover, be counted among the most significant female characters in world drama, along with Antigone, Medea and Juliet.[23] How can such an astounding and durable success be accounted for? The theatre historian Julie Holledge identifies three key factors which most often come up in response to this question. The first is aesthetic innovation, with the play being seen as introducing a new form of psychological realism in the theatre, not least in its representation of female characters. The second is Nora's iconic status in women's struggle for subjective freedom, and the third the special connection created between the audience and the play's lead character. One of the reasons behind Ibsen's phenomenal success in the theatre is no doubt related to his appeal within the profession, and particularly to actresses.

When he wrote to his Danish publisher three months before the play's publication, Ibsen claimed that the play would 'touch on problems, which must be called particularly topical'.[24] The title *Et Dukkehjem* creates the impression that we, as readers and spectators, are invited to peer into a home where human beings, and women in particular, are, metaphorically, reduced to dolls. There is a contraction here of the larger social world we have witnessed in *Pillars of the Community*, and the action takes place over only a few days, showing Nora Helmer's transformation from doll to independent woman.

A Doll's House has no genre designation other than 'A Play in Three Acts', though Ibsen had referred to it as 'the tragedy of contemporary life' ('nutids-tragedien', literally 'the tragedy of the now') in his notes.[25] The play was published in Copenhagen on 4 December 1879, and the first edition of 8,000 copies sold out almost immediately. *A Doll's House* in fact had a relatively positive first reception in Norway, and Ibsen was almost universally praised for the play's formal features, even if some queried its ideas. The reviews were followed, however, by a more heated debate on Nora's choice, supposed immorality and on gender roles more generally.

So what does Nora in the end react or rebel against? Torvald Helmer is a lawyer who, when the play begins, has finally achieved financial security as director of the local bank. After years of illness and financial struggle, a new life seems to open up for his family of five. The first act gives us an irresponsible and rather lightheaded Nora, a product of a patronizing and protective husband and, before that, we later learn, a similarly minded father, who has treated her as his 'doll child'. The power of naming, as well as the power to make laws and establish norms, the play suggests, is a male form of power. Torvald's use of a variety of pet names for her, such as 'squirrel' and 'song-lark', is one of the ways in which the relationship is performed. In the first act it is already hinted that Nora has taken on responsibility, however, if in a misguided way, and that there are other sides to her than those which she displays in her husband's presence. When she understands that what she sees as her own brave action is not exempt from punishment by the legal system, she observes that this must be a 'bad law'. The statement is on one level naive; on another level it is an indictment on how the law more generally regards women in her society. As the plot gradually unravels and the tension builds, Nora matures, so rapidly that it has always represented an artistic challenge to the actress playing the lead role.

The tarantella dance at the end of Act Two is a key scene, one which is equally characterized by authenticity and theatricality, in which the other and new Nora surfaces.[26] She dances, her husband observes, 'as if your life depended on it', and when he later, in Act Three, considers her performance, he notes that there may have been something just a little 'over-natural' about it. At this stage Nora decides to throw off her 'masquerade costume' and utters the now famous words: 'you and I have a lot to talk about'. The ensuing conversation not only demonstrates her quest for autonomy and freedom, and Torvald's inadequate responses to her arguments and demands, it also shows how deeply connected her unhappy situation is with society's regulation of the relationship between the sexes. I am 'first and foremost a human being' (often, in ideologically significant ways, mistranslated as 'individual' in English), Nora asserts, and her strong conviction that her womanhood, and the expectations invested in that womanhood, are secondary strengthens her resolve to make a radical choice: a break with both husband and – with necessity, due to her legal position – her children:

> HELMER: Leave your home, your husband and your children! And you haven't a thought for what people will say.
> NORA: I can't take that into consideration. I just know that it'll be necessary for me.
> HELMER: Oh, this is outrageous. You can abandon your most sacred duties, just like that?
> NORA: What, then, do you count as my most sacred duties?
> HELMER: And I really need to tell you that! Aren't they the duties to your husband and your children?
> NORA: I have other equally sacred duties.
> HELMER: You do not. What duties could *they* be?
> NORA: The duties to myself.

Nora's existential choice seems to be forced upon her by society. But in adopting her husband's and society's language, so often used to contain and control women, she now speaks of her 'duties' towards herself, even 'sacred' ones. For some early Ibsen critics this meant that the play was 'all self, self, self!'; for others, such as the feminists who gathered to watch the first proper London production of the play, it represented 'either the end of the world or the beginning of a new world for women'.[27]

One of the recurring issues in the criticism of *A Doll's House* is whether it is a play about the emancipation of women or about human freedom more generally. From a gender perspective, Toril Moi notes, the play's key sentence is precisely Nora's insistence that she is first and foremost a human being.[28] In a radical refusal to stick to inherited notions of women's role in family and society, Nora rejects the other identities available to her, both as 'doll' and as self-sacrificing 'wife and mother', and the play captures a historical transition of women moving from a status of 'generic family member' to becoming 'individuals'.[29] It is also, it may be added, a rejection of Torvald's 'pet names' for her.

How can the fact of two people living together (the 'samliv' of the original) become a true marriage, Nora wonders. If *A Doll's House* is nothing less than 'a revolutionary reconsideration of the very meaning of love', it is because it articulates new demands on the institution of marriage, as one between equals.[30] And these demands originate in the situation of a particular individual, a woman. In spite of Ibsen's early ideas about certain essential differences between man and woman, as expressed in his notes, the play itself effectively breaks with the notion of 'separate spheres'.[31] And it finds its dramatic material in the tension between 'difference' and 'equality'. While at first seemingly basing his claim for equality on difference, in the end the play may seem to stress sameness. But it is not quite as simple as this, and Ibsen refused to give an answer. Does Nora want to be an 'individual' in Helmer's sense? Her situation and longings can of course be generalized or shared by other human beings, but historically the performance of this play, it may be worth remembering, has 'depend[ed] on a *female* body'.[32] Sameness and difference continue to play themselves out as an unresolved paradox, and this tension is part of the continued attraction of *A Doll's House*.

Variations on the key term 'vidunderlig' occur throughout *A Doll's House* and are central to the play's conclusion. In a fashion typical of Ibsen's language, these central clusters of words expand and gather weight through being used in a number of different contexts, here, from the play's beginning, with reference to material well-being and then to Nora's romantic fictions.[33] The term is close to 'wonderful', but stronger, and while 'the miracle' contains too powerfully religious connotations, this translation has opted for the somewhat weaker adjectival forms, such as 'the miraculous' and 'the miraculous thing'. At the end of the play, something larger than a carefree material life or romantic love is shown to be at stake, something relating to a new, shared consciousness of mutuality.

The custom on the Victorian stage was to subject foreign drama, which was primarily imported from Paris, to thorough domestication. Characters, plots, cultural and moral codes were anglicized. Upon his arrival in the English-speaking world, Ibsen was initially exposed to the same treatment. In the soppy 1884 London adaptation of *A Doll's House*, called *Breaking a Butterfly*, the Torvald Helmer figure (renamed Goddard) takes the blame for his wife's forgery upon himself and forgives her (Flora or 'Flossie') in an intensely patronizing way. Towards the end of the play she proclaims that her husband has shown himself to be 'a thousand times too good for me', and in his last line, as he burns the compromising, forged note, Goddard can happily observe that 'Nothing has happened, except that Flossie was a child yesterday: to-day she is a woman.'[34] And no one leaves; the status quo is re-established.

It is difficult to get further away from the original, and it took five more years until the play was successfully performed in English, and in a more faithful version. This was the famous Novelty Theatre production, which premiered in London on 7 June 1889 and then went on a tour to Australia and New Zealand. The play's theme and supposed message led to heated debate, but even the most conservative critics did not deny its effect on stage, or how it provided the leading actress, Janet Achurch, with a great role. The fact that a contemporary foreign playwright was treated with such respect, rather than being freely adapted and domesticated, was in itself striking. 'Word for word Mr. Archer has faithfully translated the original play and not allowed one suggestion, however objectionable, to be glossed over,' the conservative critic of the *Daily Telegraph*, Clement Scott, remarked.[35] In a small way, this production also pointed towards more realistic staging and acting conventions in the Victorian theatre. The Novelty production made Ibsen's name in Britain. On 1 July 1889 William Archer would note that 'Ibsen has for the past month been the most famous man in the English literary world.'[36]

George Bernard Shaw, socialist and early 'Ibsenite', saw *A*

Doll's House as a radical turning point, and claimed that its crucial 'new technical feature' was 'the discussion'.[37] Until a certain point in the last act, Shaw noted in his polemical pamphlet *The Quintessence of Ibsenism* (1891), *A Doll's House* might, if a few lines were excised, be turned into a conventional French play with its secrets, devices such as the letter box and sudden turns in the plot. But at that crucial moment the heroine 'stops her emotional acting and says: "We must sit down and discuss all this that has been happening between us."' Here, Shaw claimed, this play founded 'a new school of dramatic art'.[38]

Many contemporary critics found this move fundamentally untheatrical, however, due to its lack of dramatic action, and later writers on the drama have also characterized Ibsen's form as novelistic.[39] It was not only a matter of a new and more complex psychology which broke with the old dramaturgy of stock characters and clear, easily recognizable gestures and emotions. Ibsen's 'retrospective technique', in which many of the most significant events have taken place before the play begins, and are only gradually revealed, is even more prominent in the next play, *Ghosts*. This technique had its antecedents in Greek tragedy and Sophocles in particular, but what was new was Ibsen's reactivation of it at a new juncture in history, at a different point in the development of the genre.

The final slamming of the street door remains one of the most famous endings in the history of Western theatre and it may, as much as Shaw's favoured 'discussion', symbolically represent the beginning of modern drama. But this ending, including the expressed longing for the 'miraculous thing', is, importantly, one without definite closure. From the first publication of *A Doll's House* the play has engendered alternative endings, sequels, prequels, adaptations, parodies and new artistic responses of all kinds, like few other plays in the canon. *A Doll's House* has, more generally, proved itself astonishingly adaptable to new contexts; it still seems to contain stories that need to be told.

Ghosts

A Doll's House was seen as a strong challenge to society's gender and family norms. But it was his next play, which Ibsen finished during the autumn of 1881, which he ended up calling 'A Family Drama'. After the reception of *A Doll's House*, Ibsen, so often the master of reinvention, set himself a new task. *Ghosts* can be read as an exploration of what would have happened if Nora had chosen to stay, although the play should not, of course, be reduced to this. Mrs Alving is a woman who, we learn, left her husband after a year of marriage, but was subsequently persuaded to return. This episode and this choice come back to haunt her.

The setting is Mrs Alving's estate by a 'large fjord in West Norway', and the scene is one of rain, fog and general greyness. As with *Pillars of the Community* and *A Doll's House*, the movement is again one between an enclosed space and another, larger and freer one, outdoors or elsewhere. In Mrs Alving's son Osvald's case this elsewhere is Paris.[40] But the movement is also, and perhaps more significantly, between different times, between a now and various thens; the ghosts ('Gengangere') of the play are reminders of the fact that the now is full of continuities, of different pasts that collide in violent and sometimes shocking ways in the present. In its slow, retrospective unravelling of the past, the play concerns itself with such issues as heredity, memory, causality and history, quite apart from Ibsen's familiar explorations of truth and freedom.

Ghosts was Ibsen's greatest *succès de scandale* and helped place him as a central figure of the European avant-garde. Thematizing, among other subjects, divorce, venereal disease, prostitution, incest and euthanasia, the play was bound to challenge not only the dominant aesthetic idealism of the time, but also various forms of censorship, official and unofficial. *Ghosts* became a central play for the new, independent theatre movement in Europe in the 1880s and '90s.

Within the play, a battle of ideas, ideals, beliefs and conventions is being played out between Mrs Alving and Pastor

Manders. Like Nora, albeit belatedly and too late, Mrs Alving claims that she has to work her way 'out to freedom'. The idea of her son Osvald having inherited his father's disease functions as an image, as one of several manifestations of the past in the present, of the things that come back to haunt the characters. In Mrs Alving's definition of 'ghosts' or the 'ghost-like' ('gengangeragtige') in the second act, these are not just matters of inheritance from mother and father, but also of all sorts of dead ideas and beliefs. This general idea of inheritance is one that overrides what we now know are incorrect facts – the hints that syphilis, although it is never mentioned explicitly in the play, is being passed down from father to son – which Ibsen employs to such dramatic and philosophical effects. We are so 'wretchedly frightened of the light, all of us', Mrs Alving concludes. The word 'lysrædd' is one of the Dano-Norwegian compounds that tend to defy translation, but it also belongs to a group of Ibsenian neologisms which draw particular attention to themselves in the original. These coinages are not common colloquial expressions; they are more than 'the sum of the two words yoked together', and create a new unit, 'much like the two halves of a metaphor'.[41] To be 'mørkerædd' is to be afraid of the dark, a common enough ailment and expression. But on this model Ibsen coins 'lysrædd', afraid of the light. Another central compound in the original is 'livsglæden', the joy of life, and at the end of the play Osvald, against his mother's expressed wish – in a futile, utopian gesture – asks for the sun, having long since noted that the 'joy of life' is not really known here, at home.

The official date of publication of *Ghosts* was 13 December 1881, and a stoical Ibsen anticipated violent reactions. If the play did not create an uproar, it would not have been necessary to write it, he told his Danish publisher.[42] As the author had predicted, *Ghosts* created a sensation. It was deemed not just to be deeply immoral, but also to break with established aesthetic norms, and the main Scandinavian theatres refused to stage it. At the beginning of 1882, Ibsen, who began to worry about book sales, wrote to the Danish author and theatre critic Sophus Schandorph, pointing out that he was not responsible for the opinions uttered by the characters of the play. In no other of his plays had the author been 'so completely absent' as in this last one.[43] In fact, not 'a single opinion, not a single utterance' could be attributed to the author, Ibsen claimed. 'I took great care in avoiding that.'

When the play was given its first British performance, ten years later, on 13 March 1891, the shock effect of *Ghosts* had certainly not worn out. The production staged by the Independent Theatre, which avoided the censor's interference by formally organizing itself as a private club, has been called the 'most sensational of all nineteenth-century premières'.[44] The editorial of the country's biggest newspaper, the *Daily Telegraph*, did what it could to appeal to the theatre censor, the Lord Chamberlain's Office. *Ghosts* was simple 'in the sense of an open drain; of a loathsome sore unbandaged; of a dirty act done publicly; or of a lazar-house with all its doors and windows open'.[45] This was not art. Rather than being an 'Æschylus of the North', Ibsen was like 'one of his own Norwegian ravens' hungry for 'decayed flesh'. The ensuing debate led to well over 500 newspaper and journal items on Ibsen. When William Archer in an article called 'Ghosts and Gibberings' listed some of the abuse levelled at the Norwegian playwright, it became an effective piece of polemic, causing embarrassment to at least some of Ibsen's most intemperate critics.[46] But it was not until 1913 that the play was given a licence by the censor, and then after considerable debate within the Lord Chamberlain's Office.

For a long time, *Ghosts* continued to be associated with scandal, and twenty years after its publication it stopped the ageing Ibsen from being awarded the Nobel Prize in Literature. The statutes of the prize, established in 1901, demanded that it go to the person who had produced the most excellent work 'in an idealist direction'.[47] Considering his candidature in 1902, the Swedish Academy found that Ibsen was simply too enigmatic and negative.

An Enemy of the People

In the later part of his career, Ibsen got into the habit of publishing a new play every other year. One of the unusual things about his next play, *En folkefiende*, *An Enemy of the People*, was that it appeared only one year after *Ghosts*. The book was available in Scandinavia on 28 November 1882. It no doubt stands in a fairly direct relationship to *Ghosts*, or, rather, to the public reactions to *Ghosts*. Ibsen was bitterly disappointed with the lack of support from the liberals at home in connection with the play. But while *An Enemy of the People* was in part intended as an attack on the 'compact majority', and on a press that was becoming a powerful factor in contemporary life, the playwright also wanted to produce a play that was different in kind from *Ghosts*. For a while he even considered calling it a 'lystspil', a light comedy with satirical dimensions, and in March 1882 he assured his Danish publisher that the play would be 'peaceful', and that it could be read by pillars of the community and their ladies, as well as played at the theatres.[48] He was to be proven right.

This time the action takes place in 'a coastal town in southern Norway', which has set great hopes on the income from its new baths. When Dr Stockmann, the town spa's medical officer, discovers that the baths are infected, he naively thinks that the town will honour him for his discovery. Instead he manages to unite the liberals and conservatives against him. Ibsen again, and perhaps more harshly than ever, satirizes the blinkered, self-interested and provincial perspectives of the small-town bourgeoisie.

While it is possible to approach the play biographically and see Dr Stockmann as the playwright's self-portrait, a number of features complicate such readings. Stockmann is too much of a naive idealist, and to an extent too self-destructive. He does much to injure his own chances of succeeding, his fiery temperament leads him to extreme characterizations of his opponents, and his quest for recognition and authority comes across as slightly ridiculous and pompous. But he exists in a society built on a lie, and among people who are content with their old ideas and beliefs, whether the new ones be good or bad. There can be little doubt as to the play's critical perspective on Stockmann's small-town opponents, both old-time conservatives like his elder brother, the mayor, and new-time liberals like Aslaksen and Hovstad. The play's didactic climax comes in the public meeting in the fourth act, where Stockmann formulates his philosophy of the one against the many: 'The minority is always in the right.' While the argument can be made that the play brings up the problem of a minority's position within majority rule, it is difficult not to recognize the political implications of Dr Stockmann's views, at a time when large democratizing processes were being both supported and resisted all over Europe. He is out to provoke:

And now let me turn to dogs, to whom we humans are so closely related. First, imagine a simple common dog – I mean, the kind of vile, ragged, badly behaved mongrels that run around in the streets fouling the house walls.

In contrast to such creatures, Stockmann points to 'a poodle whose pedigree goes back several generations, and who comes from a noble house where it's been fed with good food and had the chance to hear harmonious voices and music'. It is hardly odd that such a poodle is ahead of its mongrel relatives, the doctor suggests, that its 'cranium has developed quite differently from that of the mongrel': an 'ordinary peasant mongrel' would never be able to do the kind of tricks performed by a poodle.

Stockmann clearly wants to contrast the frustratingly conformist and unthinking masses with a progressive, noble minority, but these are ideas influenced by some of the more questionable Social Darwinist ideas of the time. The play's ambiguous hero also questions the durability of truths, however, insisting that an 'averagely built truth' is rarely valid much longer than twenty years. It is such attacks on society's seemingly stable values which help turn him into an 'enemy of the people'. The result is broken glass, and isolation. At the end of the play, Stockmann does not claim that 'the strongest man in the world is he who stands alone', but, tellingly, 'most alone'.

Even this famous statement has a potentially ironic effect, surrounded as the protagonist is, in the play's final tableaux, by wife and daughter. And while Petra seems to have faith in her father, his wife only smiles and shakes her head.

Soon the play was produced on all the main Scandinavian stages, and ten years later it became the first commercial success of sorts for Ibsen in Britain, when the actor-manager Herbert Beerbohm Tree brought it to the West End in June 1893. It happened in an admittedly domesticated and farce-like version, with Tree even impersonating Ibsen in the lead role. After this the critic of *The Times*, in a representative early response, expressed his pleasant surprise that this was a play 'which everybody can understand', rather than the usual Ibsen 'full of enigmas and obscurities, intelligible only to the elect'.[49] The Norwegian reception had been mixed but relatively friendly, even if a number of critics found it a weaker play than its predecessors. The play does not have characters with the kinds of complex inner lives characteristic of a Nora or a Mrs Alving. But a number of critics saw Dr Stockmann as a secular version of Brand, the fiery vicar protagonist of Ibsen's great drama in verse.

Even if *An Enemy of the People* on the whole adheres to a classical construction, it has less of the discipline and artistic control generally associated with the mature Ibsen; there is more of the comic and outright burlesque. One of the fundamental conflicts is, as so often in Ibsen's plays, that between the individual and society, only here it is distilled or heightened. Another tension is that between truth and convention, again portrayed in starker terms than before, and with greater and more obvious political implications. The five-act play's somewhat caricatured lone hero has been subjected to a wide variety of appropriations, from those of early anarchists to German Nazis, who recognized a strong man opposed to the masses, to Arthur Miller's adaptation for a McCarthyite America in the 1950s.

In the year 1900 the eighteen-year-old James Joyce wrote an essay on Ibsen's last play, *When We Dead Awaken* (1899), in which he observed a tendency in the playwright's later work 'to get out of closed rooms'.[50] While the four plays in this volume mostly take place within closed rooms, they display the beginnings of the same tendency. Lona Hessel pulls away the curtains and longs for fresh air, while Hovstad in *An Enemy of the People* speaks of 'air[ing] this place out', without, admittedly, ever getting around to doing it. The thematics of indoors and outdoors is there from the beginning of what, as Ibsen saw it, became a cycle of plays, and the broken windows after the public meeting in the fourth act of the last play in this volume may represent the difficulty of upholding clear boundaries between out there and in here, abroad and home, province and centre.

Radical Classics

We treat Ibsen as a prominent figure in the Western canon, hailed as one of its great 'titans'.[51] That is testified to through the sheer number of performances, translations, editions and individual readings of his works throughout the world. The plays in this volume have, since *Pillars of the Community* was first published in 1877, continued to perform their 'world-making'. And this has, of course, been dependent on the rapid canonization of these texts, on the fact that they have been made available to ever-new audiences, on page and stage. But it is important, because potentially more rewarding, that we try both to stage and to read Ibsen in ways which do not simply take his canonization for granted.[52] One of the ways this can be done is perhaps in 'reprovincializing' him, remembering where he came from, not smoothing out his strangeness. In the process of these plays becoming classics certain things have been forgotten or erased, certain ghosts have not been evoked.

It is worth remembering that the specialness of a writer can be lost if we take him for granted, if we domesticate him too strongly, if we assume that he is too much like us. This Penguin edition wants to contribute to opening Ibsen up, to establishing premises for fresh approaches, through capturing the strangeness of his language, the individuality of his plays, how they each create their own storyworlds, through making readers and audiences aware of the historical contexts of these texts and some of the most significant of the many choices made in the process of translation.

From an early stage there was a sense in certain radical and avant-garde milieux throughout Europe that the new literature from Scandinavia and Russia was 'the "classical" literature of their own time, or at least the artistic precursors of a coming classical literature'.[53] The waves of cultural export from these hitherto peripheral regions became significant factors in the renewal of nineteenth-century literature, both the novel and the drama. But world literature and theatre always come from somewhere, and a work manifests itself differently at home than abroad, in another language and in other cultural contexts. At the same time, world literature, David Damrosch notes, is 'always as much about the host culture's values and needs as it is about a work's source culture'.[54] A reflection on such matters of exchange ought to be part of any approach to reading, studying, teaching and performing Ibsen in English.

One of the tasks the contemporary reader and interpreter of Ibsen (whether they encounter him on page or stage) may face, then, is to discover or rediscover the playwright's strangeness; that is, to pull him off centre, to resist the many habitual readings to which he has been exposed, to avoid 'reducing him to the familiar', even as we try to understand him.[55] At the same time, it is notable how Ibsen has been put to use, and to all kinds of different uses, for around 150 years since his Scandinavian breakthrough with *Brand* and how he is still being put to use today. In numerous languages, forms, adaptations and versions he still affects us, his plays continue to touch us, to stir and surprise us, to change the way we feel about and perceive reality.

With the major exception of Shakespeare, Ibsen is played more often around the world than any other playwright, most strikingly perhaps in countries like India, Bangladesh and China, and in parts of Africa, in addition to being alive in the classical repertory of European and American theatres. Ibsen's plays, in short, still seem capable of letting in fresh air, of creating newness or otherness in the world, of gaining in translation. And even if some of his plays are less polyphonous and composite than others, his own genuinely quizzical poetics can be adopted in relation to them all. As Ibsen put it in a much-quoted 'rhymed letter' written for the Danish critic Georg Brandes's journal *Det nittende Aarhundrede* (*The Nineteenth Century*) in 1875: 'I do but ask; my call is not to answer'.[56] The answering or interpreting must be up to us, his readers, spectators, co-creators.

                                        Tore Rem, University of Oslo

NOTES

1. Franco Moretti, *The Bourgeois: Between History and Literature* (London: Verso, 2013), p. 181.

2. William Archer, 'The Real Ibsen' [1901], in Thomas Postlewait, ed., *William Archer on Ibsen: The Major Essays, 1889–1919* (London: Greenwood Press, 1984), pp. 53–68 (p. 54).

3. David Damrosch, *What Is World Literature?* (Princeton: Princeton University Press, 2003), p. 288.

4. See 'A Note on the Translation' in this volume.

5. See Emily Apter and her criticism of world literature and a 'translatability assumption', *Against World Literature: On the Politics of Untranslatability* (London: Verso, 2013), p. 3.

6. Rolf Fjelde chose *A Doll House* for his translation, thus correctly rejecting the genitive form, while not substituting 'Home' for 'House'; see *Ibsen: The Complete Major Prose Plays* (New York: Penguin, 1978). The Norton edition of *Ibsen's Selected Plays*, translated by Rick Davis and Brian Johnston, has followed suit. This alternative cannot be said to have won out in popular usage, though.

7. Frederic Wedmore, 'Ibsen in London', *The Academy*, 15 June 1889, xxxv, pp. 419–20, in Michael Egan, ed., *Henrik Ibsen: The Critical Heritage* (London: Routledge, 1972), pp. 107–8 (p. 108).

8. Frederic Wedmore, 'Ibsen Again', *The Academy*, 27 July 1889, pp. 60–61, in Egan, ed., *Henrik Ibsen*, p. 132.

9. Henry James, review of *John Gabriel Borkman*, *Harper's Weekly*, 6 February 1897, xlv, no. 2094, p. 78, in Egan, ed., *Henrik Ibsen*, pp. 364–5; and 'On the Occasion of *Hedda Gabler*', *New Review*, June 1891, iv, pp. 519–30, in Egan, ed., *Henrik Ibsen*, pp. 234–44 (p. 244).

10. Henrik Ibsen to Frederik V. Hegel, 12 July 1871, http://www. ibsen.uio.no/brev.xhtml.

11. Henrik Ibsen to Edmund Gosse, 15 January 1874, http://www. ibsen.uio.no/brev.xhtml.

12. 'Literatur. Bjørnstjerne Bjørnson: "En Fallit" og "Redaktøren"', Det nittende Aarhundrede (1875), p. 241.

13. Henrik Ibsen to Lucie Wolf, 25 May 1883, http://www.ibsen. uio.no/brev.xhtml.

14. Moretti, The Bourgeois, p. 169.

15. It should be noted, however, that Ibsen's success in Germany was more tentatively connected with his name at this stage; it was primarily a matter of traditional theatre conventions and star actresses. See Ståle Dingstad, Den smilende Ibsen (Oslo: Akademika Forlag, 2013), pp. 167–80.

16. The Sunday Times, 21 July 1889, p. 7, quoted in Egan, ed., Henrik Ibsen, p. 3.

17. Inga-Stina Ewbank, 'Ibsen's Language: Literary Text and Theatrical Context', in The Yearbook of English Studies (Birmingham: MHRA, 1979), pp. 102–15 (p. 115).

18. Cf. Bjørn Hemmer, 'Ibsen and the Realistic Problem Drama', in James McFarlane, ed., The Cambridge Companion to Ibsen (Cambridge: Cambridge University Press, 1994), pp. 68–88 (pp. 77–8).

19. See Toril Moi, Henrik Ibsen and the Birth of Modernism: Art, Theater, Philosophy (Oxford: Oxford University Press, 2006), p. 221, and Hemmer, 'Ibsen and the Realistic Problem Drama', p. 77.

20. Henrik Ibsens Skrifter (HIS), vol. 7k, p. 191 (digital edition: www.ibsen.uio.no).

21. See James W. McFarlane, ed. and trans., The Oxford Ibsen, 8 vols. (London: Oxford University Press, 1961), vol. 5, pp. 436–7.

22. For a short version of this story in English, see e.g. Joan Templeton, Ibsen's Women (Cambridge: Cambridge University Press, 1997), pp. 135–7.

23. Julie Holledge, 'Addressing the Global Phenomenon of A Doll's House: An Intercultural Intervention', Ibsen Studies 8, no. 1 (2008), pp. 13–28.

24. Henrik Ibsen to Frederik V. Hegel, 2 September 1879. http:// www.ibsen.uio.no/brev.xhtml.

25. HIS, vol. 7k, p. 210.

26. See Moi, Henrik Ibsen and the Birth of Modernism, pp. 236–42.

27. Clement Scott, 'A Doll's House', Theatre (July 1889), xiv, pp. 19–22, in Egan, ed., Henrik Ibsen, p. 114; Edith Lees Ellis, Stories and Essays (Berkeley Heights: Free Spirit Press, 1924), p. 128.

28. Moi, Henrik Ibsen and the Birth of Modernism, p. 226.

29. Ibid., pp. 244 and 247; for another discussion of the tensions between 'universalist' and 'feminist' readings, see Templeton, Ibsen's Women, pp. 110–45.

30. Moi, Henrik Ibsen and the Birth of Modernism, p. 247.

31. Templeton, Ibsen's Women, p. 137.

32. Julie Holledge, 'Pastor Hansen's Confirmation Class: Religion, Freedom, and the Female Body in Et Dukkehjem', Ibsen Studies 10, no. 1 (2010), pp. 3–16 (p. 3).

33. For a longer discussion of the uses of this word, see Brian Johnston, ed., 'Introduction', in Ibsen's Selected Plays, pp. xi–xxi (p. xix). But Johnston's edition has chosen to translate 'det vidunderlige' with 'wonderful'.

34. Henry Arthur Jones and Henry Herman, Breaking a Butterfly: A Play in Three Acts, LCC 53271, British Library.

35. Scott, unsigned notice, Daily Telegraph, 8 June 1889, p. 3, in Egan, ed., Henrik Ibsen, pp. 101–3 (p. 101).

36. Cf. Michael Egan, 'Introduction', in Egan, ed., Henrik Ibsen, pp. 1–39 (p. 5).

37. Bernard Shaw, 'The Quintessence of Ibsenism', in Major Critical Essays (London: Penguin, 1986), pp. 23–176 (pp. 160–64).

38. Ibid., pp. 163–4.

39. Cf. Peter Szondi, 'Ibsen', in Charles R. Lyons, ed., Critical Essays on Henrik Ibsen (Boston, Mass.: G. K. Hall, 1987), pp. 106–11 (pp. 110–11).

40. See Paul Binding's assessment of Osvald the artist, With Vine-Leaves in His Hair (Norwich: Norvik Press, 2006), pp. 21–46.

41. Ewbank, 'Ibsen's Language: Literary Text and Theatrical Context', pp. 107–8.

42. Henrik Ibsen to Frederik V. Hegel, 23 November 1881, http://www.ibsen.uio.no/brev.xhtml.

43. Henrik Ibsen to Sophus Schandorph, 6 January 1882, http://www.ibsen.uio.no/brev.xhtml.

44. Nicholas de Jongh, Politics, Prudery and Perversions (London: Methuen, 2000), p. 29. See also theatre historian Jean Chothia's account, English Drama of the Early Modern Period, 1890–1940 (London: Longman, 1996).

45. Editorial comment in the *Daily Telegraph*, 14 March 1891, p. 5, in Egan, ed., *Henrik Ibsen*, pp. 189–93 (p. 190).

46. William Archer, 'Ghosts and Gibberings', *Pall Mall Gazette*, 8 April 1891, in Egan, ed., *Henrik Ibsen*, pp. 209–14.

47. Cf. Tore Rem, 'Afterword to *Ghosts*', in *Said about Ibsen – By Norwegian Writers*, trans. Robert Ferguson (Oslo: Gyldendal, 2006), pp. 34–40 (p. 34); Moi, *Henrik Ibsen and the Birth of Modernism*, pp. 96–100.

48. Henrik Ibsen to Frederik V. Hegel, 16 March 1882. http://www.ibsen.uio.no/brev.xhtml.

49. Unsigned notice, *The Times*, 15 June 1893, in Egan, ed., *Henrik Ibsen*, pp. 298–9 (p. 298).

50. James Joyce, 'Ibsen's New Drama', in Lyons, ed., *Critical Essays*, pp. 37–53 (p. 52).

51. Harold Bloom, *The Western Canon: The Books and School of the Ages* (New York: Harcourt Brace, 1994), p. 355. See Tore Rem, '"The Provincial of Provincials": Ibsen's Strangeness and the Process of Canonisation', *Ibsen Studies* 4, no. 2 (2004), pp. 205–26.

52. Hans-Robert Jauss, 'The Identity of the Poetic Text in the Changing Horizon of Understanding', in James L. Machor and Philip Goldstein (eds.), *Reception Study* (London: Routledge, 2001), pp. 7–28 (p. 25).

53. Georg Lukács, 'Tolstoy and the Development of Realism', in Lyons, ed., *Critical Essays*, pp. 99–105 (p. 102).

54. Damrosch, *What Is World Literature?*, p. 283.

55. Derek Attridge, *J. M. Coetzee and the Ethics of Reading* (Chicago: University of Chicago Press, 2004), p. 11.

56. A somewhat freer translation has 'I'd rather ask; my job's not explanations'; cf. 'A Rhyme-Letter', in *Ibsen's Poems*, trans. John Northam (Oslo: Norwegian University Press, 1986), pp. 125–9 (p. 126).

Further Reading

Book Studies and Articles in English

Aarseth, Asbjørn, *Peer Gynt and Ghosts* (Basingstoke: Macmillan, 1989).

Anderman, Gunilla, *Europe on Stage: Translation and Theatre* (London: Oberon, 2005).

Binding, Paul, *With Vine-Leaves in His Hair: The Role of the Artist in Ibsen's Plays* (Norwich: Norvik Press, 2006).

Bloom, Harold, ed., *Henrik Ibsen*, Modern Critical Views (Philadelphia: Chelsea House, 1999).

Bryan, George B., *An Ibsen Companion* (Westport, Conn.: Greenwood Press, 1984).

Durbach, Errol, ed., *Ibsen and the Theatre* (London: Macmillan, 1980).

—— *'Ibsen the Romantic': Analogues of Paradise in the Later Plays* (London: Macmillan, 1982).

Egan, Michael, ed., *Henrik Ibsen: The Critical Heritage* (London: Routledge, 1997 [1972]).

Ewbank, Inga-Stina et al., eds., *Anglo-Scandinavian Cross-Currents* (Norwich: Norvik Press, 1999).

Fischer-Lichte, Erika et al., eds., *Global Ibsen: Performing Multiple Modernities* (London: Routledge, 2011).

Fulsås, Narve, 'Ibsen Misrepresented: Canonization, Oblivion, and the Need for History', *Ibsen Studies* 11, no. 1 (2011).

Goldman, Michael, *Ibsen: The Dramaturgy of Fear* (New York: Columbia University Press, 1999).

Helland, Frode, 'Empire and Culture in Ibsen: Some Notes on the Dangers and Ambiguities of Interculturalism', *Ibsen Studies* 9, no. 2 (2009).

Holledge, Julie, 'Addressing the Global Phenomenon of *A Doll's House*: An Intercultural Intervention', *Ibsen Studies* 8, no. 1 (2008).

Innes, Christopher, ed., *Henrik Ibsen's Hedda Gabler: A Sourcebook* (London: Routledge, 2003).

Johnston, Brian, *The Ibsen Cycle* (University Park, Pa.: Pennsylvania University Press, 1992).

Kittang, Atle, 'Ibsen, Heroism, and the Uncanny', *Modern Drama* 49, no. 3 (2006).

Ledger, Sally, *Henrik Ibsen,* Writers and Their Work (Tavistock: Northcote House, 2008 [1999]).

Lyons, Charles R., ed., *Critical Essays on Henrik Ibsen* (Boston, Mass.: G. K. Hall, 1987).

— *Henrik Ibsen: The Divided Consciousness* (Carbondale, Ill.: Southern Illinois University Press, 1972).

McFarlane, James, ed., *The Cambridge Companion to Ibsen* (Cambridge: Cambridge University Press, 1994).

— *Ibsen and Meaning: Studies, Essays and Prefaces 1953–87* (Norwich: Norvik Press, 1989).

Malone, Irina Ruppo, *Ibsen and the Irish Revival* (Basingstoke: Palgrave, 2010).

Meyer, Michael, *Henrik Ibsen* (abridged edition) (London: Cardinal, 1992 [1971]).

Moi, Toril, *Henrik Ibsen and the Birth of Modernism: Art, Theater, Philosophy* (Oxford: Oxford University Press, 2006).

Moretti, Franco, *The Bourgeois: Between History and Literature* (London: Verso, 2013).

Northam, John, *Ibsen's Dramatic Method: A Study of the Prose Dramas* (Oslo: Universitetsforlaget, 1971 [1953]).

Puchner, Martin, 'Goethe, Marx, Ibsen and the Creation of a World Literature', *Ibsen Studies* 13, no. 1 (2013).

Rem, Tore, ' "The Provincial of Provincials": Ibsen's Strangeness and the Process of Canonisation', *Ibsen Studies* 4, no. 2 (2004).

Sandberg, Mark B., *Ibsen's Houses: Architectural Metaphor and the Modern Uncanny* (Cambridge: Cambridge University Press, 2015).

Shepherd-Barr, Kirsten, *Ibsen and Early Modernist Theatre, 1890–1900* (Westport, Conn.: Greenwood Press, 1997).

Templeton, Joan, *Ibsen's Women* (Cambridge: Cambridge University Press, 1997).

Törnqvist, Egil, *Ibsen: A Doll's House* (Cambridge: Cambridge University Press, 1995).

Williams, Raymond, *Drama from Ibsen to Brecht* (Harmondsworth: Penguin, 1974).

Digital and Other Resources

Ibsen.nb.no is a website with much useful information on Ibsen and on Ibsen productions worldwide: http://ibsen.nb.no/id/83.0.

Henrik Ibsens Skrifter is the new critical edition of Ibsen's complete works. So far only available in Norwegian: http://www.ibsen.uio.no/forside.xhtml.

Ibsen Studies is the leading Ibsen journal.

A Note on the Translation

Henrik Ibsen's reputation as one of the world's greatest playwrights is today, well over a hundred years after his death, firmly established. His international popularity naturally owes much to the translation of his work into a large number of languages over the years, and several versions of most of his plays already exist in English. When being translated again, for these Penguin editions, Ibsen no longer needs to be 'introduced' or 'rediscovered' – as was the case a hundred years ago or during the 1960s and '70s – and this has given us the confidence to delve deeper into the texture of his writing, safe in the knowledge that Ibsen's brilliance in turning social, political and psychological subject matters into compelling theatre is beyond dispute. Looking closely at the plays, it soon became apparent to us that Ibsen's theatrical genius is found not only at the structural level but with equal precision at the micro-level of his texts. We discovered that the preservation of even seemingly insignificant linguistic details might enhance the reader's interpretation of a character or scene. In particular we became alert to the theatrical significance of the repetition of words and phrases within Ibsen's texts, and to the imagery used by his characters that is both explicitly and subtly embedded in everyday language. Attention to linguistic accuracy also allowed for some of the more idiosyncratic aspects of Ibsen's characters to emerge more clearly. During our work we have consulted electronic versions of all Ibsen's plays, comparing them to the works of other Norwegian writers at the time, fiction as well as non-fiction, in addition to a five-volume contemporary encyclopaedia. Doing so made it possible for us to quantify phrase and word frequency within and between Ibsen's plays, and with greater accuracy to identify instances when Ibsen was being creative with the verbal conventions of his time. Our aim has been the recreation of dialogue that preserves the plays' dramatic 'performability', while paying closer attention to the linguistic fabric of Ibsen's original than has been ventured in previous translations. We have selected here a few representative examples to illustrate our approach.

One example pertaining to linguistic fidelity is to be found in *Ghosts*, where Pastor Manders in Act One suggests that children are best brought up in 'fædrenehjemmet', literally the *patriarchal home*. The temptation for a translator is to use the colloquial *family home*. Ibsen could, however, easily have used this term in Norwegian, and here in fact gender is important: far from being the morally upright patriarch to whom Osvald should look up, his father is revealed as a wastrel. Indeed, it was precisely to avoid the potential infection of the *patriarchal home* that Mrs Alving sent Osvald away to school.

Previous translations of Pastor Manders' lines have preserved his eloquence and self-importance but overlooked the linguistically violent aspect of some of them. In the same act, Manders recounts with pride how he once made Mrs Alving submit to her moral duty and return to her husband, employing a turn of phrase that in Norwegian is very brutal. He uses the words 'jeg fik Dem bøjet ind under pligt og lydighed', which literally translates as *I got you bent in under duty and obedience*. It is significant that this is not the most obvious choice to describe submission in Norwegian. Whether this reflects an earlier passion or an aggressive aspect of Pastor Manders' character is open to interpretation, but the challenge it gives the translator in producing convincing dialogue makes it all too tempting to tone down.

All of Ibsen's characters have distinct voices that in previous translations often have been normalized: Hilmar Tønnesen's ineffectual bravado, Dr Rank's dark humour, the childish eagerness of Mr Billing's revolutionary interjections, Nora's effusive language, the impulsive and belligerent tone of Dr Stockmann, the mysterious and spiteful voice of Old Morten

Kiil, the outspokenness of Miss Hessel, the malapropisms of Mr Engstrand and Regine. All of these are dependent on the translator giving close attention not only to the rhythm, register and speech patterns, but also each character's idiosyncratic use of vocabulary and imagery.

Mr Rummel, in *Pillars of the Community*, is in many translations made to speak in quite everyday terms, yet in Norwegian he talks with a distinctly brusque and rumbustious tone. In Act Four Mr Rummel tries to convince a jittery Consul Bernick that their opponents must be suppressed by an overwhelming display of confidence. He uses words associated with weight, such as *heavy*, *crush*, *swell* and *ample*, to create a graphic image of manipulation of the townsfolk. Beyond its semi-political resonance, there may also be a comic dimension to this speech: Rummel not only speaks loudly (as his wife tells us), but is possibly an overweight character – his name in Norwegian suggests hollow noise and rotundity. It would at any rate be remiss of us to ignore the associations with weight in the words Ibsen has chosen for him.

By contrast Mr Krap, in the same play, speaks with absolute directness, regularly omitting the grammatical subject in his speech. This not only serves to create a specific idiolect, but brings pace to the opening scene of the play and strengthens the tension between the modern, efficient bureaucrat (Mr Krap) and the older, working-class shipbuilder (Aune), a tension that is central to the play, in which the new industrial world is replacing the old order. It also undoubtedly reflects Ibsen's determination to bring to the stage Norwegian as it was really spoken.

An aspect of Ibsen's writing that has affected much of our translation work is his use of repeated words and phrases. It is generally recognized that there are a number of key words that correspond to key themes in Ibsen's plays, but Ibsen goes much further. Certain words may only ever be used by one character, or may be shared by two, or used in *one* play by several characters. Repetition is a powerful tool in the theatre: while an audience may not consciously notice the repetition of a word or phrase, it will nonetheless resonate subliminally. By limiting his vocabulary Ibsen creates a palette for each play, and thereby a unique, self-contained linguistic world carefully woven into the everyday language of its inhabitants.

This is particularly true of *A Doll's House*, in which there are several notable repeats. Among these are Nora's favourite word 'dejligt' (lovely), which is used by or about her twenty-four times, Helmer's 'lille' (little), employed twenty-seven times only to describe Nora, and the crucial 'vidunderlig' (wonderful/miraculous), which stands in contrast to 'forfærdelig' (dreadful/disastrous), appearing nineteen and fourteen times respectively throughout the play. Nora also views life or emotional experiences as either 'let' (light/easy) or 'tungt' (heavy/difficult), sometimes with only a few lines between them. Other repeats, and another contrasting pair, are that of 'smukt' (beautiful) and 'stygt' (ugly). The first is used twelve times in describing Nora's dress and appearance, the house and Christmas decorations, etc. The second is used sixteen times in a variety of expressions including for unpleasant talk, bad weather, bad teeth, ugly words or foul newspapers – all things that threaten the perfection of the home or even Helmer's love for Nora. Finally, the word 'udvej' (a way out) appears in this play nine times, used only occasionally in a few of Ibsen's other plays. The word is spoken by Nora (seven times) or someone talking to her (twice). Nora says she is looking for an 'udvej' to get money, literally a way out to get money. Ibsen could easily have used the word 'måde' (method/means) or 'kilde' (source) but chooses to make Nora say 'udvej', reflecting her sense of being trapped. The challenge for the translator is that each manifestation of these words in Ibsen's Norwegian does not consistently correspond to the same word in English. This is not normally a problem in translation, unless the very act of repeating is significant – which we believe it is. Reluctantly we have occasionally had to settle for minimal variation, instead of a complete match, when no other solution was acceptable.

However, for some words it is not the high frequency that counts. The only person using the word 'bedærvet' in *A Doll's House* is Dr Rank, only twice, yet in Norwegian it is so stark and unpleasant as to stick out. The physician jokes to a slightly fatigued Mrs Linde that perhaps she is a tad 'bedærvet' on the inside – the word means *rotten, rancid, gone off* (indeed it is used in *Enemy of the People* to describe the putrefied waters at the Spa). Dr Rank has relatively few lines in the play, and this is almost the first thing he says. Yet only a few lines later Dr Rank repeats the word by describing Mr Krogstad as being 'bedærvet' to the very roots of his character. While previous translators have reflected the image of rottenness in relation to Krogstad, they have perhaps been too polite to parallel the unpleasantness in Dr Rank's remark to Mrs Linde. However, it seems too noticeable a wording to ignore. Dr Rank's use of the adjective is open to interpretation; it may simply mark his morbid humour induced by his own illness or his misanthropic tendencies or serve to foreshadow the relationship between Mrs Linde and Krogstad and the destruction they will bring to the Helmer household. Whatever the case, this verbal feature should be available to readers of Ibsen in English.

There is another arena for repeats in Norwegian that often automatically disappears in translation: the Norwegian predilection for creating compounds, where simpler words are combined to make a new concept. A noun like 'stridslyst' (directed at Dr Stockmann in *Enemy of the People*) might well be translated as *belligerence*, but it is actually made up of *battle* and *wish* and will therefore resonate with the two words 'strid' or 'lyst' elsewhere in the play. Similarly, Mr Billing uses 'stridsmod', which can mean *determination* or *pluck*, yet the word in Norwegian is made up from *battle* and *courage*. Such compounds and their simpler (often more graphic) components appear throughout the play, and to readers of the original they become part of a through-line of references to revolution, war, conflict and fighting at many points in the text. The linguistic options offered by composite words in Norwegian may be fortuitous in Ibsen's writing, but never accidental. For the translator it is a particular challenge to keep this tightly woven textuality intact in English.

Finally, humour is always difficult to preserve in translation, but all the more important when we consider that Ibsen is mainly known as a serious, naturalistic dramatist. In particular, *Pillars of the Community*, in many respects a joyously theatrical play predating Ibsen's more naturalistic works, moves with a rhythmic tempo largely sustained by comedic stage business.

Ibsen has a distinct tendency to poke fun at characters who think too highly of themselves, most often minor characters, including Aslaksen and Billing in *Enemy of the People*, and Rummel and Rørlund in *Pillars of the Community*. In the latter play Bernick's egotistical view of the world is mostly expressed in unconscious little remarks, revealing his lack of self-awareness. Talking about his single sister, Bernick reassures Johan, who suspects she is rather unhappy, that she has plenty to keep her occupied: 'hun har jo mig og Betty og Olaf og mig' (literally meaning 'after all, she has me and Betty and Olaf and me'), thus mentioning himself twice. Surprisingly, Ibsen's carefully placed verbal slip has been 'tidied up' in previous translations.

We should also mention the difficulties of translating swear-words in Ibsen – a type of vulgarity that may also have a humorous effect – since these are impossible to reflect accurately, as indeed they generally are from language to language. The distribution of the related swear-words 'fanden' or 'fan'/ fa'n' is telling in Ibsen's plays. Both have their origin in the word for *devil*, and both words turn up in other plays, generally serving as a marker of class. The former, longer version is tolerable for a man of the middle class if used in a moment of exasperation and is used liberally by Dr Stockmann and Mr Billing. The shorter pronunciation is far more vulgar and is generally used by working-class characters, and at a lower threshold of emotion. Those who use it in these plays are the carpenter Mr Engstrand in *Ghosts*, the old tanner Morten Kiil in *An Enemy of the People* and a couple of people in the crowd scene in *Enemy of the People*, one of whom shouts 'fy for fan''. This, even to a modern Norwegian, is as offensive as the f-word in today's English.

Although these four plays are translated with the reader in mind, we have sought to reflect the spirit and playability of Ibsen's dialogue. For a long time there has been a tendency, particularly in the social dramas featured in this volume, to focus wholly on the moment-by-moment believability of the dialogue. Yet Ibsen's genius lies in his capacity to create an intricate dramatic tapestry that works on multiple levels, simultaneously naturalistic and highly theatrical. Ultimately it is this craftsmanship that we hope we have captured. Most importantly, we hope that these translations offer the Anglophone reader without direct access to the original the possibility of interrogating and interpreting these texts anew.

Of course, however hard a translator aims at objectivity, translation is always a matter of interpretation, and true 'meaning' a source of endless debate. Ultimately our translations can only contribute to the on-going discussion about Ibsen's work. We have to thank our editorial team for setting the exciting parameters within which we have worked, and our expert readers, who have often presented us with alternative and insightful readings and who have contributed so generously and patiently to our journey of investigation.

Deborah Dawkin
Erik Skuggevik

A Note on the Text

This Penguin edition is the first English-language edition based on the new historical-critical edition of Henrik Ibsen's work, *Henrik Ibsens Skrifter* (2005–10) (*HIS*). The digital edition (*HISe*) is available at http://www.ibsen.uio.no/forside.xhtml. The texts of *HIS* are based on Ibsen's first editions.

PILLARS OF THE
COMMUNITY[1]

CHARACTERS

CONSUL[2] KARSTEN BERNICK
MRS[3] BETTY BERNICK, *his wife*
OLAF, *their son, thirteen years old*
MISS MARTA BERNICK, *the consul's sister*
JOHAN TØNNESEN, *Mrs Bernick's younger brother*
MISS LONA HESSEL, *Mrs Bernick's older step-sister*
MR HILMAR TØNNESEN, *Mrs Bernick's cousin*
MR RØRLUND, *a schoolmaster*[4]
MR RUMMEL, *a merchant*[5]
MR VIGELAND, *a tradesman*
MR SANDSTAD, *a tradesman*
DINA DORF, *a young girl living in the Bernicks' house*
MR KRAP, *the consul's chief clerk*
MR AUNE, *shipwright at Bernick's yard*
MRS RUMMEL, *wife of Mr Rummel*
MRS HOLT, *wife of the postmaster*
MRS LYNGE, *wife of the doctor*
MISS RUMMEL
MISS HOLT
THE TOWN'S CITIZENS AND OTHER INHABITANTS, FOREIGN SAILORS, STEAMSHIP PASSENGERS, ETC.

The action takes place in Consul Bernick's house in a moderately small Norwegian coastal town.

ACT ONE

A spacious garden room in Consul Bernick's house. In the foreground to the left a door leads into the consul's room; further back on the same wall is a similar door. In the middle of the opposite wall is a large entrance door. The wall in the background consists almost completely of plate glass with a door opening out on to wide garden steps, over which hangs a sunshade. Below the steps, part of the garden can be seen, enclosed by a fence with a small gate. Beyond this and running along the fence is a street, lined on the opposite side with small wooden houses painted in light colours. It is summer, and the sun is shining warmly. Now and then people walk past in the street, some stopping to talk, some doing their shopping at a little shop on the corner, etc.

A group of ladies is seated round a table in the garden room. At the centre of the table sits MRS BERNICK. *To her left sits* MRS HOLT *with her daughter, followed by* MRS RUMMEL *and* MISS RUMMEL. *To the right of* MRS BERNICK *sit* MRS LYNGE, MISS BERNICK *and* DINA DORF. *All the ladies are busy sewing. On the table lie big piles of half-finished and cut-out linen garments and other articles of clothing. Further back, at a small table, on which there are two potted plants and a glass of squash, sits the schoolmaster,* MR RØRLUND, *reading aloud from a book with gilt edges, although only the occasional word is audible to the audience. Outside in the garden* OLAF BERNICK *runs about, shooting at things with a bow and arrow.*

A short while later MR AUNE *comes quietly in through the door on the right. The reading is temporarily interrupted;* MRS BERNICK *nods to him and points towards the door on the left.* AUNE *goes quietly over and knocks gently twice on the consul's door, pausing between each knock.* KRAP, *the* CONSUL's *chief clerk, carrying his hat in his hand and papers under his arm, comes out of the room.*

KRAP: Oh, it's *you* knocking?

AUNE: The consul sent for me.

KRAP: He did indeed; but can't see you; he's delegated it to me to –

AUNE: To you? I'd have preferred –

KRAP: – delegated it to me to tell you this. You have to put a stop to these Saturday lectures for the workers.

AUNE: Oh? But I thought I could use my free time –

KRAP: You can't go using your free time to make the men useless in their work time. Last Saturday you were speaking on the harm that would come to the workers from our new machinery and the new working methods in the shipyard. Why are you doing this?

AUNE: I do it to uphold[6] the community.

KRAP: Extraordinary! The consul says it destabilizes the community.

AUNE: My community is not the consul's community, Mr[7] Chief Clerk! As foreman of the Workers' Association[8] I have to –

KRAP: You are first and foremost foreman of Consul Bernick's shipyard. You have first and foremost a duty towards the community which is Consul Bernick's company; because it's what we all live by. – So, now you know what the consul had to say to you.

AUNE: The consul wouldn't have said it in *that* way, Mr Chief Clerk, sir! But I know who I have to thank for this. It's that damned American ship that's in for repairs. Those people want the job done in the way they're accustomed to over there, and that's –

KRAP: Yes, yes, yes; I can't get involved in long-winded discussions. You know the consul's opinion now, and that's that!

Could you go back down to the yard; that might be useful; I'll come down myself in a bit. – Excuse me, ladies.

He nods and exits through the garden and down the street. MR AUNE *walks quietly out to the right. The* SCHOOL-MASTER, *who during the preceding hushed conversation has continued reading aloud, finishes the book soon afterwards and snaps it closed.*

MR RØRLUND: And that, my dear lady listeners, brings us to the end.

MRS RUMMEL: Oh, what an instructive tale!

MRS HOLT: And so moral!

MRS BERNICK: Such a book gives us a great deal to think about.

MR RØRLUND: Oh yes; it forms a salutary contrast to what we unfortunately see in the newspapers and magazines every day. The gilded and rouged exterior that these larger societies and communities[9] present us with – what does it actually conceal? Hollowness and decay, if you ask me. No moral bedrock under their feet. In a word – they are whited sepulchres,[10] these great modern-day societies.

MRS HOLT: Yes, how terribly true.

MRS RUMMEL: We need only look at the American crew docked here right now.

MR RØRLUND: Yes well, such dregs of humanity I'd really rather not discuss. But even in more elevated circles – how are things *there*? Doubt and fermenting disquiet on every side; discord and uncertainty in everything. Just look at how family life is undermined out there. Look how the voice of wanton revolt shouts down the most solemn of truths.

DINA [*without looking up*]: But aren't lots of great things being done out there too?

MR RØRLUND: Great things –? I don't understand –

MRS HOLT [*amazed*]: Good heavens, Dina –!

MRS RUMMEL [*at the same time*]: Really, Dina, how could you –?

MR RØRLUND: I don't think it would be healthy if such things were to gain entry here. No, we should thank our Lord that things are as they are, here at home. Admittedly tares grow in amongst the wheat here too,[11] unfortunately; but then we strive to weed them out as best we can. We must keep our community pure, dear ladies – keep out all the untested things that an impatient age wishes to force upon us.

MRS HOLT: And there are more than enough of those, unfortunately.

MRS RUMMEL: Yes, it was by a hair's breadth we didn't end up with a railway into town last year.

MRS BERNICK: Well, Karsten put a stop to that.

MR RØRLUND: Providence, Mrs Bernick. You can be sure your husband was an instrument in the hand of one higher when he refused to take on that scheme.

MRS BERNICK: And yet he had to read so many malicious things in the papers. But we're completely forgetting to thank you, Mr Rørlund. It really is more than kind of you to sacrifice so much time to us.

MR RØRLUND: Not at all; now with the school holidays –

MRS BERNICK: Yes, yes, but it's a sacrifice nonetheless, Mr Rørlund.

MR RØRLUND [*moves his chair in closer*]: Don't mention it, my good lady. Aren't you all making a sacrifice for a good cause? And making it willingly and gladly, too? These morally corrupted individuals for whose betterment we work are like wounded soldiers on a battlefield. You, my dear ladies, are the Volunteer Nurses,[12] kind-hearted sisters plucking the lint for these unhappy injured souls, tenderly dressing their wounds, mending and healing them –

MRS BERNICK: What a heavenly gift it must be to be able see everything in such a beautiful light.

MR RØRLUND: As regards that, a great deal is inborn; although a great deal can also be developed. It's simply a matter of seeing things in the light of a solemn vocation. Yes, what do you say, Miss Bernick? Don't you find that you've somehow found a firmer foundation to stand on since you offered yourself up to your school work?

MISS BERNICK: Oh, I'm not sure what to say. When I'm down there in the schoolroom, I often wish I was far out on the wild sea.

MR RØRLUND: Well, these are the things we wrestle with, my dear Miss Bernick. But we must close the door against such restless guests. The wild sea – well naturally you don't mean that literally; you mean the vast swell of human society where so many run aground. And do you really put so much value on the life that you hear buzzing and bubbling away outside? Just look down into the street. Out there people are going about in the hot sun, sweating and fretting over their petty concerns. No, those of us sitting here in the cool, our backs turned to the source of this disturbance, are most definitely better off.

MISS BERNICK: Yes, you're right, I'm sure –

MR RØRLUND: And in a house like this – in a good, pure home, where family life reveals itself in its most beautiful form – where peace and harmony preside – [*To* MRS BERNICK] What are you listening to, Mrs Bernick?

MRS BERNICK [*turned towards the door furthest forward to the left*]: They're getting rather loud in there.

MR RØRLUND: Is something in particular going on?

MRS BERNICK: I don't know. I can hear somebody's in there with my husband.

   HILMAR TØNNESEN, *with a cigar in his mouth, enters the door from the right, but pauses at the sight of the large group of ladies.*

HILMAR TØNNESEN: Oh, I do apologize – [*Wants to withdraw.*]

MRS BERNICK: No, Hilmar, do come in, you're not disturbing us. Did you want something?

HILMAR TØNNESEN: No, I just wanted to look in. – Good morning, ladies. [*To* MRS BERNICK] So, what's the outcome?

MRS BERNICK: Of what?

HILMAR TØNNESEN: Bernick's drummed up this meeting.

MRS BERNICK: Oh? About what exactly?

HILMAR TØNNESEN: Oh, it's this railway nonsense again.

MRS RUMMEL: No, is that possible?

MRS BERNICK: Poor Karsten, is he to have still more unpleasantness –

MR RØRLUND: But what should we make of this, Mr Tønnesen? Consul Bernick made it absolutely clear last year that he didn't want any railway.

HILMAR TØNNESEN: Yes, I thought that too, but I met Chief Clerk Krap, and he told me that this railway business[13] was back on the agenda, and that Bernick was holding a meeting with three of the town's investors.

MRS RUMMEL: Yes, that's what I thought – that I heard Rummel's voice.

HILMAR TØNNESEN: Oh yes, Mr Rummel's in on it naturally, and then there's Mr Sandstad from up the hill, and Mikkel Vigeland – 'Holy Mikkel' as they call him.

MR RØRLUND: Hrrm –

HILMAR TØNNESEN: Apologies, Mr Rørlund.

MRS BERNICK: And it was so nice and peaceful here just now.

HILMAR TØNNESEN: Well, I, for my part, wouldn't object to them starting to quarrel again. It would be a diversion at least.

MR RØRLUND: Oh, I think we could do without that kind of diversion.

HILMAR TØNNESEN: That's all according to one's constitution. Certain natures require the occasional harrowing battle. But sadly that's not something provincial life offers much of, and it isn't given to everyone to – [Leafs through the SCHOOLMASTER's book] 'Woman as Servant to the Community'.[14] What sort of bunkum is this?

MRS BERNICK: Goodness, Hilmar, you oughtn't say that. You've obviously not read the book.

HILMAR TØNNESEN: No, and nor do I intend to read it.

MRS BERNICK: You're not quite yourself today, it seems.

HILMAR TØNNESEN: No, I am not.

MRS BERNICK: Didn't you sleep well last night, perhaps?

HILMAR TØNNESEN: No, I slept very badly. I took a stroll yesterday evening on account of my illness. Drifted up to the club and read a travelogue from the North Pole. It has a certain galvanizing effect, following people in their battles with the elements.

MRS RUMMEL: But it doesn't seem to have agreed with you too well, Mr Tønnesen.

HILMAR TØNNESEN: No, it agreed with me extremely badly; I lay the entire night tossing and turning in a half sleep, dreaming I was being pursued by some ghastly walrus.

OLAF [*who has walked up on to the garden steps*]: Were you pursued by a walrus, Uncle?

HILMAR TØNNESEN: I dreamed it, you clothead! But are you still running around playing with that ludicrous bow? Why don't you get hold of a proper gun?

OLAF: Oh yes, I'd love that, but –

HILMAR TØNNESEN: Because a proper gun, there's some sense in that; there's always certain nervous thrill to be had when one's about to fire.

OLAF: And then I could shoot bears, Uncle. But Father won't let me.

MRS BERNICK: You really mustn't put things like that into his head, Hilmar.

HILMAR TØNNESEN: Hm – well, it's some generation being raised nowadays! All this talk about sports and more sports[15] – heavens preserve us – it's all nothing but play, never any serious drive towards the toughening-up process that comes from staring danger manfully in the eye. Don't stand there pointing that bow at me, you clot; it might go off.

OLAF: No, Uncle, there's no arrow in it.

HILMAR TØNNESEN: You can't be sure of that; there might just be an arrow in it after all. Put it away, I say! – Why in hell have you never gone over to America with one of your father's ships? There you might see a buffalo hunt or a battle with Redskins.

MRS BERNICK: But Hilmar –

OLAF: Oh, I'd love that, Uncle; and then perhaps I could meet Uncle Johan and Aunt Lona.

HILMAR TØNNESEN: Hm – stuff and nonsense.

MRS BERNICK: You can go back down into the garden now, Olaf.

OLAF: Can I go out into the street too, Mummy?

MRS BERNICK: Yes, but not too far.

OLAF *runs out through the metal gate.*

MR RØRLUND: You oughtn't to put such notions into the child's head, Mr Tønnesen.

HILMAR TØNNESEN: No, naturally, he ought to hang about here and turn into a stay-at-home, like so many others.

MR RØRLUND: Why don't you travel over there yourself?

HILMAR TØNNESEN: Me? With my illness? Yes, well, goes without saying, nobody gives much consideration to *that* here in town. But, that aside – one does have certain duties towards the community one is a part of. There's got to be *somebody* here to hold the flag of ideas aloft. Oof, now he's screaming again!

THE LADIES: Who's screaming?

HILMAR TØNNESEN: Oh, I don't know. Their voices are a little raised in there, and it makes me nervous.

MRS RUMMEL: That's probably my husband, Mr Tønnesen. But you mustn't forget, he's so used to speaking at big meetings –

MR RØRLUND: The others aren't too quiet either, if you ask me.

HILMAR TØNNESEN: No, heavens preserve us, when it comes to guarding their wallets, then –. Everything's reduced to petty materialistic calculation round here. Oof!

MRS BERNICK: It's better than before at least, when everything was reduced to the pursuit of pleasure.

MRS LYNGE: Was it really that bad here before?

MRS RUMMEL: Oh yes, believe you me, Mrs Lynge. You can count yourself lucky you didn't live here at the time.

MRS HOLT: Yes, we've certainly had some changes here! When I think back to my girlhood –

MRS RUMMEL: Oh, just think back fourteen, fifteen years. Mercy upon us, what goings-on! Back then we had the Ballroom Society and the Music Society –

MISS BERNICK: And the Dramatics Society. I remember that well.

MRS RUMMEL: Yes, that's where your play was put on, Mr Tønnesen.

HILMAR TØNNESEN [*moving away into the background*]: Ah, what, what –?!

MR RØRLUND: A play – by our student Tønnesen?[16]

MRS RUMMEL: Yes, it was a long time before *you* came here, Mr Rørlund. Besides, it was only performed *once*.

MRS LYNGE: Wasn't *that* the play you told me about – where you played the mistress, Mrs Rummel?

MRS RUMMEL [*shoots a glance at the* SCHOOLMASTER]: Me? What, I certainly can't remember *that*, Mrs Lynge. But I do remember all the noisy socializing that went on in some families.

MRS HOLT: Yes, I even know houses where they had two big dinner parties a week.

MRS LYNGE: And there was a company of travelling actors here, so I've heard.

MRS RUMMEL: Yes, now that really was the worst –!

MRS HOLT [*uneasy*]: Hrrm, hrrm –

MRS RUMMEL: Ah, actors? No, not at all, I don't remember that.

MRS LYNGE: Yes, they're meant to have done so many crazy things, I hear. What was actually behind these stories?

MRS RUMMEL: Oh, nothing at all really, Mrs Lynge.

MRS HOLT: Dina, my sweet, hand me that piece of linen.

MRS BERNICK [*at the same time*]: Dina dear, go out and ask Katrine to bring the coffee.

MISS BERNICK: I'll come with you, Dina.

DINA *and* MISS BERNICK *exit through the door at the back to the left.*

MRS BERNICK [*gets up*]: And you'll have to excuse me for a moment too, ladies; I think we'll take our coffee outside.

She goes out on the garden steps and lays a table; the SCHOOLMASTER *stands in the doorway talking with her.* HILMAR TØNNESEN *sits outside smoking.*

MRS RUMMEL [*quietly*]: Goodness, Mrs Lynge, you gave me a fright there!

MRS LYNGE: Me?

MRS HOLT: Well, you were the one who actually started it, Mrs Rummel.

MRS RUMMEL: Me? How can you say that, Mrs Holt? Not one word crossed my lips.

MRS LYNGE: But what *is* all this?

MRS RUMMEL: How could you start talking about –! Just think – didn't you see that Dina was here?

MRS LYNGE: Dina? But, my goodness, has it got something to do with –?

MRS HOLT: And in *this* house! You must know it was Mrs Bernick's brother –?

MRS LYNGE: What – him? I know nothing at all; I *am* very new here –

MRS RUMMEL: So you've not heard –? Hmm – [*To her daughter*] You can go down into the garden for a bit, Hilda.

MRS HOLT: You too, Netta. And be really friendly to that poor Dina when she comes.

   MISS RUMMEL *and* MISS HOLT *go out into the garden.*

MRS LYNGE: Well, so what was this about Mrs Bernick's brother?

MRS RUMMEL: Don't you know he's the one that was involved in that awful story?

MRS LYNGE: Mr Tønnesen, the student – in some awful story?

MRS RUMMEL: Good Lord, no, Mrs Lynge, the student is her cousin of course. I'm talking about her brother –

MRS HOLT: – the Prodigal Tønnesen –[17]

MRS RUMMEL: Johan was his name. He ran off to America.

MRS HOLT: *Had* to run off, you see.

MRS LYNGE: And *he* was in this awful story?

MRS RUMMEL: Yes, it was something – how should I describe it? It was something to do with Dina's mother. Oh, I remember it as though it were yesterday. Johan Tønnesen was working in old Mrs Bernick's office at the time; Karsten Bernick had just come home from Paris – wasn't yet engaged –

MRS LYNGE: Yes, but the awful story?

MRS RUMMEL: Well, you see – that winter Møller's Actors' Company was here in town –

MRS HOLT: – and among this company were the actor Dorf and his wife. All the young men were completely besotted with her.

MRS RUMMEL: Yes, Lord knows how they could find *her* attractive. But then Dorf came home late one evening –

MRS HOLT: – rather unexpectedly –

MRS RUMMEL: – and found – no, it really doesn't bear telling.

MRS HOLT: And found *nothing*, Mrs Rummel, because the door was locked from the inside.

MRS RUMMEL: Yes, that's exactly what I'm saying; he found the door locked! And just imagine, the man who's inside has to leap out of the window.

MRS HOLT: All the way from the loft window!

MRS LYNGE: And that was Mrs Bernick's brother?

MRS RUMMEL: It was indeed.

MRS LYNGE: And that was when he ran off to America?

MRS HOLT: Yes, he had to, you'll understand.

MRS RUMMEL: Because later something was discovered that was almost as bad; just think, he'd had his hands in the till –

MRS HOLT: But nobody knows that for sure, Mrs Rummel; it may just have been a rumour.

MRS RUMMEL: Really now, I must say –! Wasn't it known all over town? Wasn't old Mrs Bernick close to going bankrupt because of it? I have it from Rummel himself. But heaven guard my tongue.

MRS HOLT: Well, one thing's certain, Madam Dorf didn't get the money, because she –

MRS LYNGE: Yes, how did things go between Dina's parents afterwards?

MRS RUMMEL: Well, Dorf went off, leaving his wife and child behind. But she was brazen enough to stay here for a whole year. She didn't dare appear at the theatre again, of course, but she made a living by washing and sewing for people –

MRS HOLT: And then she tried to get a dancing school going.

MRS RUMMEL: That didn't work, of course. What parent would entrust their children to a person like that? Not that she lasted very long anyway; that fine madam clearly wasn't used to work; something went to her chest, and she died.

MRS LYNGE: Oh, that really is an awful story!

MRS RUMMEL: Yes, believe me, it's been very painful for the Bernicks. It is, as Rummel once put it, the murky blot on their sun of happiness. So you must never ever mention these things in this house, Mrs Lynge.

MRS HOLT: Nor, for heaven's sake, her half-sister!

MRS LYNGE: Yes, Mrs Bernick has a half-sister too, hasn't she?

MRS RUMMEL: *Did* have – fortunately. I'd say any sense of kinship is over between the two of them now. Oh yes, she was one of a kind! Imagine, she cut off her hair and wore men's boots when it rained.

MRS HOLT: And when her half-brother – that prodigal creature – had run off, and the whole town was naturally in an uproar over him – do you know what she does? She follows him over!

MRS RUMMEL: Yes, but the scandal she made before she left, Mrs Holt!

MRS HOLT: Shush, don't talk about it.

MRS LYNGE: Goodness, did she make a scandal too?

MRS RUMMEL: Well, it was like this, Mrs Lynge. Bernick had just got engaged to Betty Tønnesen; and just as he comes in with her on his arm to announce to her aunt –

MRS HOLT: The Tønnesens were parentless, you see –

MRS RUMMEL: – Lona Hessel gets up from the chair she's sitting on and slaps that fine, cultured Karsten Bernick so hard his ears rang.

MRS LYNGE: No, well I never –!

MRS HOLT: Yes, it's the truth.

MRS RUMMEL: And then she packed her suitcase and went to America.

MRS LYNGE: But then she must have had an eye for him herself.

MRS RUMMEL: You can be sure of it. She'd gone about here deluding herself that they'd be a couple when he got home from Paris.

MRS HOLT: Yes, to think she could believe such a thing! Bernick – that young, charming man of the world – an absolute gentleman – darling of all the ladies –

MRS RUMMEL: – and yet so respectable, Mrs Holt; and such a moral man.

MRS LYNGE: But what did this Miss Hessel do with herself in America?

MRS RUMMEL: Well, you see, thereover rests, as Rummel once put it, a veil that ought not to be lifted.

MRS LYNGE: Meaning what?

MRS RUMMEL: She no longer has any contact with the family, of course; but this much the whole town knows: she's sung for money in the taverns over there –

MRS HOLT: – and held lectures in public halls –[18]

MRS RUMMEL: – and published some crackpot book.

MRS LYNGE: Never –!

MRS RUMMEL: Oh, yes, Lona Hessel is yet another murky blot on the sun of the Bernick's family happiness. Anyway, you've been informed now, Mrs Lynge. I have, God knows, only mentioned this so you'll exercise caution.

MRS LYNGE: Absolutely, you can rest assured I shall. – But that poor Dina Dorf! I feel so dreadfully sorry for her.

MRS RUMMEL: Well, for her it was rather lucky of course. Imagine, if she'd remained in her parents' hands! We took care of her, all of us, naturally, and we offered her instruction as best we could. Later Miss Bernick insisted on her coming here into this house.

MRS HOLT: But she's always been a difficult child. You can just imagine – with all those bad examples. That sort isn't like one of our own, of course; she must be taken as she comes, Mrs Lynge.

MRS RUMMEL: Shh – here she is. [*Loudly*] Yes, that Dina, she's such a clever girl. Oh, is that you, Dina? We were just sitting here putting our needlework away.

MRS HOLT: I say, how delicious your coffee smells, Dina darling. A nice cup of afternoon coffee –

MRS BERNICK [*out on the garden steps*]: Here we are, ladies! MISS BERNICK *and* DINA *have meanwhile helped the maid bring out the coffee things. All the ladies take their places outside; they talk to* DINA *in an exaggeratedly friendly tone. Moments later she goes into the room and looks for her needlework.*

MRS BERNICK [*outside by the coffee table*]: Dina, don't you want to join us –?

DINA: No, thank you, I don't.

She sits down with her sewing. MRS BERNICK *and the*
SCHOOLMASTER *exchange a few words; a moment later*
he comes into the room.

MR RØRLUND [*makes an excuse to go over to the table and*
says quietly]: Dina.

DINA: Yes.

MR RØRLUND: Why didn't you want to be out there?

DINA: When I came in with the coffee, I saw from the new
lady's expression that they'd talked about me.

MR RØRLUND: Then you must also have seen how friendly she
was to you out there.

DINA: But I can't bear it!

MR RØRLUND: You have a stubborn spirit, Dina.

DINA: Yes.

MR RØRLUND: But why?

DINA: I can't be any different.

MR RØRLUND: Couldn't you at least try to be different?

DINA: No.

MR RØRLUND: Why not?

DINA [*looks at him*]: I am one of the morally depraved.

MR RØRLUND: Dina, really!

DINA: Mother was also one of the morally depraved.

MR RØRLUND: Who's been talking to you about such things?

DINA: Nobody; they never talk. Why don't they? Everybody
always treats me so delicately, as if I'd break if –. Oh, how I
loathe all their good-heartedness.

MR RØRLUND: My dear Dina, I do understand your finding it
rather oppressive here, but –

DINA: Yes, if only I could get away, far away. I'm sure I'd be
able to help myself get on if I didn't live amongst people who
were so – so –

MR RØRLUND: So what?

DINA: So respectable and so moral.

MR RØRLUND: But, Dina, you don't mean that.

DINA: Oh, you know very well what I mean. Every day Hilda
and Netta come here so that I'll model myself on them. I'll
never be as proper as they are. I don't want to be. Oh, if I
was some place far away, I'm sure I'd prove myself capable.

MR RØRLUND: But you already *are* capable, Dina dear.

DINA: What good is that to me here?

MR RØRLUND: But to leave –. Are you considering that seriously?

DINA: I wouldn't stay one day longer if *you* weren't here.

MR RØRLUND: Dina, tell me – why exactly do you like to spend time with me?

DINA: Because you teach me so much that's beautiful.

MR RØRLUND: Beautiful? You call what I can teach you beautiful?

DINA: Yes. Or, rather – you don't exactly teach me anything, but when I hear you speak I see so much that's beautiful.

MR RØRLUND: What exactly do you understand by a beautiful thing?

DINA: That's not something I've ever thought about.

MR RØRLUND: Think about it now, then. What do you understand by a beautiful thing?

DINA: A beautiful thing is something big – and far away.

MR RØRLUND: Hm. – Dina my dear, I am deeply concerned about you.

DINA: Nothing *more*?

MR RØRLUND: You know very well how unutterably dear you are to me.

DINA: If I were Hilda or Netta you wouldn't be frightened of people noticing it.

MR RØRLUND: Oh, Dina, you have such scant insight into the hundreds of considerations –. When a man is tasked with being a moral pillar of the community in which he lives, well – one just can't be too careful. If I could only be sure that people would really know how to interpret my motives correctly. – But never mind that; you *must* and *shall* be helped up. Are we agreed, Dina, that when I come – when circumstances allow me to come – and I say: here is my hand – then will you take it and be my wife? – Do you promise me, Dina?

DINA: Yes.

MR RØRLUND: Thank you, thank you. And the same goes for me –. Oh, Dina, I really do hold you so very dear –. Shh; someone's coming. Dina, for my sake – go out to the others.

She goes outside to the coffee table. At the same moment
RUMMEL, SANDSTAD *and* VIGELAND *come out from the*
room in the foreground to the left, followed by CONSUL
BERNICK, *who has a pile of papers in his hand.*

KARSTEN BERNICK: Right, so the matter's settled.

VIGELAND: In the name of our Lord, let us hope so.

RUMMEL: It's settled, Bernick! A Norseman's word[19] stands as
solid as the rocks of Dovre Mountain, you know that!

KARSTEN BERNICK: And none shall waver; none shall fall
away, whatever opposition we might meet.

RUMMEL: We stand or fall together, Bernick!

HILMAR TØNNESEN [*who has appeared at the garden door*]:
Fall? Permit me, isn't it the railway that's to take the fall here?

KARSTEN BERNICK: Quite the contrary; it's going to run –

RUMMEL: – full steam, Mr Tønnesen.

HILMAR TØNNESEN [*closer*]: Oh?

MR RØRLUND: How?

MRS BERNICK [*at the garden door*]: But, Karsten dear, what is
all this –?

KARSTEN BERNICK: Oh, Betty my dear, how could it possibly
interest *you*? [*To the three gentlemen*] But we must get the
subscription lists ready now, the sooner the better. Needless
to say, the four of us will sign up first. The position we
occupy in the community makes it our duty to stretch ourselves to the utmost.

SANDSTAD: Of course, Mr Consul, sir.

RUMMEL: It *will* happen, Bernick; we're sworn to it.

KARSTEN BERNICK: Oh, I'm not the least worried about the
outcome. We must make sure that each of us works on our own
circle of contacts; as soon as we can point to a really lively
participation in every level of the community, it'll follow
that the council[20] will have to make its contribution too.

MRS BERNICK: But, Karsten, you really must come out and
explain to us –

KARSTEN BERNICK: Oh, Betty my dear, this isn't something
ladies can understand.

HILMAR TØNNESEN: So you really want to take this railway
business on after all?

KARSTEN BERNICK: Naturally.

MR RØRLUND: But last year, consul –?

KARSTEN BERNICK: Last year was quite a different matter. Then the talk was of a coastal line –

VIGELAND: – which would have been quite superfluous, schoolmaster, since of course we have steamships –

SANDSTAD: – and which would have been ridiculously expensive –

RUMMEL: – yes, and would have been downright damaging to important interests here in town.

KARSTEN BERNICK: The main issue was that it wouldn't have benefited the greater community. That was why I opposed it, and then the inland route[21] was granted approval.

HILMAR TØNNESEN: Yes, but that's not going to affect the towns around here.

KARSTEN BERNICK: It'll affect *our* town, my dear Hilmar, because we're going to lay a branch line down here now.

HILMAR TØNNESEN: Aha; so some new scheme.

RUMMEL: Yes, a marvellous scheme isn't it? Eh?

MR RØRLUND: Hm –

VIGELAND: It can't be denied that Providence has almost laid the terrain out perfectly for a branch line.

MR RØRLUND: Are you really saying that, Mr Vigeland?

KARSTEN BERNICK: Yes, well, I must admit that I too view it as a form of guidance that I should go up that way on business this spring and chance upon a valley I'd never previously been in. It struck me like a bolt of lightning that we should be able to lay a branch line down to us. I've had an engineer survey the area; I have here the preliminary calculations and estimates. There's nothing to stand in the way.

MRS BERNICK [*still standing with the other ladies gathered by the garden door*]: But, Karsten dear, how could you keep all this hidden from us?

KARSTEN BERNICK: Oh, Betty my sweet, you ladies would never have been able to grasp the intricacies of it. Besides, I've not talked about it to a living soul before today. But now the critical moment is arrived; now we will execute it in the open and with absolute vigour. Yes, even if it means investing my entire being in it, I shall drive this matter through.

RUMMEL: And we with you, Bernick; you can rely on it.

MR RØRLUND: You really expect so much of this enterprise then, gentlemen?

KARSTEN BERNICK: Yes, I think so, absolutely. Imagine what a powerful lever it'll represent for our entire community. Think of the enormous tracts of forest[22] that'll be made accessible; think of all the rich seams of ore that can be worked; think of the river with one waterfall after the other. Just imagine all the industry that can be established there.

MR RØRLUND: And you don't fear that more frequent intercourse with a corrupt outside world might –?

KARSTEN BERNICK: No, you can rest easy, schoolmaster. Our industrious little town stands, thank the Lord, upon good, sound moral soil these days, which all of us, if I may say, have helped to drain; and we shall continue to do so, each in our own way. You, schoolmaster, will continue your spiritually uplifting work in our school and our homes. We, the men of practical affairs, will support our community by spreading well-being in as wide a circle as possible – and our women – yes, ladies, come closer now, you're welcome to listen – our women, I say, our wives and our daughters – you will continue uninterrupted in your service to charity, dear ladies, and, I might also add, be a help and comfort to those closest to you, just as my darling Betty and Marta are to myself and Olaf – [Looking around] But where is Olaf today?

MRS BERNICK: Oh, it's impossible to keep him at home in the holidays.

KARSTEN BERNICK: So I take it he's down by the water again! You'll see; he won't stop before there's an accident.

HILMAR TØNNESEN: Bah – a little toying with the forces of nature –

MRS RUMMEL: How beautiful that you should be so family-minded,[23] Mr Bernick.

KARSTEN BERNICK: Well, the family is after all the kernel of society. A good home, honourable and loyal friends, a tight-

knit little circle into which no disturbing elements cast their
shadow –

    KRAP *comes in from the right with letters and newspapers.*

KRAP: The overseas post, Mr Consul, sir – and a telegram[24]
from New York.

KARSTEN BERNICK: Ah, the owners of the *Indian Girl*.

RUMMEL: So the post has come? Then I must ask you to
excuse me.

VIGELAND: As must I.

SANDSTAD: Goodbye, Mr Consul.

KARSTEN BERNICK: Goodbye, goodbye, gentlemen. And do
remember, we have a meeting at five o'clock this afternoon.

THE THREE GENTLEMEN: Yes; right, of course.

    They exit to the right.

KARSTEN BERNICK [*who has read the telegram*]: Well, this is
typically American! Downright shocking –

MRS BERNICK: Heavens, Karsten, what is it?

KARSTEN BERNICK: Just look, Mr Krap; read that!

KRAP [*reading*]: 'Make minimum repairs; despatch *Indian
Girl* as soon as able to sail; good time of year; at worst the
cargo will keep her afloat.' Well, I must say –

KARSTEN BERNICK: The cargo keep her afloat! These gentlemen know full well that with that cargo the ship will sink to
the bottom like a stone, should anything happen.

MR RØRLUND: Yes well, there we see how things are in these
much-lauded larger communities.

KARSTEN BERNICK: You're right there; no regard even for
human life, the moment profits come into play. [*To* KRAP]
Can the *Indian Girl* sail in four or five days?

KRAP: Yes, if Mr Vigeland agrees to our stopping work on the
Palm Tree in the meantime.

KARSTEN BERNICK: Hm, he won't. Now, perhaps you could
look through the post. Listen, you didn't see Olaf down on
the quay, did you?

KRAP: No, Mr Consul, sir.

    He goes into the room to the left nearest the front.

KARSTEN BERNICK [*looks again at the telegram*]: These
gentlemen think nothing of risking eighteen human lives –

HILMAR TØNNESEN: Well, it's a sailor's calling to challenge the elements; there must be a certain nervous thrill in having just a thin plank between oneself and the abyss –

KARSTEN BERNICK: Well, I'd like to see the shipowner over here who'd bring himself to do such a thing! Not *one*, not a single one – [*Spots* OLAF] Oh, thank heavens, he's in one piece.

> OLAF, *with a fishing rod in his hand, has come running up the street and through the garden gate.*

OLAF [*still in the garden*]: Uncle Hilmar, I've been down looking at the steamship.

KARSTEN BERNICK: Have you been on the quay again?

OLAF: No, I was only out in a boat. But imagine, Uncle Hilmar, a whole circus troupe[25] came ashore with their horses and animals; and there were such a lot of passengers too.

MRS RUMMEL: No, are we really going to see circus riders?

MR RØRLUND: We? I trust not.

MRS RUMMEL: Well, of course not *we*, but –

DINA: I'd love to see circus riders.

OLAF: Me too.

HILMAR TØNNESEN: You are a clothead. Is *that* something to see? Mere dressage. It would be something quite different, of course, to see the gaucho chase across the Pampas on his snorting mustang. But, heavens, here in the provinces –

OLAF [*tugging at* MISS BERNICK] Aunty Marta, look, look – here they come!

MRS HOLT: Yes, Lord above, there they are.

MRS LYNGE: Oof, such dreadful people!

> *A large number of* PASSENGERS *and a great crowd of the* TOWNSFOLK *come up the street.*

MRS RUMMEL: Yes, a real bunch of rogues and vagabonds. Just look at that woman in the grey dress, Mrs Holt; she's carrying her travel bag on her back.

MRS HOLT: And to think, she's carrying it on the handle of her parasol! That's the manager's madam of course.

MRS RUMMEL: And that must be the manager himself; the one with the beard. Yes, he looks like an absolute rogue. Don't look at him, Hilda!

MRS HOLT: Nor you, Netta!

OLAF: Mummy, the manager's waving up at us.

KARSTEN BERNICK: What?

MRS BERNICK: What are you saying, child?

MRS RUMMEL: Yes, Lord above, now the woman's[26] waving too!

KARSTEN BERNICK: Well, that really is *too* outrageous!

MISS BERNICK [*with an involuntary gasp*]: Ah –!

MRS BERNICK: What is it, Marta?

MISS BERNICK: Oh, no, nothing; I just thought –

OLAF [*shrieks with joy*]: Look, look, there are the others with the horses and animals! And the Americans are there too! All the sailors from the *Indian Girl* –

> '*Yankee Doodle*' *can be heard, accompanied by clarinet and drum.*

HILMAR TØNNESEN [*holding his ears*]: Oof! Oof! Oof!

MR RØRLUND: I think we should shut ourselves off a little from this, ladies; it's nothing for us. Let's return to our work.

MRS BERNICK: Should we perhaps draw the curtains?

MR RØRLUND: My thoughts precisely.

> *The ladies take their places by the table; the* SCHOOL-MASTER *closes the garden door and draws the curtains on the door and windows; the room is in semi-darkness.*

OLAF [*peeping out*]: Mummy, the manager's madam is standing by the pump now, washing her face.

MRS BERNICK: What? In the middle of the square!

MRS RUMMEL: And in broad daylight!

HILMAR TØNNESEN: Well, if I was out on a desert expedition and stumbled on a water butt, then neither would I hesitate to –. Oof, that dreadful clarinet!

MR RØRLUND: Surely this is provocation enough for the police to step in.

KARSTEN BERNICK: Oh come now; one shouldn't be unduly strict when judging foreigners; these people don't have the deep-rooted sense of propriety that keeps *us* within the proper bounds. Let them kick over the traces. How does it affect us? This uncouth behaviour that flaunts proper convention fortunately bears no kinship with our community, if I may say. – What's this!

An unknown LADY *strides quickly in through the door to the right.*

LADIES [*startled but quietly*]: The circus-rider! The manager's madam!

MRS BERNICK: Lord above, what's the meaning of this?

MISS BERNICK [*leaps up*]: Ah –!

THE LADY: Afternoon, Betty dear! Afternoon, Marta! Afternoon, brother-in-law!

MRS BERNICK [*with a shriek*]: Lona –!

KARSTEN BERNICK [*takes an unsteady step back*]: Well, I never –!

MRS HOLT: Lord have mercy –!

MRS RUMMEL: It's impossible –!

HILMAR TØNNESEN: What! Oof!

MRS BERNICK: Lona –! Is it really –?

MISS HESSEL: Is it really me? Yes, it most certainly is; well, feel free to fall about my neck.

HILMAR TØNNESEN: Oof; oof!

MRS BERNICK: And you've come back as a –?

KARSTEN BERNICK: – you're really going to perform –?

MISS HESSEL: Perform? What do you mean, perform?

KARSTEN BERNICK: Well, I mean – with the circus riders –

MISS HESSEL: Ha-ha-ha! Are you mad, brother-in-law? You think I'm with the circus riders? Well, I've certainly learned a few tricks and made a fool of myself in various ways –

MRS RUMMEL: Hm –

MISS HESSEL: – but tricks on horseback – no, never.

KARSTEN BERNICK: So, you're not –

MRS BERNICK: Ah, thank God!

MISS HESSEL: No, we came, of course, like other respectable folk – in second class right enough, but we're used to that.

MRS BERNICK: *We*, you say?

KARSTEN BERNICK: Who's *we*?

MISS HESSEL: Me and the kid, of course.

LADIES [*in exclamation*]: Kid!

HILMAR TØNNESEN: What?

MR RØRLUND: Well, I must say –!

MRS BERNICK: But what do you mean, Lona?

MISS HESSEL: I mean John, of course; I don't have any other kid but John, that's for sure – or Johan, as you called him.

MRS BERNICK: Johan –!

MRS RUMMEL [*quietly to* MRS LYNGE]: The prodigal brother.

KARSTEN BERNICK [*hesitantly*]: Is Johan with you?

MISS HESSEL: Of course; of course; I'd not travel without him. But you all look so grim. And you're sitting here in the twilight, stitching away at some white cloth or other. Not been a death in the family, has there?

MR RØRLUND: Madam, you find yourself here among the Association for the Morally Corrupt –

MISS HESSEL [*half to herself*]: What are you saying? That these sweet, retiring ladies are –?

MRS RUMMEL: Now, I *must* say –!

MISS HESSEL: Oh, I get it, I get it! But damned if it isn't Mrs Rummel! And sitting right there, Mrs Holt too! Well, we three haven't got any younger since the last time. But listen, my good people, let the morally corrupt wait a day; they won't get any worse for that. A joyous occasion like this –

MR RØRLUND: A homecoming is not always a joyous occasion.

MISS HESSEL: Oh? How do you read your Bible, pastor?

MR RØRLUND: I'm not a pastor.

MISS HESSEL: Oh, but you will be, I'm sure. – But dear, dear, dear me – this moral linen has a certain corrupt odour about it – like a shroud. I'm used to the air out on the prairies, I'll tell you.

KARSTEN BERNICK [*wipes his forehead*]: Yes, it really is rather stuffy in here.

MISS HESSEL: Wait, wait; I'm sure we can find a way up from this burial chamber. [*Pulls the curtains open*] Full daylight is what's needed here when my boy arrives. Then you'll see a young man who's scrubbed up well –

HILMAR TØNNESEN: Oof!

MISS HESSEL [*opening doors and windows*]: – when he's *had* a scrub, that is – over at the hotel; he got as filthy as a pig on the steamship.

HILMAR TØNNESEN: Oof, oof!

MISS HESSEL: Oof? Goodness me, if it isn't –! [*Points to* HILMAR *and asks the others*] Is *he* still drifting about here saying oof all the time?

HILMAR TØNNESEN: I do not drift about; I am here because of my illness.

MR RØRLUND: Ahem, ladies, I don't think –

MISS HESSEL [*has spotted* OLAF]: Is *that yours*, Betty? – Give us a paw, boy! Or maybe you're scared of your ugly old aunt?

MR RØRLUND [*as he takes his book under his arm*]: Ladies, I don't think the mood here is conducive to our working any further today. But we'll meet up again tomorrow, yes?

MISS HESSEL [*as the lady visitors get up to take their leave*]: Oh yes, let's do that. I'll be right here.

MR RØRLUND: *You*? With permission, madam, what would *you* do in *our* association?

MISS HESSEL: Let some fresh air in, pastor.

ACT TWO

The garden room in Consul Bernick's house.

MRS BERNICK *is sitting alone by the work table with her sewing. Shortly after,* CONSUL BERNICK *arrives from the right with his hat on and carrying his gloves and walking stick.*

MRS BERNICK: Back home already, Karsten?

KARSTEN BERNICK: Yes. There's somebody I've arranged to meet.

MRS BERNICK [*with a sigh*]: Oh right, Johan's coming down here again, I suppose.

KARSTEN BERNICK: It's a man, I tell you. [*Puts his hat aside.*] Where have all the ladies got to today?

MRS BERNICK: Mrs Rummel and Hilda hadn't the time.

KARSTEN BERNICK: Oh? Sent their excuses?

MRS BERNICK: Yes; they had so much to do at home.

KARSTEN BERNICK: I see. And the others aren't coming either, I take it?

MRS BERNICK: No, *they* sent their apologies too.

KARSTEN BERNICK: I could have told you that beforehand. Where's Olaf?

MRS BERNICK: I let him go out with Dina for a bit.

KARSTEN BERNICK: Hm; Dina, that flighty little hussy –. The way she was so quick yesterday to make all that fuss over Johan –.

MRS BERNICK: But, Karsten dear, Dina has no idea –

KARSTEN BERNICK: But then Johan should have had the tact not to pay her any attention at least. I saw the looks Mr Vigeland was giving them.

MRS BERNICK [*with her sewing in her lap*]: Karsten, have you any idea what they want here at home?

KARSTEN BERNICK: Hm; he's got a farm over there that doesn't seem to be going particularly well; and *she* mentioned something yesterday about their having to travel second class –

MRS BERNICK: Yes, unfortunately it must be something like that. But for *her* to come with him! Her! After the dreadful way she insulted you –!

KARSTEN BERNICK: Oh, don't think about those old stories.

MRS BERNICK: How can I think about anything else right now? He is my brother after all – well, of course, it isn't for his sake, it's all the discomfort it might cause *you*. – Karsten, I'm terribly frightened that –

KARSTEN BERNICK: What are you frightened of?

MRS BERNICK: Mightn't it occur to someone to have him put away for the money that went missing from your mother?

KARSTEN BERNICK: Oh, nonsense! Who can prove any money went missing?

MRS BERNICK: Good Lord, the whole town knows it, unfortunately; and you've said yourself –

KARSTEN BERNICK: I've not said anything. The town knows nothing about those matters; idle rumours, that's all they were.

MRS BERNICK: Oh, how noble you are, Karsten!

KARSTEN BERNICK: Just leave these old memories, I say! You don't know how you torment me by raking all this up. [*He paces up and down; then he throws his stick aside.*] And to think that they should come home now – now, when I need an unequivocally positive mood in the town and in the press. It'll be written about in all the newspapers in the neighbouring towns. Whether I give them a *warm* reception or a *cold* reception, it'll be discussed and expounded upon. They'll stir up all this old stuff – just as *you*'re doing. In a community like ours –. [*Throws his gloves on to the table.*]

And I haven't got one single person here I can talk to or seek any support from.

MRS BERNICK: Nobody at all, Karsten?

KARSTEN BERNICK: No, who would *that* be? – And to get them around my neck right now! There's no doubt they'll cause a scandal in one way or another – particularly her. What a calamity it is to have people like that in one's family!

MRS BERNICK: Yes, but *I* can't help it if –

KARSTEN BERNICK: What can't you help? That you're related to them? No, never a truer word.

MRS BERNICK: I didn't ask them to come home.

KARSTEN BERNICK: Oh, yes, here we go! I didn't ask them to come home; I didn't write and invite them; I didn't drag them home by the hair! Oh, I know the whole litany by heart.

MRS BERNICK [*breaks down in tears*]: You really are so unkind sometimes –

KARSTEN BERNICK: Yes, that's right; turn on the tears, so the town has *that* to talk about too. Leave off this foolishness, Betty. Go and sit outside; somebody might come. Should they perhaps see madam with red eyes? Oh yes, it would be lovely if it got out among people that –. There, I can hear somebody in the hallway. [*There is a knock.*] Come in!

> MRS BERNICK *walks out on to the garden steps with her sewing.*

> AUNE *the shipwright enters from the right.*

AUNE: Good morning, Mr Consul, sir.

KARSTEN BERNICK: Good morning. Well, you can probably guess what I want with you?

AUNE: The chief clerk mentioned yesterday that you weren't pleased with –

KARSTEN BERNICK: I am displeased with the entire running of the shipyard, Aune. You're getting nowhere with the ships that are in for repairs. The *Palm Tree* should have been under sail long ago. Mr Vigeland comes here every day pestering me; he's a difficult man to have as co-shipowner.[27]

AUNE: The *Palm Tree* can sail the day after tomorrow.

KARSTEN BERNICK: At last. But the American ship, the *Indian Girl*, that's been docked here for five weeks now –

AUNE: The American? I understood we were to put all our efforts into your own ship first and foremost.

KARSTEN BERNICK: I've given you no cause to think that. Everything was to be done to push on as fast as possible with the American vessel too; but it's not happening.

AUNE: The bottom of the ship's completely rotten, Mr Consul, sir; the more we patch it up, the worse it gets.

KARSTEN BERNICK: That's not the real reason. Mr Krap has told me the whole truth. You don't know how to work with the new machines I've procured – or more precisely, you don't *want* to work with them.

AUNE: Mr Consul, sir, I'm in my fifties now,[28] and I've been accustomed to the old working methods since I was a boy –

KARSTEN BERNICK: We can't use those nowadays. You mustn't believe it's for the sake of profit, Aune; fortunately I have no need of that; but I must consider the community in which I live, and the business of which I am the head. It's from me progress must come, or it'll never come.

AUNE: I want progress too, Mr Consul, sir.

KARSTEN BERNICK: Yes, for your own narrow circle, for the working class. Oh, I'm well aware of your political agitations; you hold speeches, you whip the people up, but when tangible progress offers itself, as now with our machines, then you want no part of it; you get scared.

AUNE: Yes, I do indeed get scared, Mr Consul, sir; I get scared on behalf of the many who are robbed of their bread by these machines. The consul[29] talks so often about taking the community into consideration; but I think the greater community has its duties too. How can science and capital employ these new inventions in the workplace before the community has trained a generation who can use them?

KARSTEN BERNICK: You read and brood over things too much, Aune; it does you no good; *that's* what makes you dissatisfied with your position.

AUNE: It is not, Mr Consul, sir; but I can't bear to see one good worker after another dismissed and losing their daily bread because of these machines.

KARSTEN BERNICK: Hm; when the printing press was invented many a scribe lost his bread.

AUNE: Would the consul have been so fond of that art if he'd been a scribe back then?

KARSTEN BERNICK: I didn't send for you to have a debate. I called you in to tell you that the *Indian Girl* must be ready to sail the day after tomorrow.

AUNE: But, Mr Consul –

KARSTEN BERNICK: The day after tomorrow, you hear; at the same time as our own ship, not an hour later. I've got my reasons for pressing on with this. Have you read this morning's paper? Well, then you'll know the Americans have been causing havoc again. That dissolute mob is turning the whole town upside down; not a night goes by without fighting in the taverns and streets; their more vile excesses I shan't even mention.

AUNE: Yes, they're wicked folk, that's for sure.

KARSTEN BERNICK: And who gets the blame for this uncouth behaviour? Me! Yes, I'm the one who bears the brunt of it. These newspapermen are making snide insinuations, embroidering on the fact that we've been putting all our resources into the *Palm Tree*. I, whose task it is to lead my fellow citizens by the power of example, have to have that thrown at me! I won't tolerate it. It doesn't serve my interests to have my name tarnished like that.

AUNE: Ah, the consul has such a good name, it can withstand that and more.

KARSTEN BERNICK: Not now; at this precise moment I need all the respect and goodwill my fellow citizens can afford me. I've a big enterprise in the offing, as you've probably heard; but if these ill-meaning people are successful in shaking the unconditional faith in my person, it could cause me the greatest difficulties. That's why I want to avoid these malicious, insinuating newspaper scribblings at any price, and why I have set the deadline for the day after tomorrow.

AUNE: Mr Consul, you might just as well set the deadline for this afternoon.

KARSTEN BERNICK: You mean I'm demanding the impossible?

AUNE: Yes, with the workforce we have now –

KARSTEN BERNICK: Very well; then we'll have to look elsewhere.

AUNE: You really want to dismiss even more of the old workers?

KARSTEN BERNICK: No, that isn't what I'm considering.

AUNE: Because I reckon it would cause bad blood in both the town and the newspapers if you did that.

KARSTEN BERNICK: Quite possibly; so we shan't do that. But if the *Indian Girl* isn't signed off the day after tomorrow, I shall dismiss *you*.

AUNE [*with a jolt*]: Me! [*He laughs.*] You're joking, Mr Consul, sir.

KARSTEN BERNICK: I wouldn't count on it.

AUNE: You could think of dismissing *me*? A man whose father and grandfather served in the shipyard their entire lives, just as I have –

KARSTEN BERNICK: Who's forcing me to it?

AUNE: You're demanding the impossible, sir.

KARSTEN BERNICK: Oh, with a little goodwill nothing's impossible. Yes or no; give me a decisive answer, or you're dismissed here and now.

AUNE [*a step closer*]: Mr Consul, sir, have you really thought about what it means to give an old worker his notice? You think perhaps he'll just go and look for something else? Yes, he may well do; but is that all there is to it? You should be there, just once, in a dismissed worker's house the night he comes home and puts his toolbox down inside the door.

KARSTEN BERNICK: Do you think I'm dismissing you with a light heart? Haven't I always been a fair employer?

AUNE: So much the worse, sir. That's exactly why they won't lay the blame on you, back at home. They won't say anything to me, because they wouldn't dare, but they'll look at me when I'm not watching and think: he must have brought it on himself. You must see, sir, that's – that's something I couldn't bear. However lowly a man I may be, I've always been used to being counted as the first among my own. My humble home is a little community too, Mr Consul, sir. I've been able to support and hold up this little community because my wife has believed in me, and because my children have believed in me. And now all this is going to fall apart.

KARSTEN BERNICK: Yes, if there's no other solution the lesser must fall to the greater; the individual must in God's name be sacrificed to the common good. I don't know what other answer to give you, things don't work any other way in this world. But you're a stubborn man, Aune! You're opposing me, not because you can't do otherwise, but because you won't acknowledge the superiority of machines over manual labour.

AUNE: And you're holding to this so hard, Mr Consul, sir, because you know that by getting rid of me, you'll convince the press at least of your goodwill.

KARSTEN BERNICK: And if that was so? I've told you what's at stake for me – to get the press at my throat or have it sympathetically disposed towards me, just when I'm working on a big project for the advancement of the common good. Well? Can I really act in any other way? The question here, let me tell you, is whether to hold up your home, as you put it, or to perhaps hold down hundreds of new homes, hundreds of homes that'll never come into existence, that'll never have a smoking chimney, if I don't succeed in implementing what I am now working towards. That's why I've given you the choice.

AUNE: Well, if that's the case, I've no more to say.

KARSTEN BERNICK: Hm – my dear Aune, it pains me deeply that we must part ways.

AUNE: We'll not part ways, Mr Consul, sir.

KARSTEN BERNICK: Oh?

AUNE: Even an ordinary man has something to defend here in this world.

KARSTEN BERNICK: Yes, quite – so you do really believe you can promise –?

AUNE: The *Indian Girl* can be signed off the day after tomorrow.

He nods and exits to the right.

KARSTEN BERNICK: Hah, I got the better of that stiff-neck. I
take that as a good omen –

> HILMAR TØNNESEN, *cigar in mouth, comes through the
> garden gate.*

HILMAR TØNNESEN [*on the garden steps*]: Good morning,
Betty! Good morning, Bernick!

MRS BERNICK: Good morning.

HILMAR TØNNESEN: Oh, you've been crying I see. You know
then?

MRS BERNICK: I know what?

HILMAR TØNNESEN: That the scandal's in full swing? Oof!

KARSTEN BERNICK: What do you mean?

HILMAR TØNNESEN [*comes inside*]: Well, the two Americans
are walking about the streets displaying themselves in the
company of Dina Dorf.

MRS BERNICK [*following him*]: But, Hilmar, surely not –?

HILMAR TØNNESEN: Oh yes, it's the absolute truth, unfortunately. Lona was even tactless enough to call out after me;
but naturally I pretended not to hear.

KARSTEN BERNICK: And that won't have gone unnoticed.

HILMAR TØNNESEN: Quite, you can be sure of it. People
stopped and stared after them. It seemed to go like wildfire
across town – much like a blaze on the Western Prairies. In
all the houses people stood there at their windows waiting for the parade to pass by; cheek by jowl behind the
curtains – oof! Well, you'll excuse me, Betty, I'm saying oof
because this is making me nervous – if it carries on I shall be
forced to consider taking a rather long trip.

MRS BERNICK: But you should have talked to him and made it
clear –

HILMAR TØNNESEN: In the middle of the street? No, really,
excuse me. But how that man dares to show himself here in
town at all! Well, we'll see if the press can't put a stopper on
him; yes, I'm sorry Betty; but –

KARSTEN BERNICK: The press, you say? Have you heard any
suggestion of that sort?

HILMAR TØNNESEN: Well, yes, you might say that. When I
left here yesterday afternoon, I drifted up to the club on

account of my illness. It was clear from the silence that descended that the two Americans had been under discussion. Then in comes that impertinent editor, Hammer, and congratulates me rather loudly on the homecoming of my wealthy cousin.

KARSTEN BERNICK: Wealthy –?

HILMAR TØNNESEN: Yes, that's how he put it. Naturally, I looked him up and down with a well-deserved glare and let him know I knew nothing of Johan Tønnesen's wealth. 'Oh', he says, 'that's very peculiar; people generally make it big in America when they have something to start out with, and your cousin didn't exactly go over empty-handed.'

KARSTEN BERNICK: Oh, spare me –

MRS BERNICK [anxious]: There you see, Karsten –

HILMAR TØNNESEN: Well, I for one have had a sleepless night on account of that man. And yet he goes about the streets looking as though there was nothing in the least wrong with him. Why didn't he just stay gone, once and for all? It really is intolerable the way some people cling on to life.

MRS BERNICK: Goodness, Hilmar, what are you saying?

HILMAR TØNNESEN: Oh, I'm not saying anything. But there he goes escaping railway accidents and attacks by Californian bears and Blackfoot Indians without a scratch; not so much as scalped. – Oof, there they are.

KARSTEN BERNICK [looks up the street]: Olaf's with them too!

HILMAR TØNNESEN: Well, naturally, they want to remind everybody that they belong to the town's first family. Look, look, there are all the layabouts drifting out from the pharmacy, gawping at them and passing commentary. This really isn't good for *my* nerves; how a man's supposed to hold the flag of ideas aloft under such circumstances, is quite –

KARSTEN BERNICK: They're coming this way. Now listen, Betty, it's my firm wish that you show them every possible kindness.

MRS BERNICK: You'd allow that, Karsten?

KARSTEN BERNICK: Absolutely, absolutely; and you too, Hilmar. With luck they won't be here too long; and even when we're among ourselves – no insinuations; we mustn't offend them in any way.

MRS BERNICK: Oh Karsten, how noble you are.

KARSTEN BERNICK: Yes, yes, just leave it now.

MRS BERNICK: No, let me thank you; and forgive me for getting so worked up earlier. You had good reason to –

KARSTEN BERNICK: Leave it, leave it, I say.

HILMAR TØNNESEN: Oof!

JOHAN TØNNESEN *and* DINA, *followed by* MISS HESSEL *and* OLAF, *arrive through the garden.*

MISS HESSEL: Morning, morning, dear people.

JOHAN TØNNESEN: We've been out taking a look at some of the old haunts, Karsten.

KARSTEN BERNICK: Yes, so I hear. A lot of changes, don't you think?

MISS HESSEL: Yes, Consul Bernick's great and good works[30] everywhere. We've been up in the public gardens that you donated to the town.

KARSTEN BERNICK: Oh *there?*

MISS HESSEL: 'Karsten Bernick's Gift' as it says over the entrance. Well, you're certainly *the* man around here.

JOHAN TØNNESEN: And you've got some grand ships too. I met the captain of the *Palm Tree*, my old school friend –

MISS HESSEL: And you've built a new schoolhouse too; and you were responsible for the gas pipe[31] and water mains, so I hear.

KARSTEN BERNICK: Well, one must serve the community one lives in, after all.

MISS HESSEL: Yes, that's lovely, brother-in-law; but it's also pleasing to see what high esteem you're held in. I don't think I'm vain, but I couldn't resist reminding one or two people we spoke to that we belonged to the family.

HILMAR TØNNESEN: Oof –!

MISS HESSEL: Are you saying oof to that?

HILMAR TØNNESEN: No, I said hm –

MISS HESSEL: Well, we'll allow you that, poor thing. So, Betty, you've not got any visitors today?

MRS BERNICK: No, we're alone today.

MISS HESSEL: Yes, we met a couple of those moral ladies up in the market square; they did seem awfully busy. But we still haven't had the chance to talk properly ourselves, have we; yesterday those three pioneers were here, and then we had that pastor –

HILMAR TØNNESEN: Schoolmaster.

MISS HESSEL: *I* call him the pastor. But what do you all reckon to *my* great work of these fifteen years? Hasn't he grown into a good, solid lad? Who'd recognize the madcap who ran away from home?

HILMAR TØNNESEN: Hm –!

JOHAN TØNNESEN: Oh, Lona, don't brag too much now.

MISS HESSEL: Yes, but I'm mighty proud of it. Good Lord, it's my only achievement here in this world; but it gives me some kind of right to exist at least. Yes, Johan, when I think how the two of us started out over there, with just our bare mitts –

HILMAR TØNNESEN: Hands you mean.

MISS HESSEL: *I* say mitts; because they were so grubby –

HILMAR TØNNESEN: Oof!

MISS HESSEL: – and empty too.

HILMAR TØNNESEN: Empty? Well, I must say –!

MISS HESSEL: What must you say?

KARSTEN BERNICK: Hm!

HILMAR TØNNESEN: Well, I must say – oof!

He walks down the garden steps.

MISS HESSEL: What is the matter with that man?

KARSTEN BERNICK: Oh, pay no attention to him; he's a bit nervous these days. But wouldn't you like to take a little look around the garden? You've not been there yet, and I happen to have an hour spare.

MISS HESSEL: Yes, I'd love that; I've often visited your garden in my thoughts, believe me.

MRS BERNICK: There have been some big changes there too, you'll see.

The CONSUL, *his* WIFE *and* MISS HESSEL *walk down to the garden, where they can be glimpsed now and then during the following.*

OLAF [*in the doorway to the garden*]: Uncle Hilmar, d'you know what Uncle Johan asked me? He asked if I wanted to go with him to America.

HILMAR TØNNESEN: A clothead like you, who goes around here clinging to his mother's skirts –

OLAF: But I don't want to do that any more. You'll see when I'm big –

HILMAR TØNNESEN: Oh, piffle, you've no real urge for the steeling effect that comes from –

They walk down into the garden together.

JOHAN TØNNESEN [*to* DINA, *who has taken her hat off and now stands in the doorway to the right, shaking the dust off her dress*]: You worked up quite a heat with that walk.

DINA: Yes, it was a lovely walk; I've never had such a lovely walk.

JOHAN TØNNESEN: You don't often go for morning walks perhaps?

DINA: Yes, but only with Olaf.

JOHAN TØNNESEN: Well, now. – Perhaps you'd prefer to go down into the garden rather than staying here?

DINA: No, I'd prefer to stay here.

JOHAN TØNNESEN: Me too. So it's agreed then, that we'll take a walk together every morning.

DINA: No, Mr Tønnesen, you shouldn't.

JOHAN TØNNESEN: What shouldn't I? But you promised me.

DINA: Yes, but now that I think it over, well –. You're not to go around with me.

JOHAN TØNNESEN: But why not?

DINA: Well. You're not from these parts. You wouldn't understand; but I can tell you –

JOHAN TØNNESEN: Well?

DINA: No, I'd rather not talk about it.

JOHAN TØNNESEN: Oh, but surely you can talk to me about anything at all.

DINA: All right, I'll tell you. I'm not like the other young girls; there's something – something different about me. That's why you're not to.

JOHAN TØNNESEN: But I really don't understand. You've not done anything bad, have you?

DINA: No, not me, but – no, I don't want to talk about it any more. I'm sure you'll hear about it from the others.

JOHAN TØNNESEN: Hm.

DINA: But there was something else I wanted to ask you about.

JOHAN TØNNESEN: And what was that?

DINA: They say it's so easy to make something of yourself over in America?

JOHAN TØNNESEN: Well, it's not always that easy; one often has to struggle hard and work tirelessly to begin with.

DINA: Yes, I'd like that –

JOHAN TØNNESEN: You?

DINA: I can certainly work; I'm strong and healthy, and Aunt Marta has taught me a good deal.

JOHAN TØNNESEN: But then, dammit, come and travel with us.

DINA: Oh, you're just joking now; you said the same thing to Olaf. But what I wanted to know was *this*: are the people very, very – sort of moral over there?

JOHAN TØNNESEN: Moral?

DINA: Yes, I mean, are they as – respectable and proper as they are here?

JOHAN TØNNESEN: Well, they're not as wicked as everybody here believes at least. You shouldn't worry on that account.

DINA: You don't understand. I'd like it very much if they weren't so proper and moral.

JOHAN TØNNESEN: Oh really? How would you like them to be?

DINA: I'd like them to be natural.

JOHAN TØNNESEN: Well, yes, perhaps *that's* exactly what they are.

DINA: Well, then it would be good for me if I could go over.

JOHAN TØNNESEN: Most certainly it would; that's why you should travel with us.

DINA: No, I wouldn't want to travel with you; I'd have to travel on my own. Oh, I'm sure I'd make something of it; I'm sure I'd prove myself capable –

KARSTEN BERNICK [*at the bottom of the garden steps with both ladies*]: Just stay there, I'll fetch it, Betty dear. You could easily catch a cold.

    He enters the living room, looking for his wife's shawl.

MRS BERNICK [*out in the garden*]: You must come too, Johan; we're going down to the grotto.

KARSTEN BERNICK: No, no, Johan must stay here now. Here, Dina; take my wife's shawl and go with them. Johan's staying here with me, Betty dear. I really must hear a bit about life over there.

MRS BERNICK: Yes, of course, but do come on afterwards; you know where you'll find us.

    MRS BERNICK, MISS HESSEL *and* DINA *walk down through the garden to the left.*

KARSTEN BERNICK [*follows them with his gaze for a moment, then walks over to close the left-hand door to the rear; after that, he crosses over to* JOHAN, *grabs both his hands, shakes and squeezes them*]: So, Johan, we're alone. Allow me now to thank you.

JOHAN TØNNESEN: Oh, come, come!

KARSTEN BERNICK: My house and home, my family happiness, my entire status as a citizen in this community – I owe it all to you.

JOHAN TØNNESEN: Well, my dear Karsten, I'm pleased that something good came out of that mad story.

KARSTEN BERNICK [*shakes his hands again*]: Still, thank you, thank you! There's not *one* in ten thousand would have done what you did for me back then.

JOHAN TØNNESEN: Oh, nonsense! We were both young and reckless, weren't we? One of us had to carry the guilt –

KARSTEN BERNICK: Yes, but who better placed than the guilty man?

JOHAN TØNNESEN: Stop! At the time the innocent man was best placed for it. I was footloose and fancy-free; without parents; it was a complete joy to get away from the drudgery of that office. But you, in contrast, still had your elderly mother alive, and besides you'd just got secretly engaged to

Betty, who was so taken with you. How would it have been for her if she'd found out –?

KARSTEN BERNICK: True, true, but –

JOHAN TØNNESEN: And wasn't it precisely for Betty's sake that you broke off this liaison with Madam Dorf? It was, after all, specifically to break it off for good that you were up at her place that evening –

KARSTEN BERNICK: Yes, that disastrous evening, when that drunken individual arrived home –! Yes, Johan, it was for Betty's sake; but still – that you could be noble enough to turn appearances against yourself, and leave –

JOHAN TØNNESEN: Have no qualms, my dear Karsten. After all, we agreed that it should be that way; you needed rescuing and you were my friend. Oh yes, that was a friendship I was mighty proud of. There was I, slogging away like some poor local yokel, and then you come back, so fine and distinguished from your great foreign travels; been to London and Paris. And then you pick me to be your pal even though I was four years younger than you – well, that was, of course, because you'd started courting Betty; I see that *now*. But how proud I was of it! And who wouldn't have been? Who wouldn't have sacrificed themselves gladly for you, particularly when it meant nothing more than a month of town gossip, and along with that the chance to run off into the big wide world.

KARSTEN BERNICK: Hm, my dear Johan, I have to be honest and tell you; this story still isn't quite forgotten.

JOHAN TØNNESEN: It isn't? Well, what's that to me, once I'm sitting over there on my farm again –

KARSTEN BERNICK: So you'll be going back?

JOHAN TØNNESEN: Of course.

KARSTEN BERNICK: But not too soon, I hope?

JOHAN TØNNESEN: As soon as possible. It was only to please Lona that I came over.

KARSTEN BERNICK: Really? How's that?

JOHAN TØNNESEN: Well, you see, Lona isn't young any more, and lately the longing for home seemed to haunt her,

tug at her; though she'd never admit it; [*smiles*] how could
she dare leave me behind all alone, feckless individual that I
am, when, aged only nineteen, I'd already got myself mixed
up in –

KARSTEN BERNICK: And so?

JOHAN TØNNESEN: Well, Karsten, this brings me to something I'm ashamed to confess.

KARSTEN BERNICK: You haven't told her what happened,
have you?

JOHAN TØNNESEN: Well yes. It wasn't right of me; but I
couldn't do otherwise. You can't begin to imagine what
Lona has been for me. You've never been able to stand her;
but to me she's been like a mother. During those first years,
when things were so tight for us over there – how she worked!
And when I was laid up sick for a long time, unable to earn
anything, and incapable of preventing her, she took up singing ballads in coffee houses – gave lectures that people poked
fun at; and then she wrote a book that she's laughed and
cried over ever since – all this to keep me alive. Could I
watch her fade away last winter, the woman who'd sweated
and toiled for me? No, I couldn't, Karsten. And so I said:
Lona you go; you don't need to worry about *me*; I'm not as
irresponsible as you think. And then – well, then I told her.

KARSTEN BERNICK: And how did she take it?

JOHAN TØNNESEN: Well, she reckoned, quite rightly, that
since I knew myself to be innocent I couldn't have anything
against taking a trip here with her. But don't worry; Lona
won't reveal a thing, and *I* shall certainly guard my tongue
a second time.

KARSTEN BERNICK: Yes, yes, I'm sure.

JOHAN TØNNESEN: Here's my hand on it. We won't talk about
that old story any more; fortunately it's the only bit of mischief either of us was guilty of, I think. And now I want to
enjoy the few days I have here. You won't believe what a
grand walk we had this morning. Who'd have thought the
little scamp who once ran around here and played the angel
at the theatre –! But tell me – what happened to her parents
afterwards?

KARSTEN BERNICK: Oh, my dear Johan, I don't know that there's more to tell, other than what I wrote to you right after you'd left. You got my two letters, I take it?

JOHAN TØNNESEN: Yes, yes, of course; I have them both. The drunkard ran off and left her, didn't he?

KARSTEN BERNICK: And knocked his brains out later in a drunken stupor.

JOHAN TØNNESEN: And *she* died not long afterwards too? But I expect you did everything you could for her discreetly?

KARSTEN BERNICK: She was proud; she betrayed nothing and would accept nothing.

JOHAN TØNNESEN: Well, anyway, it was the right thing to do when you took Dina into your home.

KARSTEN BERNICK: Yes, it certainly was. Although, it was actually Marta who drove that through.

JOHAN TØNNESEN: So it was Marta? Yes, Marta – but – where is she today?

KARSTEN BERNICK: Oh, Marta – when she hasn't got the school to look after, she's got her invalids.

JOHAN TØNNESEN: So, it was really Marta who took care of her.

KARSTEN BERNICK: Yes, Marta's always had a certain weakness for the business of child-raising. Which is why she's taken on a post at the poor school[32] as well. A capital folly on her part.

JOHAN TØNNESEN: Yes, she looked extremely tired yesterday; *I'm* afraid too that her health might not be up to it.

KARSTEN BERNICK: Oh, health-wise, I'm sure she could always keep at it. But it's unpleasant for *me*; it looks as if I, her brother, weren't willing to provide for her.

JOHAN TØNNESEN: Provide for her? I thought she had a small inheritance of her own –

KARSTEN BERNICK: Not a penny. I take it you remember how tough times were for Mother when you left. She carried on for a while with my assistance; but that naturally wasn't going to serve my interests in the long term. Then I was taken on in the firm; but *that* didn't work either. So I had to take over the whole thing, and when we drew up the balance sheets, it emerged that there was practically nothing left of my mother's share. Then when Mother died shortly afterwards, Marta was left high and dry too, of course.

JOHAN TØNNESEN: Poor Marta!

KARSTEN BERNICK: Poor? Why? You surely don't think I let her want for anything? Oh, no, I venture to say I'm a good brother. She lives with us, of course, and eats at our table; her teaching salary allows her to clothe herself comfortably, and a single woman – what more could she want?

JOHAN TØNNESEN: Hm; that's not the way we think in America.

KARSTEN BERNICK: No, that I can believe; in an agitated society like America. But here in our small circle where up to now, thank heavens, corrupting influences haven't gained entry, women are content to occupy a seemly if modest position. It is, by the way, Marta's own fault; she could easily have been provided for long ago, if she'd wanted.

JOHAN TØNNESEN: You mean she could have got married?

KARSTEN BERNICK: Yes, and very favourably placed she could have been too. She's had several good offers, remarkably enough; a girl of limited means, no longer young, and rather insignificant with it.

JOHAN TØNNESEN: Insignificant?

KARSTEN BERNICK: Yes, well, I don't hold that against her. I wouldn't want her any other way. You can imagine – in a big house like ours – it's always good to have a steady-going person, whom one can put to any task, as and when.

JOHAN TØNNESEN: But for *her* –?

KARSTEN BERNICK: Her? What do you mean? Ah, I see; well, *she* has enough to interest her, of course; she's got me and Betty and Olaf and me. People really shouldn't think of themselves first, least of all women. We do, after all, each of us, have a larger or smaller community to uphold and serve. That's *my* approach at least. [*Gestures towards* MR KRAP, *who enters from the right.*] And here you have instant proof. You think my own affairs are what occupy me? Not in the slightest. [*Quickly to* KRAP] Well?

KRAP [*quietly, shows a pile of papers*]: All the sales contracts
   in order.

KARSTEN BERNICK: Splendid! Excellent! – Well, brother-
   in-law, you really must excuse me for now. [*Lowering
   his voice and shaking* JOHAN'*s hand*] Thank you, thank
   you, Johan; and rest assured that whatever I can do to be
   of service – well, I'm sure you understand. – Come on in,
   Mr Krap.

   They go into the CONSUL'*s room.*

JOHAN TØNNESEN [*gazes after him for a moment*]: Hm –
   He heads for the garden. At the same time MISS BERNICK
   enters from the right, carrying a small basket.

JOHAN TØNNESEN: Oh, hello there, Marta!

MISS BERNICK: Ah – Johan – it's you?

JOHAN TØNNESEN: Out and about early too, are you?

MISS BERNICK: Yes. Wait a bit; I'm sure the others will be
   along soon. [*Wants to go out to the left.*]

JOHAN TØNNESEN: Hey, Marta, are you always in such a
   rush?

MISS BERNICK: Me?

JOHAN TØNNESEN: Well, yesterday you seemed almost to be
   keeping away, so I didn't get one word with you; and today –

MISS BERNICK: Yes, but –

JOHAN TØNNESEN: But we were always together before – we
   two old playmates.

MISS BERNICK: Oh, Johan, that was many, many years ago.

JOHAN TØNNESEN: Good Lord, it's fifteen years ago, neither
   more nor less. You think perhaps I've changed so very much?

MISS BERNICK: You? Yes, you too, although –

JOHAN TØNNESEN: What do you mean?

MISS BERNICK: Oh, it's nothing.

JOHAN TØNNESEN: You don't seem very excited to see me
   again.

MISS BERNICK: I've waited so long, Johan – *too* long.

JOHAN TØNNESEN: Waited? For me to come?

MISS BERNICK: Yes.

JOHAN TØNNESEN: And why did you think I would come?

MISS BERNICK: To atone for what you did.

JOHAN TØNNESEN: Me?

MISS BERNICK: Have you forgotten that a woman died in penury and shame on your account? Have you forgotten that on your account a growing child's best years were marred with bitterness?

JOHAN TØNNESEN: And I have to hear this from you? Marta, hasn't your brother ever –?

MISS BERNICK: What?

JOHAN TØNNESEN: Hasn't he ever – I mean, hasn't he ever had so much as a mitigating word for me?

MISS BERNICK: Oh, Johan, you know Karsten's strict principles.

JOHAN TØNNESEN: Hm – yes, quite, quite, I think I know my old friend Karsten's strict principles. – But this really is –! Right, well. I was talking with him a minute ago. I think he's greatly changed.

MISS BERNICK: How can you say that? Karsten has always been an excellent man.

JOHAN TØNNESEN: Yes, that wasn't quite what I meant, but anyway. – Hm; so now I know what light you've seen me in; it's the prodigal's homecoming you've been waiting for.

MISS BERNICK: Listen, Johan, I'll tell you what light I've seen you in. [*Pointing down into the garden*] You see that girl, playing down there in the grass with Olaf? That's Dina. Do you recollect the confused letter you wrote to me when you left? You wrote that I should believe in you. I have believed in you, Johan. All those wicked things that were rumoured here after you'd gone must have happened in bewilderment, impulsively, with no forethought –

JOHAN TØNNESEN: What do you mean?

MISS BERNICK: Oh, I'm sure you know what I mean – not a word more about it. But you had to get away, naturally, start afresh – a new life. You see, Johan, I've been your stand-in here at home, me, your old playmate. The duties that you didn't remember to attend to here, or couldn't attend to, I have attended to for you. I'm telling you this, so you won't have *that* to blame yourself for too. I have been a mother to that wronged child, and raised her, as best I could –

JOHAN TØNNESEN: And wasted your entire life on that cause –

MISS BERNICK: It's not been wasted. But you were late coming, Johan.

JOHAN TØNNESEN: Marta – if I could only tell you –. Well, at least let me thank you for your loyal friendship.

MISS BERNICK [*with a sad smile*]: Hm – Well, we've both had our say now, Johan. Shh; somebody's coming. Goodbye, I really can't now –

> *She goes out through the rear door to the left.*
>
> MISS HESSEL *is coming from the garden, followed by* MRS BERNICK.

MRS BERNICK [*still in the garden*]: But, for heaven's sake, Lona, what are you thinking of?

MISS HESSEL: Let me be, I tell you; I must and I will talk to him.

MRS BERNICK: But that really would be the biggest scandal! Ah, Johan, are you still here?

MISS HESSEL: Out you go now, boy; don't hang around in this stuffy air;[33] go down into the garden and talk to Dina.

JOHAN TØNNESEN: Yes, I was thinking I might.

MRS BERNICK: But –

MISS HESSEL: Listen, John dear, have you taken a proper look at Dina?

JOHAN TØNNESEN: I believe so, yes.

MISS HESSEL: Well, you should take a proper, thorough look at her, my boy. *That* would be something for *you*!

MRS BERNICK: But, Lona –!

JOHAN TØNNESEN: Something for me?

MISS HESSEL: To look at, I mean. Off you go!

JOHAN TØNNESEN: Yes, yes, I'm more than happy to go.

> *He goes out into the garden.*

MRS BERNICK: Lona, I am mortified by you. You can't possibly be serious about this.

MISS HESSEL: Oh, I most certainly am. Isn't she good and fit and healthy? That's just the wife for John. That's the sort he needs over there; that would be something altogether different from an old half-sister.

MRS BERNICK: Dina! Dina Dorf! Just consider –

MISS HESSEL: I am considering the boy's happiness first and foremost. I have to help things along, after all; he's not very advanced in such matters himself; he's never had a proper eye for the girls or the ladies.

MRS BERNICK: He? Johan! Well, I certainly think we had unfortunate proof that –

MISS HESSEL: Oh, to hell with that stupid story! Where's Bernick gone? I want to talk to him.

MRS BERNICK: Lona, you're not to do it, I tell you!

MISS HESSEL: I am doing it. If the boy likes her – and she him – they shall have each other. Bernick's a man of such wisdom; he'll have to find a way –

MRS BERNICK: And you imagine this unseemly American behaviour would be tolerated here –

MISS HESSEL: Oh nonsense, Betty –

MRS BERNICK: – that a man like Karsten, with his strict, moral outlook –

MISS HESSEL: Oh, pff, I shouldn't think it's so overly strict.

MRS BERNICK: What are you daring to suggest?

MISS HESSEL: I'm daring to suggest that Bernick isn't any more uniquely moral than other menfolk.

MRS BERNICK: So that's how deep your hatred is for him still! But then what do you want here, since you've never been able to forget that –? I don't understand how you dared to look him in the eye after that shameful insult you inflicted on him back then.

MISS HESSEL: Yes, Betty, back then I overstepped myself dreadfully.

MRS BERNICK: And how noble-minded he was in forgiving you, this man who hadn't done a thing wrong! *He* couldn't help it if you went about here building up your hopes. But ever since that time you've hated *me* too. [*Bursts into tears.*] You've always begrudged me my happiness. And now you've come here to bring all this down on me – to show the town what sort of family I've brought Karsten into. Yes, I'm the one who'll bear the brunt of it, and *that's* what you want. Oh, it's despicable of you!

She leaves, still crying, through the left-hand door to the back.

MISS HESSEL [*gazes after her*]: Poor Betty.

CONSUL BERNICK *comes out of his room.*

KARSTEN BERNICK [*still at his door*]: Yes, yes, that's good, Mr Krap; that's splendid. Send four hundred kroner[34] towards food for the poor. [*Turns around*] Lona! [*Closer*] You're alone? Betty's not coming?

MISS HESSEL: No. Shall I fetch her perhaps?

KARSTEN BERNICK: No, no, no, leave it! Oh, Lona, you don't know how I've burned to speak with you openly – to implore your forgiveness.

MISS HESSEL: Listen, Karsten, let's not get sentimental; it doesn't suit us.

KARSTEN BERNICK: You *must* listen to me, Lona. I do realize that appearances are against me, now that you know all about this thing with Dina's mother. But I swear to you, it was nothing but a fleeting aberration; I really did, honestly and truthfully, love you once.

MISS HESSEL: What do you think I've come home for?

KARSTEN BERNICK: Whatever you've got in mind, I beg you not to act on it before I've vindicated myself. And I can, Lona; I can at least explain myself.

MISS HESSEL: You're scared now. – You loved me once, you say. Yes, you assured me of it often enough in your letters; and perhaps it was true too – in a way, as long as you were living out there in a big and free world, it gave you the courage to think bigger and more freely yourself. Perhaps you found rather more character and will and independence in me than in most people here at home. And, of course, it was a secret between the two of us; so nobody could poke fun at your bad taste.

KARSTEN BERNICK: Lona, how can you think –?

MISS HESSEL: But then when you came back; when you heard the jeers that were raining down on me; when you sensed the way everybody here laughed at what they called my peccadilloes –

KARSTEN BERNICK: You *were* reckless back then.

MISS HESSEL: Mostly to annoy those beskirted and betrou-
sered prudes that dragged about town. And then, when you
met that beguiling young actress –

KARSTEN BERNICK: That was a silly bout of vanity; nothing
more; I swear to you; not one tenth of the rumour and gossip
that went round was true.

MISS HESSEL: Maybe so; but then when Betty returned home,
beautiful, blooming, worshipped by all – and when it was
made known that she was to inherit all Auntie's money and
that I'd get nothing –

KARSTEN BERNICK: Yes, there's the nub of it, Lona; and now
I'll tell you without embellishment. I didn't love Betty back
then; and I didn't break with you because of some new
infatuation. It was quite simply for the sake of the money; I
was forced to it; I *had* to secure that for myself.

MISS HESSEL: And you're telling me that to my face?

KARSTEN BERNICK: Yes, I am. Listen, Lona –

MISS HESSEL: And yet you wrote and told me you were gripped
by an irrepressible love for Betty, appealed to my noble-
mindedness, made me swear for Betty's sake to keep quiet
about what had been between us –

KARSTEN BERNICK: I had to, I say.

MISS HESSEL: Then, by God in heaven, I don't regret overstep-
ping myself the way I did that day.

KARSTEN BERNICK: Let me explain, coolly and calmly, what
the position was at the time. My mother was, as you remember, the head of the firm; but she had absolutely no business
sense whatever. I was called home urgently from Paris; times
were critical; I was to get the business up and running. What
did I find? I found something that had to be kept in deepest
secrecy, a house that was as good as ruined. Yes, it was as
good as ruined, this old, respected house that had stood for
three generations. What was I, the son, the only son, to do
but look around for some means of rescue?

MISS HESSEL: And so you rescued the House of Bernick at a
woman's expense.

KARSTEN BERNICK: You know very well Betty loved me.

MISS HESSEL: Yes, but me?

KARSTEN BERNICK: Believe me, Lona – you would never have been happy with me.

MISS HESSEL: Was it out of concern for my happiness that you sacrificed me?

KARSTEN BERNICK: You think perhaps I was motivated by self-interest in acting as I did? Had I stood alone at the time, I'd have started afresh with cheerful courage. But you've no understanding for how a businessman, under such an inordinate weight of responsibility, grows as one with the company he inherits. Do you realize that the welfare of hundreds, nay, thousands of people depends upon him? Doesn't it occur to you that the entire community which both you and I call our home would have been affected in the most drastic way if the House of Bernick had collapsed?

MISS HESSEL: Is it for the community's sake, too, that you've stood fixed for these fifteen years in a lie?

KARSTEN BERNICK: In a lie?

MISS HESSEL: What does Betty know of what lay behind or happened before her involvement with you?

KARSTEN BERNICK: Can you believe I'd want to hurt her to no advantage by revealing these things?

MISS HESSEL: No advantage, you say. Oh yes, you're the businessman of course; you must know what's advantageous. – But listen now, Karsten, now I *too* wish to speak coolly and calmly. Tell me – are you really happy?

KARSTEN BERNICK: In my family you mean?

MISS HESSEL: Perhaps.

KARSTEN BERNICK: I am, Lona, yes. Oh, your self-sacrifice to me as a friend has not been in vain. I venture to say I've grown happier year by year. Betty is amenable and good. And the way she's learned with the years to bend her nature to all my little idiosyncrasies –

MISS HESSEL: Hm.

KARSTEN BERNICK: Initially, of course, she had lots of over-excited notions about love; she couldn't settle with the idea that it would, little by little, turn into a mild flame of companionship.

MISS HESSEL: But now she's reconciled to that?

KARSTEN BERNICK: Absolutely. You can be sure that her day-to-day association with *me* has not been without a maturing influence upon her. People must learn to exercise mutual restraint in their demands if they're to fulfil their purpose in their community here on earth. That too Betty learned little by little to see, and as a result our house is now a model to our fellow citizens.

MISS HESSEL: But these fellow citizens know nothing about the lie?

KARSTEN BERNICK: About the lie?

MISS HESSEL: Yes, the lie you've now stood in for fifteen years.

KARSTEN BERNICK: And you call that –?

MISS HESSEL: A lie, I call it. A threefold lie. First the lie towards me; then the lie towards Betty; then the lie towards Johan.

KARSTEN BERNICK: Betty never demanded I should speak out.

MISS HESSEL: Because she knew nothing.

KARSTEN BERNICK: And *you* won't demand it – out of consideration for her.

MISS HESSEL: No indeed, I think I can bear the volleys of laughter; I have broad shoulders.

KARSTEN BERNICK: And Johan won't demand it either; he's promised me that.

MISS HESSEL: But you, Karsten? Is there nothing within you that wants to come out of this lie?

KARSTEN BERNICK: I should voluntarily sacrifice my family happiness and my position in the community!

MISS HESSEL: What right have you to stand where you stand?

KARSTEN BERNICK: Every day for fifteen years I've bought myself a little of that right – by my conduct, and with everything I've worked for and the progress I've achieved.

MISS HESSEL: Yes, you've worked and achieved a great deal, both for yourself and for others. You're the town's richest and most powerful man; they don't dare do anything but bend under your will, any of them, because you're reckoned to be without fault and flaw; your home passes for a model home, your conduct passes for model conduct. But all this splendour, and you with it, stands on an uncertain quagmire. A moment may come, a word be spoken – and both you and all this splendour will sink right to the bottom, if you don't save yourself in time.

KARSTEN BERNICK: Lona – what is it you want over here?

MISS HESSEL: I want to help you get to ground that's firm underfoot, Karsten.

KARSTEN BERNICK: Revenge! You want revenge? I suspected as much. But you won't succeed! There's only *one* person here who has the authority to speak, and he is silent.

MISS HESSEL: Johan?

KARSTEN BERNICK: Yes, Johan. If anybody else wishes to accuse me, I'll deny everything. If somebody wants to annihilate me, I shall fight for my life. You'll never succeed, I tell you! The man who could topple me, he is keeping quiet – and he is leaving again.

RUMMEL *and* VIGELAND *enter from the right.*

RUMMEL: Good morning, good morning, my dear Bernick; you must come up with us to the Business Association; we've got a meeting about the railway, remember.

KARSTEN BERNICK: I can't. Impossible right now.

VIGELAND: You ought, really, Mr Consul, sir –[35]

RUMMEL: You[36] must, Bernick. There are people working against us. Hammer and the others who backed the coastal line are claiming there are private interests behind this new proposal.

KARSTEN BERNICK: So explain to them –

VIGELAND: It won't help, whatever *we* explain, Mr Consul, sir –

RUMMEL: No, no, you must come yourself; naturally nobody would dare suspect you of any such thing.

MISS HESSEL: No, I should think not.

KARSTEN BERNICK: I can't, I tell you; I'm not well – or at least, wait – let me gather myself.

MR RØRLUND *enters from the right.*

MR RØRLUND: Excuse me, Mr Consul, sir; you see me here in a violent state of agitation –

KARSTEN BERNICK: Well, what's the matter with you?

MR RØRLUND: I must ask you a question, Mr Consul, sir. Is it with your consent that the young girl who's found refuge under your roof shows herself in the public street in the company of a person who –

MISS HESSEL: What person, pastor?

MR RØRLUND: With the very person she should, of all people in the world, be kept furthest from.

MISS HESSEL: Oh, come now!

MR RØRLUND: Is it with your consent, Mr Consul, sir?

KARSTEN BERNICK [*who is looking for his hat and gloves*]: I know nothing of it. I'm sorry, I'm in a hurry. I'm on my way up to the Business Association.

HILMAR TØNNESEN [*enters from the garden and walks over towards the left-hand door to the rear*]: Betty, Betty, listen!

MRS BERNICK [*in the doorway*]: What is it?

HILMAR TØNNESEN: You've got to go down into the garden and put an end to this flirtation that a certain somebody is engaging in with that Dina Dorf. It's made me quite nervous just listening to it.

MISS HESSEL: And? What has this somebody said?

HILMAR TØNNESEN: Oh, only that he wants her to go to America with him. Oof!

MR RØRLUND: Can that be possible?

MRS BERNICK: What are you saying!

MISS HESSEL: But that would be marvellous.

KARSTEN BERNICK: It's impossible. You've misheard.

HILMAR TØNNESEN: Ask him yourself then. Here comes the couple. But just leave me out of it.

KARSTEN BERNICK [*to* RUMMEL *and* VIGELAND]: I'll follow on – in a moment –

    RUMMEL *and* VIGELAND *exit to the right.* JOHAN TØNNESEN *and* DINA *enter from the garden.*

JOHAN TØNNESEN: Hurrah, Lona, she's coming with us!

MRS BERNICK: But, Johan – you irresponsible –!

MR RØRLUND: Unbelievable! A first-class scandal! With what tricks of seduction have you –!

JOHAN TØNNESEN: Steady, man; what are you saying?

MR RØRLUND: Answer me, Dina; is this your purpose – your full and free decision?

DINA: I *have* to get away from here.

MR RØRLUND: But with *him* – with *him*!

DINA: Name me anyone else here who's had the courage to take me with them.

MR RØRLUND: I see, you must be told who he is, then.

JOHAN TØNNESEN: Do not speak!

KARSTEN BERNICK: Not a word more!

MR RØRLUND: Then I'd be serving the community, for whose morals and conduct I'm placed as custodian, very poorly indeed; and acting irresponsibly towards this young girl, in whose upbringing I have also borne a significant share and for whom I feel –

JOHAN TØNNESEN: Careful what you do!

MR RØRLUND: She *shall* know it! Dina, this is the man who caused all your mother's unhappiness and shame.

KARSTEN BERNICK: Mr Rørlund –!

DINA: He! [*To* JOHAN TØNNESEN] Is this true?

JOHAN TØNNESEN: You answer, Karsten.

KARSTEN BERNICK: Not a word more! There'll be silence here today.

DINA: So it's true.

MR RØRLUND: Absolutely true. And there's more. This person, in whom you've put your trust, did not run away from home empty-handed: Widow Bernick's money – the consul can testify to it!

MISS HESSEL: Liar!

KARSTEN BERNICK: Ah –!

MRS BERNICK: Oh my God, oh my God!

JOHAN TØNNESEN [*towards him with raised arm*]: And you dare to –!

MISS HESSEL [*checking him*]: Don't hit him, Johan!

MR RØRLUND: Yes, assault me, why don't you. But the truth will out; and it *is* the truth; Consul Bernick said it himself, and the entire town knows it. – So, Dina, now you know who he is.

Short silence.

JOHAN TØNNESEN [*quietly, grabbing* BERNICK*'s arm*]: Karsten, Karsten, what have you done!

MRS BERNICK [*subdued and in tears*]: Oh, Karsten, that I
should bring such disgrace on you.

SANDSTAD [*enters quickly from the right, shouting, with his
hand on the door handle*]: You must come straight away,
Mr Consul, sir. The entire railway hangs by a thread.

KARSTEN BERNICK [*distractedly*]: What's that? What am I to –?

MISS HESSEL: You're to go and uphold the community,
brother-in-law.

SANDSTAD: Yes, come on now; we need every ounce of your
moral weight.

JOHAN TØNNESEN [*close to him*]: Bernick – you and I will
talk tomorrow.

> He exits through the garden; CONSUL BERNICK, *as if in a
> daze, goes out to the right with* SANDSTAD.

ACT THREE

The garden room in Consul Bernick's house.

CONSUL BERNICK, *a cane*[37] *in his hand, comes out in a fierce temper from the room nearest to the back on the left, leaving the door half-open behind him.*

KARSTEN BERNICK: There; at long last I've finally shown him what's what; I doubt he'll forget that beating in a hurry. [*To somebody in the room*] What are you saying? – And I'm saying you're an irresponsible mother! You make excuses for him, give him approval in all his wicked pranks. – Not wicked? What do you call it then? Sneaking out of the house at night, going out to sea with the fishing boat, staying away until long into the day, and putting the fear of death into me when I've so much else to do. And then the scoundrel dares to threaten he'll run away! Well, just let him try! – You? Oh, yes, I can believe that all right, you don't worry yourself much over his welfare. Even if it cost him his life, I think you'd –! – Really? Yes, but *I* have a vocation to pass on after me here in this world; it won't serve my interests to be made childless. – No objections, Betty; it'll be as I've said; he's grounded – [*listens*] Hush; don't let anybody notice anything.

    KRAP *enters from the right.*

KRAP: Have you got a moment, Mr Consul, sir?

KARSTEN BERNICK [*throws the cane aside*]: Yes, yes, of course. You've come up from the shipyard?

KRAP: Just now. Hrm –

KARSTEN BERNICK: Well? Nothing wrong with the *Palm Tree* is there?

KRAP: The *Palm Tree* can sail tomorrow, but –

KARSTEN BERNICK: So it's the *Indian Girl* is it? I had a feeling that stiff-neck would –

KRAP: The *Indian Girl* can also sail tomorrow; but – she probably won't get far.

KARSTEN BERNICK: What do you mean?

KRAP: Pardon me, Mr Consul, sir; that door is slightly ajar, and I think somebody's in there –

KARSTEN BERNICK [*closes the door*]: Right. But what is it that nobody should hear?

KRAP: It's this: it seems Aune's of a mind to let the *Indian Girl* go to the bottom – crew and all.

KARSTEN BERNICK: But Lord preserve us, how can you think –?

KRAP: Can't see any other explanation, Mr Consul, sir.

KARSTEN BERNICK: Well, tell me briefly, then –

KRAP: Right you are. You know yourself how slowly things have been going at the shipyard since we got the new machinery and the new, inexperienced workers.

KARSTEN BERNICK: Yes, yes.

KRAP: But this morning, when I got down there, I noticed that the repairs on the American had taken a conspicuous leap forward; around the large valve in the bottom – you know, the area that's rotten –

KARSTEN BERNICK: Yes, yes, what about it?

KRAP: Completely repaired – seemingly at least; sheathed; looked like new; heard that Aune had worked down there by lamplight all night.

KARSTEN BERNICK: Yes, and so –?

KRAP: Mulled it over a bit; the men had just broken off for breakfast,[38] so I took the opportunity to look around unobserved, both outside and on board; had trouble getting below in the loaded vessel; but had my suspicions confirmed. There are dodgy goings-on, Mr Consul, sir.

KARSTEN BERNICK: I can't believe it, Mr Krap. I can't, I won't believe such a thing of Aune.

KRAP: Pains me – but it's the plain truth. Dodgy goings-on I tell you. No new timber put in, as far as I could make out; just shifted and plugged and riveted with boards and tarpaulin and the like. Total sham! The *Indian Girl* will never reach New York; she'll go to the bottom like a cracked pan.

KARSTEN BERNICK: Well, this is dreadful! But what do you think he can hope to achieve?

KRAP: Wants to bring the machines into disrepute no doubt; wants his revenge; wants the old workforce restored to favour.

KARSTEN BERNICK: And for that he'd sacrifice all those human lives.

KRAP: He said recently: there are no human beings on board the *Indian Girl* – just beasts.

KARSTEN BERNICK: Well, leave that now; but has he no regard for the big capital investment that'll be lost?

KRAP: Aune doesn't look kindly on big capital, Mr Consul, sir.

KARSTEN BERNICK: True; he's an agitator and troublemaker; but such an unscrupulous act –. Listen, Mr Krap; this matter must be double-checked. Not a word to anyone about it. It reflects badly on our shipyard if people get to know of something like this.

KRAP: Of course, but –

KARSTEN BERNICK: During lunch-break you must go down there again; I need absolute certainty.[39]

KRAP: You shall have it, Mr Consul, sir; but with permission, what will you do then?

KARSTEN BERNICK: Report the matter, of course. After all, we can't make ourselves accessories to an outright crime. I can't have my conscience burdened.[40] Besides, it will make a good impression in the press and the community at large when it's seen that I'm sweeping all personal interest aside and allowing justice to run its course.

KRAP: Very true, Mr Consul, sir.

KARSTEN BERNICK: But first and foremost, absolute certainty. And silence for now –

KRAP: Not a word, Mr Consul, sir; and you will have certainty.

He leaves through the garden and walks down the street.

KARSTEN BERNICK [*half aloud*]: Most disturbing! But no, it's
impossible – unthinkable!

Just as he is going to his room, HILMAR TØNNESEN
comes from the right.

HILMAR TØNNESEN: Good afternoon, Bernick! Well, congratulations on your victory at the Business Association
yesterday.

KARSTEN BERNICK: Oh, thank you.

HILMAR TØNNESEN: It was a splendid victory, so I hear; the
victory of intelligent public spirit over self-interest and
prejudice – much like a French raid on the Kabyles.[41]
Extraordinary, how after those unpleasant scenes here, you –

KARSTEN BERNICK: Yes, well, leave that now.

HILMAR TØNNESEN: But the major battle's yet to be fought.

KARSTEN BERNICK: About the railway, you mean?

HILMAR TØNNESEN: Yes, I take it you know what Hammer's
brewing up?

KARSTEN BERNICK [*anxiously*]: No! What's *that*?

HILMAR TØNNESEN: He's latched on to that rumour that's
going about and wants to write a newspaper article about it.

KARSTEN BERNICK: What rumour?

HILMAR TØNNESEN: That thing about those big property
acquisitions along the branch line, of course.

KARSTEN BERNICK: What do you mean? Is such a rumour
going round?

HILMAR TØNNESEN: Yes, it's all over town. I heard it at the
club when I drifted in. It seems one of our lawyers has been
commissioned to quietly buy up all the forests, all the min-
eral deposits, all the waterfalls –

KARSTEN BERNICK: And they don't say who for?

HILMAR TØNNESEN: Up at the club they reckoned it must be
for some out-of-town company that had got wind of your
plans and rushed in before property prices rose –. Despicable, isn't it? Oof!

KARSTEN BERNICK: Despicable?

HILMAR TØNNESEN: Yes, for outsiders to encroach on our
territory like that. And that one of the town's own lawyers

could lend himself to such a thing! Now it'll be out-of-town people who go off with the profits.

KARSTEN BERNICK: Yes, but it's only a rumour.

HILMAR TØNNESEN: But people believe it, and tomorrow or the day after, our editor Hammer will nail it down as a fact. There was already general resentment up there. I heard several of them say that if the rumour's confirmed they'll cross themselves off the lists.

KARSTEN BERNICK: Impossible!

HILMAR TØNNESEN: Really? Why do you think these mercenary souls were so eager to go along with your enterprise? You don't think perhaps they'd sniffed out the possibility of –?

KARSTEN BERNICK: Impossible, I say; there's surely *that* much public spirit here in our little community –

HILMAR TØNNESEN: Here? Well, you are, of course, an optimist, and you judge others by yourself. But I, as a well-seasoned observer –. No, there's not *one* man here – with the exception of ourselves naturally – not *one*, I say, who holds the flag of ideas aloft. [*Up towards the background*] Oof, I can see them!

KARSTEN BERNICK: Who?

HILMAR TØNNESEN: The two Americans. [*Looks out to the right*] And who are they with? Yes, by God, if it isn't the captain of the *Indian Girl*. Oof!

KARSTEN BERNICK: What can they want with *him*?

HILMAR TØNNESEN: Oh, it's very fitting company, I'd say. He was a slave trader or a pirate apparently; and who knows what those two have been up to all these years.

KARSTEN BERNICK: Hilmar, now, it would be a terrible wrong to think such things of them.

HILMAR TØNNESEN: Well, you're an optimist, as I said. And we're about to get them round our necks again, of course; so I'll make a timely – [*Walks up towards the door on the left.*]

   MISS HESSEL *enters from the right.*

MISS HESSEL: Ah, Hilmar! Not chasing you from the sitting room, am I?

HILMAR TØNNESEN: No, absolutely not; I was just standing here in a most urgent hurry; got to have a word with Betty. [*Walks into the room on the left towards the back.*]

KARSTEN BERNICK [*after a short silence*]: Well, Lona?

MISS HESSEL: Yes.

KARSTEN BERNICK: Where do I stand in your opinion today?

MISS HESSEL: As yesterday. One lie more or less –

KARSTEN BERNICK: I need to put this in its proper light. Where's Johan gone?

MISS HESSEL: He's coming; he had to talk to a man about something.

KARSTEN BERNICK: After what you heard yesterday, you'll understand that my entire existence is destroyed if the truth comes to light.

MISS HESSEL: I understand that.

KARSTEN BERNICK: It goes without saying of course that *I* am not guilty of the crime that was rumoured round here.

MISS HESSEL: Self-evidently. But who was the thief?

KARSTEN BERNICK: There was no thief. There was no money stolen; not a shilling went missing.

MISS HESSEL: What?

KARSTEN BERNICK: Not a shilling I say.

MISS HESSEL: But the rumour? How did this shameful rumour get out that Johan –?

KARSTEN BERNICK: Lona, with you I think I can speak as with nobody else; I'll conceal nothing from you. *I* played my part in the spreading of this rumour.

MISS HESSEL: You? And you could do that to the man who for your sake –!

KARSTEN BERNICK: You shouldn't pass judgement without remembering how things were at the time. I did explain it to you yesterday. I came home to find my mother tangled up in a whole series of unwise enterprises; disasters of all sorts kept piling up; it was as if everything evil was storming in on us; our house was on the edge of ruin. I was half reckless and half desperate, Lona, I think it was mainly to drown out my thoughts that I got involved in the affair that led to Johan leaving.

MISS HESSEL: Hm –

KARSTEN BERNICK: I'm sure you can imagine how all kinds of rumours were set in motion after he, and you, had gone. This wasn't his first reckless act, it was said. Some claimed Dorf was given a large sum of money from him to keep quiet and go; others reckoned *she*'d been given it. At the same time it was no secret that our house had difficulties meeting its obligations. What could be more natural than for the scandalmongers to put these two rumours together? When she went on living here in abject poverty, then people said he'd gone of with the money to America, and as the rumour went on the amount grew continually larger and larger.

MISS HESSEL: And you, Karsten –?

KARSTEN BERNICK: I grabbed this rumour like a raft.

MISS HESSEL: You spread it wider?

KARSTEN BERNICK: I didn't contradict it. The creditors had started hounding us; it was essential I calm them, and that was reliant on people not doubting the solidity of the house; we'd taken an unfortunate little knock, they oughtn't to put pressure on; just give it time; everybody would get their dues.

MISS HESSEL: And did everybody get their dues?

KARSTEN BERNICK: Yes, Lona, that rumour saved our house and made me the man I am now.

MISS HESSEL: So a lie has made you the man you are now.

KARSTEN BERNICK: Who was harmed back then? It was Johan's intention never to come back.

MISS HESSEL: You ask who it harmed. Look within yourself and tell me whether you've not been harmed by it.

KARSTEN BERNICK: Look within any man you choose, and in every single one you'll find *one* dark point at least that he has to conceal.

MISS HESSEL: And you call yourselves the pillars of the community.

KARSTEN BERNICK: No community has better.

MISS HESSEL: And what does it matter whether such a community is upheld or not? What is it that counts round here?

A sham and lies – and nothing else. You live here, the first man in the town, in luxury and happiness, with power and glory – you – who branded an innocent man a criminal.

KARSTEN BERNICK: Don't you think I feel the wrong I've done him deeply enough? And don't you think I'm prepared to make amends?

MISS HESSEL: How? By speaking out?

KARSTEN BERNICK: You could demand that?

MISS HESSEL: What else could right such a wrong?

KARSTEN BERNICK: I'm wealthy, Lona; Johan can demand whatever he wants –

MISS HESSEL: Yes, offer him money, and you'll hear what he says.

KARSTEN BERNICK: Do you know what his intentions are?

MISS HESSEL: No. Since yesterday he's been silent. It's as though all this had suddenly made him into a full-grown man.

KARSTEN BERNICK: I must talk to him.

MISS HESSEL: Well, there you have him.

JOHAN TØNNESEN *enters from the right.*

KARSTEN BERNICK [*towards him*]: Johan –!

JOHAN TØNNESEN [*warding him off*]: Me first. Yesterday morning I gave you my word to keep quiet.

KARSTEN BERNICK: Yes you did.

JOHAN TØNNESEN: But I didn't yet know –

KARSTEN BERNICK: Johan, just let me explain the situation in two words –

JOHAN TØNNESEN: No need; I understand the situation very well. The house was in a difficult position at the time; and then, when I was gone and you had my defenceless name and reputation to use at will –. Well, I don't blame you too harshly for that; we were young and reckless in those days. But now I need the truth, now you must speak out.

KARSTEN BERNICK: And right now I need all my moral prestige, which is why I *can't* speak now.

JOHAN TØNNESEN: I'm not too bothered by these fabrications that you set in motion about me; it's the other thing you'll take the blame for yourself. Dina is going to be my wife, and I want to stay here, here in this town, and build a life with her.

MISS HESSEL: You do?

KARSTEN BERNICK: With Dina? As your wife? Here in town?

JOHAN TØNNESEN: Yes, right here; I want to stay here to defy all these liars and backbiters. But if I'm to win her, it's necessary that you set me free.

KARSTEN BERNICK: Have you considered that, by admitting to the one thing, I'll have admitted to the other? You'll suggest I could prove from the books that nothing dishonest took place? But I can't; our books weren't kept as accurately then. And even if I could – what would be gained? Wouldn't I still be seen as the man who once saved himself by a falsehood and who, for fifteen years, allowed this falsehood and everything else to gain hold, without taking one step to prevent it? You no longer know our community, or you'd know that this would break me, utterly and completely.

JOHAN TØNNESEN: All I can tell you is that I'm going to take Madam Dorf's daughter as my wife and live with her here in this town.

KARSTEN BERNICK [wipes the sweat from his forehead]: Hear me out, Johan – and you too, Lona. It is no ordinary situation I am faced with at this moment. My position means that if this blow is directed at me, the two of you will have destroyed me, and not me alone, but also a great and promising future for this community, which after all is your childhood home.

JOHAN TØNNESEN: And if I don't direct this blow against you, then I will ruin my own future happiness.

MISS HESSEL: Speak on, Karsten.

KARSTEN BERNICK: All right, listen. It's linked to this railway business, and that's not quite as straightforward as you think. You've probably heard talk that there were proposals for a coastal line last year? It had the support of numerous and influential voices both here in town and the region, and notably in the press; but I prevented it because it would have harmed our steamship activity along the coast.

MISS HESSEL: And you have an interest in this steamship activity?

KARSTEN BERNICK: Yes. But nobody dared suspect me on that count; I had my well-respected name to shield and shelter me. Besides I could have borne the loss anyway; but the town couldn't have borne it. Then the decision was passed about the inland route. When that happened, I established, on the quiet, that a local branch line could be laid down to the town here.

MISS HESSEL: Why on the quiet, Karsten?

KARSTEN BERNICK: Have you heard about the large purchases of forests, of mines and waterfalls –?

JOHAN TØNNESEN: Yes, there's some out-of-town company –

KARSTEN BERNICK: As these properties lie now, they're as good as worthless to their widely dispersed owners; as a result they've been sold relatively cheaply. If the buyer had waited until the branch line was in the offing, the owners would have demanded the most outrageous prices.

MISS HESSEL: I see; so what then?

KARSTEN BERNICK: Well, this brings us to something that can be interpreted variously – something a man in our community can only confess to if he has a well-respected and untarnished name to uphold him.

MISS HESSEL: Well?

KARSTEN BERNICK: I'm the one who's bought everything.

MISS HESSEL: You?

JOHAN TØNNESEN: On your own?

KARSTEN BERNICK: On my own. If the branch line goes ahead, I'm a millionaire; if it doesn't, I'm ruined.

MISS HESSEL: This is risky, Karsten.

KARSTEN BERNICK: I've risked all my assets on it.

MISS HESSEL: I'm not thinking of assets; but when it comes to light that you –

KARSTEN BERNICK: Yes, there's the nub. With the untarnished name that I've borne thus far, I can take this on my shoulders, carry it forward and say to my fellow citizens: look, I've risked all this for the benefit of the community.

MISS HESSEL: Of the community?

KARSTEN BERNICK: Yes; and not *one* person would doubt my intentions.

MISS HESSEL: But there are men here who have acted more openly than you, without hidden agendas, or ulterior motives.

KARSTEN BERNICK: Who?

MISS HESSEL: Rummel and Sandstad and Vigeland, of course.

KARSTEN BERNICK: To win them over I was obliged to let them in on it.

MISS HESSEL: And?

KARSTEN BERNICK: They made it a condition that they share a fifth of the profits between them.

MISS HESSEL: Oh, these pillars of the community!

KARSTEN BERNICK: And isn't it the community itself that forces us to take the crooked byway? What would have happened if I hadn't acted on the quiet? Everybody would have thrown themselves into the enterprise, divided, dispersed, bungled and botched the whole thing. There's not a single man in this town besides me who has the knowhow to lead as large a project as this will be; in this country the only people with any aptitude at all for bigger business operations are the immigrant families.[42] This is why my conscience acquits me in this. Only in my hands can these properties become a lasting blessing for the many, a means for them to earn their bread.

MISS HESSEL: You're probably right, Karsten.

JOHAN TØNNESEN: But I don't know 'the many', and my life's happiness is at stake.

KARSTEN BERNICK: The welfare of your birthplace is also at stake. If things emerge to cast a shadow on my earlier conduct, then all my opponents will combine forces to come down on me. A youthful indiscretion is never erased in our community. People will sift through all the intervening years of my life, drag a thousand little episodes out, interpret and construe them in the light of what's been revealed; I'll be broken under the weight of rumours and backbiting. I'll have to withdraw from the railway project; and once I take my hand from that, it'll collapse, and at a stroke I'll be both financially ruined and dead as a citizen.[43]

MISS HESSEL: After what you've heard here, Johan, you must leave and keep quiet.

KARSTEN BERNICK: Yes, yes, Johan, you must!

JOHAN TØNNESEN: Yes, I will leave and keep quiet too; but I'll be back and then I'll speak out.

KARSTEN BERNICK: Stay over there, Johan; keep quiet and I'm willing to give you a share –

JOHAN TØNNESEN: Keep your money, but give me my name and reputation back.

KARSTEN BERNICK: And sacrifice my own!

JOHAN TØNNESEN: That's for you and your community to deal with. I have to, want to and am going to win Dina for myself. Which is why I'm leaving with the *Indian Girl* tomorrow –

KARSTEN BERNICK: With the *Indian Girl*?

JOHAN TØNNESEN: Yes, the captain has promised to take me with him. I'm going over, as I said; I'm selling my farm and sorting out my affairs. In two months I'll be back.[44]

KARSTEN BERNICK: And then you'll speak out?

JOHAN TØNNESEN: Then the guilty party will take the guilt on himself.

KARSTEN BERNICK: Are you forgetting I'd then also have to take upon me the thing of which I am *not* guilty?

JOHAN TØNNESEN: Who was it that benefited from that shameful rumour fifteen years ago?

KARSTEN BERNICK: You're driving me to despair! But if you speak out, I'll deny everything! I'll say there's a conspiracy against me; revenge; that you've come here to extort money from me!

MISS HESSEL: Shame on you, Karsten!

KARSTEN BERNICK: I'm desperate, I tell you; and I'm fighting for my life. I'll deny everything, everything!

JOHAN TØNNESEN: I've got your two letters. I found them in my suitcase among my other papers. I read through them this morning; they're plain enough.

KARSTEN BERNICK: And you'll produce those?

JOHAN TØNNESEN: If necessary.

KARSTEN BERNICK: And in two months you'll be back?

JOHAN TØNNESEN: I hope so. The wind's fair. In three weeks I'll be in New York – as long as the *Indian Girl* doesn't go down.

KARSTEN BERNICK [*looking startled*]: Go down? Why should the *Indian Girl* go down?

JOHAN TØNNESEN: No, why indeed?

KARSTEN BERNICK [*barely audible*]: Go down?

JOHAN TØNNESEN: Well, Bernick, now you know what's in store; you'd better consider your options in the meantime. Goodbye! You can say goodbye to Betty for me, she's hardly given me a sisterly welcome. But Marta I do want to see. She must tell Dina – must promise me –

He leaves through the furthest door to the left.

KARSTEN BERNICK [*to himself*]: The *Indian Girl* –? [*Urgently*] Lona, you *must* prevent this!

MISS HESSEL: You can see for yourself, Karsten – I no longer have any power over him.

She follows JOHAN *into the room to the left.*

KARSTEN BERNICK [*troubled*]: Go down –?

AUNE *enters from the right.*

AUNE: With permission, is it convenient to the consul –?

KARSTEN BERNICK [*turns abruptly*]: What do you want?

AUNE: To ask if I may put a question to the consul.

KARSTEN BERNICK: Well then; hurry up. What d'you want to ask?

AUNE: I wanted to ask if it still stands firm – if it's irreversible – that I'd be dismissed from the yard if the *Indian Girl* couldn't sail tomorrow?

KARSTEN BERNICK: What? The ship *will* be ready to sail, won't it?

AUNE: Yes – it will. But if it wasn't – would I be dismissed?

KARSTEN BERNICK: What is the point of such idle questions?

AUNE: I'd like very much to know, Mr Consul, sir. Just answer me *that*; would I then be dismissed?

KARSTEN BERNICK: Does my word usually stand firm or not?

AUNE: So, tomorrow I'd have lost the position I have in my house and among those closest to me – lost my influence in the workers' circles – lost the opportunity to do anything of benefit for those of low and modest status in the community.

KARSTEN BERNICK: Mr Aune, we've done with that subject.

AUNE: Right, then the *Indian Girl* will sail.

Short silence.

KARSTEN BERNICK: Listen here; I can't have eyes everywhere; can't be responsible for everything. You can, I presume, assure me that the repairs are beyond criticism?

AUNE: You gave me a tight deadline, Mr Consul, sir.

KARSTEN BERNICK: But the repairs are satisfactory, you say?

AUNE: We do have good weather, and it's the middle of summer.

Renewed silence.

KARSTEN BERNICK: Do you have anything else to say to me?

AUNE: I don't know of anything else, Mr Consul, sir.

KARSTEN BERNICK: So – the *Indian Girl* will sail –

AUNE: Tomorrow?

KARSTEN BERNICK: Yes.

AUNE: Right.

He nods and leaves.

CONSUL BERNICK *stands in doubt for a moment; then he walks quickly to the exit door, as if to call* AUNE *back, but stands uneasily with his hand on the door handle. At that moment the door is opened from the outside and* MR KRAP *steps in.*

KRAP [*hushed*]: Aha, he was here. Has he confessed?

KARSTEN BERNICK: Hm – have you discovered anything?

KRAP: What's the need? Couldn't the consul see that evil conscience flashing out of his eyes?

KARSTEN BERNICK: Come, come, now – such things aren't visible. I asked if you'd discovered anything?

KRAP: Couldn't get access; was too late; they were already towing the ship out of dock. But this very haste indicates clearly –

KARSTEN BERNICK: It indicates nothing. So the inspection's taken place?

KRAP: Of course; but –

KARSTEN BERNICK: There you see. And naturally they found nothing to criticize.

KRAP: Mr Consul, sir, you know very well how these inspections are conducted, particularly at a yard with as good a name as ours.

KARSTEN BERNICK: Nonetheless; we're beyond reproach then.

KRAP: Sir, did you really notice nothing in Aune that –?

KARSTEN BERNICK: Aune has reassured me absolutely, I tell you.

KRAP: And I'm telling you that I am morally convinced that –

KARSTEN BERNICK: What are you getting at, Mr Krap? I realize you bear a grudge against the man; but if you want rid of him, you'll have to choose some other occasion. You know how crucial it is for me – or to put it more accurately the shipping company – that the *Indian Girl* sets sail tomorrow.

KRAP: Well, well, so be it; but when we'll hear from *that* ship again, I – hm!

MR VIGELAND *enters from the right.*

VIGELAND: A very good day to you, Mr Consul. Do you have a moment?

KARSTEN BERNICK: At your service, Mr Vigeland.

VIGELAND: I just wanted to hear if you're also in favour of the *Palm Tree* setting sail tomorrow?

KARSTEN BERNICK: Well, of course; that's agreed.

VIGELAND: But now the captain's come to me, reporting signs of a storm.

KRAP: The barometer's fallen sharply since this morning.

KARSTEN BERNICK: Oh? Can we expect a storm?

VIGELAND: Strong winds at least; but no headwind; quite the contrary –

KARSTEN BERNICK: Hm; so what do *you* say?

VIGELAND: Well, I say, as I said to the captain, that the *Palm Tree* rests in the hands of Providence. And besides, she's only crossing the North Sea to begin with; and with freights[45] being so high in England right now –

KARSTEN BERNICK: Yes, it would probably mean a loss for us if we waited.

VIGELAND: And the ship is solid all right, and besides she's fully insured. No, when it comes to it, the *Indian Girl* is at much greater risk.

KARSTEN BERNICK: How do you mean?

VIGELAND: Well, she's sailing tomorrow too.

KARSTEN BERNICK: Yes, her owners have put the pressure on, and besides –

VIGELAND: Well, if that old crate can brave it – and with a crew like that into the bargain – it'd be a shame if we didn't –

KARSTEN BERNICK: Well, well. I take it you have the ship's papers with you?

VIGELAND: Yes, here.

KARSTEN BERNICK: Good; then do go in with Mr Krap.

KRAP: After you; it'll be sorted out in no time.

VIGELAND: Thank you. – And we shall place the outcome in the hands of the Almighty, Mr Consul.

> *He walks together with* MR KRAP *into the nearest room to the left.* SCHOOLMASTER RØRLUND *comes through the garden.*

MR RØRLUND: Ah, at home at this time of day, Mr Consul, sir?

KARSTEN BERNICK [*in thought*]: As you see.

MR RØRLUND: Well, it was for your wife's sake I dropped by actually. I thought she might need a few words of comfort.

KARSTEN BERNICK: Indeed she might. But I'd like to speak with you too.

MR RØRLUND: With pleasure, Mr Consul, sir. But what's troubling you? You look rather pale and upset.

KARSTEN BERNICK: Oh? Do I? Yes, how could it be otherwise – with things towering up around me as they are just now? My whole business – and then the railway –. Listen, tell me something, schoolmaster; let me put a question to you.

MR RØRLUND: With pleasure, sir.

KARSTEN BERNICK: It's a thought that's occurred to me. When one stands on the threshold of a far-reaching enterprise which aims at the improved well-being of thousands –. If this thing were to require one single sacrifice –?

MR RØRLUND: In what way, sir?

KARSTEN BERNICK: Suppose, for example, that a man is considering building a large factory. He knows for certain – since experience has taught him this – that sooner or later during the running of this factory human life will be lost.

MR RØRLUND: Yes, that's only too probable.

KARSTEN BERNICK: Or a man embarks on a mining business. He takes family men and youngsters in the prime of life into his service. It can be said with absolute certainty, can it not, that they won't all come out of it alive?

MR RØRLUND: Yes, unfortunately, that's probably so.

KARSTEN BERNICK: Well. Such a man knows beforehand, then, that the enterprise he wants to set in motion will undoubtedly cost human lives at some point. But this enterprise is for the common good; for every human life it costs, it will just as undoubtedly further the welfare of hundreds.

MR RØRLUND: Aha, you're thinking of the railway – all that dangerous excavation work and mountain blasting and such –

KARSTEN BERNICK: Yes, yes; I am indeed thinking of the railway. And, well yes – the railway will, of course, give rise to both factories and mines. But nonetheless don't you think –?

MR RØRLUND: My dear consul, you have almost too great a conscience. I feel that when you place the matter in the hands of Providence –

KARSTEN BERNICK: Yes; yes, of course; Providence –

MR RØRLUND: – you are then beyond reproach. You just build your railway with confidence.

KARSTEN BERNICK: Yes, but now I'll suggest a specific instance. Suppose there is a borehole that has to be blasted in a dangerous place; but without the blasting of this borehole, the railway will never be realized. And now let's suppose that the engineer knows it will cost the life of the worker who'll light the explosive; yet lit it must be, and it's the engineer's duty to send a worker out to do it.

MR RØRLUND: Hm –

KARSTEN BERNICK: I know what you'll say. It would be heroic if the engineer took the fuse himself and went over to light the borehole. But nobody does that. So, he must sacrifice a worker.

MR RØRLUND: No engineer here would ever do that.

KARSTEN BERNICK: No engineer in one of the larger countries would hesitate to do it.

MR RØRLUND: The larger countries? Yes, that I can believe. In those corrupt and unscrupulous communities –

KARSTEN BERNICK: Oh, there are many good things about *those* communities.

MR RØRLUND: And you can say that, when you yourself –?

KARSTEN BERNICK: In these larger communities people do at least have room to further a beneficial enterprise; they have the courage over there to sacrifice something for a great cause; but here people are restricted by all sorts of petty considerations and misgivings.

MR RØRLUND: Is a human life a petty consideration?

KARSTEN BERNICK: When this human life represents a threat to the welfare of thousands.

MR RØRLUND: But you're presenting utterly inconceivable examples, Mr Consul, sir! I don't understand you at all today. And then you point to these larger communities. Well, yes, out there – what's a human life worth? There they calculate human lives as they do capital. But *we* take quite a different moral standpoint, I should think. Look at our honest shipowners! Name one single shipowner here at home who would sacrifice a human life for paltry gain! And then think of those crooks out there in these larger communities, who for profit's sake send one unseaworthy ship out after another –

KARSTEN BERNICK: I'm not talking about unseaworthy ships!

MR RØRLUND: But I am talking about them, Mr Consul, sir.

KARSTEN BERNICK: Yes, but what's your point? That's irrelevant, isn't it. – Ah, these craven little considerations! If a general here at home led his men into the line of fire and got them shot down, he'd have sleepless nights afterwards. Things aren't like that elsewhere. You should hear what the man in there says –

MR RØRLUND: Who? The American –?

KARSTEN BERNICK: Yes. You should hear how in America they –

MR RØRLUND: He's in *there*? And you didn't tell me. I'm going right –

KARSTEN BERNICK: It'll do you no good; you won't get anywhere with him.

MR RØRLUND: We'll see about that. Well now, here he is.

JOHAN TØNNESEN *comes from the room on the left.*

JOHAN TØNNESEN [*speaks back through the open door*]: All right, Dina, that's fine; but I shan't give up on you even so. I'll come back, and then everything will come good between us.

MR RØRLUND: With permission, what are you suggesting with those words? What is it you want?

JOHAN TØNNESEN: What I want is for the young girl for whom you blackened my character yesterday to be my wife.

MR RØRLUND: Your –? And you think you can –?

JOHAN TØNNESEN: I want her as my wife.

MR RØRLUND: All right, then you must be told – [*Walks over to the half-open door*] Mrs Bernick, be so good as to act as witness. And you too, Miss Marta. And Dina must come. [*Sees* MISS HESSEL] Ah, you're here as well?

MISS HESSEL [*in the doorway*]: Shall I come too?

MR RØRLUND: As many as wish; the more the better.

KARSTEN BERNICK: What have you in mind?

MISS HESSEL, MRS BERNICK, MISS BERNICK, DINA *and* HILMAR TØNNESEN *come out of the room.*

MRS BERNICK: Mr Rørlund, hard as I tried, I couldn't stop him –

MR RØRLUND: I shall stop him, Mrs Bernick. – Dina, you are a thoughtless girl. But I don't reproach you harshly. You've been left much too long without the moral support that ought to have upheld you. It's myself I reproach, for not having been that pillar of support earlier.

DINA: Do not speak now!

MRS BERNICK: But what is this?

MR RØRLUND: It is *now* that I must speak, Dina, even though your conduct both yesterday and today has made it ten times harder for me. But for your rescue all other considerations must give way. You remember the pledge I made you. You remember what you promised to answer, when I found that the time had come. I dare hesitate no longer [*to* JOHAN TØNNESEN] – the young girl whom you are pursuing, is my fiancée.

MRS BERNICK: What!

KARSTEN BERNICK: Dina!

JOHAN TØNNESEN: She! Your –?

MISS BERNICK: No, Dina, no!

MISS HESSEL: Lies!

JOHAN TØNNESEN: Dina – is this man speaking the truth?

DINA [*after a short pause*]: Yes.

MR RØRLUND: So now, hopefully, any tricks of seduction are rendered powerless. I am happy for this step, which I have resolved upon for Dina's benefit, to be announced to our whole community. I cherish the sure hope that it will not be misconstrued. But now, Mrs Bernick, I think it best we escort her from here and seek to bring calm and equilibrium to her mind once more.

MRS BERNICK: Yes, come. Oh, Dina, how wonderful for you!
    She leads DINA *out to the left;* MR RØRLUND *follows them.*

MISS BERNICK: Farewell, Johan!
    She leaves.

HILMAR TØNNESEN [*in the garden doorway*]: Hm – well, I really must say –

MISS HESSEL [*who has watched* DINA *leave*]: Don't lose heart, boy! I'll stay here and keep watch on the pastor.
    She goes out to the right.

KARSTEN BERNICK: Well, Johan, you won't be going with the *Indian Girl* now!

JOHAN TØNNESEN: I certainly will.

KARSTEN BERNICK: But you won't be coming back?

JOHAN TØNNESEN: I'll come back.

KARSTEN BERNICK: After this? What would you want here after this?

JOHAN TØNNESEN: To avenge myself on all of you; to crush as many of you as I can.

He leaves to the right. MR VIGELAND *and* MR KRAP *enter from the* CONSUL's *room.*

VIGELAND: Right, the documents are in order now, Mr Consul, sir.

KARSTEN BERNICK: Good, good –

KRAP [*quietly*]: And it stands firm that the *Indian Girl* sails tomorrow?

KARSTEN BERNICK: She sails.

He goes into his room. MR VIGELAND *and* MR KRAP *leave to the right.* HILMAR TØNNESEN *wants to follow them, but just then* OLAF *sticks his head hesitantly round the door to the left.*

OLAF: Uncle! Uncle Hilmar!

HILMAR TØNNESEN: Oof! It's you? Why aren't you upstairs? You're grounded.

OLAF [*a couple of steps forward*]: Ssh! Uncle Hilmar, have you heard the news?

HILMAR TØNNESEN: Well, I know you got a thrashing today.

OLAF [*casts a threatening glance towards his father's room*]: He'll never ever hit me again. But did you know Uncle Johan's sailing tomorrow with the Americans?

HILMAR TØNNESEN: What's that got to do with you? Take yourself upstairs again.

OLAF: Maybe I can go on a buffalo hunt too one day, Uncle.

HILMAR TØNNESEN: Oh, rubbish; a wimp like you –

OLAF: Oh, just wait; you'll know different tomorrow!

HILMAR TØNNESEN: Clothead!

He walks out through the garden. OLAF *runs back into the room and closes the door when he sees* MR KRAP *coming in from the right.*

KRAP [*walks over to the* CONSUL's *door and opens it halfway*]: Excuse my coming back, Mr Consul, sir; but there's a violent storm gathering. [*Waits a little; no reply*] Will the *Indian Girl* sail just the same?

After a short pause CONSUL BERNICK *answers from inside the room.*

KARSTEN BERNICK: The *Indian Girl* sails just the same.

MR KRAP *closes the door and again leaves to the right.*

ACT FOUR

The garden room at Consul Bernick's. The work table has been removed. It is a stormy afternoon. It is already half dark and gets darker during the following.

A SERVANT *lights the chandelier; a couple of* SERVANT GIRLS *bring in pots of flowers, lamps and candles, which are placed on tables and ledges along the walls.* RUMMEL, *wearing a dinner suit, gloves and a white cravat, stands in the room, giving instructions.*

RUMMEL [*to the* SERVANT]: Only every other candle, Jakob. It oughtn't to look too festive; it's supposed to come as a surprise after all. And all these flowers –? Oh all right, just leave them; it can look as if they were here every day –
   CONSUL BERNICK *comes out of his room.*
KARSTEN BERNICK [*in the doorway*]: What's going on?
RUMMEL: Oh heck, are you here? [*To the* SERVANTS] Well, you can go for now.
   The SERVANT *and the* MAIDS *leave through the door furthest back on the left.*
KARSTEN BERNICK [*comes closer*]: But Rummel, what's the meaning of all this?
RUMMEL: It means your proudest moment is come. The town is holding a parade this evening for its top man.
KARSTEN BERNICK: What?
RUMMEL: A parade with banners and music! We were going to have torches too; but we didn't dare in this stormy weather.

Still, the illuminations[46] will be there; and *that* will sound pretty good too when it comes in the papers.

KARSTEN BERNICK: Listen, Rummel, I don't want any part in this.

RUMMEL: Well, it's too late now; they'll be here in half an hour.

KARSTEN BERNICK: But why didn't you tell me before?

RUMMEL: Precisely because I was afraid you'd make objections. But I got together with your wife; she allowed me to make a few arrangements and she's attending to the refreshments.

KARSTEN BERNICK [*listening*]: What's that? Are they coming already? I think I can hear singing.

RUMMEL [*by the garden door*]: Singing? Oh, that's just the Americans. It's the *Indian Girl* being towed out to the buoy.

KARSTEN BERNICK: Being towed out! I see – no, I can't do this tonight, Rummel; I'm ill.

RUMMEL: Yes, you do look rather poorly. But you've got to buck up.[47] You must, for crying out loud, buck up! We've all, myself and Sandstad and Vigeland, put a lot of weight behind getting this event organized. Our opponents must be crushed under the amplest demonstration of public opinion possible. Rumours are multiplying around town; the announcement of the land purchases can't be held back any longer. You've got to let them know this very evening, amid singing and speeches and the clinking of glasses, in short, amid a swell of festivity, what you've risked for the good of the community. In such a swell of festivity, as I just put it, one can achieve a great deal here in our town. But *that*'s what you need, or it won't work.

KARSTEN BERNICK: Yes, yes, yes –

RUMMEL: Especially when such a delicate and ticklish matter is to be raised. Well, you have, thank God, a name that can take it, Bernick. But listen now; we need to finalize a few little details. Mr Tønnesen has written a song for you. It starts very nicely with the words: 'Raise the flag of ideas aloft'. And Mr Rørlund has been assigned the task of giving the speech of honour. To which you must obviously respond.

KARSTEN BERNICK: I can't tonight, Rummel. Couldn't you –?

RUMMEL: Impossible, however much I'd want to. The speech will, as you'd expect, be directed mainly at you. Although there might be the odd word for the rest of us too. I've spoken to Vigeland and Sandstad about it. We thought you could answer with a toast to the well-being of our community; Sandstad will say a few words about the harmony that exists between all levels of our community; Vigeland will doubtless say a bit about how essential it is that this new enterprise shouldn't disturb the moral foundation upon which we presently stand, and I am thinking of saying a few appropriate words in remembrance of our womenfolk, whose more modest works are not altogether without significance to the community. But you're not listening –

KARSTEN BERNICK: Yes – yes, of course I am. But tell me, do you think the sea is that violent out there?

RUMMEL: Oh, you're worried about the *Palm Tree*? She's well insured.

KARSTEN BERNICK: Yes, insured; but –

RUMMEL: And in good repair; and that's what's most important.

KARSTEN BERNICK: Hm –. If something happens to a vessel, it doesn't necessarily follow, of course, that human lives will be lost. A ship and cargo can go down – and one can lose suitcases and papers –

RUMMEL: Christ almighty, suitcases and papers aren't of any great consequence.

KARSTEN BERNICK: They're not? No, of course, I just meant –. Ssh – they're singing again.

RUMMEL: It's aboard the *Palm Tree*.

MR VIGELAND *enters from the right.*

VIGELAND: Well, the *Palm Tree* is putting out to sea now. Good afternoon, Mr Consul, sir.

KARSTEN BERNICK: And you, with your knowledge of the oceans, you still hold that –?

VIGELAND: I hold firmly by Providence, I do, Mr Consul, sir; besides I've been on board and distributed a few short tracts, which will, I hope, act as a blessing.

MR SANDSTAD *and* MR KRAP *enter from the right.*

SANDSTAD [*in the doorway*]: Yup, if *that* doesn't end in disaster, anything's possible. Ah, afternoon all, afternoon!

KARSTEN BERNICK: Something wrong, Mr Krap?

KRAP: I'm saying nothing, Mr Consul, sir.

SANDSTAD: The entire crew of the *Indian Girl* are drunk; I wouldn't be an honest man if I said those beasts would make it over alive.

MISS HESSEL *arrives from the right.*

MISS HESSEL [*to* CONSUL BERNICK]: Right, now I can say goodbye to you from him.

KARSTEN BERNICK: Already on board?

MISS HESSEL: Soon at least. We parted outside the hotel.

KARSTEN BERNICK: And his intentions still stand firm?

MISS HESSEL: Firm as rock.

RUMMEL [*up by the windows*]: Damn these new-fangled fittings; I can't get these curtains down.

MISS HESSEL: Are they to come down? I rather thought –

RUMMEL: Down to start with, Miss Hessel. You do know[48] what's happening here, I take it?

MISS HESSEL: Indeed. Let me help; [*grabs the strings*] I'll let the curtains down for my brother-in-law – though I'd rather have it go up.

RUMMEL: Well, you can do that later. When the garden is filled with the swelling crowd the curtains will go up, and people will see a surprised and happy family within –. A citizen's home should be like a glass cabinet.

CONSUL BERNICK *seems to want to say something but turns abruptly and goes into his room.*

RUMMEL: Right, let's have our final conference. You too, Mr Krap; you need to assist us with a few facts here.

All the gentlemen walk into the CONSUL's *room.* MISS HESSEL *has closed the curtains over the windows and is about to do the same with the curtains on the open glass door when* OLAF *jumps down on to the garden steps from above; he is carrying a small blanket over his shoulder and a bundle in his hand.*

MISS HESSEL: Oh, God forgive you, boy, you frightened me!

OLAF [*hides his bundle*]: Shhh, Auntie!

MISS HESSEL: Did you just jump out of your window? Where
 are you off to?

OLAF: Shhh; don't say anything. I want to go to Uncle Johan;
 just to the harbour, you understand – just to say goodbye to
 him. Good night, Auntie!

 He runs through the garden.

MISS HESSEL: No, stay! Olaf – Olaf!

 JOHAN TØNNESEN *in travel clothes, with a bag over
 his shoulder, enters hesitantly through the door to the
 right.*

JOHAN TØNNESEN: Lona!

MISS HESSEL [*turns*]: What! Are you back?

JOHAN TØNNESEN: There are still a few minutes left. I have to
 see her one more time. We can't part like this.

 MISS BERNICK *and* DINA, *both with coats on, and the
 latter with a small travel bag in her hand, enter from the
 furthest door on the left.*

DINA: To him; to him!

MISS BERNICK: Yes, you shall go to him, Dina!

DINA: There he is!

JOHAN TØNNESEN: Dina!

DINA: Take me with you!

JOHAN TØNNESEN: What –!

MISS HESSEL: You want to go?

DINA: Yes, take me with you! The other one's written to me
 and said it'll be announced publicly this evening –

JOHAN TØNNESEN: Dina – you don't love him?

DINA: I've never loved that man. I'll throw myself to the bottom of the fjord if I have to be his fiancée! Oh, the way he
 tried to make me grovel with his arrogant words yesterday!
 The way he made me feel he was lifting some despised creature up to his level! I don't want to be despised any more. I
 want to travel. Can I come with you?

JOHAN TØNNESEN: Yes, yes – a thousand times yes!

DINA: I shan't be a burden to you for long. Just help me get
 over there; help me settle in a bit at the start –

JOHAN TØNNESEN: Hurrah, everything will sort itself out, Dina!

MISS HESSEL [*points to the* CONSUL's *door*]: Shh, quietly, quietly!

JOHAN TØNNESEN: Dina, I'll carry you in my arms!

DINA: I won't let you carry me. I want to make my own way; and over there I'm sure I can. Just so long as I get away from here. Oh, these respectable wives – you've no idea – they also wrote to me today; they urged me to recognize my good fortune, lectured me on how noble-minded he's been. Tomorrow and for ever after, they'll watch over me to see if I'm proving worthy of it all. Oh, all this respectability terrifies me!

JOHAN TØNNESEN: Tell me, Dina, is that the only reason for your leaving? Am I nothing to you?

DINA: Yes, Johan. You mean more to me than anyone else.

JOHAN TØNNESEN: Oh, Dina –!

DINA: Everybody here says that I ought to hate and detest you; that it's my duty. But I don't understand this thing about duty; I'll never understand it.

MISS HESSEL: Nor should you, my child!

MISS BERNICK: No, nor should you; and that's why you shall go with him as his wife.

JOHAN TØNNESEN: Yes! Yes!

MISS HESSEL: What? Now I've got to kiss you, Marta! I'd never have expected *that* from *you*.

MISS BERNICK: No, that I can believe; I didn't expect it myself. But something was bound to burst out in me at some point. Oh, how we suffer here under the abuse of conventions and rules! Rebel against it, Dina. Be his wife. Do something that defies all these dos and don'ts.

JOHAN TØNNESEN: What's your answer, Dina?

DINA: Yes, I want to be your wife.

JOHAN TØNNESEN: Dina!

DINA: But first I want to work, make something of myself, just as you have. I don't want to be a thing that's taken.

MISS HESSEL: Yes, quite right too.

JOHAN TØNNESEN: Fine; I shall wait and hope –

MISS HESSEL: – and win her, my boy. But now, aboard!

JOHAN TØNNESEN: Yes, aboard! Ah, Lona, my dear sister, a word; listen now –

He takes her towards the background and speaks urgently with her.

MISS BERNICK: Dina, you lucky thing – let me look at you, kiss you one more time – the last time.

DINA: Not the last; no, dear darling Aunt, I'm sure we'll see each other again.

MISS BERNICK: Never! Promise me that, Dina, never come back. [*Grasps both her hands and looks at her*] You're going to your happiness now, my darling child – over the sea. Oh, how often in the schoolhouse I've dreamed of it! It must be beautiful out there; wider skies, clouds drifting higher than here, a freer air flowing cool above people's heads –

DINA: Oh, Auntie Marta, you'll come too some time.

MISS BERNICK: Me? Never; never. It's here I have my little life vocation, and I do believe now that I can become wholly and completely what I should be.

DINA: I can't imagine parting from you.

MISS BERNICK: Oh, a person may be parted from a great deal, Dina. [*Kisses her.*] But that's not for you to experience, my sweet child. Promise me to make him happy.

DINA: I don't want to promise anything; I hate making promises; everything must come as it can.

MISS BERNICK: Yes, yes, it must; you must stay just as you are – honest and true to yourself.

DINA: I will, Auntie.

MISS HESSEL [*hides some papers in her pocket that* JOHAN *has given her*]: Good, very good, my sweet boy. But now, off you go.

JOHAN TØNNESEN: Yes, there's no time to waste. Goodbye, Lona; thank you for all your love. Goodbye, Marta, and thanks to you too, for your loyal friendship.

MISS BERNICK: Goodbye, Johan! Goodbye, Dina! And life-long happiness to you both!

> MISS HESSEL *and* MISS BERNICK *usher them towards the door in the background.* JOHAN TØNNESEN *and* DINA *walk quickly through the garden.* MISS HESSEL *closes the door and then draws the curtain in front of it.*

MISS HESSEL: Now we're alone, Marta. You've lost her and
I him.

MISS BERNICK: You – him?

MISS HESSEL: Oh, I'd half lost him over there already. The boy
was longing to stand on his own two feet; so I made him
think I was yearning for home.

MISS BERNICK: Was that why? Yes, now I understand why
you came. But he'll want you back there, Lona.

MISS HESSEL: An old half-sister – what use is she to him
now? – Men tear apart so much and so many things in their
quest for happiness.

MISS BERNICK: It happens on occasion.

MISS HESSEL: But we'll stick together, Marta.

MISS BERNICK: Can I be anything to you?

MISS HESSEL: Who more? Us two foster mothers – haven't we
both lost our children? We're alone now.

MISS BERNICK: Yes, alone. And that's why you should know
this – I've loved him more than anything in the world.

MISS HESSEL: Marta! [*Grabs her arm.*] Is that true?

MISS BERNICK: The entire content of my life lies in those
words. I've loved him and waited for him. Every summer
I've waited for him to come. And then he came – but he
didn't see me.

MISS HESSEL: Loved him! And yet you were the one who put
happiness in his hands.

MISS BERNICK: Shouldn't I put happiness in his hands, when
I loved him? Yes, I have loved him. My whole life has been a
life for him, from the moment he left. What reason had I to
hope, you're wondering? Oh, I do believe I had some reason
for it. But when he came back – it was as though everything
was wiped from his memory. He didn't see me.

MISS HESSEL: It was Dina who overshadowed you, Marta.

MISS BERNICK: A good thing she did. At the time when he left,
we were the same age; when I saw him again – oh, that dreadful moment – it dawned on me that I was now ten years older
than him. He'd journeyed out into the bright, shimmering
sunlight and sucked youth and health in with every breath of
air; and meanwhile I'd sat in here spinning and spinning –

MISS HESSEL: – the thread of his happiness, Marta.

MISS BERNICK: Yes, it was gold that I spun. No bitterness! Isn't that so, Lona, we've been two good sisters to him?

MISS HESSEL [*throws her arms around her*]: Marta!

    KARSTEN BERNICK *comes out of his room.*

KARSTEN BERNICK [*to the gentlemen in his room*]: Yes, yes, organize everything as you please. I'm sure, when the time comes, I'll – [*Closes the door.*] Ah, so you're here? Listen, Marta, you must dress up a bit. And tell Betty to do the same. I don't want anything showy, of course; just a neat, homely touch. But you've got to hurry.

MISS HESSEL: And a bright, cheerful expression, Marta; happy faces all round.

KARSTEN BERNICK: Olaf should come down too; I want to have him next to me.

MISS HESSEL: Hm; Olaf –

MISS BERNICK: I'll let Betty know.

    She leaves through the door furthest back on the left.

MISS HESSEL: So, the great and solemn moment is come.

KARSTEN BERNICK [*walks back and forth*]: Yes, it has indeed.

MISS HESSEL: At a moment like this a man must feel proud and happy, I'd imagine.

KARSTEN BERNICK [*looks at her*]: Hm!

MISS HESSEL: The whole town is to be illuminated, I hear.

KARSTEN BERNICK: Yes, they've come up with something of the sort.

MISS HESSEL: The associations will all turn up with their banners. Your name will be lit up in burning letters. It'll be telegraphed to every corner of the land tonight: 'Surrounded by his happy family, Consul Bernick was hailed by his fellow townsfolk as one of the pillars of the community.'

KARSTEN BERNICK: That's right; and the crowd will cheer outside, and shout excitedly for me to appear in that doorway there; and I shall be compelled to bow and thank them.

MISS HESSEL: *Compelled* to –

KARSTEN BERNICK: Do you think I feel happy at this moment?

MISS HESSEL: No, *I* don't think you can be feeling very happy at all.

KARSTEN BERNICK: Lona, you despise me.

MISS HESSEL: Not yet.

KARSTEN BERNICK: Nor do you have a right to. Not to *despise* me! – Lona, you have no idea how unutterably lonely I stand here in this mean-spirited and crippled community – how year upon year I've had to cut back on any expectation of a wholly fulfilling vocation in life. What have I accomplished, however great and varied it might appear? Patchwork – petty trivialities. But nothing else, nothing more, is tolerated here. If I wanted to move one step ahead of the mood or opinion of the moment, all my power would be gone. Do you know what we are – those of us who are reckoned pillars of the community? We are the instruments of the community, that's all.

MISS HESSEL: Why have you only just seen this?

KARSTEN BERNICK: Because I've been thinking a lot recently – since you came back – and most of all this evening. – Oh Lona, why didn't I know you for who you really are – in the old days.

MISS HESSEL: What then?

KARSTEN BERNICK: Then I'd never have let you go; and if I'd had you, I wouldn't be standing where I'm standing now.

MISS HESSEL: And you've no thought for what *she* might have grown to be for you, the woman you chose in my place?

KARSTEN BERNICK: I know at least that she never became anything for me that I needed.

MISS HESSEL: Because you've never shared your life's vocation with her; because you've never put her in a place where she could be honest and free in relation to you; because you've allowed her to sink under the weight of accusation and blame for the disgrace that *you* poured over her family.

KARSTEN BERNICK: Yes, yes, yes; it all stems from the lies and hollow deceit.

MISS HESSEL: So why don't you break with the lies and hollow deceit?

KARSTEN BERNICK: Now? Now it's too late, Lona.

MISS HESSEL: Tell me, Karsten, what sort of satisfaction does this sham and deception bring you?

KARSTEN BERNICK: It brings me none. I'll go under like the rest of this tired community. But a generation is growing up after us; it's my son I'm working for; it's for *him* I'm building up a life's work. There'll come a time when truth will descend on the life of our community, and on that he'll found a happier existence than his father's.

MISS HESSEL: With a lie as its basis? Think carefully what it is that you're giving your son as an inheritance.

KARSTEN BERNICK [*in suppressed despair*]: The inheritance I'm giving him is a thousand times worse than you know. But the curse must lift some day surely. Then again – perhaps – [*Bursting out*] How could you two bring all this down on me! But it's happened now. I must move forward. You *won't* succeed in crushing me!

 HILMAR TØNNESEN, *with an opened note in his hand, arrives quickly and in a state of agitation from the right.*

HILMAR TØNNESEN: But this is utterly –. Betty, Betty!

KARSTEN BERNICK: What now? Are they coming already?

HILMAR TØNNESEN: No, no; but I really must talk to somebody –

 He goes out through the door furthest back to the left.

MISS HESSEL: Karsten: you talk of our coming to crush you. Then let me tell you what stuff[49] he's made of, this prodigal son your moral community shuns like the plague. He can do without all of you, because he's gone now.

KARSTEN BERNICK: But he wanted to come back –

MISS HESSEL: Johan won't ever come back. He's gone for good, and Dina's gone with him.

KARSTEN BERNICK: Won't come back? And Dina with him?

MISS HESSEL: Yes, to be his wife. That's their way of slapping your virtuous community in the face, just as I once – well!

KARSTEN BERNICK: Gone; her too – with the *Indian Girl* –!

MISS HESSEL: No; he didn't dare entrust such a precious cargo to that dissolute mob. Johan and Dina have gone with the *Palm Tree*.

KARSTEN BERNICK: Ah! So – all for nothing – [*Walks quickly over to his room, flings the door open and shouts*] Krap, stop the *Indian Girl*; she mustn't sail tonight!

KRAP [*inside*]: The *Indian Girl* has already put to sea, Mr Consul, sir.

KARSTEN BERNICK [*closes the door and says dully*]: Too late – and to no purpose –

MISS HESSEL: What do you mean?

KARSTEN BERNICK: Nothing, nothing. Get away from me –![50]

MISS HESSEL: Hm. Look here, Karsten. Johan wants you to know that he's entrusted me with the name and reputation he once lent you, and the one you robbed him of in his absence. Johan will keep quiet, and I can do exactly as I please in the matter. Look, I have your two letters here in my hand.

KARSTEN BERNICK: You've got them! And so – now you'll – this very evening – perhaps when the parade –

MISS HESSEL: I didn't come here to expose you, but to shake you up so that you'd speak of your own free will. It's not succeeded. So go on standing there in your lie. Look: I'm tearing your two letters up. Take the scraps; there you have them. Now there's nothing to bear witness against you, Karsten. You're safe now; be happy now too – if you can.

KARSTEN BERNICK [*completely shaken*]: Lona – why didn't you do this before! It's too late now; my whole life is in ruins; I can't go on living after this day.

MISS HESSEL: What's happened?

KARSTEN BERNICK: Don't ask me. – But I *must* live even so! I *want* to live – for Olaf's sake. He'll rectify and atone for everything –

MISS HESSEL: Karsten –!

HILMAR TØNNESEN *comes hurrying back in.*

HILMAR TØNNESEN: Nobody to be found; gone; not Betty either!

KARSTEN BERNICK: What's the matter with you?

HILMAR TØNNESEN: I don't dare tell you.

KARSTEN BERNICK: What is it? You must and will tell me!

HILMAR TØNNESEN: All right; Olaf's run away on the *Indian Girl*.

KARSTEN BERNICK [*stumbles backwards*]: Olaf – on the
  Indian Girl! No, no!

MISS HESSEL: He has, yes! I understand now –. I saw him
  jump out of the window.

KARSTEN BERNICK [*in the doorway to his room, cries out in
  despair*]: Krap, stop the *Indian Girl* at any price!

KRAP [*comes out*]: Impossible, Mr Consul, sir. How d'you
  think –?

KARSTEN BERNICK: We *must* stop her; Olaf's on board!

KRAP: What!

RUMMEL [*comes out*]: Olaf's run away? Impossible!

SANDSTAD [*comes*]: He'll be sent back with the harbour pilot,
  Mr Consul, sir.

HILMAR TØNNESEN: No, no; he's written to me; [*shows the
  note*] he says he'll hide in the cargo until they're on the
  open sea.

KARSTEN BERNICK: I'll never see him again!

RUMMEL: Oh, nonsense; a strong, sound ship, newly repaired –

VIGELAND [*who has also come out*]: – from your own yard,
  Mr Consul, sir!

KARSTEN BERNICK: I'll never see him again, I tell you. I've
  lost him, Lona, and – now I see it – he was never mine.
  [*Listens*] What's that?

RUMMEL: Music. Here comes the parade.

KARSTEN BERNICK: I can't, I don't want to receive anyone!

RUMMEL: What are you thinking of? That's impossible.

SANDSTAD: Impossible, Mr Consul, sir; consider what's at
  stake for you.

KARSTEN BERNICK: What does all this matter to me now!
  Who have I got to work for now?

RUMMEL: How can you ask that? You have ourselves and the
  community.

VIGELAND: Yes, never a truer word.

SANDSTAD: And surely the consul's not forgetting that we –
      MISS BERNICK *comes through the furthest door to the
      left. The music can be heard muffled, far down the street.*

MISS BERNICK: Here comes the parade; but Betty's not at
  home; I can't understand where she –

KARSTEN BERNICK: Not at home! You see, Lona; no support, either in joy or in sorrow.

RUMMEL: Away with the curtains! Come and help me, Mr Krap. You too, Mr Sandstad. A wretched shame that the family should be so split right now; utterly contrary to the programme.

The curtains are pulled at the windows and doorway. The whole street can be seen lit up. On the house opposite there is a large transparency[51] with the words 'Long Live Karsten Bernick, Pillar of our Community!'

KARSTEN BERNICK [*shies away*]: Take it all away! I don't want to see it! Put out the lights, put them out!

RUMMEL: With due respect, are you out of your mind?

MISS BERNICK: What's the matter with him, Lona?

MISS HESSEL: Shh! [*Speaks quietly with her.*]

KARSTEN BERNICK: Take away that mocking inscription, I say! Can't you all see these lights are poking their tongues out at us?

RUMMEL: Now, I must say –

KARSTEN BERNICK: Oh, what would any of you know –! But I, I –! They're candles in a death chamber.

KRAP: Hm –

RUMMEL: No, but really – you're taking this much too hard.

SANDSTAD: The boy gets a trip over the Atlantic, and then you get him back.

VIGELAND: Just put your trust in the Almighty's hand, Mr Consul, sir.

RUMMEL: And in the ship, Bernick; it's hardly about to sink.

KRAP: Hm –

RUMMEL: If it was one of those floating coffins we hear of in those larger communities –

KARSTEN BERNICK: I feel my hair turning grey at this moment.
    MRS BERNICK *with a large shawl over her head comes in through the garden door.*

MRS BERNICK: Karsten, Karsten, did you know –?

KARSTEN BERNICK: Yes, I do know – but you – who see nothing – you, who can't keep a mother's eye on him –!

MRS BERNICK: Oh, do listen now –!

KARSTEN BERNICK: Why didn't you watch over him! Now I've lost him. Give him back to me, if you can!

MRS BERNICK: Yes, I can; I've got him!

KARSTEN BERNICK: You've got him!

THE GENTLEMEN: Ah!

HILMAR TØNNESEN: Well, I thought as much.

MISS BERNICK: You've got him back, Karsten!

MISS HESSEL: So win him now too.

KARSTEN BERNICK: You've got him! Is it true – what you're saying? Where is he?

MRS BERNICK: You shan't know before you've forgiven him.

KARSTEN BERNICK: Oh what, forgive –! But how did you find out –?

MRS BERNICK: You don't think a mother sees? I was frightened to death you'd get to know. A couple of words he let slip yesterday – and when his room was empty, and his backpack and clothes gone –

KARSTEN BERNICK: Yes, yes –?

MRS BERNICK: I ran; got hold of Aune; we went out in his sailboat; the American ship was about to set sail. Thank God, we got there in time – got on board – searched the hold, found him. Oh, Karsten, you mustn't punish him!

KARSTEN BERNICK: Betty!

MRS BERNICK: Nor Mr Aune!

KARSTEN BERNICK: Aune? What do you know about him? Is the *Indian Girl* under sail again?

MRS BERNICK: No, that's just it –

KARSTEN BERNICK: Speak, speak!

MRS BERNICK: Aune was as shaken as me; the search took time; darkness was falling so the harbour pilot was making objections; and then Aune took the liberty – in your name –

KARSTEN BERNICK: Well?

MRS BERNICK: Of stopping the ship till tomorrow.

KRAP: Hm –

KARSTEN BERNICK: Oh, what unspeakable good fortune!

MRS BERNICK: You're not angry?

KARSTEN BERNICK: Oh, what extraordinary good fortune, Betty!

RUMMEL: You really do have far too great a conscience.

HILMAR TØNNESEN: Yes, the instant it means a little battle with the elements, then – oof!

KRAP [*up by the windows*]: The parade's coming through the garden gate now, Mr Consul, sir.

KARSTEN BERNICK: Yes, they can come now.

RUMMEL: The whole garden's filling up with people.

SANDSTAD: The whole street's chock-a-block.

RUMMEL: The whole town's come out, Bernick. A truly blazingly inspirational moment.

VIGELAND: Let's take this in a spirit of humility, Mr Rummel.

RUMMEL: All the banners are out. What a parade! There we have the events committee with Mr Rørlund at the front.

KARSTEN BERNICK: Let them come, I say!

RUMMEL: But listen; given your present state of agitation –

KARSTEN BERNICK: What of it?

RUMMEL: I might just be persuaded to give a speech in your place.

KARSTEN BERNICK: No, thank you; tonight I shall speak for myself.

RUMMEL: But you do know what you've got to say?

KARSTEN BERNICK: Yes, trust me, Rummel – now I know what I must say.

> *The music has stopped in the meantime. The garden door is opened.* RØRLUND, *leading the* EVENTS COMMITTEE, *steps in, followed by a few* HIRED SERVANTS *carrying a draped basket. Behind them the* TOWN'S INHABITANTS *of all classes follow, as many as the room can hold. A vast* CROWD *with banners and flags can be made out in the garden and in the street.*

MR RØRLUND: Most highly esteemed Mr Consul, sir! I see by the amazement painted on your face that it is as unexpected guests we intrude upon you in your happy family circle, at your peaceful hearth and surrounded by loyal, industrious friends and fellow citizens. But our hearts have compelled us to pay you homage. This is not the first time such a thing has happened, but it *is* the first on such a grand scale. We have

come to you with our thanks many times, for the broad
moral foundation on which you have, so to speak, built
our community. This time we salute you especially as the
clear-sighted, untiring, unselfish, nay, self-sacrificing citizen, who has grasped the initiative for an enterprise which
according to all expert opinion will give a powerful impetus
to this community's earthly comfort and well-being.

VOICES IN THE CROWD: Bravo, bravo!

MR RØRLUND: Mr Consul, sir, for many years you have led
our town by the light of your example. I am not speaking of
your exemplary family life, or your spotless moral conduct
in general. Such things are for contemplation in the private
chamber and not for the grand hall! No, I speak now of your
civic contributions, such as are apparent for all eyes to see.
Well-equipped ships leave your yards and fly the flag upon
the furthest seas. A contented and numerous workforce
looks up to you as to a father. In bringing new branches of
industry to life you have laid the foundations for the
well-being of hundreds of families. You are, in the most emi-
nent sense, the cornerstone of this community.

VOICES: Hear, hear, bravo!

MR RØRLUND: And it is this altruism that touches your every
action with its radiance, which has such an indescribably
beneficial effect, especially in these times. You stand now on
the threshold of bringing us – well, I shan't hesitate to give it
its plain and prosaic name – a railway line.

MANY VOICES: Bravo! Bravo!

MR RØRLUND: But this enterprise appears to be running into
difficulties, mostly dictated by narrow and selfish concerns.

VOICES: Hear; hear!

MR RØRLUND: It has not passed unnoticed that certain individuals who do not belong to our community have stolen the
march on our hard-working citizens and taken ownership of
certain advantages for themselves that ought rightly to have
been to our own town's benefit.

VOICES: Yes! Yes! Hear! Hear!

MR RØRLUND: This regrettable fact has of course come to
your attention too, Mr Consul, sir. Yet you remain as

unshakeable as ever in the pursuit of your project, knowing as you do that a citizen of the state[52] should not merely favour his own borough.

DISPARATE VOICES: Hm! No, no! Yes, yes!

MR RØRLUND: It is as a true citizen[53] of the state then – man as he should and ought to be – that we salute you this evening. May your enterprise prove a true and lasting success for this community! The railway line can, of course, become a pathway by which we expose ourselves to the influx of corrupting outside elements, but also one by which we might swiftly remove them. And even now we are unable to keep ourselves free of such unsavoury outside elements. Yet the very fact that upon this festive evening we have been blessed, or so rumour has it, by the unexpectedly swift removal of precisely such elements –

VOICES: Shh! Shh!

MR RØRLUND: – this fact, I take as a happy omen for the enterprise. That I even touch upon this particular issue *here* is proof we are in a house where ethical principles are placed above family ties.

VOICES: Hear! Hear! Bravo!

KARSTEN BERNICK [*simultaneously*]: Allow me –

MR RØRLUND: Just a word more, Mr Consul, sir. What you've done for this borough has clearly not been motivated by the thought that it might bring you any tangible reward. But you surely couldn't decline a humble token of appreciation from your grateful fellow citizens, least of all at this significant moment, when, according to the assurances of practical men, we stand at the start of a new age.

MANY VOICES: Bravo! Hear! Hear!

> *He gives the* HIRED SERVANTS *a signal; they bring the basket closer; the* MEMBERS OF THE EVENTS COMMITTEE *take out and present during the following the objects as they are mentioned.*

MR RØRLUND: So, Mr Consul, sir, we shall now present you with a silver coffee service. May it grace your table when in the future, as so often before, we have the joy of gathering in this hospitable house. And you too, gentlemen, who have been so ready and willing to stand by our community's first man, we ask to accept a small memento. This silver goblet is for you, Mr Rummel, sir. You have so often with your eloquent words, amid the clinking of goblets, championed our community's civic interests; may you find many a worthy occasion to lift and drain this goblet. – To you, Mr Sandstad, sir, I present this album of photographs of your fellow citizens. Your widely credited and creditable humanity puts you in the pleasant position of counting friends in every section of our community. – And to you, Mr Vigeland, sir, I give, to adorn your private chamber, this book of family devotions,[54] on vellum and in luxury binding. With the ripening of the years, you have gained a solemn view of life; your everyday business activities have for many a year been purified and ennobled by thoughts of higher things and of the hereafter. [*Turns to the* CROWD] And with that, my friends, long live Consul Bernick and his fellow men-at-arms! Three cheers for the pillars of our community!

THE WHOLE CROWD: Long live Consul Bernick! Long live the pillars of the community! Hurrah, hurrah, hurrah!

MISS HESSEL: Congratulations, brother-in-law!

Expectant silence.

KARSTEN BERNICK [*begins seriously and slowly*]: My fellow citizens – it has been said through your spokesman that we stand this evening at the start of a new age – and I hope this may indeed prove right. But for this to come about we must take possession of the truth – the truth which has, wholly and comprehensively, until this evening, been reduced to a homeless wanderer in our community.

Surprise among the CROWD.

KARSTEN BERNICK: So I must begin by declining the praises which you, Mr Rørlund, according to the custom on such occasions, have showered upon me. I do not deserve them, because I have not, up to this day, been a selfless man. Even if I have not always sought financial reward, I am aware, now at least, that a desire and hunger for power, influence and esteem have been the driving force for most of my actions.

RUMMEL [*quietly*]: Oh, what now?

KARSTEN BERNICK: Standing here before my fellow citizens, I do not upbraid myself for this, since I still believe that I can count myself in the first rank among the competent men of our town.

MANY VOICES: Yes, yes, yes!

KARSTEN BERNICK: But what I do condemn myself for is that I have so often been weak enough to take the crooked byway, because I knew and feared our community's tendency to see impure motives behind anything a man does around here. And now I come to a subject that relates to this.

RUMMEL [*uneasily*]: Hm – hm!

KARSTEN BERNICK: Rumours are circulating about substantial property purchases further inland. I have bought these properties, all of them. I alone.

HUSHED VOICES: What did he say? The consul? Consul Bernick?

KARSTEN BERNICK: They are, for the moment, in my hands. Naturally I have confided in my companions, Messrs Rummel, Vigeland and Sandstad, and we have agreed that –

RUMMEL: This isn't true! Proof – proof –!

VIGELAND: We've not agreed anything!

SANDSTAD: Well, I must say –

KARSTEN BERNICK: No, that is absolutely right; we've not yet agreed on what I wanted to say now. But then I hope that these three gentlemen will concur with me when I announce that I have, this evening, agreed, with myself at least, that these properties shall be offered up for general subscription; anyone who wants may have a share in them.

MANY VOICES: Hurrah! Long live Consul Bernick!

RUMMEL [*quietly to* BERNICK]: What base treachery –!

SANDSTAD [*likewise*]: Fooling us like that –!

VIGELAND: May the devil take –! Oh, God forgive me, what am I saying?

THE CROWD [*outside*]: Hurrah, hurrah, hurrah!

KARSTEN BERNICK: Silence, gentlemen. I have no right to this applause, since what I have now decided upon was not my intention at the outset. My intention was to hold on to it all for myself, and I am still of the opinion that these properties can be put to best use if they remain together in the hands of *one* man. But the choice is there. If it's your wish, then I am willing to administer them to the best of my ability.

VOICES: Yes! Yes! Yes!

KARSTEN BERNICK: But first my fellow citizens must know me as I really am. Let each of you examine himself, and let it then stand firm that from tonight we begin a new age. The old, with its hypocrisy, its painted exterior and its hollowness, with its sham respectability and miserable deference, will stand in our minds as a museum, open for our edification; and to this museum we will donate – you agree, gentlemen? – the coffee service, the goblet, the album and the family devotions on vellum and with luxury binding.

RUMMEL: Well, naturally.

VIGELAND [*mumbles*]: You've taken everything else so –

SANDSTAD: Here you are.

KARSTEN BERNICK: And now, to the main issue that must be settled with my community. It has been said here that unsavoury elements took their leave of us this evening. I might add something people don't know: the man in question has not travelled alone; accompanying him to be his wife was –

MISS HESSEL [*loudly*]: Dina Dorf!

MR RØRLUND: What!

MRS BERNICK: What are you saying!

Great commotion.

MR RØRLUND: Fled? Run away – with *him*! Impossible!

KARSTEN BERNICK: To be his wife, Mr Rørlund. And I have more to add. [*Lowering his voice*] Betty, brace yourself and be strong for what's coming. [*Loudly*] I say, hats off to that man, for he has, most nobly, taken another man's sin upon him. My fellow citizens, I seek release from this untruth; it has come close to poisoning each and every fibre in me. You shall know everything. Fifteen years ago, *I* was the guilty one.

MRS BERNICK [*in a quiet and trembling voice*]: Karsten!

MISS BERNICK [*likewise*]: Ah, Johan –!

MISS HESSEL: There, finally you've won yourself back!

Speechless surprise among those present.

KARSTEN BERNICK: Yes, my fellow citizens, I was the guilty one, and he left. The malicious and false rumours that were spread afterwards are now beyond human power to disprove. But that isn't for me to lament. Fifteen years ago I lifted myself aloft on these rumours; whether I am now to fall by them is for each of you to consider for yourself.

MR RØRLUND: What a thunderbolt! The town's first man –! [*Quietly to* MRS BERNICK] Oh, I feel so sorry for you, Mrs Bernick!

HILMAR TØNNESEN: What a confession! Well, I must say –!

KARSTEN BERNICK: But no decisions this evening. I ask each of you to return home – to collect yourselves – to look within yourselves. When calm is descended upon you, it will emerge whether I have lost or won by speaking. Goodbye! I still have much, much to repent of; but that concerns my conscience alone. Good night! Away with all these festive trappings. We all feel it – such things have no place here.

MR RØRLUND: They most certainly don't. [*Aside to* MRS BERNICK] Ran away! So she was completely unworthy of me after all. [*Quietly to the* EVENTS COMMITTEE] Yes, well, gentlemen, after all this I think it best we withdraw discreetly.

HILMAR TØNNESEN: How one's to hold the flag of ideas aloft after this, is –. Oof!

The information has meanwhile been whispered from person to person. All the participants in the parade leave through the garden. RUMMEL, SANDSTAD *and* VIGELAND *leave in heated but muffled debate.* HILMAR TØNNESEN *sneaks off to the right.* KARSTEN BERNICK, MRS BERNICK, MISS BERNICK, MISS HESSEL *and* MR KRAP *remain standing in silence.*

KARSTEN BERNICK: Betty, can you forgive me?

MRS BERNICK [*looks at him with a smile*]: Do you realize, Karsten, you've opened up the happiest prospect I've had for years?

KARSTEN BERNICK: What do you mean –?

MRS BERNICK: For years I believed that I had once owned you and then lost you. Now I know that I've never owned you; but I shall win you.

KARSTEN BERNICK [*throws his arms around her*]: Oh, Betty, you *have* won me! Through Lona I've finally learned to know you properly. But let Olaf come in now.

MRS BERNICK: Yes, now you shall have him. – Mr Krap –!
She speaks quietly with him in the background. He exits through the garden door. During the following all the transparencies and lights in the houses are gradually extinguished.

KARSTEN BERNICK [*in a hushed voice*]: Thank you, Lona, you've rescued the best in me – and for me.

MISS HESSEL: Was there anything else I wanted?

KARSTEN BERNICK: Well, was there – or wasn't there? I can't make you out.

MISS HESSEL: Hm –

KARSTEN BERNICK: So, it wasn't hatred? Wasn't revenge? Why did you come back over then?

MISS HESSEL: Old friendship doesn't rust.[55]

KARSTEN BERNICK: Lona!

MISS HESSEL: When Johan told me about the lie, then I swore to myself: the hero of my younger days shall stand free and true.

KARSTEN BERNICK: Oh, how little this miserable creature has deserved that of you.

MISS HESSEL: Well, if we women asked what was deserved, Karsten –!
AUNE arrives with OLAF from the garden.

KARSTEN BERNICK [*turning towards him*]: Olaf!

OLAF: Father, I promise you, I won't ever –

KARSTEN BERNICK: Run away?

OLAF: Yes, yes, I promise you, Father.

KARSTEN BERNICK: And I promise you that you'll never have reason to. From now on you'll be allowed to grow up, not as an heir to *my* life's work,[56] but as someone who has his own life's work ahead.

OLAF: And am I allowed to become whatever I want?

KARSTEN BERNICK: Yes, you are.

OLAF: Thank you. Then I don't want to be a pillar of the community.

KARSTEN BERNICK: No? Why not?

OLAF: No, because I think that must be really boring.

KARSTEN BERNICK: You shall be yourself, Olaf; and the rest must come as it may. – And you, Aune –

AUNE: I know, Mr Consul, sir. I am dismissed.

KARSTEN BERNICK: We stay together, Aune; and forgive me –

AUNE: But how? The ship's not sailing tonight.

KARSTEN BERNICK: Nor will it sail tomorrow. I gave you too short a deadline. It must be seen to more thoroughly.

AUNE: It will be, Mr Consul, sir – and with the new machines!

KARSTEN BERNICK: That's the way! But thoroughly and honestly. There are many things round here that need thorough and honest repair. Well, good night, Aune.

AUNE: Good night, sir – and thank you, thank you, thank you! *He exits to the right.*

MRS BERNICK: Now they've all gone.

KARSTEN BERNICK: And we're alone. My name's no longer lit up in flaming letters; all the lights are out in the windows.

MISS HESSEL: Would you want them lit again?

KARSTEN BERNICK: Not for anything in the world. Wherever have I been? You'll be appalled when you get to hear. It's as though I'd returned to my faculties after being consumed by poison. But I feel it – I *can* be young and healthy again. Oh, come closer – tighter around me. Come here, Betty! Come here, Olaf, my boy! And you, Marta – I don't think I've really seen you in all these years.

MISS HESSEL: No, I don't think you have; this community of yours is a community of old bachelor-souls; you don't see women.

KARSTEN BERNICK: True, true; which is precisely why – and *this* is definite, Lona – you're not leaving Betty and me.

MRS BERNICK: No, Lona, you mustn't!

MISS HESSEL: No, how could I think of leaving you two youngsters when you're about to set up home? I'm a foster mother, aren't I? Me and you, Marta, us two old aunties –. What are you looking at out there?

MISS BERNICK: The skies are clearing. Look how light it is over the sea. The *Palm Tree* has good fortune with her.

MISS HESSEL: And happiness on board.

KARSTEN BERNICK: And we – well, we have a long serious working day awaiting us; I most of all. But let that come; just gather closely around me, you loyal and truthful women. *That's* something I've learned too over the last few days: it is you women who are the pillars of the community.

MISS HESSEL: Then you have learned a frail wisdom, brother-in-law. [*Places her hand solemnly on his shoulder*] No, my friend; the spirit of truth, the spirit of freedom[57] – *they* are the pillars of the community.

A DOLL'S HOUSE[1]

CHARACTERS

HELMER, *a lawyer*[2]
NORA, *his wife*
DR RANK
MRS[3] LINDE
NILS KROGSTAD, *a lawyer*
HELMER'S THREE SMALL CHILDREN
ANNE-MARIE, *the Helmers' nanny*
THE MAID[4]
A PORTER

ACT ONE

A comfortably[5] and tastefully, though not expensively, furnished room. A door on the right in the background leads out into the hallway.[6] Another door to the left in the background leads towards Helmer's office. Against the wall between these two doors, a piano. In the middle of the wall to the left, a door, and further forwards, a window. Near the window, a round table with an armchair and a small sofa. On the side-wall to the right some way back, a door, and on the same wall closer to the foreground a ceramic stove with a pair of armchairs and a rocking-chair in front of it. Between the stove and the side door a small table. Copperplate engravings on the walls. A display cabinet filled with china objects and other little ornaments; a small bookcase with finely bound books. A carpet on the floor; a fire in the stove. A winter's day.

The doorbell rings outside in the hallway; a moment later we hear the front door being opened. NORA *comes into the room, contentedly humming a tune; she is dressed in outdoor clothes and carries a number of parcels, which she puts down on the table to the right. She leaves the door to the hall open after her, and we see a* PORTER *outside carrying a Christmas tree and a basket, which he gives to the* MAID, *who has opened the door to them.*

NORA: Hide the Christmas tree[7] well, Helene. The children mustn't see it until this evening when it's decorated. [*To the* PORTER; *taking her purse out*] How much –?
PORTER: Half a krone.[8]

NORA: There's a krone. No, keep it all.

The PORTER *thanks her and leaves.* NORA *closes the door. She continues to laugh in quiet contentment as she takes off her outdoor clothes.*

NORA [*takes a bag of macaroons from her pocket and eats a couple; then she goes cautiously over to listen at her husband's door*]: Ah yes, he's home. [*Hums again as she goes over to the table on the right.*]

HELMER [*from in his room*]: Is that my song-lark chirruping out there?

NORA [*busy opening some of the parcels*]: Yes, it is.

HELMER: Is that my squirrel rummaging in there?

NORA: Yes!

HELMER: When did my squirrel get home?

NORA: Just now. [*Puts the bag of macaroons in her pocket and wipes her mouth.*] Come out here, Torvald, and you'll see what I've bought.

HELMER Do not disturb! [*A moment later; opens the door and looks in, with pen in hand*] Bought, you say? All that? Has my little spending-bird[9] been out frittering money again?

NORA: Yes but, Torvald, surely we must be able to let ourselves go a little this year. After all, this is the first Christmas we don't need to save.

HELMER: Yes, but really, we can't be extravagant.

NORA: Oh but, Torvald, we can be a little extravagant now, surely. Can't we? Just a teeny-weeny bit. After all, you'll have a big salary now and be earning lots and lots of money.

HELMER: Yes, from the New Year; but it'll be a whole quarter before my salary is due.

NORA: Pff; surely we can borrow in the meantime.

HELMER: Nora! [*Goes over to her and jokingly tweaks her ear.*] Is frivolity out for a stroll again? Suppose I borrowed a thousand kroner today, and you frittered it away in the Christmas week, and then on New Year's Eve I got a roof tile on my head and I lay –

NORA [*puts her hand over his mouth*]: Oh shush; don't say anything so ugly.

HELMER: Well, suppose such a thing happened – what then?

NORA: If something that ghastly happened, it would make no odds to me whether I was in debt or not.

HELMER: Perhaps so, but to the people I'd borrowed from?

NORA: Them? Who's bothered about them? They're just strangers.

HELMER: Nora, Nora, a woman thou art![10] No, but seriously, Nora; you know my thoughts on this issue. No debts! Never borrow! There's something unfree, and so something unlovely, that comes over the home that's founded on loans and debts. Now, we've both held out very bravely until today; and we'll go on doing so for the short time it's still necessary.

NORA [moves over to the stove]: Yes, yes, as you wish, Torvald.

HELMER [follows her]: There, there; my little songbird shan't go trailing her wings now. Hmm? Is my squirrel standing there sulking? [Takes out his wallet.] Nora; what do you think I have here?

NORA [turns around quickly]: Money!

HELMER: There you are. [Hands her some banknotes.] Good Lord, I know, of course, that a great deal goes on house-keeping at Christmas.

NORA [counting]: Ten – twenty – thirty – forty. Oh thank you, thank you, Torvald; I'll make it go a long way.

HELMER: Yes, you certainly must.

NORA: Yes, yes, I will, really. But come here, and I'll show you everything I've bought. And so cheaply! Look, here are new clothes for Ivar – and a sword too. Here's a horse and a trumpet for Bob. And here's a doll with a doll's bed for Emmy; it's rather plain; but she'll soon rip it to pieces anyway, of course. And here I've got dress material[11] and headscarves for the maids; old Anne-Marie really should have had a lot more.

HELMER: And what's in that parcel there?

NORA [shrieks]: No, Torvald, you shan't see that till this evening!

HELMER: All right. But now tell me, you little spendthrift: what have you got in mind for yourself?

NORA: Oh, pff; for me? I'm not bothered with anything for myself.

HELMER: Oh, yes you are. Name me something reasonable now that you'd most like.

NORA: Oh, I don't know, really. Although perhaps, Torvald –

HELMER: Well?

NORA [*fiddling with his buttons; without looking at him*]: If you want to give me something, you could of course – you could –

HELMER: Well; out with it.

NORA [*quickly*]: You could give me money, Torvald. Only as much as you feel you can afford; and then I'll buy something with it over the next few days.

HELMER: But Nora –

NORA: Oh yes, please, darling Torvald; I'm begging you. Then I'd hang the money[12] in a lovely gold paper wrapper on the Christmas tree. Wouldn't that be fun?

HELMER: What are those birds called that are always frittering money away?

NORA: Yes, yes; spending-birds, I know. But Torvald, let's do as I say; and then I'll have time to give careful consideration to what I need most. Isn't that very sensible? Hmm?

HELMER [*smiling*]: Yes, of course it is; that's to say, if you really could hold on to the money I give you and really bought something for yourself with it. But it'll go towards the house and on one useless thing after another, and then I'll have to fork out again.

NORA: Oh but, Torvald –

HELMER: Can't be denied, my dear little Nora. [*He puts his arm around her waist.*] My spending-bird is sweet; but it uses up an awful lot of money. It's incredible how expensive it is for a man to keep a spending-bird.

NORA: Oh shush, how can you possibly say that? I really do save everything I can.

HELMER [*laughs*]: Yes, never a truer word. Everything you *can*. But you can't at all.

NORA [*humming and smiling in quiet contentment*]: Mmm, if you only knew what a lot of expenses we larks and squirrels have, Torvald.

HELMER: You're a strange little one. Just as your father was. You're forever on the lookout for ways to get money; but as soon as you get it, it's as though it slips through your fingers; you never know what you've done with it. Well, we must take you as you are. It's in the blood. Oh yes it is, these things are hereditary, Nora.

NORA: Well, I wish I'd inherited a great many of Daddy's qualities.

HELMER: And I wouldn't wish you any other way than exactly as you are, my sweet little songbird. But listen; something occurs to me. You look so – so – what shall I call it? – so sneaky today –

NORA: Do I?

HELMER: You certainly do. Look me straight in the eyes.

NORA [*looks at him*]: Well?

HELMER [*wags a stern finger*]: My sweet-tooth wouldn't perhaps have been on the rampage in town today?

NORA: No, how can you think such a thing.

HELMER: Did my sweet-tooth really not make a detour into the confectioner's?

NORA: No, I assure you, Torvald –

HELMER: Not nibbled at a little jam?

NORA: No, absolutely not.

HELMER: Not even gnawed a macaroon or two?

NORA: No, Torvald, I assure you really –

HELMER: Well, well; I'm only joking of course –

NORA [*goes to the table on the right*]: It would never occur to me to go against you.

HELMER: Yes, I know that; and you've given me your word –. [*Moving towards her*] Well, keep your little Christmas secrets to yourself, darling Nora. They'll be revealed this evening, no doubt, when the Christmas tree is lit.

NORA: Have you remembered to invite Dr Rank?

HELMER: No. But there's no need; it goes without saying that he'll eat with us. Besides I'll invite him when he comes this afternoon. I've ordered a good wine. Nora, you can't believe how I'm looking forward to this evening.

NORA: Me too. And how thrilled the children will be, Torvald!

HELMER: Ah, but it certainly is splendid to think that one's got oneself a secure, safe post; that one has a generous income. It's a huge pleasure to think of, isn't that right?

NORA: Oh, it's miraculous![13]

HELMER: Do you remember last Christmas? A whole three weeks beforehand, you locked yourself in every evening until way past midnight to make flowers for the Christmas tree and all those other splendid things you planned to surprise us with. Ugh, that was the most boring time I've ever been through.

NORA: I wasn't the least bored.

HELMER [smiling]: But the results were rather measly, Nora.

NORA: Oh, are you going to tease me about that again? How could I help it if the cat got in and ripped everything to pieces?

HELMER: No, of course you couldn't, my poor little Nora. You had the best of intentions, you wanted to make us all happy, and that's the main thing. But it really is so good those pinched times are over.

NORA: Yes, it's absolutely miraculous.

HELMER: Now I won't need to sit here alone and bored; and you won't need to torture your darling eyes and your fair, delicate little hands –

NORA [clapping her hands]: Yes, isn't that so, Torvald, it's no longer necessary? Oh, how lovely that is to hear! [Takes his arm.] Now I'll tell you how I thought we should arrange things, Torvald. As soon as Christmas is over – [There is a ring in the hallway.] Oh, that's the doorbell. [Tidying the room a bit] Someone must be coming. What a bore.

HELMER: I'm not at home for visitors, remember.

MAID [in the door to the hall]: Madam, there's a lady – a stranger –

NORA: Very well, ask her to come in.

MAID [to HELMER]: And the doctor's come too.

HELMER: Did he go straight into my study?

MAID: Yes, he did.

HELMER *goes into his study. The* MAID *shows* MRS
LINDE, *who is in travelling clothes,*[14] *into the living room
and closes the door after her.*

MRS LINDE [*timidly and a little hesitantly*]: Good morning,
Nora.

NORA [*uncertainly*]: Good morning –

MRS LINDE: You probably don't recognize me.

NORA: Well, I don't know – ah yes, I seem to – [*Bursting out*]
What! Kristine! Is it really you?

MRS LINDE: Yes, it's me.

NORA: Kristine! And there I was, not recognizing you! But
then how could I possibly – [*More quietly*] How you've
changed, Kristine!

MRS LINDE: Yes, I probably have. In nine or ten long years –

NORA: Is it that long since we saw each other? Yes, so it is. Oh,
these last eight years have been a happy time, believe you
me. And now you've come here to town? Made that long
journey in the winter. That was very brave.

MRS LINDE: I arrived on the steamer just this morning.

NORA: To enjoy yourself over Christmas, naturally. Oh, but
how lovely! Yes, and enjoy ourselves we certainly shall. But
do take your coat off. You're not cold, are you? [*Helps her.*]
There; now we'll sit ourselves comfortably here by the stove.
No, in the armchair there! I'll sit here in the rocking-chair.
[*Grasps* MRS LINDE's *hands*] Yes, you've got your old face
again now; it was just in that first moment –. You've grown
a little paler, though, Kristine – and a little thinner
perhaps.

MRS LINDE: And much, much older, Nora.

NORA: Yes, a little older perhaps, a teeny little bit; not much at
all. [*Stopping herself suddenly, serious*] Oh, what a thoughtless person I am, sitting here and chattering away. Sweet,
darling Kristine, can you forgive me?

MRS LINDE: What do you mean, Nora?

NORA [*softly*]: Poor Kristine, you're a widow now, of course.

MRS LINDE: Yes, it happened three years ago.

NORA: Oh, I did know about it; I read it in the newspapers.
Oh, Kristine, you must believe me, I often thought about

writing to you at the time; but I always put it off, something
always got in the way.

MRS LINDE: Nora dear, I completely understand.

NORA: No, it was bad of me, Kristine. Oh, you poor thing, you
must have gone through so much. – And he didn't leave you
anything to live on?

MRS LINDE: No.

NORA: And no children?

MRS LINDE: No.

NORA: Absolutely nothing, then?

MRS LINDE: Not even a sense of grief or loss to sustain me.

NORA [looks at her in disbelief]: But Kristine, how can that be
possible?

MRS LINDE [smiles sadly and strokes NORA's hair]: Oh, these
things happen, Nora.

NORA: To be so utterly alone. What a heavy sadness that must
be for you. I have three lovely children. Though you can't see
them at the moment, they're out with their nanny. But now,
you must tell me everything –

MRS LINDE: No, no, no, you tell.

NORA: No, you start. Today I don't want to be selfish. Today I
want only to think of your concerns. Although there is *one*
thing I really must tell you. Do you know what wonderful
good fortune we've had recently?

MRS LINDE: No. What's *that*?

NORA: Just think, my husband's been made director of the
Commercial Bank.

MRS LINDE: Your husband? Oh, what luck –!

NORA: Yes, tremendous! As a lawyer one's income is so unreliable, especially when one doesn't want to handle any affairs
except those that are right and proper. And that's something
Torvald's never wanted to do, of course; and I'm entirely
with him there. Oh, believe me, we're so looking forward to
it! He's starting at the bank right after the New Year, and
then he'll have a big salary and lots of bonuses. From now
on we'll be able to live quite differently – just as we want.
Oh, Kristine, I feel so light and happy! Yes, because it's so

lovely to have a proper amount of money and not to have to go worrying over things. Isn't it?

MRS LINDE: Well, it must be lovely at least to have what's necessary.

NORA: No, not just what's necessary, but a proper, proper amount of money!

MRS LINDE [smiles]: Nora, Nora, you've not grown sensible yet? Back at school you were a big spendthrift.

NORA [laughs softly]: Yes, Torvald still says that too. [Wags a finger sternly.] But 'Nora, Nora' isn't as crazy as you all think. – We've certainly been in no position for me to be extravagant. We've had to work, both of us.

MRS LINDE: You too?

NORA: Yes, with little things, with handiwork, with crocheting and embroidery, things like that, [casually] and with other things too. You know presumably that Torvald left the Department[15] when we got married? There were no prospects for promotion in his office, and of course he needed to earn more money than before. But he exhausted himself dreadfully in that first year. He had to seek out all kinds of extra income, as you can imagine, and to work from morning till night. But it was more than he could take, and he became dangerously ill. So the doctors declared that it was vital he travel south.

MRS LINDE: Yes, you stayed for a whole year in Italy, didn't you?

NORA: That's right. It wasn't easy to get away, believe me. Ivar had only just been born then. But we had to go, of course. Oh, it was a miraculous, lovely trip. And it saved Torvald's life. But it cost an awful lot of money, Kristine.

MRS LINDE: I can well imagine.

NORA: Twelve hundred speciedaler[16] it cost. Four thousand eight hundred kroner. That's a huge amount of money, you know.

MRS LINDE: Yes, but in such a situation it's a great blessing to have it at least.

NORA: Yes, I'll say, though we got it from Daddy of course.

MRS LINDE: Oh, I see. It was at around that time your father died, I believe.

NORA: Yes, Kristine, it was just at that time. And imagine, I couldn't travel to him and nurse him. I was here, of course, waiting for little Ivar to come into the world any day. And then I had my poor mortally ill Torvald to look after. My dear kind Daddy! I never got to see him again, Kristine. Oh, that's the heaviest thing I've gone through since I was married.

MRS LINDE: I know you were very fond of him. But then you went to Italy?

NORA: Yes; well, we had the money then; and the doctors were pressing us to go. So we left a month later.

MRS LINDE: And your husband returned in full health.

NORA: Fit as a fiddle!

MRS LINDE: But – the doctor?

NORA: How do you mean?

MRS LINDE: I thought the maid said he was the doctor, that man who came at the same time as me.

NORA: Oh, that was Dr Rank; but he doesn't come on patient visits; he's our closest friend and looks in at least once a day. No, Torvald hasn't had one hour of illness since. And the children are fit and healthy, and so am I. [*She jumps up and claps her hands.*] Oh God, oh God, Kristine, it's lovely and miraculous to be alive and happy! – Oh, but this really is loathsome of me – I'm talking about my own concerns again. [*Sits on a footstool close to* MRS LINDE *and rests her arms on her knees.*] Oh, you mustn't be cross with me! – Tell me, is it really true that you didn't love your husband? Why did you marry him, then?

MRS LINDE: My mother was still alive; and she was bedridden and helpless. And I also had my two younger brothers to provide for. I didn't really see how I could justify declining his offer.

NORA: No, perhaps you're right. He was rich at the time, then?

MRS LINDE: He was reasonably well off, I think. But his business interests were unreliable, Nora. When he died, everything collapsed and there was nothing left over.

NORA: And then –?

MRS LINDE: Well, then I had to struggle on with a little shop and a little school[17] and whatever else I could think of. The last three years have been like one long, unremitting workday for me. Now it's at an end, Nora. My poor mother no longer needs me, now that she's passed away. And neither do the boys; they've got jobs now and can provide for themselves.

NORA: You must feel a good deal lighter –

MRS LINDE: No, Nora. Just unspeakably empty. With nobody to live for any more. [*Gets up restlessly.*] That's why I couldn't stand it any longer out there in that little backwater. It must surely be easier to find something here to engage you and occupy your thoughts. If I could just be lucky enough to get a permanent post, some sort of office work –

NORA: Oh but, Kristine, that's so terribly exhausting; and you already look exhausted before you've begun. It would be much better for you to go to a spa.[18]

MRS LINDE [*moves towards the window*]: I don't have any daddy who can present me with travel money, Nora.

NORA [*gets up*]: Oh, don't be angry with me!

MRS LINDE [*moves towards her*]: Nora dear, don't *you* be angry with *me*. That's the worst thing about a situation like mine, it leaves such a deep trace of bitterness in your mind. You have nobody to work for; but you still have to be on the lookout, fighting your corner. We have to live after all; and then we get self-centred. When you told me about the happy change in your circumstances[19] – can you believe it? – I wasn't so pleased on your behalf, as on my own.

NORA: In what way? Oh, I see. You mean that Torvald could maybe do something for you.

MRS LINDE: Yes, that was my thought.

NORA: And so he will, Kristine. Just leave it to me; I'll bring it up so, so delicately – I'll think up something that'll charm him, that'll capture his approval. Oh, I do so sincerely want to be of help to you.

MRS LINDE: How sweet of you, Nora, to be so eager on my behalf – doubly sweet of *you*, when you know so little of life's burdens and hardships yourself.

NORA: I –? I know so little of –?

MRS LINDE [*smiling*]: Well. Good Lord, a little bit of hand-work and the like –. You're a child, Nora.

NORA [*tosses her head and crosses the room*]: You oughtn't to say that so condescendingly.

MRS LINDE: Oh?

NORA: You're like the others. You all think I'm incapable of anything really serious –

MRS LINDE: Now, now –

NORA: – that I've experienced nothing of this difficult world.

MRS LINDE: Nora dear, you've just told me about all your hardships.

NORA: Pfff – those trifles! [*Softly*] I haven't told you about the biggest.

MRS LINDE: Biggest? What do you mean?

NORA: You're far too dismissive of me, Kristine; but you shouldn't be. You're proud that you worked so hard and so long for your mother.

MRS LINDE: I certainly don't dismiss anyone. But it *is* true: I am both proud and happy that it was granted me to make my mother's last years relatively free from care.

NORA: And you're proud too, when you think about what you've done for your brothers.

MRS LINDE: I think I have a right to be.

NORA: I think so too. But now I'm going to tell you something, Kristine. I also have something to be proud and happy about.

MRS LINDE: I don't doubt it. But how do you mean?

NORA: Speak quietly. Imagine if Torvald heard this! He mustn't at any price – nobody must get to know this, Kristine; nobody but you.

MRS LINDE: But what is it?

NORA: Come here. [*Pulls her down on the sofa beside her.*] Well, Kristine – I also have something to be proud and happy about. It was I who saved Torvald's life.

MRS LINDE: Saved –? In what way saved?

NORA: I told you about our trip to Italy. Torvald could never have pulled through if he hadn't gone down there –

MRS LINDE: Right; and your father gave you the necessary money –

NORA: Yes, that's what Torvald and all the others believe; but –

MRS LINDE: But –?

NORA: Daddy didn't give us a penny. It was I who raised the money.

MRS LINDE: You? That entire sum?

NORA: Twelve hundred speciedaler. Four thousand eight hundred kroner. What do you say to that?

MRS LINDE: Yes, but, Nora, how was that possible? Had you won the lottery?[20]

NORA [with scorn]: The lottery? [Gives a little snort.] Where would the skill be in that?

MRS LINDE: But then where did you get it from?

NORA [hums and smiles secretively]: Hm; tra la la la!

MRS LINDE: After all, you couldn't borrow it.

NORA: Oh? Why not?

MRS LINDE: Well, of course, a wife can't borrow without her husband's consent.[21]

NORA [tosses her head]: Oh, when it's a wife with a touch of business flair – a wife who knows how to go about things a little cleverly, then –

MRS LINDE: But, Nora, I simply don't understand –

NORA: Nor do you need to. Nobody's said that I borrowed the money. After all, I might have got it in other ways. [Throws herself back in the sofa.] I might have got it from some admirer or other. When you're as relatively attractive as I am –

MRS LINDE: You're a crazy one!

NORA: You're tremendously curious now, aren't you, Kristine?

MRS LINDE: Now listen, Nora my dear – haven't you acted rather imprudently?

NORA [sitting upright again]: Is it imprudent to save one's husband's life?

MRS LINDE: I think it's imprudent that, without his knowing, you –

NORA: But that's exactly it, he wasn't meant to know anything! Good Lord, don't you understand? He wasn't even meant to know how much danger he was in. I was the one the doctors came to, saying that his life was at risk; that nothing could save him except a stay in the south. Don't you think I tried to coax him at first? I talked to him about how lovely it would be for me to travel abroad like other young wives; I cried and I begged; I said he should please remember my condition, that he must be kind and give in to my wishes; and then I suggested that he could perhaps take out a loan. But then he almost went into a fury, Kristine. He said I was frivolous, and that it was his duty as a husband not to give way to me in my whims and caprices – I think he called it. Well, I thought, you've got to be rescued; and so I found a way out –

MRS LINDE: And your husband didn't discover from your father that the money hadn't come from him?

NORA: No, never. Daddy died at just around that time. I'd thought to let him in on it and ask him not to reveal anything. But then he was so ill –. Sadly, it was never necessary.

MRS LINDE: And you've not confided in your husband since?

NORA: No, for heaven's sake, how can you think that? When he's so strict on the issue of borrowing! And besides, just think how awkward and humiliating it would be for Torvald – with his manly self-esteem – to know he owed me something. It would upset the entire balance of our relationship; our beautiful, happy home would no longer be what it is.

MRS LINDE: Will you never tell him?

NORA [thoughtfully, half smiling]: Yes – perhaps one day – many years from now, when I'm no longer as pretty. You shouldn't laugh! I mean, of course, when Torvald no longer admires me as much as he does now; when he no longer finds it amusing to have me dance for him, and dress up and recite things. Then it might be good to have something in reserve – [Breaks off.] Oh, rubbish, rubbish! That time will never come. – So, what do you say to my big secret, Kristine? Aren't I also capable of something? – And you can be sure too that this matter has caused me a great many worries. It certainly hasn't been easy for me to fulfil my obligations on time. In the business world, let me tell you, there's something called quarterly interest, and something called instalments; and they're always terribly difficult to get hold of. So I've had to save a bit here and a bit there, wherever I could, you see. Naturally, I couldn't put much aside from the housekeeping money, since Torvald had to live comfortably. And I couldn't let the children go badly dressed; whatever I got for them, I had to use every bit. My sweet little angels!

MRS LINDE: So I suppose your own necessities took the brunt of it, my poor Nora?

NORA: Yes, of course. But I was also best placed. Whenever Torvald gave me money for new dresses and the like, I never used more than half of it; always bought the plainest and cheapest thing. It was a blessing from heaven that everything suits me so well, so Torvald didn't notice. But many a time it weighed heavily on me, Kristine; after all it is lovely to be elegantly dressed. Isn't that so?

MRS LINDE: It certainly is.

NORA: And then I've had other sources of income too, of course. Last winter I was lucky enough to get a fair bit of copying work. So I locked myself in and sat there writing every evening, long into the night. Oh, I was often so tired, so tired. But it was terribly fun, nonetheless, to sit like that, working and earning money. It was almost as though I was a man.

MRS LINDE: But how much have you been able to pay off in this way?

NORA: Well, I can't say exactly. These kinds of transactions, you see, are so extremely difficult to keep track of. All I know is that I've paid everything I could scrape together. I've often been at my wits' end. [Smiles.] Then I'd sit here and imagine that an elderly rich gentleman had fallen in love with me –

MRS LINDE: What? Which gentleman?

NORA: Oh, pff! – that he'd died, and when they opened his will, it said in capital letters: 'All my money is to be immediately paid to the charming Mrs Nora Helmer in cash.'

MRS LINDE: But my dear Nora – who was this gentleman?

NORA: Good heavens, don't you understand? The elderly gentleman didn't exist at all; that was just something I sat here imagining again and again when I couldn't see a way out to get hold of any money. But it makes no odds now; as far as I'm concerned that boring old personage can stay right where he is; I'm not bothered about him or his will, because now I haven't a care. [*Jumps up.*] Oh God, but it's so lovely to think, Kristine! Not a care! To be able to be carefree, absolutely carefree; to be able to play and romp about with the children; to be able to make the house nice and pretty, everything just as Torvald likes it! And just think, the spring will come soon with big blue skies. Then we might get to travel a little. I might get to see the sea again. Oh yes, yes, it certainly is miraculous to be alive and to be happy!

The doorbell is heard in the hall.

MRS LINDE [*gets up*]: The doorbell; perhaps it's best I go.

NORA: No, you stay; nobody's coming here, I'm sure; it must be for Torvald –

MAID [*in the doorway to the hall*]: Excuse me, madam – there's a gentleman wants to speak with the lawyer –

NORA: With the bank director, you mean.

MAID: Yes, with the bank director; but I didn't know – since the doctor's in there –

NORA: Who is this gentleman?

KROGSTAD [*in the doorway to the hall*]: It's me, madam.

    MRS LINDE *starts, then shrinks back and turns towards the window.*

NORA [*takes a step towards him, tense, her voice lowered*]: You? What is it? What do you want to speak to my husband about?

KROGSTAD: Bank matters – in a way. I've a modest position at the Commercial Bank, and I hear your husband's going to be our new boss –

NORA: So it's –

KROGSTAD: Just some boring business, madam; nothing more at all.

NORA: Right, be so good then as to go through to the office. [*Nods offhandedly, as she closes the door to the hall*; *then walks over to attend to the stove.*]

MRS LINDE: Nora – who was that man?

NORA: It was a certain Mr Krogstad.

MRS LINDE: So it really was him.

NORA: You know the man?

MRS LINDE: I knew him once – many years ago. He worked as a solicitor's clerk[22] for a while in our parts.

NORA: Ah yes, so he did.

MRS LINDE: How changed he was.

NORA: He was very unhappily married, I believe.

MRS LINDE: And now he's a widower?

NORA: With a lot of children. There now; it's burning. [*Closes the stove door and moves the rocking-chair a little to one side.*]

MRS LINDE: He's involved in a variety of business activities, they say?

NORA: Oh? Well, that's possible; I wouldn't know –. But let's not think about business; it's so boring.

DR RANK *comes from* HELMER's *room.*

RANK [*still in the doorway*]: No, no, Helmer; I don't want to intrude; I'd rather go in to your wife for a bit. [*Closes the door and notices* MRS LINDE] Oh, apologies; it seems I'm intruding here too.

NORA: No, not at all. [*Introduces*] Dr Rank. Mrs Linde.

RANK: Aha. A name that's frequently heard in this house. I believe I passed you on the stairs as I arrived.

MRS LINDE: Yes, I climb rather slowly; a bit too much for me to take.

RANK: Ah, a slight touch of the internal rots, eh?

MRS LINDE: More a case of exhaustion actually.

RANK: Nothing else? So, I take it you've come to town to unwind at our various festive gatherings.

MRS LINDE: I've come here to look for work.

RANK: That's supposed to be a proven remedy for exhaustion, is it?

MRS LINDE: We have to live, doctor.

RANK: Yes, it is indeed a commonly held belief that such a thing is necessary.

NORA: Come, come, Dr Rank – you want very much to live too.

RANK: Yes, of course I do. However miserable I may be, I still prefer to be tormented for as long as is possible. And the same goes for all of my patients. As it does for the morally afflicted too. Right now, in fact, there's just such a moral invalid in there with Helmer –

MRS LINDE [*quietly*]: Ah!

NORA: Who do you mean?

RANK: Oh, it's one Krogstad, an individual of whom you know nothing. Rotten right down to the roots of his character, Mrs Helmer. But even he started to talk as though it was of some magnificent import, about his having to *live*.

NORA: Oh? What did he want to talk to Torvald about?

RANK: I have absolutely no idea; all I heard was that it was something about the Commercial Bank.

NORA: I didn't know that Krog – that this man Krogstad had anything to do with the Commercial Bank.

RANK: Yes, he's got some sort of a job down there. [*To* MRS LINDE] I don't know if you also, over in your parts, have the kind of people who scamper breathlessly about sniffing for moral decay, only to get the individual admitted for observation in some favourable position or other. The healthy people just have to put up with being left outside.

MRS LINDE: But surely it's the sick who most need to be brought into the fold.

RANK [*shrugs his shoulders*]: Yes, there we have it. It's that attitude that turns society into an infirmary.

   NORA, *in her own thoughts, bursts into quiet laughter and claps her hands.*

RANK: Why are you laughing at that? Do you actually know what society is?

NORA: What do I care about boring society? I was laughing at something quite different – something terribly amusing. – Tell me, Dr Rank – everybody who's employed at the Commercial Bank will now be dependent on Torvald, yes?

RANK: Is *that* what you find so terribly amusing?

NORA [*smiling and humming*]: Never you mind! Never you mind! [*Walks to and fro.*] Well, it certainly is tremendously pleasing to think that we – that Torvald has such influence over so many people now. [*Takes the paper bag out of her pocket.*] Dr Rank, a little macaroon perhaps?

RANK: I say, macaroons. I thought they were forbidden goods here.

NORA: Yes, but Kristine gave me these.

MRS LINDE: What? I –?

NORA: Now, now; don't be frightened. You couldn't know, of course, that Torvald had forbidden them. He's worried, you see, that they'll give me bad teeth. But pff – just for once –! Don't you agree, Dr Rank? There you go! [*Puts a macaroon in his mouth.*] And you too, Kristine. And I'll have one too, just a little one – or two at most. [*Wanders about again.*] Yes, now I really am terribly happy. Now there's only one thing in the world that I have a most tremendous desire to do.

RANK: Oh? And what's that?

NORA: There's something I have a tremendous desire to say, so Torvald hears it.

RANK: And why can't you say it?

NORA: No, I daren't, it's so hideous.

MRS LINDE: Hideous?

RANK: Then it's not advisable. But you can to us, of course –. What is it you have such a desire to say, so Helmer hears it?

NORA: I have a most tremendous desire to say: bloody hell!

RANK: Are you mad!

MRS LINDE: For heaven's sake, Nora –!

RANK: Say it then. There he is.

NORA [*hides the bag of macaroons*]: Ssh, ssh, ssh!

 HELMER, *with his overcoat on his arm and his hat in his hand, comes from his room.*

NORA [*facing him*]: So, Torvald dear, did you get rid of him?

HELMER: Yes, he's just gone.

NORA: I must introduce you – this is Kristine, who's arrived in town.

HELMER: Kristine –? Apologies, but I don't know –

NORA: Mrs Linde, Torvald dear; Mrs Kristine Linde.

HELMER: Oh right. A childhood friend of my wife's, I take it?

MRS LINDE: Yes, we knew each other in earlier days.

NORA: And imagine, she's made the long journey to town in order to speak to you.

HELMER: How's that?

MRS LINDE: Well, not exactly –

NORA: Yes, because Kristine is terribly clever at office work, and she has a tremendous desire to come under a capable man's leadership and learn more than she already knows –

HELMER: Most sensible, Mrs Linde.

NORA: And when she heard that you'd been made bank director – a telegram[23] came about it – well, then she travelled here as fast as she could and –. I'm right, aren't I, Torvald – for my sake, you can do something for Kristine? Yes?

HELMER: Well, it's certainly not impossible. You are a widow I take it, Mrs Linde?

MRS LINDE: Yes.

HELMER: And have experience of office work?

MRS LINDE: Yes, a fair bit.

HELMER: Well, then it's highly likely that I can get you some employment –

NORA [claps her hands]: You see; you see!

HELMER: You've come at a propitious moment, Mrs Linde –

MRS LINDE: Oh, how can I thank you –?

HELMER: There's really no need. [Puts on his overcoat.] But today you'll have to excuse me –

RANK: Wait; I'll come with you. [Fetches his fur coat from the hall and warms it by the stove.]

NORA: Don't stay out long, Torvald dear.

HELMER: An hour; no more.

NORA: Are you leaving too, Kristine?

MRS LINDE [putting on her outdoor clothes]: Yes, I must go out now to look for a room.

HELMER: Perhaps we'll walk down the street together.

NORA [helping her]: What a bore that we're so cramped for space here; but we really can't –

MRS LINDE: Oh, don't even think about it! Goodbye, dear Nora, and thank you for everything.

NORA: Goodbye for now. But you'll come back this evening, of course. And you too, Dr Rank. Hmm? If you feel well enough? Oh, of course you will; just wrap up well.

Amidst general conversation they go into the hallway. Children's voices are heard outside, on the stairs.

NORA: There they are! There they are!

She runs over and opens the door.

The nanny, ANNE-MARIE, *is coming with the* CHILDREN.

NORA: Come in; come in! [*Bends down and kisses them.*] Oh you sweet little angels –! You see them, Kristine? Aren't they lovely!

RANK: Enough pleasantries out here in the draught!

HELMER: Come on, Mrs Linde; it'll be intolerable here now for anybody but a mother.

DR RANK, HELMER and MRS LINDE go down the stairs. The NANNY *comes into the living room with the* CHILDREN, *as does* NORA, *who closes the door to the hall.*

NORA: How fresh and healthy you look! What red cheeks you've got! Like apples and roses. [*The* CHILDREN *are talking at her during the following.*] Have you enjoyed yourself that much? That's marvellous. Really; you pulled both Emmy and Bob on the sledge? What, really, both at once? Yes, you are a clever boy, Ivar. Oh, let me hold her for a bit, Anne-Marie. My sweet little doll! [*Takes the youngest from the* NANNY *and dances with her.*] Yes, yes, Mummy will dance with Bob, too. What? Have you been throwing snowballs? Oh, I wish I'd been there! No, don't; I'll take their coats off myself, Anne-Marie. Oh yes, do let me; it's such fun. Go inside for now; you look frozen through. There's some hot coffee for you on the stove.

The NANNY *goes into the room on the left.* NORA *takes the* CHILDREN's *outdoor clothing off and drops it all over the place as she lets them all talk excitedly at once.*

NORA: No, really? So there was a big dog that ran after you? But it didn't bite? No, dogs don't bite lovely little baby dolls. Don't look in the parcels, Ivar! What is it? Yes, wouldn't you like to know? Oh no, no; it's something really horrid. Well? Shall we play? What shall we play? Hide and seek. Yes, let's play hide and seek. Bob can hide first. Shall I? All right, let me hide first.

She and the CHILDREN *play, laughing and shouting, in the living room and in the adjoining room to the right. Finally* NORA *hides under the table; the* CHILDREN *come storming in, look, but cannot find her, hear her muffled laughter, dash*

over to the table, lift the cloth, see her. Squeals of delight.
She creeps out as if to scare them. More squeals of delight.
Meanwhile someone has been knocking on the door;
nobody has noticed. Now the door is pushed ajar, and
KROGSTAD *appears; he waits a little; the game continues.*

KROGSTAD: Excuse me, Mrs Helmer –

NORA [*with a muffled cry, turns, startled*]: Ah! What do *you* want?

KROGSTAD: I'm sorry; the front door[24] was ajar; someone must have forgotten to close it –

NORA [*gets up*]: My husband's not at home, Mr Krogstad.

KROGSTAD: I know.

NORA: Right – so what do you want here?

KROGSTAD: To have a word with you.

NORA: With –? [*To the* CHILDREN, *quietly*] Go in to Anne-Marie now. What? No, the strange man won't hurt Mummy. When he's gone, we'll play again.
      She ushers the CHILDREN *into the room on the left and closes the door behind them.*

NORA [*nervous, tense*]: You want to talk to me?

KROGSTAD: Yes, I do.

NORA: Today –? But we've not got to the first of the month yet –

KROGSTAD: No indeed, it's Christmas Eve. It'll be up to you how merry your Christmas is.

NORA: What do you want? Today I can't possibly –

KROGSTAD: We shan't talk about that for now. There's something else. You do have a moment?

NORA: Well yes; yes, of course I have, although –

KROGSTAD: Good. I was sitting in Olsen's café and I saw your husband walking down the street –

NORA: Yes?

KROGSTAD: – with a lady.

NORA: What about it?

KROGSTAD: May I be so bold as to ask; wasn't the lady a certain Mrs Linde?

NORA: Well, yes it was.

KROGSTAD: Just arrived in town?

NORA: Yes, today.

KROGSTAD: And she's a good friend of yours?

NORA: Yes, she is. But I don't see –

KROGSTAD: I knew her too once.

NORA: I know.

KROGSTAD: Oh? So you do know about it. I thought as much. Well, to get straight to the point, might I ask: is Mrs Linde to have some kind of employment at the Commercial Bank?

NORA: How can *you* permit yourself to quiz *me*, Mr Krogstad, *you*, one of my husband's subordinates? But since you ask, you shall get your answer: Yes, Mrs Linde is to have employment. And it was I who recommended her, Mr Krogstad. Now you know.

KROGSTAD: So I was right to put two and two together.

NORA [*walks to and fro*]: Oh, I'd have thought one always has a little grain of influence. Just because one is a woman really doesn't mean –. Being in a subordinate position, Mr Krogstad, one really should take care not to offend someone who – hmm –

KROGSTAD: – who has influence?

NORA: Yes, exactly.

KROGSTAD [*changing tone*]: Mrs Helmer, would you have the kindness perhaps to employ your influence for my benefit?

NORA: What? What do you mean?

KROGSTAD: Would you be kind enough to ensure I hold on to my subordinate post in the Bank?

NORA: How do you mean? Who's thinking of taking your post from you?

KROGSTAD: Oh, you don't need to play ignorant with me. I quite understand that it can't be comfortable for your friend to risk having to bump into me; and now I know too who I'll have to thank when I'm chased out.

NORA: But I can assure you –

KROGSTAD: Yes, yes, but to the point now: there's still time, and I advise you to use your influence to prevent it.

NORA: But, Mr Krogstad, I *have* absolutely no influence.

KROGSTAD: Really? I thought you said a moment ago –

NORA: Not in that sense of course. Me? How can you think I have that kind of influence over my husband?

KROGSTAD: Oh, I've known your husband since our student days. I don't imagine our Mr Bank Director is any less biddable than other husbands.

NORA: If you speak disrespectfully of my husband, I'll show you the door.

KROGSTAD: Madam is brave.

NORA: I'm not afraid of you any more. Once the New Year is over, I'll soon be out of this whole thing.

KROGSTAD [*more controlled*]: Listen to me, Mrs Helmer. If it proves necessary, I'll fight as though my life depended on it to keep my little job in the Bank.

NORA: Yes, so it seems.

KROGSTAD: Not just for the sake of the income; that's the least of my worries. But there's something else –. Yes well, out with it! It's this, you see. You know, of course, as well as everybody else, that some years ago I was guilty of an imprudence.

NORA: I think I've heard something of the sort.

KROGSTAD: The matter didn't go to court; but it meant all avenues were somehow closed to me. So I struck out into the line of business you know about. I had to grab on to something after all; and I think I can say I've not been amongst the worst. But now I must get out of all this. My sons are growing older; for their sake I must try to reclaim all the social respectability I can. This post in the Bank was to be the first step on the ladder for me. And now your husband wants to kick me off that ladder, so I'll end up down in the dirt again.

NORA: But, for God's sake, Mr Krogstad, it really isn't in my power to help you.

KROGSTAD: That's because you don't have the will; but I have the means to force you.

NORA: You wouldn't tell my husband that I owe you money, surely?

KROGSTAD: Hm; and if I did tell him?

NORA: It would be a shameful thing to do. [*Tears rising in her throat*] That secret, my pride and joy, to think he should find out about it in such a hideous, clumsy way – get to know about it from *you*! You'd expose me to the most fearful unpleasantness –

KROGSTAD: Merely unpleasantness?

NORA [*vehemently*]: Well, just do it then; you'll be the one to come off worst, because then my husband will really get to see what a despicable individual you are, and then you certainly won't keep your job.

KROGSTAD: I was asking if it was merely domestic unpleasantness you feared?

NORA: If my husband finds out, he will, of course, pay whatever's outstanding immediately; and then we'll have nothing more to do with you.

KROGSTAD [*a step closer*]: Listen, Mrs Helmer – either you have a rather weak memory, or then again, perhaps you don't have much understanding of business. I'd better explain the situation to you in a little more depth.

NORA: How do you mean?

KROGSTAD: When your husband was ill, you came to me to borrow twelve hundred speciedalers.

NORA: I knew nobody else.

KROGSTAD: So I promised to get you that sum –

NORA: And you did.

KROGSTAD: I promised to get you that sum on certain conditions. You were so preoccupied at the time with your husband's illness, and so keen to get the travel money, that I don't think you gave much consideration to all the incidental circumstances. It would not, therefore, be inappropriate to remind you of this. Now: I promised to find you the money against an IOU, which I drew up.

NORA: Yes, and which I signed.

KROGSTAD: Correct. But beneath that I added a few lines in which your father stood as guarantor for the debt. It was these lines that your father was supposed to sign.

NORA: Supposed to –? He did sign them.

KROGSTAD: I'd left the date blank; that is, your father himself was supposed to enter the date on which he signed the document. Do you remember this, Mrs Helmer?[25]

NORA: Yes, I believe –

KROGSTAD: I then handed the IOU over to you, so that you could send it by post to your father. Isn't that so?

NORA: Yes.

KROGSTAD: And of course you did so immediately; since no more than five or six days later you brought me the bond with your father's signature. The sum was then paid out to you.

NORA: Well, yes; haven't I made all my payments properly?

KROGSTAD: Reasonably, yes. But – to come back to what we were discussing – it must have been a difficult time for you, Mrs Helmer?

NORA: Yes, it was.

KROGSTAD: Your father was extremely ill, I believe.

NORA: He was dying.

KROGSTAD: Died shortly afterwards?

NORA: Yes.

KROGSTAD: Tell me, Mrs Helmer, you wouldn't happen to remember the day your father died? The day of the month, I mean.

NORA: Daddy died on the 29th of September.

KROGSTAD: That's quite right; I've verified it for myself. Which is why there's a peculiarity here [takes a document out] that I simply can't explain.

NORA: What peculiarity? I don't know –

KROGSTAD: The peculiarity is this, madam, that your father signed this IOU three days after his death.

NORA: How? I don't understand –

KROGSTAD: Your father died on the 29th of September. But look at this. Here your father has dated his signature the 2nd of October. Isn't that peculiar, Mrs Helmer?

NORA *is silent.*

KROGSTAD: Can you explain that to me?

NORA *remains silent.*

KROGSTAD: It's rather curious too that the words '2nd of October' and the year are not written in your father's hand, but in a hand I seem perhaps to recognize. Well, that can be explained, of course: your father may have forgotten to date his signature, and then someone or other has done it at random, before knowing about his death. There's no harm in that. It's the person's signature it comes down to. And *that* is authentic, isn't it, Mrs Helmer? It is your father, of course, who has written his name here?

NORA [*after a short silence, tosses her head and looks defiantly at him*]: No, it isn't. *I'm* the one who wrote Daddy's name.

KROGSTAD: Listen, Mrs Helmer – you do realize that this is a dangerous admission?

NORA: Why? You'll have your money soon.

KROGSTAD: May I put a question to you – why didn't you send the document to your father?

NORA: It was impossible. With Daddy being ill. If I'd asked him for his signature, I'd have had to tell him what the money was to be used for. But I couldn't tell him, of course, when he was so ill, that my husband's life was in danger. That was impossible.

KROGSTAD: Then it would have been better for you to have abandoned this trip abroad.

NORA: No, that was impossible. That trip was to save my husband's life. I couldn't abandon it.

KROGSTAD: But didn't you consider the fact that you were committing fraud against me –?

NORA: I couldn't take that into account. I wasn't the least bothered about you. I couldn't stand you and the coldness with which you put obstacles in my way, when you knew the danger my husband was in.

KROGSTAD: Mrs Helmer, you obviously have no clear understanding of what it is you are actually guilty of. But let me tell you, the thing I once did was neither something greater nor something worse, and it wrecked my entire social standing.

NORA: You? You'd have me believe that you did something brave to save your wife's life?

KROGSTAD: The law doesn't ask about motives.

NORA: Then it must be an extremely bad law.

KROGSTAD: Bad or not – if I produce this document in court, you will be condemned according to the law.

NORA: I don't believe that for a moment. Hasn't a daughter the right to protect her old and mortally ill father from worries and anxieties? Hasn't a wife the right to save her husband's life? I don't know the law too well; but I'm certain it must say somewhere that such things are permitted. And you have no knowledge of this – you, as a lawyer? You must be a very bad lawyer, Mr Krogstad.

KROGSTAD: That may be. But business agreements – the kind you and I have with one another – you must surely believe I have an understanding of those? Very well. Do whatever you please. But *this much* I tell you: if I find myself pushed out a second time, you'll be keeping me company.

He makes a farewell gesture and goes out through the hall.

NORA [*thoughtful for a moment; then tosses her head*]: What nonsense! – Trying to frighten me! I'm not that gullible. [*Busies herself with gathering up the* CHILDREN's *clothes; soon stops.*] But –? – No, but it's impossible! I did it out of love after all.

THE CHILDREN [*in the doorway to the left*]: Mummy, that man just went out of the door downstairs.

NORA: Yes, yes, I know. But you're not to tell anyone about the man. You hear? Not even Daddy!

THE CHILDREN: No, Mummy, but will you play with us again now?

NORA: No, no; not now.

THE CHILDREN: Oh but, Mummy, you promised.

NORA: Yes, but I can't right now. Go inside; I've got so much to do. Go in, go in, my dear, sweet children.

She hurries them gently back into the room and closes the door after them.

NORA [*sits on the sofa, picks up some embroidery and does a few stitches but soon stops*]: No! [*Throws the embroidery aside, gets up, goes to the hall door and shouts*] Helene! Let me have the tree in here. [*Goes to the table on the left and opens the drawer; stops again.*] No, but it's utterly impossible, surely!

MAID [*with the Christmas tree*]: Where shall I put it, madam?

NORA: There; in the middle of the room.

MAID: Shall I fetch anything else?

NORA: No thank you; I've got what I need.

The MAID *has put the tree down, she goes out again.*

NORA [*busy decorating the tree*]: Candles here – and flowers here. – That despicable person! Oh, nonsense, nonsense! There's nothing the matter. The Christmas tree is going to be lovely. I'll do whatever you want, Torvald – I'll sing for you, dance for you –

HELMER, *with a bundle of papers under his arm, comes in from outside.*

NORA: Ah – are you back already?

HELMER: Yes. Has anybody been here?

NORA: Here? No.

HELMER: That's peculiar. I saw Krogstad come out of the downstairs door.

NORA: Really? Oh yes, that's right, Krogstad was here for a moment.

HELMER: Nora, I can see it in your face: he's been here and asked you to put in a good word for him.

NORA: Yes.

HELMER: And you were meant to do it as if of your own accord? You were meant to conceal it from me that he'd been here. He asked that of you too, didn't he?

NORA: Yes, Torvald; but –

HELMER: Nora, Nora, how could you go along with something like that? Engage in conversation with a man of that sort, and then give him a promise! And then to top it, tell me an untruth!

NORA: An untruth –?

HELMER: Didn't you say nobody had been here? [*Wags a stern finger.*] My little songbird must never do that again. A songbird needs a clean beak to chirrup with; never a false note. [*Holds her round her waist.*] Isn't that how it should be? Yes, that's what I thought. [*Lets her go.*] And now, no more about it. [*Sits down in front of the stove.*] Ah, how cosy and comfortable it is in here. [*Leafs through his papers a little.*]

NORA [*busy with the Christmas tree, after a short pause*]: Torvald!

HELMER: Yes.

NORA: I'm looking forward so tremendously to the fancy dress ball at the Stenborgs' the day after tomorrow.

HELMER: And I'm tremendously curious to see what you're going to surprise me with.

NORA: Ah, that stupid idea.

HELMER: Oh?

NORA: I can't think of anything that'll do; everything seems so pathetic, so meaningless.

HELMER: Has my little Nora come to *that* realization?

NORA [*behind his chair, leaning with her arms on the back of it*]: Are you very busy, Torvald?

HELMER: Well –

NORA: What sort of papers are those?

HELMER: Bank matters.

NORA: Already?

HELMER: I got the outgoing management to give me authority to undertake the necessary changes in the staff and business plan. I'll have to spend Christmas week on it. I want to have everything in order by New Year.

NORA: So that's why this poor Krogstad –

HELMER: Hm.

NORA [*still leaning on the back of his chair and slowly running her fingers through the hair at the nape of his neck*]: If you'd not been so busy, I'd have asked you for a tremendously big favour, Torvald.

HELMER: Tell me. What could that be?

NORA: Nobody has such excellent taste as you. And I do so want to look good at the ball. Torvald, couldn't you take me in hand and decide what I should be, and how my costume should be arranged?

HELMER: Aha, is little Miss Wilful out looking for a man to rescue her?

NORA: Yes, Torvald, I can't get anywhere without your help.

HELMER: Very well. I'll give it some thought; we'll manage something.

NORA: Oh, how kind of you. [*Goes back to the Christmas tree; pause.*] How pretty these red flowers look. – But tell me,

is it really so bad, whatever it was that this Krogstad was
guilty of?

HELMER: Falsifying signatures. Have you any idea what that
means?

NORA: Mightn't he have done it out of necessity?

HELMER: Indeed, or, as so many do, in a moment of imprudence. I'm not so heartless as to condemn a man categorically
for the sake of one such isolated act.

NORA: No, isn't that so, Torvald!

HELMER: Many may rise and redeem themselves morally, if
only they confess their misdeeds openly and take their
punishment.

NORA: Punishment –?

HELMER: But that wasn't the path Krogstad chose; he managed to slip away with tricks and manoeuvres; and that's
what has eroded him morally.

NORA: You think that would –?

HELMER: Just imagine how such a guilt-ridden person has to
lie and dissemble and pretend to all and sundry, has to wear
a mask even for those closest to him, yes, even for his own
wife and his own children. And the children, well, that really
is the worst of it, Nora.

NORA: Why?

HELMER: Because such an atmosphere[26] of lies brings conta-
gion and disease into the very life of a home. Every breath
the children take in such a house is filled with the germs of
something ugly.

NORA [closer behind him]: Are you sure of that?

HELMER: My dear, I've experienced it often enough as a lawyer. Almost all those who are corrupt from an early age have
had mothers who were liars.

NORA: Why precisely – mothers?

HELMER: It's mostly ascribable to the mothers; but fathers, of
course, have the same effect; every lawyer knows that. And
yet, this Krogstad has gone about his home, year in year out,
poisoning his own children with lies and hypocrisy; that's
why I say he is morally destitute. [Holds his hands out to
her.] And that's why my sweet little Nora must promise me

not to plead his cause. Your hand on it. Now, now, what's this? Give me your hand. There now. That's settled. It would, I assure you, have been impossible for me to work with him; I literally feel physically ill in the proximity of such individuals.

NORA [*pulls her hand back and goes round to the other side of the Christmas tree*]: How hot it is in here. And I've got so much to do.

HELMER [*gets up and gathers his papers together*]: Yes, and I should think about getting some of this read before dinner. Your costume – I'll give some thought to that as well. And something to hang in gold wrapping on the Christmas tree; I might just perhaps have that in store too. [*Puts his hand on her head.*] Oh, my darling little songbird. [*Goes into his room and closes the door behind him.*]

NORA [*quietly, after a silence*]: Oh, surely! It isn't true. It's impossible. It *must* be impossible.

NANNY [*in the doorway on the left*]: The little ones are asking so prettily if they can come in to their mummy.

NORA: No, no, don't let them come in here to me! You stay with them, Anne-Marie.

NANNY: Very well, madam. [*Closes the door.*]

NORA [*pale with fear*]: Corrupt my little children –! Poison our home? [*Brief pause; she lifts her head high.*] It isn't true. It can't ever possibly be true.

ACT TWO

The same room. Up in the corner by the piano stands the Christmas tree, stripped, dishevelled and with its candles burned down to the stubs. Nora's outdoor clothes are lying on the sofa.

NORA, *alone in the room, walks about anxiously; finally she stops at the sofa and picks up her coat.*

NORA [*dropping her coat again*]: Someone's coming! [*Goes to the door, listens.*] No – nobody's there. Of course – nobody will come today, Christmas Day;[27] – and not tomorrow either. – But perhaps – [*opens the door and looks out*] No; nothing in the letterbox; quite empty. [*Moves forward across the room.*] Oh, it's ludicrous! Of course he won't actually do it. Something like that *can't* happen. It's impossible. I've got three young children, after all.

The NANNY, *carrying a large cardboard box, comes in from the room on the left.*

NANNY: There now, I've finally found the box of fancy dress costumes.

NORA: Thank you; put it on the table.

NANNY [*does so*]: But they're in rather a bad way, I'm afraid.

NORA: Oh, I wish I could rip them into a hundred thousand pieces!

NANNY: Heavens; they can easily be put right; just a little patience.

NORA: Yes, I'll go over and get Mrs Linde to help me.

NANNY: Out again? In this foul weather? Miss Nora[28] will catch a chill – get sick.

NORA: Well, that wouldn't be the worst. – How are the children?

NANNY: The poor little mites are playing with their Christmas presents, but –

NORA: Are they asking for me a lot?

NANNY: Well, they are very used to having Mummy around.

NORA: Yes but, Anne-Marie, from now on I *can't* be with them as much as before.

NANNY: Well, little ones get used to all sorts.

NORA: Do you believe that? Do you believe they'd forget their mummy if she was gone altogether?

NANNY: Heavens; gone altogether!

NORA: Listen, tell me, Anne-Marie – I've often thought – how could you overrule your heart and place your child with strangers?

NANNY: But I had to, of course, when I was going to be wet-nurse for little Nora.

NORA: Yes, but that you'd *want* to?

NANNY: When I could get such a good job? A penniless girl who's got herself into trouble[29] has to be grateful for whatever she gets. After all, that scoundrel did nothing for me.

NORA: But your daughter must have forgotten you.

NANNY: Oh no, she most certainly hasn't. She wrote to me, you know, both when she was confirmed and after she was married.

NORA [*caresses her neck*]: Dear old Anne-Marie, you were a good mother to me, when I was little.

NANNY: Little Nora, poor thing, didn't have any other mother but me.

NORA: And if my little ones didn't have any other, I know that you'd –. Oh, nonsense, nonsense. [*Opens the box.*] Go in to them. Now, I must –. Tomorrow you'll see how lovely I'll be.

NANNY: Ah, there'll certainly be nobody at the whole ball as lovely as Miss Nora.

She goes into the room on the left.

NORA [*starts to unpack the box but soon throws it all aside*]: Oh, if I dared to go out. If only I knew nobody would come. That nothing would happen here at home in the meantime.

Stuff and nonsense; nobody's coming. Just don't think. Brush my muff. Lovely gloves, lovely gloves. Push it away; push it away! One, two, three, four, five, six – [*Screams.*] Ah, they're coming – [*Starts for the door, but stands irresolute.*]

MRS LINDE *comes in from the hall, where she has left her outdoor things.*

NORA: Oh, is it you, Kristine? There's nobody else out there, is there? – It's so good you came.

MRS LINDE: I hear you've been up asking for me.

NORA: Yes, I was just passing. There's something you really must help me with. Let's sit here on the sofa. Look. There's going to be a fancy dress ball tomorrow evening, upstairs at Consul[30] Stenborg's, and Torvald wants me to be a Neapolitan fisher-girl[31] and dance the tarantella[32] – I learned it on Capri.

MRS LINDE: I say; so you'll be giving a whole performance?

NORA: Yes, Torvald says I should. Look, I've got the outfit here; Torvald had it sewn for me down there; but now the whole thing's in such tatters, and I simply don't know –

MRS LINDE: Oh, we'll soon get that put right; it's just the trimmings that have come a bit loose here and there. Needle and thread? Right, we've got everything we need.

NORA: Oh, it's so kind of you.

MRS LINDE [*sewing*]: So you'll be in disguise tomorrow, Nora? You know what, I'll pop by for a moment then, to see you in your finery. But, of course, I've clean forgotten to thank you for that nice evening yesterday.

NORA [*gets up and walks across the room*]: Oh, I don't think it was as nice here yesterday as it usually is. – You should have come to town a bit sooner, Kristine. – But yes, Torvald certainly knows how to make a home lovely and beautiful.

MRS LINDE: And yourself no less, I'd say; you're not your father's daughter for nothing. But tell me, is Dr Rank always as gloomy as he was yesterday?

NORA: No, it was particularly noticeable yesterday. But then he does suffer from a very dangerous illness. He has consumption of the spine,[33] poor man. His father was a revolting man, let me tell you, who kept mistresses and that sort of thing; which is why his son was sickly from childhood, you understand.

MRS LINDE [*lowers her sewing*]: But my dearest, sweetest Nora, where do you get to know about such things?

NORA [*strolling about*]: Pff – when you have three children, you get an occasional visit from – from ladies who are half-way knowledgeable in medical matters, and they tell you this and that.

MRS LINDE [*sewing again; brief silence*]: Does Dr Rank come to the house every day?

NORA: Every single day. He's been Torvald's best friend since they were young, and he's *my* good friend too. Dr Rank's almost a part of the house.

MRS LINDE: But tell me, Nora: is the man completely sincere? I mean, doesn't he rather like saying things to please people?

NORA: No, on the contrary. What makes you think that?

MRS LINDE: When you introduced me to him yesterday, he assured me he'd often heard my name mentioned in this house; but later I noticed that your husband had no idea who I actually was. So how could Dr Rank –?

NORA: No, but that's quite right, Kristine. Torvald is so indescribably devoted to me; so he wants to have me all for himself, alone, as he says. In the beginning he'd almost get jealous if I so much as mentioned any of the dear people from home. So, naturally, I avoided it. But I often talk to Dr Rank about such things, because he's so happy to hear about them, you see.

MRS LINDE: Now listen, Nora; you are in many respects like a child still; I'm considerably older than you, of course, and have a little more experience. I want to tell you something: you must get out of this thing with Dr Rank.

NORA: What exactly must I get out of?

MRS LINDE: Of this, that and the other, I'd say. Yesterday you mentioned something about a rich admirer who was going to give you money –

NORA: Yes, a man who doesn't exist – unfortunately. But what of it?

MRS LINDE: Is Dr Rank wealthy?

NORA: Yes, he is.

MRS LINDE: And has no dependants?

NORA: No, none; but –?

MRS LINDE: And he comes to this house every day?

NORA: Yes, you heard what I said.

MRS LINDE: But how could such a distinguished man be so persistent?

NORA: I really don't follow you.

MRS LINDE: Don't pretend now, Nora. Don't you think I know who you borrowed the twelve hundred speciedaler from?

NORA: Are you completely out of your mind? Can you imagine such a thing! A friend of ours, who comes here every single day! Just think how terribly awkward that would be!

MRS LINDE: So it really isn't him?

NORA: No, I assure you. It never occurred to me for a moment –. He didn't have any money to lend out at the time anyway; he only inherited it later.

MRS LINDE: Well, I think that was lucky for you, my dear Nora.

NORA: No, it could never occur to me to ask Dr Rank –. Having said that, I'm pretty certain that if I were to ask him –

MRS LINDE: But naturally you won't.

NORA: No, naturally. I don't think I can imagine it ever being necessary. But I'm pretty sure that if I *were* to speak to Dr Rank –

MRS LINDE: Behind your husband's back?

NORA: I must get out of this other business; *that's* behind his back too. I *must* get out of all this.

MRS LINDE: Yes, yes, that's exactly what I said yesterday; but –

NORA [*walks back and forth*]: A man can handle this sort of thing so much better than a mere woman –

MRS LINDE: One's own husband, yes.

NORA: Oh stuff and nonsense. [*Stops.*] When you pay everything you owe, you get your IOU back, yes?

MRS LINDE: Yes, obviously.

NORA: And can rip it into a hundred thousand pieces and burn it up – that filthy revolting bit of paper!

MRS LINDE [*looks stiffly at her, puts her sewing down and gets up slowly*]: Nora, you're hiding something from me.

NORA: Does it show?

MRS LINDE: Something's happened to you since yesterday morning. Nora, whatever is it?

NORA [*towards her*]: Kristine! [*Listens.*] Ssh! Torvald's just got home. Look; you go and sit with the children for now. Torvald can't bear to see mending and darning. Let Anne-Marie help you.

MRS LINDE [*collects some of the sewing things together*]: Yes, all right, but I'm not leaving until we've had a proper talk together.

She goes into the room on the left, just as HELMER *comes from the hall.*

NORA [*goes to meet him*]: Oh, how I've waited for you, Torvald dear.

HELMER: Was that the seamstress?

NORA: No, it was Kristine; she's helping me put my costume right. I'm going to look wonderful, believe me.

HELMER: Yes, rather an inspired idea of mine, wasn't it?

NORA: Marvellous! But aren't I nice too, to give in to you?

HELMER [*takes her chin in his hand*]: Nice – for giving in to your husband? Well, well, you crazy little thing, I know you didn't mean it that way. Still, I don't want to intrude; you'll be trying on your costume, I expect.

NORA: And you'll be working?

HELMER: Yes. [*Showing her a bundle of papers*] Look at this. I've been down at the Bank – [*About to go into his room.*]

NORA: Torvald.

HELMER [*stops*]: Yes.

NORA: If your little squirrel asked you ever so prettily, for just one thing –?

HELMER: Well?

NORA: Would you do it?

HELMER: I'd need to know what it is first, naturally.

NORA: Your squirrel would run about and do tricks, if you were nice and gave in to her.

HELMER: Out with it then.

NORA: Your skylark would chirrup in all the rooms, both high and low –

HELMER: Oh, but my skylark does that anyway.

NORA: I'd play elfin-girl[34] and dance for you in the moonlight, Torvald.

HELMER: Nora – surely it's never that thing you started on this morning?

NORA [closer]: Yes, Torvald, I beg and beseech you!

HELMER: And you have the courage to rake that business up again?

NORA: Yes, yes, you *have* to give in to me; you *have* to let Krogstad keep his post at the Bank.

HELMER: But my dear Nora, it's *his* job I've allotted to Mrs Linde.

NORA: Yes, that's extremely kind of you; but surely you can just dismiss another clerk instead of Krogstad.

HELMER: This really is the most incredible obstinacy! Just because you go making some thoughtless promise to speak on his behalf, I'm supposed to –!

NORA: That's not why, Torvald. It's for your own sake. This person writes in the foulest newspapers; you've said so yourself. He can do you such unutterable harm. I'm so deadly afraid of him –

HELMER: Aha, now I understand; old memories – that's what's putting you into this fearful flutter.

NORA: What do you mean?

HELMER: You're thinking of your father, of course.

NORA: Oh yes, that's it, yes. Remember how those evil-minded people wrote in the newspapers about Daddy and slandered him so horribly. I think they would have got him dismissed, if the Department hadn't sent you over to look into it, and if you hadn't been so obliging and helpful to him.

HELMER: My little Nora, there is a significant difference between your father and myself. Your father wasn't an unimpeachable public servant. But I am and hope to remain so for as long as I am in my post.

NORA: Oh, nobody knows what things evil people can think up. Things could be so nice now, so calm and happy for us here in our peaceful and carefree home – you and I and the children, Torvald! That's why I beg you, earnestly –

HELMER: And it's precisely by pleading for him that you make it impossible for me to keep him. It's already known at the Bank that I intend to dismiss Krogstad. If it were rumoured now that the new Bank director allowed his mind to be changed by his wife –

NORA: Would that matter –?

HELMER: No, naturally; so long as this little Miss Wilful could get her way –. I'm supposed to go in and make myself ridiculous in front of the entire staff – give people the idea I'm subject to all kinds of external influence? Well, believe me, I'd soon feel the consequences! And besides – there's one factor that makes it absolutely impossible to have Krogstad at the Bank, as long as I am director.

NORA: And what's that?

HELMER: I could, at a pinch, perhaps have overlooked his moral defects –

NORA: Yes, isn't that so, Torvald?

HELMER: And I hear that he's pretty good at his job too. But he's an acquaintance from my youth. It was one of those rash associations that one's so often embarrassed by later in life. Well, I may as well tell you straight: we're on first-name terms.[35] And this tactless individual does nothing to hide it in the presence of others. Quite the contrary – he thinks it entitles him to take a familiar tone with me; so he constantly gets one over me with his 'Torvald this' and 'Torvald that'. I assure you, it is highly embarrassing. He'd make my position at the Bank intolerable.

NORA: Torvald, you don't mean anything by this.

HELMER: Oh really? Why not?

NORA: Because it's such a petty concern.

HELMER: What are you saying? Petty! You think I am petty!

NORA: No, quite the contrary, Torvald dear; and that's precisely why –

HELMER: Nevertheless; you're calling my motives petty; so I must be too. Petty! I see! – Right, this will be brought to a decisive end. [Goes to the hall door and calls] Helene!

NORA: What are you doing?

HELMER [*searching among his papers*]: Settling the matter.

    The MAID *comes in.*

HELMER: Here; take this letter; go down with it immediately. Get hold of a messenger and have him deliver it. But quickly. The address is on it. Look, there's the money.

MAID: Very well.

    She leaves with the letter.

HELMER [*assembles his papers*]: So, my little Miss Stubborn.

NORA [*with bated breath*]: Torvald – what was that letter?

HELMER: Krogstad's notice.

NORA: Call it back, Torvald! There's still time. Oh, Torvald, call it back! Do it for my sake – for your own sake; for the children's sake! Are you listening, Torvald? Do it! You don't realize what this can bring down on us all.

HELMER: Too late.

NORA: Yes, too late.

HELMER: My dear Nora, I forgive you the anxiety you're going through here, even if it's essentially an insult to me. Oh yes, it is! Or isn't it perhaps an insult to believe that *I* would be worried about some wretched hack lawyer's revenge? But I do nevertheless forgive you, because it's such sweet testimony to your great love for me. [*Takes her in his arms.*] That's how it should be, my own darling Nora. Let whatever comes come.[36] When it really counts, you can be sure, I have both strength and courage. You'll see, I am man enough to take everything upon myself.

NORA [*terrified*]: What do you mean?

HELMER: *Everything,* I say –

NORA [*firmly*]: No, you shall never, never do that.

HELMER: All right; then we'll share it, Nora – as husband and wife. That's how it should be. [*Caresses her.*] Are you satisfied now? There, there, now; not these terrified doves' eyes! This is nothing, really, but the emptiest figment of your imagination. – You should run through the tarantella and practise with the tambourine now. I'll sit in the inner office and close the door between, so I won't hear a thing; you can make as much noise as you want. [*Turns around in the doorway.*] And when Rank arrives, tell him where he can find me.

He nods to her, goes into his room with his papers and closes the door.

NORA [*in bewildered fear, stands as if rooted to the spot, whispers*]: He was prepared to do it. He'll do it. He'll do it, in the face of everything. – No, never that, never! Before all else! Rescue –! A way out – [*The doorbell rings in the hall.*] Dr Rank –! Before all else! Before *anything*, whatever it takes!

She runs her hands over her face, pulls herself together and goes over to open the door to the hall. DR RANK *is standing out in the hall, hanging up his fur coat. During the following scene darkness begins to fall.*

NORA: Hello, Dr Rank. I recognized you by the way you rang. But you mustn't go in to Torvald just now; I think he's busy with something.

RANK: And you?

NORA [*as he enters the living room, and she closes the door behind him*]: Oh, you know very well – for you, I always have a moment to spare.

RANK: Thank you. I shall avail myself of that for as long as I can.

NORA: What do you mean? For as long as you can?

RANK: Yes. Does *that* alarm you?

NORA: Well, it's such a strange turn of phrase. Is anything going to happen?

RANK: What's going to happen is what I've long been prepared for. But I really didn't think it would come so soon.

NORA [*clutching his arm*]: What have you found out? Dr Rank, you're to tell me!

RANK [*sits next to the stove*]: It's downhill for me. There's nothing to be done about it.

NORA [*sighs with relief*]: Oh, is it you –?

RANK: Who else? There's no point lying to oneself. I am the most miserable of all my patients, Mrs Helmer. In the last few days I've carried out a complete assessment of my internal status. Bankrupt. Before the month is out I'll be lying, perhaps, rotting up at the churchyard.

NORA: Shame on you, what an ugly way to talk.

RANK: Well, this thing is damned ugly. But the worst is that there'll be so much other ugliness to come beforehand. There's only one final investigation to be carried out now; when I'm finished with that, I'll know the approximate hour that the disintegration will set in. There's something I want to tell you. Helmer, with his fine sensibilities, has such a marked loathing for anything hideous. I don't want him in my sickroom –

NORA: Oh, but Dr Rank –

RANK: I don't want him there. Under any circumstance. I'm closing my door to him. – As soon as I'm fully informed of the worst, I shall send you my visiting-card with a black cross on it, and then you will know that the abominable process of destruction[37] has begun.

NORA: Oh, you're being quite unreasonable today. And just when I wanted you to be in a really good mood.

RANK: With death at hand? – And to pay like this for another man's sin. Is there any justice in that? And every single family is in some way or other governed by this kind of inexorable retribution –

NORA [covers her ears]: Oh, stop now! Merry; merry!

RANK: Yes, there's really no alternative but to laugh at the whole thing. My poor innocent spine[38] has to suffer for my father's merry days as a lieutenant.

NORA [at the table on the left]: He had such a weakness for asparagus and pâté de foie gras. Wasn't that it?

RANK: Yes; and for truffles.

NORA: Yes, truffles, yes. And then oysters, I think?

RANK: Yes, oysters, oysters; that goes without saying.

NORA: And then all that port and champagne. It's sad that all these delicious things should affect the spine.

RANK: Particularly that they should affect an unfortunate spine that hasn't had the least pleasure from them.

NORA: Ah me, yes, that's what's saddest of all.

RANK [looks at her searchingly]: Hm –

NORA [after a brief pause]: Why did you smile?

RANK: No, it was you who laughed.

NORA: No, it was you who smiled, Dr Rank!

RANK [*getting up*]: You really are a bigger scamp than I thought.

NORA: I'm so bent on mischief today.

RANK: So it seems.

NORA [*with both hands on his shoulders*]: My dear, dear Dr Rank, you're not to go and die on Torvald and me.

RANK: Oh, you'd soon recover from the loss. Those who depart are soon forgotten.

NORA [*looks anxiously at him*]: You think so?

RANK: One forms new bonds, and then –

NORA: Who forms new bonds?

RANK: You and Helmer both will, when I'm gone. *You've* already made a good start, I'd say. What was this Mrs Linde doing here yesterday evening?

NORA: Aha – you're not jealous of poor Kristine, are you?

RANK: Yes, I am. She'll be my successor here in this house. When I've got my final leave of absence, perhaps that woman will –

NORA: Hush; don't talk so loud; she's in there.

RANK: Today too? You see.

NORA: Only to sew my costume. Good Lord, you're so unreasonable. [*Sits down on the sofa.*] Be nice now, Dr Rank; tomorrow you'll see how prettily I shall dance; and then you'll imagine that I'm doing it just for your sake – well, and for Torvald's too, of course – that goes without saying. [*Takes various things out of the box.*] Dr Rank, sit down here, and I'll show you something.

RANK [*sits down*]: What is it?

NORA: Look here. Look!

RANK: Silk stockings.

NORA: Flesh-coloured. Aren't they *lovely*? Well, it's dark in here now; but tomorrow –. No, no, no; you're only to see the foot. Oh all right then, of course you can look higher up[39] too.

RANK: Hm –

NORA: Why are you looking so critical? You think perhaps they won't fit me?

RANK: Well, on *that* I couldn't possibly have an informed opinion.

NORA [*looks at him for a moment*]: Shame on you! [*Hits him lightly on the ear with the stockings.*] Take that. [*Puts them back in the box.*]

RANK: And what other glorious things am I to see?

NORA: You shan't see a scrap more, because you're naughty.

She hums to herself a little, and searches among the things.

RANK [*after a brief silence*]: When I sit here like this with you in such close confidence, then I can't imagine – no, I can't conceive – what would have become of me if I'd never come into this house.

NORA [*smiles*]: Yes, I do believe you actually enjoy yourself here with us.

RANK [*more quietly, looking straight in front of him*]: And then to have to leave it all –

NORA: Oh stuff and nonsense. You're not leaving it.

RANK [*as before*]: – without being able to leave behind even a humble token of gratitude; scarcely a fleeting sense of loss – nothing but a vacant place that can be filled by the first person to come along.

NORA: And if I were to ask you for –? No –

RANK: For what?

NORA: For a great proof of your friendship –

RANK: Yes, yes?

NORA: No, I mean – for a tremendously big favour –

RANK: Would you really, just this *one* time, make me so happy?

NORA: Oh, but you don't have any idea what it is.

RANK: All right; so tell me.

NORA: No, but really I can't, Dr Rank; it's so unreasonably much: advice, and help and a favour too –

RANK: The more the better. It's a mystery to me what you might mean. Well, speak out. Haven't I your confidence?

NORA: Yes, you have, like nobody else. You're my truest and best friend, I know that. And that's also why I shall tell you. You see, Dr Rank: there's something you must help me to prevent. You know how deeply, how indescribably Torvald loves me; he wouldn't hesitate for a moment to give his life for my sake.

RANK [*leaning towards her*]: Nora – do you think he's the only one –?

NORA [*with a slight start*]: Who would –?

RANK: Who would gladly give his life for your sake.

NORA [*sadly*]: I see.

RANK: I swore to myself that you'd know it before I went away. I'll never find a better opportunity. – Yes, Nora, now you know. And now you also know that you can confide in me as in nobody else.

NORA [*gets up; steadily and calmly*]: Let me pass.

RANK [*makes room for her, but remains seated*]: Nora –

NORA [*in the doorway to the hall*]: Helene, bring in the lamp. – [*Walks over towards the stove.*] Oh, my dear Dr Rank, that was really horrid of you.

RANK [*gets up*]: To have loved you as deeply as anyone else? Was *that* horrid?

NORA: No, but that you should go and tell me. That was absolutely unnecessary –

RANK: What do you mean? Did you know –?

The MAID *comes in with the lamp, puts it on the table and goes out again.*

RANK: Nora – Mrs Helmer – I'm asking you: did you know something?

NORA: Oh, how do I know what I knew or didn't know? I really can't say –. That you could be so clumsy, Dr Rank! Everything was so good a moment ago.

RANK: Well, at least you can be quite sure now that I'm here at your disposal, body and soul. So if you do want to speak out –

NORA [*looks at him*]: After this?

RANK: I beg you, let me know what it is.

NORA: I can't tell you anything now.

RANK: Oh please. You mustn't punish me like this. Let me do whatever's humanly possible for you.

NORA: You can't do anything for me now. – Anyway, I probably don't need any help. You'll see, the whole thing is just a figment of my imagination. Of course it is! Naturally. [*Sits down in the rocking-chair, looks at him, smiles.*] Well, you really are a fine gentleman, Dr Rank! Aren't you ashamed of yourself, now that the lamp's come in?

RANK: No, not really. But perhaps I should go – for ever?

NORA: No, you certainly mustn't do that. Naturally you'll come here as before. You know very well Torvald can't do without you.

RANK: Yes, but *you*?

NORA: Oh, I always think it's tremendously amusing here when you come by.

RANK: Yes, it was that that led me astray. You're an enigma to me. I've often had the sense that you'd almost as soon be with me as with Helmer.

NORA: Well, you know, there are certain people one loves most, and others one might almost prefer to be with.

RANK: Indeed, there's something in that.

NORA: When I was at home, I loved Daddy best, of course. But I always thought it was tremendous fun when I could steal down to the maids' room; they never ever tried to guide or instruct[40] me; and they always talked so amusingly among themselves.

RANK: Aha. So it's *them* I've replaced.

NORA [*jumps up and goes over to him*]: Oh, dear, kind Dr Rank, that's not what I meant at all. But you can understand, surely, that with Torvald it's the same as with Daddy –

The MAID *comes in from the hall.*

MAID: Madam! [*Whispers and hands her a card.*]

NORA [*glances at the card*]: Ah! [*Stuffs it in her pocket.*]

RANK: Something wrong?

NORA: No, no, not at all; it's just – it's my new costume –

RANK: Really? But your costume's over there.

NORA: Oh, yes, that one; but this is another; I've ordered it – Torvald mustn't know –

RANK: Aha, so there we have the big secret.

NORA: Yes, quite so; just go in to him; he's sitting in the inner room; keep him busy for a bit –

RANK: Don't worry; he shan't escape me.

He goes into HELMER's *room.*

NORA [*to the* MAID] And he's waiting in the kitchen?

MAID: Yes, he came up the back stairs[41] –

NORA: But didn't you tell him there was somebody here?

MAID: Yes, but it was no good.

NORA: He won't go away?

MAID: No, he won't go until he's spoken with you, madam.

NORA: Well, let him come in; but quietly. Helene, you mustn't tell anybody; it's a surprise for my husband.

MAID: Yes, yes, I understand, of course –

   She goes out.

NORA: It's happening – the most terrible thing.[42] It's coming after all. No, no, no, it can't be happening; it shan't happen. [*She goes over and bolts* HELMER's *door.*]

   The MAID *opens the door to the hallway for* KROGSTAD *and closes it after him. He is wearing a fur travel coat, boots and a fur hat.*

NORA [*going towards him*]: Talk quietly; my husband's at home.

KROGSTAD: What of it?

NORA: What do you want from me?

KROGSTAD: To get some answers.

NORA: Then hurry up. What is it?

KROGSTAD: You know presumably that I've had my dismissal.

NORA: I couldn't prevent it, Mr Krogstad. I fought my utmost on your behalf, but it was no use.

KROGSTAD: Does your husband have so little love for you? He's aware of what I can expose you to, and yet he dares –

NORA: How could you think he'd know anything?

KROGSTAD: Well, no, I didn't actually think he did. It didn't seem the least bit like dear old Torvald Helmer to show that much manly courage –

NORA: Mr Krogstad, I demand respect for my husband.

KROGSTAD: Oh, absolutely, all due respect. But since madam is so anxious to keep all this hidden, I dare to presume you're a little better informed than yesterday about what it is you've actually done.

NORA: More than *you* could ever teach me.

KROGSTAD: Yes, such a bad lawyer as I am –

NORA: What do you want from me?

KROGSTAD: Just to see how things stood with you, Mrs Helmer. I've been thinking about you all day. A debt-collector, a hack lawyer, a – well, even someone of my sort has a little of what's called compassion, you see.

NORA: Show it then; think of my young children.

KROGSTAD: Have you and your husband thought of mine? But that makes no odds now. All I wanted to tell you was this: you needn't take this affair too seriously. There won't, for the present, be any charges brought from my side.

NORA: No; that's so, isn't it; I knew it.

KROGSTAD: This entire affair can be sorted out amicably; there's absolutely no need for it to come out; it'll stay between the three of us.

NORA: My husband must never get to know about this.

KROGSTAD: How are you going to prevent it? Can you pay off what's outstanding perhaps?

NORA: No, not straight away.

KROGSTAD: Or do you perhaps have some way of raising the money over the next few days?

NORA: Not a way I want to make use of.

KROGSTAD: No, it would be of no help to you now anyway. Even if you stood here with the biggest pile of cash in your hand, you'd not get your bond from me.

NORA: Then explain to me what you want to use it for.

KROGSTAD: I just want to hold on to it – have it in my safe-keeping. Nobody else at all will get the least hint of this. So if you were going about here with some desperate solution or other –

NORA: I am.

KROGSTAD: – thinking of running away from your house and home –

NORA: I am!

KROGSTAD: – or thinking of something worse still –

NORA: How can you know?

KROGSTAD: – then forget it.

NORA: How can you know I'm thinking of *that*?

KROGSTAD: Most of us think of *that* in the beginning. I thought of it too; but I honestly didn't have the courage –

NORA [*in a dull tone*]: Neither do I.

KROGSTAD [*relieved*]: No, that's quite right; you don't have the courage for it either, do you?

NORA: No, I haven't; I haven't.

KROGSTAD: And a very foolish mistake it would be. Once the initial domestic storm is over –. I have in my pocket here a letter for your husband –

NORA: And it says everything?

KROGSTAD: Expressed as delicately as possible.

NORA [*quickly*]: He mustn't get that letter. Rip it up again. I'll find a way out, I'll get the money.

KROGSTAD: I'm sorry, Mrs Helmer, but I believe I just told you –

NORA: Oh, I'm not talking about what I owe you. Let me know exactly how much you're demanding from my husband, and I'll get the money.

KROGSTAD: I'm not demanding any money from your husband.

NORA: So what are you demanding?

KROGSTAD: I'll tell you. I want to get back on my feet, Mrs Helmer; I want to rise in the world; and your husband will help me. For a year and a half I've been guilty of nothing dishonest; I have, in all that time, battled in the most straitened circumstances; I was content to work my way up step by step. Now I've been chased out and I refuse to be content with merely being taken back into the fold. I want to rise in the world, I tell you. I want to be back in the Bank – in a higher position; your husband will create a position for me –

NORA: He'll never do that!

KROGSTAD: He will do it; I know him; he won't dare breathe a word. And once I'm in there with him, then you'll see! Within a year I shall be the director's right-hand man. It'll be Nils Krogstad and not Torvald Helmer running the Commercial Bank.

NORA: That's something you'll never see!

KROGSTAD: You might perhaps –?

NORA: I have the courage for it now.

KROGSTAD: Oh, you don't frighten me. A fine, cosseted lady like you –

NORA: You'll see; you'll see!

KROGSTAD: Under the ice perhaps? Down in the cold, coal-black water? And then to float up in the spring, hideous, unrecognizable, with your hair fallen out –

NORA: You don't frighten me.

KROGSTAD: Nor do you frighten me. People don't do such things, Mrs Helmer. Besides, what purpose would it serve? I'd have him in my pocket all the same.

NORA: Afterwards? When I'm no longer –?

KROGSTAD: Are you forgetting that *I* would *then* have control over the reputation you leave behind?

NORA *looks at him, speechless.*

KROGSTAD: Well, I've prepared you now. Don't go doing anything silly. As soon as Helmer's got my letter, I expect to hear from him. And remember, it's your husband himself who's forced me back on to such a path. And for that I shall never forgive him. Goodbye, Mrs Helmer.

He goes out through the hall.

NORA [*going to the door leading to the hall, opens it a crack and listens*]: Going. Isn't dropping the letter off. Oh no, no, of course, that would be impossible surely. [*Opens the door wider and wider.*] What's happening? He's standing outside. Isn't going down the stairs. Is he changing his mind? Might he –?

A letter falls into the letterbox; then KROGSTAD's *steps are heard as they fade down the stairwell.*

NORA [*with a stifled cry, runs across the room and towards the sofa table; brief pause*]: In the letterbox. [*Sneaks nervously over to the hall door.*] There it is. – Torvald, Torvald – we're beyond rescue now!

MRS LINDE [*comes in with the costume, from the room on the left*]: Well, I don't think there's more to put right. Should we perhaps try it on –?

NORA [*hoarsely and quietly*]: Kristine, come here.

MRS LINDE [*throws the dress on the sofa*]: What's wrong? You look quite distraught.

NORA: Come here. Do you see that letter? *There*; look –
through the glass in the letterbox.

MRS LINDE: Yes, yes; I can see it.

NORA: That letter is from Krogstad –

MRS LINDE: Nora – it's Krogstad who lent you the money!

NORA: Yes; and now Torvald will get to know everything.

MRS LINDE: Oh, believe me, Nora, it's best for both of you.

NORA: There's more to it than you know. I forged a signature –

MRS LINDE: But for heaven's sake –?

NORA: Now, there's just one thing I want to tell you, Kristine;
you've got to be my witness.

MRS LINDE: What do you mean witness? What am I to –?

NORA: In case I were to go insane – and that could well
happen –

MRS LINDE: Nora!

NORA: Or if something else were to happen to me – something
that meant I couldn't be around –

MRS LINDE: Nora, Nora, you seem quite out of your mind!

NORA: If there were someone who wanted to take everything
upon themselves, all the blame, you understand –

MRS LINDE: Yes, yes; but how can you think –?

NORA: Then you'll be a witness to it not being true, Kristine. I
am not out of my mind at all; I have full powers of reasoning
in this moment; and I am telling you: nobody else knew
about this; I did the whole thing on my own. Remember that.

MRS LINDE: Of course I will. But I don't understand any of
this.

NORA: Well, how could you understand? After all, it's the
most miraculous thing that's about to happen now.

MRS LINDE: Miraculous?

NORA: Yes, miraculous. But it's so terrible, Kristine – it *mustn't*
happen, not for anything in the world.

MRS LINDE: I'll go straight to Krogstad and talk to him.

NORA: Don't go to him; he'll only do you harm!

MRS LINDE: There was a time when he'd gladly have done
absolutely anything for my sake.

NORA: Krogstad?

MRS LINDE: Where does he live?

NORA: Oh, how do I know –? Wait, [*feels in her pocket*] here's his card. But the letter, the letter –!

HELMER [*in his room, knocking on the door*]: Nora!

NORA [*screams in terror*]: Oh, what is it? What do you want of me?

HELMER: Now, now, don't be so scared. We're not coming in; you've locked the door anyway; trying your dress on perhaps?

NORA: Yes, yes; I'm trying it on. I'll be so pretty, Torvald.

MRS LINDE [*who has read the card*]: He lives just round the corner.

NORA: Yes; but it's useless. We're beyond rescue. The letter's lying there in the box.

MRS LINDE: And your husband has the key?

NORA: Yes, always.

MRS LINDE: Krogstad must ask for his letter back unread; he must find an excuse –

NORA: But it's usually around now that Torvald –

MRS LINDE: Stall him; go in to him for now. I'll come back as quickly as I can.

She hurries out through the door to the hall.

NORA [*goes over to* HELMER's *door, opens it and peeps in*]: Torvald!

HELMER [*in the inner room*]: Well, is one finally allowed back into one's own living room? Come on, Rank, now we'll get to see – [*In the doorway*] But what's this?

NORA: What, Torvald dear?

HELMER: Rank prepared me for a scene of splendid disguise.

RANK: That's what I understood, but I was clearly mistaken.

NORA: Yes, nobody's to admire me in my full glory before tomorrow.

HELMER: But, Nora dear, you look quite exhausted. Have you been practising too hard?

NORA: No, I've not practised at all yet.

HELMER: Well, it'll be necessary –

NORA: Yes, it'll be absolutely necessary, Torvald. But I can't get anywhere without your help; I've completely forgotten it all.

HELMER: Oh, we'll soon brush it up.

NORA: Yes, do take me in hand, Torvald. Will you promise? Oh, I'm so nervous. All those people –. You must sacrifice yourself to me totally this evening. Not a scrap of work; no pen in hand. Hmm? You agree, Torvald dear?

HELMER: I promise you; this evening I shall be totally and utterly at your service – you helpless little thing. – Hmm, but that's true, there's just one thing I have to do first – [*Goes towards the door to the hall.*]

NORA: What are you looking for out there?

HELMER: Just looking to see if any letters have come.

NORA: No, no, don't do that, Torvald!

HELMER: What now?

NORA: Torvald, I beg you; there aren't any.

HELMER: Just let me look. [*Wanting to go.*]

 NORA *at the piano, plays the first few bars of the tarantella.*

HELMER [*at the door, stops*]: Aha!

NORA: I can't dance tomorrow if I don't practise with you.

HELMER [*goes over to her*]: Are you really that anxious, Nora dear?

NORA: Yes, extremely anxious. Let me practise immediately; there's still time before we have dinner. Oh, sit down and play for me, dear Torvald; correct me, instruct me as you always do.

HELMER: With pleasure, the greatest pleasure, since that's your wish.

 He sits down at the piano.

NORA [*grabs the tambourine from the box as well as a long, multi-coloured shawl, which she drapes round herself hurriedly; then she leaps into the middle of the room, stands waiting and calls out*]: Now play for me! I want to dance now!

 HELMER *plays and* NORA *dances;* DR RANK *stands at the piano behind* HELMER *and looks on.*

HELMER [*playing*]: Slower – slower.

NORA: Can't do it differently.

HELMER: Not so fiercely, Nora!

NORA: It has to be this way.

HELMER [*stops*]: No, no, this really won't do.

NORA [*laughs and swings the tambourine*]: Wasn't that what I told you?

RANK: Let me play for her.

HELMER [*gets up*]: Yes do; then I can instruct her better.

    RANK *sits down at the piano and plays.* NORA *dances increasingly wildly.* HELMER *has placed himself by the stove and issues her with corrections regularly throughout the dance; she seems not to hear; her hair comes down and falls over her shoulders; she takes no notice, but goes on dancing.*

    MRS LINDE *comes in.*

MRS LINDE [*stands by the door, dumbstruck*]: Ah –!

NORA [*dancing*]: See what fun this is, Kristine!

HELMER: But, my dear sweet Nora, you're dancing as if your life depended on it.

NORA: And so it does.

HELMER: Rank, stop; this is sheer madness. Stop, I say.

    RANK *stops playing, and* NORA *suddenly stands still.*

HELMER [*goes over to her*]: I'd never have believed this. You really have forgotten everything I taught you.

NORA [*throws down the tambourine*]: There now, you see for yourself.

HELMER: Well, there's certainly need for instruction here.

NORA: Yes, you can see how necessary it is. You must instruct me right to the very last moment. Promise me that, Torvald?

HELMER: You can depend on it.

NORA: You're not to think, either today or tomorrow, about anything but me; you're not to open any letters – not open the letterbox –

HELMER: Aha, it's still the fear of that man –

NORA: Well yes, yes, that too.

HELMER: Nora, I see it in your face, there's a letter from him already.

NORA: I don't know; I think so; but you're not to read anything of that sort now; nothing ugly must come between us before it's all over.

RANK [*quietly to* HELMER]: You'd better not contradict her.

HELMER [*throws his arm around her*]: The child shall have her way. But tomorrow night, when you've danced –

NORA: Then you're free.

MAID [*in the doorway to the right*]: Madam, dinner is served.

NORA: We'll have champagne, Helene.

MAID: Very good, madam. [*Goes out.*]

HELMER: I say – a great feast, eh?

NORA: A champagne feast until dawn. [*Calls out*] And a few macaroons, Helene, lots – for once.

HELMER [*takes her hands*]: Now, now, now; let's have none of this wild fluttering. Be my own little lark now as usual.

NORA: Oh yes, I will of course. But go in ahead, and you too, Dr Rank. Kristine, you must help me put my hair up.

RANK [*quietly, as they go*]: I don't suppose there's – well, you know – something on the way?

HELMER: Oh, not at all, my friend, it really is nothing but this childlike anxiety I was telling you about.

They go in, to the right.

NORA: Well?!

MRS LINDE: Gone to the country.

NORA: I could see by your face.

MRS LINDE: He's coming home tomorrow evening. I wrote him a note.

NORA: You shouldn't have. You're to prevent nothing. Actually it's a deep joy, to be sitting here and waiting for the miraculous to happen.

MRS LINDE: What is it you're waiting for?

NORA: Oh, you wouldn't understand. Go in to them; I'll come right away.

MRS LINDE *goes into the dining room.*

NORA [*stands for a moment as if to collect herself; then looks at her watch*]: Five. Seven hours until midnight. Then twenty-four hours until the next midnight. Then the tarantella's over. Twenty-four plus seven? Thirty-one hours left to live.

HELMER [*in the doorway to the right*]: But where's my little song-lark?

NORA [*going towards him with open arms*]: Here is your song-lark!

ACT THREE

The same room. The sofa table with chairs around it has been moved into the middle of the room. A lamp is burning on the table. The door to the hall is open. Dance music can be heard from the floor above.

MRS LINDE *is sitting at the table, leafing distractedly through a book; she tries to read but seems unable to keep her thoughts gathered; a couple of times she listens anxiously, in the direction of the front door.*

MRS LINDE [*looks at her watch*]: Still not here. And time really is running out. I just hope he hasn't – [*Listens again.*] Ah, there he is. [*Goes out into the hall and carefully opens the front door; quiet footsteps can be heard on the stairs; she whispers*] Come in. There's no one here.

KROGSTAD [*in the doorway*]: Mrs Linde, I found a note from you at home. What's all this supposed to mean?

MRS LINDE: I *have* to talk to you.

KROGSTAD: Oh? And that has to take place here in this house?

MRS LINDE: It was impossible over at my place; my room doesn't have its own entrance. Come in; we're quite alone; the maid's asleep, and the Helmers are at the ball upstairs.

KROGSTAD [*entering the room*]: Well, well. So the Helmers are dancing tonight? Really?

MRS LINDE: Yes, why not?

KROGSTAD: No, true enough.

MRS LINDE: Well, Krogstad, let's talk.

KROGSTAD: Do the two of us have anything more to talk about?

MRS LINDE: We have a great deal to talk about.

KROGSTAD: I didn't think we did.

MRS LINDE: No, because you've never understood me properly.

KROGSTAD: Was there more to understand, apart from what's entirely commonplace in this world? A heartless woman gives a man his marching orders as soon as something more advantageous presents itself.

MRS LINDE: Do you think I'm so utterly heartless? And do you think I broke it off with a light heart?

KROGSTAD: Didn't you?

MRS LINDE: Oh Krogstad, did you really think that?

KROGSTAD: If it wasn't like that, why did you write to me as you did at the time?

MRS LINDE: I couldn't do otherwise. When I had to break with you, it was also my duty to erase everything you felt for me.

KROGSTAD [*clenches his fists*]: So that was it. And this – this just for the sake of the money!

MRS LINDE: You mustn't forget that I had a helpless mother and two little brothers. We couldn't wait for you, Krogstad; your prospects were so far off back then.

KROGSTAD: That may be; but you had no right to reject me for somebody else.

MRS LINDE: Perhaps, I don't know. I've often asked myself if I had the right.

KROGSTAD [*more quietly*]: When I lost you, it was as though all solid ground slid from under my feet. Look at me now; I'm a man shipwrecked on a broken vessel.

MRS LINDE: Rescue could be close.

KROGSTAD: It was close; but then you came along and got in the way.

MRS LINDE: Without knowing it, Krogstad. I only found out today that it's you I'm taking over from at the Bank.

KROGSTAD: I believe you when I hear you say it. But now that you know, won't you step aside?

MRS LINDE: No; because that wouldn't benefit you in the least.

KROGSTAD: Oh, benefit, benefit – I'd do it even so.

MRS LINDE: I have learned to act sensibly. Life and hard, bitter necessity have taught me that.

KROGSTAD: And life has taught me not to believe in fine words.

MRS LINDE: Then life has taught you a very sensible thing. But actions, you must believe in those?

KROGSTAD: What do you mean?

MRS LINDE: You said you were like a man shipwrecked on a broken vessel.

KROGSTAD: I had good reason to say it, I think.

MRS LINDE: I too am sitting like a woman shipwrecked on a broken vessel. Nobody to grieve for, nobody to provide for.

KROGSTAD: It was your own choice.

MRS LINDE: There was no other choice, then.

KROGSTAD: Right, and so?

MRS LINDE: Krogstad, what if we two shipwrecked people were to reach across to each other –

KROGSTAD: What are you saying?

MRS LINDE: Two on *one* wreck are, after all, better off than if they each keep to their own.

KROGSTAD: Kristine!

MRS LINDE: Why do you think I came here to town?

KROGSTAD: Did you really give a thought to me?

MRS LINDE: I have to work if I'm to endure this life. Every waking day, as far back as I can remember, I've worked, and it's been my greatest and only joy. But now I am entirely alone in the world, so dreadfully empty and abandoned. There's no joy, after all, in working for oneself. Krogstad, provide me with someone and something to work for.

KROGSTAD: I can't believe this. It's nothing but overexcited female high-mindedness, driven to self-sacrifice.

MRS LINDE: Have you ever known me to be overexcitable?

KROGSTAD: You could really do this? Tell me – are you fully aware of my past?

MRS LINDE: Yes.

KROGSTAD: And do you know how I'm regarded here now?

MRS LINDE: A moment ago you seemed to think that with me you could have been another person.

KROGSTAD: I'm absolutely certain of it.

MRS LINDE: Couldn't that still happen?

KROGSTAD: Kristine – you're saying this in all seriousness, aren't you! Yes, you are. I see it in your face. Do you really have the courage –?

MRS LINDE: I need someone to be a mother to, and your children need a mother. The two of us need each other. Krogstad, I have faith in you, in what is fundamental in you; together with you, I would dare anything.

KROGSTAD [clasping her hands]: Thank you, thank you, Kristine – and now I'll find a way to raise myself up in the eyes of others too. – Oh, but I forgot –

MRS LINDE [listening]: Ssh! The tarantella! Go, go!

KROGSTAD: Why? What is it?

MRS LINDE: You hear that dance up there? When it's over, we can expect them.

KROGSTAD: Ah yes, I shall go. This is all futile anyway. You've no idea, of course, what steps I've taken against the Helmers.

MRS LINDE: Yes, Krogstad, I do know.

KROGSTAD: And you'd still have the courage to –?

MRS LINDE: I understand very well what desperation can drive a man like you to.

KROGSTAD: Oh, if I could undo what's done!

MRS LINDE: You could; your letter's still in the box.

KROGSTAD: Are you sure about that?

MRS LINDE: Quite sure; but –

KROGSTAD [looks searchingly at her]: So is that what this is about? You want to save your friend at any cost. Just say it straight. Is that it?

MRS LINDE: Krogstad, somebody who has sold themselves once for the sake of others, does not do it again.

KROGSTAD: I shall demand my letter back.

MRS LINDE: No, no.

KROGSTAD: But of course; I'll stay here until Helmer comes down; I'll tell him that he's got to give me my letter back – that it's just about my dismissal – that he's not to read it –

MRS LINDE: No, Krogstad, you're not to call your letter back.

KROGSTAD: But, tell me, wasn't that really why you set up this meeting with me?

MRS LINDE: Yes, in the initial panic; but a whole day has passed now, and the things I've witnessed in that time, here in this house, have been unbelievable. Helmer must know everything; this disastrous secret must come to light; there needs to be absolute openness between them; it's impossible to carry on with all these concealments and excuses.

KROGSTAD: Well; if you'll take the risk –. But *one* thing I can do at least, and it'll be done immediately –

MRS LINDE [*listening*]: Hurry up! Go, go! The dance is finished; we're not safe a moment longer.

KROGSTAD: I'll wait for you downstairs.

MRS LINDE: Yes, do. You must walk me to my door.

KROGSTAD: I've never been so unbelievably happy.

He goes out through the front door; the door between the room and the hall remains open.

MRS LINDE [*tidies up a little and prepares her outdoor clothes*]: What a turnaround! Yes, what a turnaround! People to work for – to live for; a home to bring comfort into. Right, there's a task to be done –. I wish they'd come soon – [*Listens.*] Aha, there they are. Coat on. [*Takes her hat and coat.*]

The voices of HELMER *and* NORA *are heard outside; a key is turned, and* HELMER *almost uses force to get* NORA *into the hall. She is dressed in her Italian costume with a large black shawl over her shoulders; he is in evening dress with an open black cloak*[43] *on top.*

NORA [*still in the doorway, resisting him*]: No, no, no; I don't want to go in yet! I want to go up again. I don't want to leave so early.

HELMER: But, my dearest Nora –

NORA: I'm asking, begging you, Torvald; I'm asking you in such earnest – just one more hour.

HELMER: Not a single minute, my sweet Nora. We agreed, you know that. Come on, now, into the living room; you'll catch a chill standing here.

He guides her, despite her opposition, gently into the room.

MRS LINDE: Good evening.

NORA: Kristine!

HELMER: Oh, Mrs Linde, are you here so late?

MRS LINDE: Yes, I do apologize, but I so wanted to see Nora in her finery.

NORA: Have you been sitting here waiting for me?

MRS LINDE: Yes, unfortunately I didn't get here on time; you were already upstairs; and then I thought I couldn't go again without seeing you.

HELMER [*taking* NORA's *shawl off*]: Well, take a good look at her. I do rather think she's worth looking at. Isn't she lovely, Mrs Linde?

MRS LINDE: Yes, I must say –

HELMER: Isn't she remarkably lovely? That was the general consensus at the party too. But frightfully obstinate, she is – this sweet little thing. What shall we do about it? Can you believe, I almost had to use force to get her away.

NORA: Oh, Torvald, you'll come to regret not letting me stay, if only for a half hour more.

HELMER: You hear that, Mrs Linde! She dances her tarantella – has a storming success – which was well deserved – although there was something a little over-natural about her rendition; I mean – a little more than was strictly speaking apposite to artistic requirements. But never mind! The main thing is – she had a success – she had a storming success. Should I have let her stay after that? Weaken the impact? No thank you; I took my lovely little Capri girl – capricious little Capri girl, I could say – by the arm; a swift tour round the room; bows on all sides, and then – as it says in romantic novels – the beautiful apparition vanishes. A finale ought always to be effective, Mrs Linde; but *that* is, it seems, quite impossible for me to get Nora to grasp. Phew, it's hot here. [*Throws his cloak on to a chair and opens the door to his room.*] What? It's dark in there. Oh yes, of course. Excuse me –

He goes inside and lights a couple of candles.

NORA [*whispers hastily and breathlessly*]: Well?

MRS LINDE [*softly*]: I've spoken to him.

NORA: And –?

MRS LINDE: Nora – you must tell your husband everything.

NORA [*in a dull tone*]: I knew it.

MRS LINDE: You have nothing to fear from Krogstad's side; but you must talk.

NORA: I shan't talk.

MRS LINDE: Then the letter will.

NORA: Thank you, Kristine; I know now what must be done. Shh –!

HELMER [*coming back in*]: Well, Mrs Linde, have you admired her?

MRS LINDE: Yes; and now I'll say good night.

HELMER: Oh really, already? Is that yours, the knitting?

MRS LINDE [*takes it*]: Yes; thank you; I almost forgot it.

HELMER: So you knit, do you?

MRS LINDE: Yes.

HELMER: You know what – you should embroider instead.

MRS LINDE: Oh? Why?

HELMER: Well, because it's much prettier. Look: you hold the embroidery like this, with the left hand, and then with the right you guide the needle – like this – out in a delicate, extended arc; isn't that so –?

MRS LINDE: Yes, very possibly –

HELMER: Whereas knitting – that can never be anything but unlovely; look here: the cramped arms – the knitting needles that go up and down – it's got something Chinese about it. – Ah, that really was a splendid champagne at dinner.

MRS LINDE: Well, good night, Nora, and don't be obstinate any more now.

HELMER: Well said, Mrs Linde!

MRS LINDE: Good night, Mr Helmer.

HELMER [*seeing her to the door*]: Good night, good night; you'll get home all right, I hope? I'd have liked to –[44] but you haven't got far to go, have you? Good night, good night.

She leaves; he closes the door behind her and comes back in.

HELMER: There; at last we've got her out of the door. She's a frightful bore, that woman.

NORA: Aren't you very tired, Torvald?

HELMER: No, not in the least.

NORA: Or sleepy?

HELMER: Absolutely not; on the contrary, I feel tremendously exhilarated. But you? Yes, you certainly look both tired and sleepy.

NORA: Yes, I'm very tired. I want to sleep soon.

HELMER: You see! You see! It was absolutely right of me that we didn't stay longer.

NORA: Oh, every single thing you do is right.

HELMER [kisses her on the forehead]: Now my skylark is talking as though it were a person. But did you notice how cheerful Rank was this evening?

NORA: Oh? Was he? I didn't get to talk to him.

HELMER: I hardly did either; but I haven't seen him in such good spirits for a long time. [Looks at her for a moment, then comes closer.] Mmm – it's glorious to be home again; to have you to myself, alone. – Oh, you entrancingly lovely young woman!

NORA: Don't look at me like that, Torvald!

HELMER: Shouldn't I look at my most precious possession? At all the glory that is mine, mine alone, mine completely and utterly.

NORA [goes over to the other side of the table]: You're not to talk like that to me tonight.

HELMER [follows her]: You've still got the tarantella in your blood, I note. And it makes you even more alluring. Listen! The guests are starting to leave now. [More quietly] Nora – soon the whole house will be quiet.

NORA: Yes, I hope so.

HELMER: Yes, isn't that right, my own darling Nora? Oh, do you know – when I'm out in company with you – do you know why I talk to you so little, keep such a distance from you, just send you the occasional stolen glance – do you know why I do that? It's because I'm imagining that you're my secret love, my young secret fiancée, and that nobody has any idea there's something between us.

NORA: Oh, yes, yes, yes; I do know that all your thoughts are with me.

HELMER: And then, when we're about to leave and I put the shawl round your fine, youthful shoulders – round that miraculous curve of your neck – then I pretend to myself that you're my young bride, that we've just come away from our wedding, that I'm leading you into my abode for the first time – that I'm alone with you for the first time – utterly alone with you – my young, trembling beauty! All this evening I've had no other desire but for you. As I watched you chasing and teasing in the tarantella – my blood fired up; I couldn't hold out any longer; that's why I took you back down with me so early –

NORA: Leave now, Torvald! You will leave me. I don't want all this.

HELMER: What are you saying? I think you're playing joker-bird with me now, my little Nora. Want, want? Aren't I your husband –?

There is a knock on the front door.

NORA [*gives a start*]: Did you hear –?

HELMER [*towards the hall*]: Who is it?

RANK [*outside*]: It's me. Might I come in for a moment?

HELMER [*quietly, annoyed*]: Oh, what does he want now? [*Loud*] Wait a second. [*He goes and unlocks the door.*] Well, how nice of you not to go past our door.[45]

RANK: I thought I heard your voice, so I wanted to look in. [*Lets his gaze travel fleetingly around*] Ah me, these dear, familiar rooms. The two of you have everything so cosy and comfortable in here.

HELMER: You seemed to make yourself very comfortable upstairs too.

RANK: Absolutely. Why shouldn't I? Why shouldn't we take from this world what it offers? As much as we can at least, and for as long as we can. The wine was excellent –

HELMER: The champagne in particular.

RANK: Noticed that too, did you? It's quite unbelievable how much I managed to swill down.

NORA: Torvald drank lots of champagne tonight too.

RANK: Really?

NORA: Yes; and then he's always so amusing afterwards.

RANK: Well, why shouldn't a man allow himself a merry evening after a day well spent?

HELMER: Well spent? That's not, I'm afraid, something *I* can boast of.

RANK [*slaps him on the shoulder*]: But *I* can, you see!

NORA: Dr Rank, I take it you conducted a scientific investigation today.

RANK: Correct.

HELMER: I say, my little Nora talking about scientific investigations!

NORA: And may I congratulate you on the result?

RANK: Yes, you certainly may.

NORA: So it was good?

RANK: The best possible for both doctor and patient – certainty.

NORA [*quickly and searchingly*]: Certainty?

RANK: Absolute certainty. So shouldn't I allow myself a cheerful evening afterwards?

NORA: Yes, you were right to, Dr Rank.

HELMER: I'd second that; as long as you don't end up suffering for it in the morning.

RANK: Well, you don't get anything for nothing in this life, you know.

NORA: Dr Rank – you're rather fond of these little masquerades, aren't you?

RANK: Yes, when there are plenty of amusing disguises –

NORA: Listen; what shall the two of us be at the next masquerade?

HELMER: You frivolous little thing – you're already thinking about the next!

RANK: The two of us? Ah, yes, I'll tell you; you must come as the child of joy and good fortune –[46]

HELMER: Yes, but find a costume that can represent *that*.

RANK: Let your wife attend exactly as she walks through this world –

HELMER: How brilliantly put. But about you, what will you be?

RANK: Well, my dear friend, of *that* I am absolutely certain.

HELMER: Well?

RANK: At the next masquerade I shall be invisible.

HELMER: That's a quaint idea.

RANK: There's a big black hat – haven't you heard tell of the cap of invisibility?[47] You put it over you, and then nobody can see you.

HELMER [*with a suppressed smile*]: Right, I see your point.

RANK: But I'm completely forgetting what I came for; Helmer, give me a cigar, one of those dark Havanas.

HELMER: With the greatest pleasure. [*Offers him the box.*]

RANK [*takes a cigar and cuts off the end*]: Thank you.

NORA [*strikes a match*]: Let me give you a light.

RANK: Thank you. [*She holds the match for him; he lights up.*] And now goodbye!

HELMER: Goodbye, goodbye, my dear friend!

NORA: Sleep well, Dr Rank.

RANK: Thank you for that kind wish.

NORA: Wish me the same.

RANK: You? Well, if you want me to –. Sleep well. And thank you for the light.

He nods to them both and goes.

HELMER [*subdued*]: He'd had a lot to drink.

NORA [*absently*]: Perhaps.

HELMER *takes his bunch of keys out of his pocket and goes out into the hall.*

NORA: Torvald – what are you doing out there?

HELMER: I have to empty the letterbox; it's pretty full; there'll be no room for the newspapers in the morning –

NORA: Will you be working tonight?

HELMER: You know very well I won't. – What's this? Someone's been at the lock.

NORA: At the lock –?

HELMER: Yes, most definitely. How can that be? I can't believe the maids –? Here's a broken hairpin. Nora, it's yours –

NORA [*quickly*]: Then it must be the children –

HELMER: You really must break them of that habit. Hm, hm –. There now, I've got it open anyway. [*Takes the contents out and calls out into the kitchen*] Helene? – Helene, put out the lamp in the hall.

   He comes back into the room and closes the door to the hall.

HELMER [*with the letters in his hand*]: Look at this. Just look how they've piled up. [*Leafs through them.*] Whatever's this?

NORA [*by the window*]: The letter! Oh no, no, Torvald!

HELMER: Two visiting cards – from Rank.

NORA: From Dr Rank?

HELMER [*looking at them*]: Dr Rank MD. They were lying on top; he must have stuck them in as he left.

NORA: Is there anything on them?

HELMER: There's a black cross over his name. Look. What a sinister idea. It's as though he were announcing his own death.

NORA: And so he is.

HELMER: What? Do you know something? Has he told you something?

NORA: Yes. When these cards come, he's taken his leave of us. He wants to shut himself away and die.

HELMER: My poor friend. I knew, of course, that I wouldn't keep him for long. But so soon –. And then to hide away like a wounded animal.

NORA: When it *has* to happen, then it's best it happens without words. Don't you think, Torvald?

HELMER [*pacing up and down*]: He'd grown so much a part of us. I don't think I can imagine him gone. With all his sufferings and his loneliness, he somehow offered a cloudy backdrop to our sunlit happiness. – Ah well, perhaps it's best this way. For him at least. [*Stops.*] And maybe for us too, Nora. Now you and I will have to look to each other alone. [*Puts his arms around her.*] Oh, my darling wife; I don't think I can hold you tightly enough. You know, Nora – many a time I've wished that some impending danger might threaten you, so I could risk life and limb and everything, everything, for your sake.

NORA [*tears herself free and says firmly and decisively*]: You should read your letters now, Torvald.

HELMER: No, no, not tonight. I want to be with you, my darling wife.

NORA: With the thought of your friend dying –?

HELMER: You're right. This has shaken us both; something unlovely has entered between us; thoughts of death and decay. From which we must seek to be absolved. Until then –. We'll go to our separate rooms.

NORA [*with her arms round his neck*]: Torvald – good night! Good night!

HELMER [*kisses her on the forehead*]: Good night, my little songbird. Sleep well, Nora. I'll read through my letters now.

He takes the bundle into his room and shuts the door after him.

NORA [*wild-eyed, fumbling around, grabs* HELMER's *cloak, throws it around herself and speaks rapidly and jerkily in a hoarse whisper*]: Never see him again. Never. Never. Never. [*Throws her shawl over her head.*] Never see the children again. Not them either. Never. Never. – Oh, the ice-cold black water. Oh, the bottomless – this –. Oh, if only this were over. – He's got it now; he's reading it. Oh no, no; not yet. Torvald, goodbye to you and the children –

She is about to rush out through the hall; at that moment HELMER *tears his door open and stands there with an open letter in his hand.*

HELMER: Nora!

NORA [*lets out a loud scream*]: Ah –!

HELMER: What is this? Do you know what's in this letter?

NORA: Yes, I do. Let me leave! Let me get out!

HELMER [*holds her back*]: Where are you going?

NORA [*tries to tear herself free*]: You're not to rescue me, Torvald!

HELMER [*stumbles backwards*]: What! Is it true what he writes here? Terrible! No, no; it can't possibly be true.

NORA: It *is* true. I've loved you above all else in the world.

HELMER: Don't come here with your pathetic evasions.

NORA [*takes a step towards him*]: Torvald –!

HELMER: You creature of ill-fortune – what have you been up to!

NORA: Let me go away. You shan't carry this for my sake. You shan't take it upon yourself.

HELMER: No playacting, now. [*Locks the front door.*] You will stay and you will stand accountable to me. Do you understand what you've done? Answer me! Do you understand?

NORA [*looks fixedly at him, her face tensing as she speaks*]: Yes, I am certainly beginning to understand.

HELMER [*walks around the room*]: Oh, how terribly I've been awakened. All these eight years – the woman who was my pleasure, my pride – a hypocrite, a liar – worse, worse – a criminal! – Oh, the depths of ugliness in all this! Shame, shame!

   NORA *remains silent and continues to look fixedly at him.*

HELMER [*stops in front of her*]: I should have sensed that something like this would happen. I should have foreseen it. All your father's frivolous attitudes. – Be quiet! You've inherited all your father's frivolous attitudes: no religion, no morals, no sense of duty –. Oh, how I've been punished for turning a blind eye to him. I did it for your sake; and this is how you repay me.

NORA: Yes, this is how.

HELMER: You've wrecked my entire happiness now. You've gambled away my entire future for me. Oh, it's too terrible to contemplate. I'm in the power of a man without conscience; he can do whatever he wants with me, demand anything at all of me, order me about as he pleases – I daren't breathe a word. And this is how miserably I must sink and be ruined for the sake of a frivolous woman!

NORA: When I'm out of this world, you'll be free.

HELMER: Oh, spare the gestures. Your father always had such phrases ready to hand too. What use would it be to me if you were out of the world, as you put it? It wouldn't be of the slightest use. He can make it public just the same; and if he does, I'll perhaps be suspected of having known about your criminal act. People will perhaps believe that I was behind it – that I was the one who incited you to it! And all this I can thank you for, you, whom I've borne in my arms[48] throughout our married life. Do you understand now what you've done against me?

NORA [*coldly and calmly*]: Yes.

HELMER: This is so unbelievable, I can't grasp it. But we'll have to come to some arrangement. Take your shawl off. Take it off, I say! I'll have to try to placate him in some way. This business must be hushed up at all costs. – And as far as you and I are concerned, it must look as though everything were the same as before between us. But obviously only in the eyes of the world. You'll go on living here; that goes without saying. But you won't be allowed to bring up the children; I daren't entrust them to you –. Oh, to have to say this to the woman I once loved so highly, and whom I still –! Well, that must be put in the past. From today it's no longer a question of happiness; it's merely a question of rescuing the remains, the scraps, the outer shell –

The doorbell rings.

HELMER [*starts*]: What's that? So late. Could the most terrible thing –? Could he –? Hide, Nora! Say you're ill.

NORA *stands motionless.* HELMER *goes over and opens the door to the hall.*

MAID [*half undressed, in the hall*]: A letter's arrived for madam.

HELMER: Give it to me.[49] [*Grabs the letter and closes the door.*] Yes, it's from him. You're not having it; I'll read it myself.

NORA: Yes, read it.

HELMER [*by the lamp*]: I scarcely have the courage. Perhaps we are lost, both you and I. No; I *must* know. [*Tears open the letter hurriedly; skims through some lines; looks at a piece of paper that is enclosed; a cry of joy*] Nora!

NORA *looks at him questioningly.*

HELMER: Nora! – No; I must read it over again. – Yes, yes; it's true. I'm saved! Nora, I'm saved!

NORA: And me?

HELMER: You too, naturally; we're both saved, both you and I. Look. He's sent you back your bond. He writes that he regrets and is sorry – that a happy change in his life – oh it makes no odds what he writes. We're saved, Nora! Nobody can do anything to you. Oh, Nora, Nora –. No, first get this repulsive thing out of the way. Let me see – [*Glances at the bond.*] No, I don't want to see it; this will be nothing more to me than a dream, this whole thing. [*Tears the bond and both letters into pieces, throws the whole lot into the stove and watches as it burns.*] There now, it's gone. – He wrote that since Christmas Eve you've –. Oh, they must have been three dreadful days for you, Nora.

NORA: I've fought a hard battle these three days.

HELMER: And been in anguish, and seen no other way out except to –. No; we'll forget this whole hideous thing. We'll just rejoice and repeat: it's over; it's over! Listen to me now, Nora; you don't seem to comprehend: it's over. But what's all this – this steely expression? Oh my poor little Nora, I understand of course; you don't feel you can believe I've forgiven you. But I have, Nora; I swear to you: I've forgiven you everything. I know, of course, that what you did, you did out of love for me.

NORA: That's true.

HELMER: You've loved me as a wife should love her husband. It was just the means that you lacked the insight to make a judgement on. But do you think you are any less dear to me because you don't know how to act independently? No; just you lean on me; I'll advise you; I'll guide and instruct you.[50] I wouldn't be a man if this feminine helplessness didn't make you doubly attractive in my eyes. You mustn't pay any attention to the harsh words I said to you in my initial shock, when I thought everything might crash down over me. I've forgiven you, Nora; I swear to you, I've forgiven you.

NORA: I thank you for your forgiveness.

She goes out through the door on the right.

HELMER: No, stay – [*Looks in.*] What are you doing there in the alcove?

NORA [*from within*]: Taking off my masquerade costume.

HELMER [*by the open door*]: Yes, you do that; be calm now, gather your mind once more into balance, my terrified little songbird. Rest safe now; I have broad wings to cover you with. [*Walks about near to the door.*] Oh, our home is so cosy and perfect, Nora. There's shelter for you here; I will hold you here like a hunted dove that I've rescued unscathed out of the hawk's claws; I'll calm the clapping of your heart. Little by little it'll happen, Nora; believe me. Tomorrow this will all look entirely different to you; soon everything will be just as it was; before long I won't need to repeat how I've forgiven you; you will feel unshakeably that I have done so. How can you think it would cross my mind to reject you, or even to reproach you for anything? Oh, you don't know the stuff of a real man's heart, Nora. For a man there's something so indescribably sweet and gratifying in knowing that he's forgiven his wife – that he has forgiven her with a full and honest heart. Yes, in a way, she has become his property in a double sense; in a way, he has brought her into the world afresh; she is, in a sense, not only his wife but also his child. That's how you'll be for me from today, you helpless, confused little creature. Don't worry about anything, Nora; just be honest of heart with me, and I will be both your will and your conscience. – What's this? Not going to bed? You've changed clothes?

NORA [*in her everyday dress*]: Yes, Torvald, I've changed clothes now.

HELMER: But why now, this late –?

NORA: I won't sleep tonight.

HELMER: But, my dear Nora –

NORA [*looks at her watch*]: It's not so late yet. Sit down here, Torvald; you and I have a lot to talk about. [*Sits on one side of the table.*]

HELMER: Nora – what is this? This steely expression –

NORA: Sit down. This will take time. I've got a lot to talk to you about.

HELMER [*sits down at the table opposite her*]: You're worrying me, Nora. And I don't understand you.

NORA: No, that's just it. You don't understand me. And I've never understood you either – before tonight. No, you shan't interrupt me. You're just going to listen to what I have to say. – This is a reckoning, Torvald.

HELMER: What do you mean by that?

NORA [*after a brief silence*]: Isn't there *something* that strikes you, Torvald, as we sit here?

HELMER: What should that be?

NORA: We have been married now for eight years. Doesn't it occur to you that this is the first time the two of us, you and I, man and wife, are talking seriously together?

HELMER: Seriously – what do you mean?

NORA: In eight whole years – no, more – ever since our first meeting, we've never exchanged a serious word about serious things.

HELMER: Should I have perpetually consulted you about worries you could do nothing to help me bear?

NORA: I'm not talking about worries. I'm saying, we have never sat down together seriously to try to get to the bottom of anything.

HELMER: But, my dearest Nora, would that really have been for you?

NORA: That's it precisely. You've never understood me. – I've been greatly wronged, Torvald. First by Daddy and then by you.

HELMER: What? By the two of us – by the two of us, who have loved you more highly than anyone else ever did?

NORA [shakes her head]: Neither of you ever loved me. You just thought it was amusing to be in love with me.

HELMER: Nora, what kind of words are these?

NORA: Well, that's how it is, Torvald. When I was at home with Daddy, he told me all his opinions, and then I had the same opinions; and if I had others, I hid them; because he wouldn't have liked it. He called me his doll-child, and he played with me, just as I played with my dolls. And then I came into your house –

HELMER: What kind of way is this to describe our marriage?

NORA [impervious]: I mean, I then went from Daddy's hands over into yours. You arranged everything according to your taste, and I acquired the same taste as you; or I only pretended to; I don't know really; I think it was both; sometimes one and sometimes the other. When I look at it now, I think I've lived like a pauper here – just from hand to mouth. I've lived by doing tricks for you, Torvald. But that was how you wanted it. You and Daddy have wronged me greatly.

The two of you are to blame for the fact that nothing has come of me.

HELMER: Nora, how unreasonable and ungrateful you are! Haven't you been happy here?

NORA: No, never. I thought so; but I have never been that.

HELMER: Not –? Not happy?

NORA: No; just cheerful. And you've always been so kind to me. But our home has never been anything other than a play-house. I've been your doll-wife here, just as at home I was Daddy's doll-child. And the children, they have in turn been my dolls. I thought it was amusing when you came and played with me, just as they thought it was amusing when I came and played with them. That's been our marriage, Torvald.

HELMER: There is some truth in what you're saying – however exaggerated and over-emotional it may be. But from now on it will be different. The time for playing is over; now comes the time for upbringing.

NORA: Whose upbringing? Mine or the children's?

HELMER: Both yours and the children's, my darling Nora.

NORA: Oh, Torvald, you're not the man to bring me up to be a proper wife for you.

HELMER: And you're saying that?

NORA: And I – how equipped am I to bring up the children?

HELMER: Nora!

NORA: Didn't you say yourself a moment ago – that that was a task you daren't entrust me with.

HELMER: In the heat of the moment! How could you take that seriously?

NORA: Yes, but what you said was very right. I'm not up to that task. There's another task that must be solved first. I must bring myself up. You're not the man to help me with that. I must do that alone. Which is why I'm leaving you now.

HELMER [jumps up]: What was that you said?

NORA: I must stand totally alone, if I'm to get an understanding of myself and of everything outside. That's why I can't stay with you any longer.

HELMER: Nora, Nora!

NORA: I shall leave here immediately. I'm sure Kristine will put me up for the night –

HELMER: You're crazed! You are not permitted! I forbid you!

NORA: It'll be no use forbidding me anything from now on. I'll take with me what belongs to me. From you I want nothing, either now or later.

HELMER: But what lunacy is this!

NORA: Tomorrow I'm travelling home – I mean, to my old hometown. It'll be easier for me to find something to do there.

HELMER: Oh you blind, inexperienced creature!

NORA: I must see to it I *get* experience, Torvald.

HELMER: Leave your home, your husband and your children! And you haven't a thought for what people will say.

NORA: I can't take that into consideration. I just know that it'll be necessary for me.

HELMER: Oh, this is outrageous. You can abandon your most sacred duties, just like that?

NORA: What, then, do you count as my most sacred duties?

HELMER: And I really need to tell you that! Aren't they the duties to your husband and your children?

NORA: I have other equally sacred duties.

HELMER: You do not. What duties could *they* be?

NORA: The duties to myself.

HELMER: You are first and foremost a wife and mother.

NORA: I don't believe that any more. I believe I am first and foremost a human being, I, just as much as you – or at least, that I must try to become one. I know, of course, that most people would say you're right, Torvald, and that something of the sort is written in books. But I can no longer allow myself to be satisfied with what most people say and what's written in books. I have to think these things through for myself and see to it I get an understanding of them.

HELMER: And you don't have an understanding of your position in your own home? Haven't you an unshakeable guide in such questions? Haven't you your religion?[51]

NORA: Oh, Torvald, I'm not even sure I know what this religion is.

HELMER: What are you saying!

NORA: I know nothing other than what Reverend Hansen said when I was prepared for confirmation. He told us that our religion was *this* and *that*. When I have come away from all this and I'm alone, I shall investigate that too. I want to see if they were right, the things Reverend Hansen said, or at least, whether they're right for *me*.

HELMER: Oh, this is unheard of from such a young woman! But if religion can't direct you, then at least let me stir your conscience. For surely you have some moral sense? Or, answer me – have you perhaps none?

NORA: Oh, Torvald, that's not easy to answer. I simply don't know. I'm in such confusion over these things. I just know that my opinion is very different from yours on such matters. And I now hear, too, that the laws are other than I'd imagined; but that these laws should be right is something I can't possibly get into my head. That a woman shouldn't have the right to spare her old and dying father, or to save her husband's life! I can't believe in such things.

HELMER: You talk like a child. You don't understand the society you live in.

NORA: No, I don't. But now I intend to look into it. I must find out who is right, society or me.

HELMER: You're ill, Nora; you're feverish; I almost think you're out of your mind.

NORA: I've never been so clear and sure as I am tonight.

HELMER: And you're clear and sure about leaving your husband and your children?

NORA: Yes; I am.

HELMER: Then there's only *one* explanation possible.

NORA: That is?

HELMER: You don't love me any more.

NORA: No, that's just the thing.

HELMER: Nora! – And you can say that!

NORA: Oh, it gives me so much pain, Torvald; because you've always been so kind to me. But I can't do anything about it. I don't love you any more.

HELMER [*struggling to stay composed*]: You're clear and sure in this conviction too?

NORA: Yes, absolutely clear and sure. That's why I don't want to be here any more.

HELMER: And can you also explain to me in what way I have forfeited your love?

NORA: Yes, I can. It was tonight, when the miraculous thing didn't happen; because then I saw that you weren't the man I'd imagined.

HELMER: Explain what you mean; I don't understand.

NORA: I've waited so patiently now for eight years; because, good Lord, I realized that miraculous things aren't exactly an everyday event. Then this crushing blow came at me; and I was so unshakeably certain: something miraculous will come now. When Krogstad's letter was out there – not for one moment did it occur to me that you'd be prepared to bend to that man's terms. I was so unshakeably certain that you would say to him: let the whole world know everything. And when that was done –

HELMER: Yes, what then? When I'd offered my wife up to shame and dishonour –?

NORA: When that had been done, I was unshakeably certain that you would step forward and take everything upon yourself and say: I am the guilty one.

HELMER: Nora –!

NORA: You're thinking I'd never have accepted such a sacrifice from you? No, of course not. But what would my assurances have counted against yours? – *That* was the miraculous thing that I went about hoping for in terror. And it was to prevent *that* that I wanted to end my life.

HELMER: I would gladly work night and day for you, Nora – bear pain and hardship for your sake. But nobody would sacrifice their *honour* for the one they love.

NORA: Hundreds of thousands of women have.

HELMER: Oh, you both think and talk like a foolish child.

NORA: Perhaps so. But you neither think nor talk like the man I could live with. Once you'd got over your fright – not at what was threatening *me*, but at what you yourself were exposed to, and when the whole danger was over – then for you, it was as if absolutely nothing had happened. I was, just as before, your little song-lark, your doll that you would carry in your arms twice as carefully hereafter, because it was so fragile and weak. [*Gets up.*] Torvald – at that moment I realized that the man I'd lived with here for eight years was a stranger and that I'd borne him three children –. Oh, I can't bear to think of it! I could rip myself to pieces.

HELMER [*sadly*]: I can see now; I see it. A chasm has indeed come between us. – Oh, but, Nora, might it not be possible to fill it?

NORA: As I am now, I am no wife for you.

HELMER: I have the strength to be a different person.

NORA: Perhaps – if your doll is taken away from you.

HELMER: To part – to part from you! No, no, Nora, I can't grasp the thought.

NORA [*goes into the room to the right*]: The more surely it must happen. [*She comes back with her outdoor clothes and a small travelling bag, which she puts on the chair by the table.*]

HELMER: Nora, Nora, not now! Wait till tomorrow.

NORA [*puts her coat on*]: I can't stay the night in a strange man's rooms.

HELMER: But then can't we live here as brother and sister –?

NORA [*tying on her hat*]: You know very well that wouldn't last long –. [*Wraps her shawl around her.*] Goodbye, Torvald. I don't want to see the little ones. I know they're in better hands than mine. As I am now, I can't be anything for them.

HELMER: But some time, Nora – some time –?

NORA: How can I know? I have no idea what I will become.

HELMER: But you're my wife, both as you are and as you will be.

NORA: Listen, Torvald; when a wife leaves her husband's house, as I am now doing, I've heard that he is freed according to the law from all obligations towards her.[52] At any rate, I'm freeing you from any obligation. You mustn't feel bound in any way, any more than I shall be. There must be complete freedom on both sides. Look, here's your ring back. Give me mine.

HELMER: This too?

NORA: Yes, this too.

HELMER: Here it is.

NORA: There. So now it's over. I'm putting the keys here. The maids know everything that needs doing in the house – better than I. Tomorrow, when I've left town, Kristine will come here to pack the things that were my property from home. I want them sent after me.

HELMER: Over; over! Nora, will you never think about me again?

NORA: Of course, I shall often think about you and about the children and about this house.

HELMER: May I write to you, Nora?

NORA: No – never. You're not to do that.

HELMER: Oh, but surely I can send you –

NORA: Nothing; nothing.

HELMER: – help you, if you should need it.

NORA: No, I say. I don't take anything from strangers.

HELMER: Nora – can I never be more than a stranger to you?

NORA [*takes her travel bag*]: Oh, Torvald, then the most miraculous thing would have to happen. –

HELMER: Name me this miraculous thing!

NORA: Then both you and I would have to change ourselves in such a way that –. Oh, Torvald, I no longer believe in the miraculous.

HELMER: But I want to believe in it. Name it! Change in such a way that –?

NORA: That our living together could become a marriage. Goodbye.

She goes out through the hall.

HELMER [*sinks down on a chair by the door and throws his hands up to his face*]: Nora! Nora! [*Looks around the room and gets up.*] Empty! She's not here any more. [*A flash of hope rises in him.*] The most miraculous –?!

The sound of the street door being slammed is heard from below.

GHOSTS[1]

A Family Drama[2] in Three Acts

CHARACTERS

MRS[3] HELENE ALVING, *widow of Captain Alving,
late chamberlain[4] to the king*
OSVALD ALVING, *her son, an artist*
PASTOR MANDERS
ENGSTRAND, *a carpenter*
REGINE ENGSTRAND, *in the service[5] of Mrs Alving*

*The action takes place at Mrs Alving's country estate
by a large fjord in West Norway.*

ACT ONE

A spacious garden room with a door in the wall to the left[6] and two doors to the right. A round table stands in the centre of the room with chairs around it: on it are books, magazines and newspapers. There is a window, and next to it a small sofa with a little sewing table in front of it. In the background the room leads on to a somewhat narrower conservatory, the walls of which are predominantly glazed. In the right wall of the conservatory is a door leading on to the garden. Through the conservatory windows a gloomy fjord landscape can be seen, veiled by steady rain.

ENGSTRAND *the carpenter is standing at the back by the garden door. His left leg is slightly crooked, and the sole of his shoe is built up with a wooden block.* REGINE, *with an empty flower mister in her hand, is stopping him from advancing further.*

REGINE [*keeping her voice low*]: What do you want? Stay right where you are. You're dripping everywhere!
ENGSTRAND: That's God's rain, that, my child.
REGINE: It's the devil's rain, more like.
ENGSTRAND: Jesus, how you talk, Regine. [*Limps forward a couple of steps into the room.*] But what I wanted to say was –
REGINE: Stop clomping about with that foot, idiot.[7] The young master's asleep upstairs.
ENGSTRAND: Lying there asleep is he? In the middle of the day?
REGINE: That's no concern of yours.
ENGSTRAND: I was out on a bender last night –

REGINE: That I can believe.

ENGSTRAND: Aye, for we are but frail,[8] my child –

REGINE: Yes, aren't we just!

ENGSTRAND: – and the temptations are manifold in this world – but, by God, I was still at my work at half past five this morning.

REGINE: Yes, yes, yes, just get out of here. I don't want to stand here rendezvousing with you.

ENGSTRAND: You don't want what?

REGINE: I don't want anyone seeing you here. Go on; get on your way.

ENGSTRAND [a couple of steps closer]: Damned if I'm going before I've talked to you. This afternoon I'll have finished with the job down there at the schoolhouse, and then tonight I'll be off on the steamship[9] to town.

REGINE [mumbles]: Pleasant trip!

ENGSTRAND: Well, thank you, my child. The orphanage will be dedicated tomorrow, so there's likely to be a right commotion here with intoxicating liquors see. And nobody's going to pin it on Jakob Engstrand that he can't stay away when temptation comes along.

REGINE: Hmm!

ENGSTRAND: Aye, 'cos there'll be lots of fine folk coming here tomorrow. Pastor Manders is expected from town too, you know.

REGINE: He's arriving today, actually.

ENGSTRAND: There, you see! And I'm damned[10] if I want him to have anything to pin on me, you understand.

REGINE: Ah. So that's it.

ENGSTRAND: What do you mean, 'that's it'?

REGINE [looks at him suspiciously]: What do you want to trick the pastor into this time?

ENGSTRAND: Shh, ssh! Are you crazy? Would I want to trick Pastor Manders into anything? Oh no, Pastor Manders has always been far too nice to me for that. But what I wanted to talk to you about, see, was that I'll be going home again tonight.

REGINE: The sooner the better, if you ask me.

ENGSTRAND: Aye, but I want you with me, Regine.

REGINE [*her jaw dropping*]: You want me –? What did you say?

ENGSTRAND: I said, I want you home with me.

REGINE [*scornfully*]: You'll never ever get me home with you.

ENGSTRAND: Oh, we'll see about that.

REGINE: Yes, you can be sure we'll see about it! *Me!* Who's grown up here with Mrs Alving, the wife of the chamberlain? *Me!* Who's been treated almost like one of the family here –? *I'm* supposed to move home to *you*? To a house like that? Ugh!

ENGSTRAND: What the hell's[11] *this*? Going against your own father, are you, girl?

REGINE [*mumbles without looking at him*]: You've said often enough that I was nothing to do with you.

ENGSTRAND: Pah. You wouldn't take *that* to heart surely –

REGINE: Haven't you yelled at me many times and called me a –? *Fi donc!*[12]

ENGSTRAND: No, by God, I never used such a foul word.

REGINE: Oh, I think I remember what word you used.

ENGSTRAND: Aye, but that was only when I'd had a drop – hm. The temptations of this world are manifold, Regine.

REGINE: Ugh!

ENGSTRAND: Or when your mother decided to be difficult. I had to find something to rile her with, my child. Always acting so prim and proper. [*Mimics*] 'Let me go, Engstrand! Leave me be. I've served three years with Chamberlain Alving's family at Rosenvold, I have!' [*Laughs.*] Jesus preserve us; she never could forget that the captain was made court chamberlain while she was in service here.

REGINE: Poor mother – you tormented the life out of her soon enough.

ENGSTRAND [*shifting his weight*]: Aye, goes without saying; I'm to blame for everything.

REGINE [*turns away, under her breath*]: Ugh –! And that leg!

ENGSTRAND: What did you say, my child?

REGINE: *Pied de mouton.*[13]

ENGSTRAND: English, that, is it?

REGINE: Yes.

ENGSTRAND: Well, well; you've got some learning out here right enough, and that might just come in useful now, Regine.

REGINE [*after a short pause*]: So what was it you wanted with me in town?

ENGSTRAND: Can you ask a father what he wants with his only child? Aren't I a lonely and forsaken widower?

REGINE: Oh, don't give me that rubbish. Why do you want me there?

ENGSTRAND: All right, I'll tell you, I've been thinking of branching into something new.

REGINE [*huffs*]: You've tried that often enough; it always ends in failure.

ENGSTRAND: Aye, but this time you'll see, Regine! – I'll bleedin' well[14] –

REGINE [*stamping her foot*]: Stop swearing!

ENGSTRAND: Hush, hush, you're right as ever, my child! But look, what I wanted to say was *this* – I've put a fair bit of money aside from the work on this new orphanage.

REGINE: Have you now? Well, good for you.

ENGSTRAND: 'Cos what's there to spend your shillings on out here in the country?

REGINE: Quite – and so?

ENGSTRAND: Well, you see, I was thinking I'd put the money into something as could pay. It would be a kind of establishment for seamen –.

REGINE: Ugh!

ENGSTRAND: A real classy establishment, you understand – not like one of those dumps for common sailors. Hell, no – this would be for ships' captains and officers and – and fine folk, you understand.

REGINE: And I would –?

ENGSTRAND: Well, you'd help out. Only for appearances' sake, you understand. It's not like you'd have such a God-awful[15] time of it, my child. You can have things just as you want.

REGINE: Right, I see!

ENGSTRAND: But there's got to be womenfolk round the house, that's plain as day. 'Cos we'll have a bit of fun in the evenings, of course, with singing and dancing and the like. You've got to remember, these are wayfaring mariners[16] upon the oceans of the world. [*Closer*] Don't be daft now and stand in your own way, Regine. What's to become of you out here? What use will you have for that education the mistress has lavished on you? You're going to take care of them kids in the new orphanage, I hear. Is *that* something for you, eh? Have you got such a slavering desire to go and work yourself to death for the sake of them filthy brats?

REGINE: No, if things went the way *I* wanted, then –. Well, it might well happen. It might well happen!

ENGSTRAND: What might happen?

REGINE: Never you mind. – Is it much money you've put aside out here?

ENGSTRAND: Altogether, I'd say it'll be about seven or eight hundred kroner.[17]

REGINE: That's not bad.

ENGSTRAND: Well, it's enough to get started with, my child.

REGINE: You're not thinking of giving me any of that money?

ENGSTRAND: No, I'm not bloody thinking of that, no.

REGINE: You're not thinking of sending me so much as a scrap of dress fabric even?

ENGSTRAND: You just come into town with me, Regine, and you'll get dress fabric aplenty.

REGINE: Pah, if I want, I can take that in hand myself.

ENGSTRAND: Aye, but with a *father's* guiding hand it's better, Regine. There's a nice house I can get in Little Harbour Street. There's not much cash needed upfront, and *that* could be like a kind of home for seamen, see.

REGINE: But I don't *want* to live with *you*! I want nothing to do with you. Now go!

ENGSTRAND: You'd not bleedin'[18] stay with me for long, child. Chance'd be a fine thing. If you knew how to handle yourself, at least. Such a pretty girl as you've grown into this last couple of years –

REGINE: Oh –?

ENGSTRAND: It wouldn't be long before some ship's mate came along – or a captain perhaps –

REGINE: I don't want to marry that sort. Sailors have no *savoir vivre*.[19]

ENGSTRAND: What don't they have?

REGINE: I know about sailors, I tell you. They're not the kind you go marrying.

ENGSTRAND: So leave off marrying them. It can still pay. [*In a more confidential tone*] That man – the Englishman – the one with the yacht – he paid three hundred speciedaler,[20] he did – and she weren't no prettier than you.

REGINE [*making for him*]: Get out!

ENGSTRAND [*retreating*]: Steady; you wouldn't hit me now, would you?

REGINE: I would! Talk about mother, and I'll hit you. Get out, I say! [*Drives him up towards the garden door.*] And don't slam the doors; young Mr Alving –

ENGSTRAND: He's sleeping, aye. You do fuss over that young Mr Alving something awful – [*Softer*] Aha; it couldn't perhaps be, that *he* –?

REGINE: Out, and quick about it! You're stark raving mad, you are. No, don't go that way. Pastor Manders is coming. Down the kitchen stairs with you.

ENGSTRAND [*towards the right*]: All right, all right, I'm going. But you just talk to *him* what's coming. *He's* the man will tell you what a child owes her father. 'Cos I am your father after all, see. I can prove that by the church register.[21]

He goes out of the other door, which REGINE *has opened, and then closes it after him.*

REGINE *looks at herself hastily in the mirror, fans herself with her handkerchief and straightens her collar; then busies herself with the flowers.*

PASTOR MANDERS, *wearing an overcoat and carrying an umbrella, and with a small travelling bag slung over his shoulder, comes into the conservatory through the garden door.*

MANDERS: Good afternoon, Miss[22] Engstrand.

REGINE [*turning round, with a look of happy surprise*]: Oh, Pastor Manders, good afternoon! Has the steamship arrived already?

MANDERS: It arrived a moment ago. [*Entering the garden room*] What tiresome wet weather we've had these last few days.

REGINE [*following him*]: But it's a blessing to the farmer,[23] pastor.

MANDERS: Yes, you are right, of course. We town folk give so little thought to these things. [*Starts taking his overcoat off.*]

REGINE: Oh, can I help? – There now. Goodness, look how wet it is! I'll just hang it up in the hallway.[24] And your umbrella – I'll open it up, so it can dry.

She goes out with the things through the second door to the right. PASTOR MANDERS *takes his travel bag off and puts it on a chair together with his hat. Meanwhile* REGINE *comes back in.*

MANDERS: Ah, it's certainly good to get inside. So, is all well here on the estate?

REGINE: Yes, thank you very much.

MANDERS: But extremely busy I imagine, preparing for tomorrow?

REGINE: Oh, yes, there's a fair bit to do.

MANDERS: And Mrs Alving is at home, I hope?

REGINE: Indeed she is, sir, she's just upstairs seeing to the young master's hot chocolate.[25]

MANDERS: Yes, do tell me – I heard down at the quayside that Osvald had come.

REGINE: Yes, he came the day before yesterday. We hadn't expected him before today.

MANDERS: And fit and well, I hope?

REGINE: Yes, thank you, quite well. But dreadfully tired from the journey. Steamed it, he did, right from Paris – I mean, he made the whole trip on just the one train. I think he's sleeping a little now, so we should probably talk a teensy bit quietly.

MANDERS: Shh, we'll be so quiet.

REGINE [*moves an armchair up to the table*]: Here you are, pastor, do sit down and make yourself at home. [*He sits down; she puts a footstool under his feet.*] There, now! Is the pastor sitting comfortably?[26]

MANDERS: Yes, thank you, I'm sitting most comfortably. [*Observing her*] You know something, Miss Engstrand, I honestly believe you've grown since I last saw you.

REGINE: Does the pastor think so? Madam says I've filled out too.

MANDERS: Filled out? Maybe, a little perhaps; well, just right. *Short pause.*

REGINE: Shall I tell madam you're here perhaps?

MANDERS: Thank you, there's no hurry, my dear child. – But tell me now, my dear Regine, how is your father doing out here?

REGINE: Thanking you, pastor, he's doing fairly well.

MANDERS: He dropped by to see me last time he was in town.

REGINE: Oh, did he? He's always so pleased when he gets to talk to the pastor.

MANDERS: And I take it you go down to see him quite regularly?

REGINE: Me? Well yes, I suppose I do; whenever I get a moment –

MANDERS: Your father's not a very strong character, Miss Engstrand. He sorely needs a guiding hand.[27]

REGINE: Yes, that may well be.

MANDERS: He needs someone around him for whom he can feel affection and upon whose judgement he can rely. He admitted it himself so open-heartedly when he was last up to see me.

REGINE: Yes, he did mention something of the sort to me. But I don't know if Mrs Alving will want to lose me – especially now we have the new orphanage to run. And I'd be dreadfully reluctant to leave Mrs Alving, when she's always been so kind to me.

MANDERS: But a daughter's duty, my good girl –. Of course, we'd have to get your mistress's consent first.

REGINE: But I'm not sure it's right for me at my age, to keep house for a single man.

MANDERS: What! But dear Miss Engstrand, this is your own father we're talking about here!

REGINE: Yes, maybe, but still –. I mean, if it was a *respectable* house and with a really proper gentleman –

MANDERS: But, my dear Regine –

REGINE: – someone I could feel a fondness for and look up to and be like a kind of daughter to –

MANDERS: Yes, but my dear, good child –

REGINE: 'Cos then I'd like ever so much to move to town. It's very lonely out here – and the pastor knows himself what it means to stand alone in the world. And I think I can say I'm both able and willing. Doesn't the pastor know of any such position for me?

MANDERS: Me? No, I can't honestly say I do.

REGINE: But dear, dear pastor – do think of me at least if –

MANDERS [*getting up*]: Yes, indeed, I will, Miss Engstrand.

REGINE: Yes, because if I –

MANDERS: Perhaps you'd be so kind as to fetch Mrs Alving?

REGINE: She'll be down right away, pastor.

She goes out to the left.

MANDERS [*walks back and forth a couple of times, stands for a moment in the background with his hands behind his back, looking out into the garden. He then comes close to the table again, picks up a book and looks at the title-page, seems surprised and looks at others*]: Hm – I see!

MRS ALVING enters through the door on the left. She is followed by REGINE, who then immediately goes out through the furthest door to the right.

MRS ALVING [*holding out her hand*]: Welcome, pastor.

MANDERS: Good afternoon, Mrs Alving. Well, here I am, as I promised.

MRS ALVING: Always on the dot.

MANDERS: It wasn't easy to get away, I can tell you. With all those blessed committees and boards I sit on –

MRS ALVING: All the kinder of you, then, to arrive in such good time. Now we can get our business done before we have supper. But where's your case?

MANDERS [*hastily*]: My things are down at the village store. I'll be staying there tonight.

MRS ALVING [*suppressing a smile*]: There's really no persuading you to stay the night under my roof this time either?

MANDERS: No, no, Mrs Alving; thank you all the same; I'll stay down there, as usual. It's so convenient when I go aboard again.

MRS ALVING: Well, you shall have it your way. Although I do really rather think that two elderly people such as ourselves –

MANDERS: Oh, heavens above, what a way to joke. Well, naturally you're in high spirits today. First with the celebrations tomorrow, and then with having Osvald home too.

MRS ALVING: Yes, imagine what a joy that is for me! It's more than two years since he was last home. And he's promised to stay with me all winter.

MANDERS: Oh, has he really? That's a fine filial gesture. After all, living in Rome and Paris must offer rather different attractions, I'd imagine.

MRS ALVING: Yes, but here at home he has his mother, you see. Oh my dear, darling boy – he certainly has room in his heart for his mother!

MANDERS: Well, it would be all too tragic if separation and the pursuit of such a thing as art were to blunt such natural sentiments.

MRS ALVING: Yes, you're quite right. But there's no risk of that with him, none at all. And now I shall enjoy seeing if you recognize him. He'll be down soon; he's upstairs at the moment taking a little rest on the sofa. – But do sit down now, my dear pastor.

MANDERS: Thank you. So it's a convenient moment –?

MRS ALVING: Yes, of course it is.

She sits down at the table.

MANDERS: Good; now let me show you –. [*Goes over to the chair on which his travel bag lies, takes a packet of papers out of it, sits on the opposite side of the table and looks for a clear space for the papers*] Firstly, we have here –. [*Breaking off*] Tell me, Mrs Alving, how do *these* books come to be here?

MRS ALVING: These books? They're books *I'm* reading.

MANDERS: You read this sort of literature?

MRS ALVING: Yes, I most certainly do.

MANDERS: Do you feel you become a better or happier person with this sort of reading?

MRS ALVING: I think I feel somehow reassured.

MANDERS: How peculiar. In what way?

MRS ALVING: Well, I find a sort of explanation and confirmation of a great many things I go around thinking myself. Yes, because *that's* what's so strange, Pastor Manders – there's actually nothing new in these books at all; they only contain what most people think and believe. It's just that most people don't formulate it for themselves, or don't want to admit it.

MANDERS: Good Lord! Do you seriously believe most people –?

MRS ALVING: Yes, I really do.

MANDERS: Yes, but not in this country, surely? Not here amongst us?

MRS ALVING: Oh most certainly, here amongst us too.

MANDERS: Well, I really must say –!

MRS ALVING: But what is it you actually object to in these books, anyway?

MANDERS: Object to? You surely don't think I spend my time perusing such offerings.

MRS ALVING: In other words you have no idea what you are condemning?

MANDERS: I've read quite enough *about* these publications to disapprove of them.

MRS ALVING: Yes, but your own opinion –

MANDERS: My dear lady, there are manifold instances in life when one must rely upon others. That's the way things are in the world; and quite right too. Where would society be otherwise?

MRS ALVING: Well, perhaps you're right.

MANDERS: Although I don't deny, of course, that there can be something rather attractive about such writings. And I can't blame you for wanting to acquaint yourself with the intellectual trends[28] which are, by all reports, current out in the wider world – where you have, of course, allowed your son to roam for so long. But –

MRS ALVING: But?

MANDERS [*lowering his voice*]: But one does not talk about it, Mrs Alving. One certainly doesn't need to give an account to all and sundry of what one reads and what one thinks inside one's own four walls.

MRS ALVING: No, of course not; I quite agree.

MANDERS: Just think, now, of the responsibility you owe this orphanage, which you decided to found at a time when your opinions on spiritual and intellectual matters were entirely different from now – as far as *I* understand, at least.

MRS ALVING: Yes, yes, that I admit absolutely. But it was about the orphanage –

MANDERS: It was about the orphanage we were going to talk, yes. But – prudence, dear lady! And now let us indeed turn to our business. [*Opens the packet and takes out some papers.*] You see these?

MRS ALVING: The documents?

MANDERS: All of them. In perfect order. It's been quite a business getting them ready in time, believe me. I had to exert a fair bit of pressure. The authorities are almost painfully conscientious when it comes to decision-making. But here they are. [*Leafs through the bundle.*] This is the deed of conveyance for the site known as Solvik,[29] being part of the Rosenvold estate,[30] together with the newly erected buildings thereon, the schoolhouse, teachers' accommodation and chapel. And here's the legal approval of the bequest and of the statutes of the foundation. Would you like to see – [*Reads*] Statutes for the orphanage known as the 'Captain Alving Memorial Foundation'.

MRS ALVING [*looks for a long time at the document*]: So there it is.

MANDERS: I've chosen the title Captain rather than Chamberlain. Captain seems less ostentatious.

MRS ALVING: Quite, whatever you think best.

MANDERS: And here you have the savings bankbook for the interest-raising capital set aside to cover the orphanage's running costs.

MRS ALVING: Thank you; but do please hold on to it for convenience's sake.

MANDERS: With pleasure. I think we'll leave the money in the savings bank to begin with. The interest rate isn't all that attractive; four per cent with six months' notice. If we could find a decent mortgage investment later – it would, of course, have to be a first mortgage with absolutely impeccable collateral – then we can discuss that further.

MRS ALVING: Quite, dear Pastor Manders, you know best about these things.

MANDERS: I'll keep my eyes open anyway. – And then there's one more thing that I've thought of asking you a few times.

MRS ALVING: And what's that?

MANDERS: Are the orphanage buildings to be insured or not?

MRS ALVING: Naturally, they must be insured.

MANDERS: Well, stop a little, Mrs Alving. Let's take a closer look at the matter.

MRS ALVING: I keep everything insured; buildings and contents, livestock and crops.

MANDERS: Of course. On your own property. I do the same – naturally. But this, you see, is quite a different matter. The orphanage is to be consecrated, as it were, to a higher purpose.[31]

MRS ALVING: Yes, but even so –

MANDERS: From my own personal perspective, I really wouldn't find it the least objectionable to cover ourselves against all eventualities –

MRS ALVING: Yes, I'm in absolute agreement.

MANDERS: – but what's the feeling among the locals out here? You know that better than I, of course.

MRS ALVING: Hm, the *feeling* –

MANDERS: Are there a significant number of men with influence out here – men with substantial influence, who might take exception?

MRS ALVING: What exactly do you mean by substantial influence?

MANDERS: Well, I'm thinking principally of men in such independent and prominent positions that one can't very well avoid giving their opinions a certain weight.

MRS ALVING: There are numerous such men here who could perhaps take exception, if –

MANDERS: Exactly! Back in town we have plenty of their sort. Just think of all my colleague's[32] staunch followers! It would be awfully easy for people to conclude that neither you nor I had the proper faith in Divine Providence.[33]

MRS ALVING: But as far as you're concerned, dear pastor, you know in yourself at least –

MANDERS: Yes, I know; I know – I'd be confident in my own mind, that's true enough. But nevertheless we'd be unable to prevent a distorted and unfavourable interpretation. And this in turn could easily have a detrimental effect on the activities of the orphanage itself.

MRS ALVING: Well, if *that's* the case, then –

MANDERS: Neither can I wholly ignore the awkward – I might say embarrassing position *I* might find *myself* in. The town's leading circles have taken a huge interest in this matter. After all, the orphanage was partially set up to be of benefit to the town too, and it'll hopefully make a significant contribution to lightening our council's social burden.[34] But since I've been your advisor and guided the business side of things, I can't but fear that the zealots would first and foremost come down on *me* –

MRS ALVING: No, you oughtn't to expose yourself to that.

MANDERS: Not to mention the attacks that would undoubtedly be directed at me in certain magazines and periodicals, which –

MRS ALVING: Enough, dear Pastor Manders; that decides the matter.

MANDERS: So you don't want it insured then?

MRS ALVING: No; we'll leave things as they are.

MANDERS [*leaning back in his chair*]: But *if* misfortune were to strike? One never can know, after all –. Would you be able to make good the damage?

MRS ALVING: No, I can tell you plainly, I certainly could not.

MANDERS: But then you know what, Mrs Alving – it's actually a rather worrying responsibility we're taking upon ourselves.

MRS ALVING: But do you think we *can* do otherwise?

MANDERS: No, that's just it; we *can't* really do otherwise. We oughtn't to expose ourselves to a skewed judgement; and we have absolutely no right to cause offence[35] among the parishioners.

MRS ALVING: You, as a clergyman, least of all.

MANDERS: And I really do think too that we should trust that such an institution has luck on its side – that it stands under special protection.

MRS ALVING: Let's hope so, Pastor Manders.

MANDERS: So we'll leave it at that, then?

MRS ALVING: Indeed we shall.

MANDERS: Good. As you wish. [*Makes a note*] So – do not insure.

MRS ALVING: It's strange though, that you should mention this today of all days –

MANDERS: I've often meant to ask you about it –

MRS ALVING: – because yesterday we very nearly had a fire down there.

MANDERS: What?

MRS ALVING: Well, it wasn't anything much. Some wood shavings caught fire in the carpenter's workshop.

MANDERS: Where Engstrand works?

MRS ALVING: Yes. He's often rather careless with matches, they say.

MANDERS: He has so many things in his head, that man – all manner of things to wrestle with.[36] But thanks be to God, he's endeavouring to lead a blameless life now, I hear.

MRS ALVING: Oh? Who told you that?

MANDERS: He assured me of it himself. And he's a good worker too.

MRS ALVING: Yes, so long as he's sober –

MANDERS: Yes, that lamentable weakness! But he's often driven to it on account of his bad leg, he says. Last time he was in town, I was truly touched by him. He came up to see me and thanked me so sincerely for having got work for him here, so he could be with Regine.

MRS ALVING: I don't think he sees much of her.

MANDERS: Oh yes, he talks to her every day, he sat there himself and told me so.

MRS ALVING: Well, well, perhaps.

MANDERS: He's so acutely aware that he needs somebody who can hold him back when temptation looms. *That's* what's so lovable about Jakob Engstrand, the fact that he comes to one so utterly helpless, berating himself and confessing his frailty. Last time he came up to talk to me –. Listen, Mrs Alving, if there were a heartfelt need in him to have Regine at home with him again –

MRS ALVING [*rises quickly*]: Regine!

MANDERS: – then you mustn't oppose it.

MRS ALVING: Oh, I most certainly will oppose it. Besides – Regine is to have a position at the orphanage, as you know.

MANDERS: But don't forget, now, he is her father –

MRS ALVING: Oh, I know best what sort of father he's been to her. No, I'll never give my blessing for her to go to him.

MANDERS [*getting up*]: But my dear lady, don't take it so violently. It's very sad that you should misjudge Engstrand like this. It seems almost as though you were terrified –

MRS ALVING [*calmer*]: That's neither here nor there. I've taken Regine in, and this is where she will stay. [*Listens.*] Shh, my dear Pastor Manders, don't talk any more about it. [*Her face lights up with happiness.*] Listen! Osvald's coming down the stairs. Now we'll only think of *him*.

OSVALD ALVING, *in a light overcoat, hat in hand and smoking a large meerschaum pipe, comes in through the door to the left.*

OSVALD [*standing by the door*]: Oh, I beg your pardon – I thought you were sitting in the office.[37] [*Coming in*] Good afternoon, Pastor Manders.

MANDERS [*staring*]: Ah –! That's quite extraordinary –

MRS ALVING: So, what do you say about *him*, Pastor Manders?

MANDERS: I – I'd say –. But is it really –?

OSVALD: Yes, it really is the Prodigal Son,[38] Pastor Manders.

MANDERS: But my dear young friend –

OSVALD: Well, the long-lost son at least.

MRS ALVING: Osvald's thinking of the time when you had so much against him becoming a painter.

MANDERS: To mortal eyes many a step may seem dubious, which later proves – [*Shakes his hand.*] Welcome, welcome! But, my dear Osvald –. I may, I presume, call you by your first name?[39]

OSVALD: Yes, what else should you call me?

MANDERS: Good. What I wanted to say was *this*, my dear Osvald – you mustn't go thinking I condemn the artistic profession indiscriminately. I imagine there are many who can preserve their inward man[40] untarnished even in that profession.

OSVALD: Let's hope so.

MRS ALVING [*beaming with pleasure*]: I know one who has preserved both his inward and his outward man untarnished. Just look at him, Pastor Manders.

OSVALD [*wandering about the room*]: All right, all right, Mother dear, that's enough.

MANDERS: Yes, absolutely – that can't be denied. And then you've started to make a name for yourself already. The newspapers have often spoken of you, and in exceedingly favourable terms. Although, I must say – recently things do seem to have gone rather quiet.

OSVALD [*standing by the flowers*]: I've not managed to paint so much lately.

MRS ALVING: Even a painter needs to take a rest once in a while.

MANDERS: Yes, I can imagine. And thus prepare himself and gather his powers for something great.

OSVALD: Quite. – Mother, are we going to eat soon?

MRS ALVING: In half an hour at most. He's certainly got an appetite, thank goodness.

MANDERS: And a taste for tobacco too.

OSVALD: I found Father's pipe up in his private room,[41] and then –

MANDERS: Ah, there we have it!

MRS ALVING: What?

MANDERS: When Osvald came into the doorway with that pipe in his mouth, it was as though I saw his father there large as life.

OSVALD: No, really?

MRS ALVING: Oh, how can you possibly say that? Osvald takes after me.

MANDERS: Yes; but there's an expression about the corners of the mouth, something about the lips, that resembles Alving precisely – when he's smoking at least.

MRS ALVING: Not at all. Osvald has something rather more priestly about his mouth, to my mind.

MANDERS: Ah yes, true, true; many of my colleagues do have a similar expression.

MRS ALVING: But put the pipe away, my dear boy; I don't want smoke in here.

OSVALD [does so]: Of course. I just wanted to try it out; because I smoked it once as a child.

MRS ALVING: You?

OSVALD: Yes. I was quite small at the time. I remember I went up into father's private room one evening, he was in such a bright, ebullient mood.

MRS ALVING: Oh, you remember nothing from those years.

OSVALD: Oh yes, I remember distinctly, he took me and sat me on his knee and let me smoke his pipe. Puff, boy, he said – puff properly, boy! And I smoked as hard as I could, until I felt myself go quite pale and the sweat break out in huge drops on my forehead. Then he roared with laughter –

MANDERS: How very peculiar.

MRS ALVING: Dear me, it's just something Osvald has dreamed.

OSVALD: No, Mother, I certainly haven't dreamed it. Because – don't you remember – you came in and carried me off to the nursery. Then I was ill, and I saw that you were crying. – Did Father often play pranks like that?

MANDERS: As a young man, he was certainly full of the joys of life.[42]

OSVALD: And still achieved so much here in the world. So much that was good and useful; despite dying so young.

MANDERS: Yes, you've certainly inherited the name of an industrious and worthy man, my dear Osvald Alving. Well, it'll hopefully be a spur to you –

OSVALD: It ought to be, yes.

MANDERS: It was, at any rate, splendid of you to come home for his day of honour.

OSVALD: It was the least I could do for Father.

MRS ALVING: And to allow me to keep him for so long, that's what's most splendid.

MANDERS: Yes, you'll be at home all winter, I hear.

OSVALD: I'm staying indefinitely, pastor. – Oh, it really is wonderful to be home again!

MRS ALVING [*radiant*]: Yes, isn't it, dear?

MANDERS [*looks sympathetically at him*]: You went out into the world early, my dear Osvald.

OSVALD: Yes, I did. Occasionally I wonder if it wasn't *too* early.

MRS ALVING: No, not at all. It's a very good thing for a healthy boy. Particularly an only child. A child like that shouldn't be at home with his mother and father getting spoiled.

MANDERS: That's a highly debatable question, Mrs Alving. The paternal home[43] is and always will be a child's rightful abode.

OSVALD: I certainly have to agree with the pastor on that.

MANDERS: Just look at your own son. We can, I'm sure, talk about this in his presence. What has the consequence been for him? He's reached the age of twenty-six or -seven, and he has never had the chance to learn what a proper home is like.

OSVALD: I'm sorry, pastor – you're quite mistaken there.

MANDERS: Oh? I thought you'd been moving in almost exclusively artistic circles.

OSVALD: And so I have.

MANDERS: And mostly among the younger artists?

OSVALD: Quite so.

MANDERS: But I thought most of those people couldn't afford to start a family and establish a home.

OSVALD: Many can't afford to get married,[44] pastor.

MANDERS: Well, that's exactly what I'm saying.

OSVALD: Yes, but they can still have a home. And one or two of them *have*; and a very proper and very pleasant home, at that.

   MRS ALVING *listens intently, nods, but says nothing.*

MANDERS: But I'm not talking about bachelors' homes. By a home I mean a family home, where a man lives with his wife and his children.

OSVALD: Yes; or with his children and his children's mother.

MANDERS [*taken aback, clasps his hands together*]: But merciful God –!

OSVALD: What?

MANDERS: Living together with – his children's mother!

OSVALD: Would you rather he disowned the mother of his children?

MANDERS: But you're talking about unlawful relationships[45] here! These so-called wild marriages![46]

OSVALD: I've never noticed anything particularly wild about the way these people live together.

MANDERS: But how is it possible for a – an even moderately well-brought-up man or young woman to bring themselves to live like that – in full view of the world!

OSVALD: But what should they do, then? A poor young artist – a poor young girl –. It costs a lot to get married. What should they do?

MANDERS: What they should do? Well, Mr Alving, I'll tell you what they should do. They should have stayed away from each other from the start – that's what!

OSVALD: That sort of talk won't get you far with young, warm-blooded people in love.

MRS ALVING: No, that won't get you far at all!

MANDERS [*persisting*]: And that the authorities tolerate such a thing! That they allow it to take place openly! [*Facing* MRS ALVING] Didn't I have grounds to be deeply worried about your son? In circles where such barefaced immorality is rampant and has somehow become the rule –

OSVALD: I'll tell you something, pastor. I have been a regular Sunday guest in a couple of these irregular homes –

MANDERS: On Sundays of all days!

OSVALD: Yes, surely a day to enjoy oneself. But not once have I heard an offensive word, far less witnessed anything that could be called immoral. No; do you know when and where *I* have come across immorality in artistic circles?

MANDERS: No, thank heavens!

OSVALD: Then permit me to tell you. I've encountered it when one of our model husbands and family men came down to take a little look around on their own – and did the artists the honour of visiting them in their lowly taverns. Then we'd hear a few realities. Those gentlemen were able to tell us about places and things we'd never dreamed of.

MANDERS: What? Are you suggesting that honourable men from home would –?

OSVALD: Have you never, when these honourable men returned home, have you never heard them pronouncing on the spread of immorality abroad?

MANDERS: Yes, naturally –

MRS ALVING: I've heard them too.

OSVALD: Well, one can safely take them at their word. Some of them are experts on the subject. [*Clutches his head.*] Oh – that this beautiful, glorious life of freedom[47] out there – that it should be sullied like this.

MRS ALVING: You mustn't over-excite yourself, Osvald; it's not good for you.

OSVALD: No, you're right, Mother. It probably isn't healthy for me. It's this damned tiredness, you see. Well, I'll go for a little walk now before dinner. I'm sorry, pastor; you've no way of understanding it, of course; but it just came over me.

He goes out through the second door on the right.

MRS ALVING: My poor boy –!

MANDERS: Yes, well may you say. So this is what he's come to.

MRS ALVING *looks at him in silence.*

MANDERS [*paces up and down*]: He called himself the Prodigal Son. Yes, alas – alas!

MRS ALVING *goes on looking at him.*

MANDERS: And what do you say to all this?

MRS ALVING: I say that Osvald was right in every word he said.

MANDERS [*stops pacing*]: Right? Right? On such fundamental issues?

MRS ALVING: Out here in my solitude I've come to think similarly, Pastor Manders. But I've never dared touch on it. But, no matter; my boy will speak for me now.

MANDERS: You're a woman deserving of great pity, Mrs Alving. But now I want to speak most sternly to you. It is no longer your business executor or advisor, nor you and your late husband's old friend, who stands before you. It is your pastor, as he stood before you at that moment in your life when you had gone so terribly astray.

MRS ALVING: And what is it the pastor has to say to me?

MANDERS: First I want to stir your memory, Mrs Alving. The moment is well chosen. Tomorrow is the tenth anniversary of your husband's death; tomorrow the memorial will be unveiled in honour of the departed; tomorrow I shall address the entire assembled crowd – but today I wish to speak to you alone.

MRS ALVING: Very well, pastor; speak!

MANDERS: Do you remember how, after less than a year of marriage, you stood on the very brink of the abyss? How you abandoned your house and home – how you fled from your husband; yes, Mrs Alving, fled – you fled and refused to go back to him, no matter how much he begged and implored you.

MRS ALVING: Have you forgotten how extremely unhappy I was in that first year?

MANDERS: It is the mark of a rebellious spirit to demand happiness here in life. What right do we mortals have to happiness? No, we must do our duty, madam! And your duty was to hold firmly to the man you'd once chosen, and to whom you were tied by holy bonds.

MRS ALVING: You know very well what sort of life my husband[48] was leading in those days; and the excesses he was guilty of.

MANDERS: I am only too aware of the rumours that circulated about him; and I am the last person to approve of his conduct in his bachelor days, assuming those rumours contained any truth. But a wife is not entitled to stand as judge over her husband.[49] It was your duty to bear with humility the cross that a higher power had deemed fit for you. But instead you rebelliously cast this cross aside, you abandon the stumbling man whom you should have supported, you gamble your good name and reputation, and – very nearly forfeit the reputation of others into the bargain.

MRS ALVING: Others? *One* other, I think you mean.

MANDERS: It was extremely inconsiderate of you to seek refuge with *me*.

MRS ALVING: With our pastor? With our good friend?

MANDERS: For that reason more than any. Yes, you may thank your Lord and God that I possessed the necessary fortitude – that I averted you from your feverish intentions and that it was granted me to lead you back to the path of duty and home to your lawful husband.

MRS ALVING: Yes, Pastor Manders, *that* certainly was your doing.

MANDERS: I was merely a humble instrument in the hand of one higher. And that I forced you to bow under your duty and obedience, didn't that blossom magnificently into a blessing for all your days thereafter? Didn't things turn out as I foretold? Didn't Alving turn his back on his dissolute ways, as befits a man? Didn't he lead a loving and blameless life with you for the rest of his days? Didn't he become a benefactor for this district, and didn't he lift you to be at his side, so that little by little you became a helpmate in all his enterprises? And a very capable helpmate too – oh, I know it, Mrs Alving, and for *that*, I give you praise. – But now I come to the next great error of your life.

MRS ALVING: What do you mean by that?

MANDERS: Just as you once renounced the duties of a wife, you have since renounced those of a mother.

MRS ALVING: Ah –!

MANDERS: You have been governed by a disastrously wilful spirit all your life. You've always been drawn to what is unconstrained and lawless. You've never been ready to tolerate any kind of bonds laid upon you. Anything that has ever inconvenienced you in life, you have recklessly and unscrupulously thrown off, like a burden you could dispose of as you pleased. It no longer suited you to be a wife, so you left your husband. You found it an inconvenience to be a mother and you sent your child away to strangers.

MRS ALVING: Yes, that's true. I did.

MANDERS: Which is why you've become a stranger to him too.

MRS ALVING: No, no; I'm not!

MANDERS: But you are; you *must* be. And in what state have you got him back? Think carefully, Mrs Alving. You've sinned gravely against your husband – that much you acknowledge in erecting the memorial down there. Now acknowledge how you've sinned against your son; there may still be time to lead him back from these wayward paths. Turn back now, and redeem whatever may still be redeemed in him. [*With raised forefinger*] For in truth, Mrs Alving, as a mother you carry a heavy burden of guilt! – This have I judged it my duty to tell you.

  Silence.

MRS ALVING [*slowly and with restraint*]: You've spoken now, pastor; and tomorrow you'll speak publicly in memory of my husband. I shan't speak tomorrow. But now I will speak to you a little, as you've spoken to me.

MANDERS: Naturally; you want to present excuses for your behaviour –

MRS ALVING: No. I just want to tell you something.

MANDERS: Well –?

MRS ALVING: Everything you've said here about my husband and me, and about our marriage, after you led me, as you put it, back to the path of duty – all this is something of which you have absolutely no knowledge from any personal observation. From that moment you – our close friend and daily guest – never set foot in our house again.

MANDERS: Well, you and your husband moved out of town soon after.

MRS ALVING: Quite; and you never came out here to see us while my husband was alive. It was business that forced you to visit me, when you got involved in organizing the orphanage.

MANDERS [*quietly and hesitantly*]: Helene[50] – if this is intended
as a reproach, then I'd ask you to bear in mind –

MRS ALVING: – the regard you owed your position; yes. And,
that I was a runaway wife. One can never be too cautious
with regard to such reckless womenfolk.

MANDERS: My dear – Mrs Alving, this is a vast exaggeration –

MRS ALVING: Yes, yes, yes, be that as it may. All I wanted to
say was that, when you pass judgement on my marital relationship, you're relying, without any thought, on common,
everyday opinion.

MANDERS: Maybe; and so?

MRS ALVING: But now, Manders, now I'll tell you the truth. I
vowed to myself that you'd come to know it one day. You
alone!

MANDERS: And what then is the truth?

MRS ALVING: The truth is that my husband died as debauched
as he had been all his life.

MANDERS [*fumbling for a chair*]: What did you say?

MRS ALVING: After nineteen years of marriage he was just as
debauched – in his desires at least – as he was before you
married us.

MANDERS: And these youthful transgressions – these irregu-
larities – excesses if you like, you call a debauched life?

MRS ALVING: That was the expression our doctor used.

MANDERS: I don't understand.

MRS ALVING: Nor do you need to.

MANDERS: I'm feeling quite dizzy. Your entire marriage – all
those years of married life with your husband were nothing
more than a concealed abyss?

MRS ALVING: Not a jot more. Now you know.

MANDERS: This – it's hard for me to take this in. I can't comprehend it! Can't grasp it! But how was it possible to –? How
could something like this be kept hidden?

MRS ALVING: That was indeed my ceaseless struggle day after
day. When we had Osvald, I felt things improved somehow
a little with Alving. But it didn't last long. And now, of
course, I had a double battle, a battle of life and death to
keep people from knowing what sort of man my child had

for a father. And you know, of course, how charming Alving was. Nobody could think anything but good of him. He was one of those people whose reputation seems undented by their conduct. But then, Manders – and this you also have to know – then the most abominable thing of all happened.

MANDERS: More abominable than this?

MRS ALVING: I would have put up with him, even though I knew very well what was going on secretly outside the house. But when this scandalous behaviour came inside our own four walls –

MANDERS: What are you saying? Here?

MRS ALVING: Yes, here in our own home. I was in there [*pointing towards the first door to the right*] in the dining room, when I first realized. I had something to do in there, and the door was ajar. I heard our housemaid come up from the garden with water for the flowers in there.

MANDERS: And then –?

MRS ALVING: A little later I heard Alving go in too. I heard him saying something quietly to her. And then I heard – [*With a short laugh*] Oh, it still rings in my ears, so dreadful and yet so ridiculous – I heard my own housemaid whisper: 'Let me go, Chamberlain Alving! Leave me alone.'

MANDERS: What an unseemly indiscretion on his part. But more than a foolish indiscretion it could not have been, Mrs Alving. You must believe me.

MRS ALVING: I soon knew what to believe. The Chamberlain had his way with that girl – and this relationship had consequences, Pastor Manders.

MANDERS [*frozen*]: And all in this house! In this house!

MRS ALVING: I had tolerated a great deal in this house. To keep him at home in the evenings – and at nights I had to act as his companion during his secret drinking bouts up in his room. I had to sit there with him, just the two of us, I had to clink glasses and drink with him, listen to all his lewd, nonsensical chatter, had to wrestle with him so as to drag him to bed.

MANDERS [*shaken*]: That you could bear all this.

MRS ALVING: I had my little boy to bear it for. But when that final humiliation came; when my own maid – well, then I vowed to myself: this will come to an end! And so I took control of the household – total control – over him and everything else. I had a weapon against him now, you see; he didn't dare object. That was when Osvald was sent away. He was coming up for seven and beginning to notice things and ask questions, as children do. I couldn't stand all that, Manders. I felt sure my child would be poisoned just by breathing in the air of this infected home. That was why I sent him away. And now you see why he was never allowed to set foot in this house as long as his father lived. Nobody knows what that has cost me.

MANDERS: Life has certainly put you to the test.

MRS ALVING: I'd never have survived if it hadn't been for my work. Yes, because I have worked, that much I dare to say. All the additions to the estate, all the improvements, all the practical innovations that Alving received such praise for – do you think *he* had the drive for that? A man who lay on the couch all day reading an old government almanac![51] No; and I'll tell you *this* too: I was the one to get him going when he occasionally had better moments; it was *I* who had to pull all the weight when he lapsed into his excesses or sank into whining self-pity.

MANDERS: And it's to this man you're raising a memorial?

MRS ALVING: There you see the power of a bad conscience.

MANDERS: Bad –? What do you mean?

MRS ALVING: It always seemed inevitable to me that the truth would come out one day and be believed. So the orphanage was somehow meant to put paid to all the rumours and sweep any doubts away.

MANDERS: Then you certainly haven't failed in your intention, Mrs Alving.

MRS ALVING: And I had an additional reason. I didn't want Osvald, my own boy, to inherit anything from his father.

MANDERS: So it's Alving's money that –?

MRS ALVING: Yes. The amounts I have donated year on year to this orphanage, make up – I've calculated it carefully – the sum that in its day made Lieutenant Alving such 'a good catch'.

MANDERS: I understand –

MRS ALVING: It was my purchase price –. I don't want that money to pass into Osvald's hands. Everything my son gets will come from me.

OSVALD ALVING *comes through the second door to the right; he has taken his hat and overcoat off outside.*

MRS ALVING [*going towards him*]: Back already? My dear, dear boy!

OSVALD: Yes; what can one do outside in this incessant rain? But I hear dinner's about to be served. That's marvellous!

REGINE [*coming from the dining room with a parcel*]: A parcel's just arrived for you, ma'am. [*Hands it to her.*]

MRS ALVING [*glancing at* PASTOR MANDERS]: The song-sheets for tomorrow, I imagine.

MANDERS: Hm –

REGINE: And dinner is served.

MRS ALVING: Good, we'll come in a moment; I just want to – [*Begins to open the parcel*]

REGINE [*to* OSVALD]: Would Mr Alving like red or white port?

OSVALD: Both please, Miss Engstrand.

REGINE: *Bien –.* Very well, Mr Alving.

She goes into the dining room.

OSVALD: I'd better help uncork the bottles – [*Goes out into the dining room too, leaving the door to swing ajar after him.*]

MRS ALVING [*who has opened the packet*]: Yes, I was right; here are the song-sheets, Pastor Manders.

MANDERS [*with clasped hands*]: How I'm to deliver my speech tomorrow with any gusto, I just –!

MRS ALVING: Oh, I'm sure you'll find a way.

MANDERS [*his voice low so as not to be heard in the dining room*]: Yes, we can't go making a scandal, can we?

MRS ALVING [*quietly, but firmly*]: No. But *then* this long, hideous farce will finally be over. For me, from the day after tomorrow, it'll be as though the dead man never lived in this house. There will be nobody here but my boy and his mother.

The sound of a chair being knocked over can be heard in the dining room; and at the same time we hear:

REGINE [*sharply, but whispering*]: Osvald! Are you mad? Let me go!

MRS ALVING [*starts with terror*]: Ah –!

As though deranged, she stares towards the half-open door. OSVALD *can be heard coughing and then humming. A bottle is uncorked.*

MANDERS [*agitated*]: What *is* going on? What *is* it, Mrs Alving?

MRS ALVING [*hoarsely*]: Ghosts. The couple in the conservatory – they walk again.

MANDERS: What are you saying? Regine –? Is *she* –?

MRS ALVING: Yes. Come on. Not a word –!

She grips MANDERS *by the arm and walks unsteadily towards the dining room.*

ACT TWO

The same room. A rainy mist still lies heavily over the land-scape. PASTOR MANDERS *and* MRS ALVING *come in from the dining room.*

MRS ALVING [*still in the doorway*]: My pleasure entirely, pastor. [*Speaking in the direction of the dining room*] Won't you join us, Osvald?

OSVALD [*from the dining room*]: No thank you. I think I'll go out for a bit.

MRS ALVING: Yes do; the rain seems to have lifted a little. [*Closes the dining-room door and goes to the hall door and calls*] Regine!

REGINE [*outside*]: Yes, ma'am?

MRS ALVING: Go down to the laundry room and help with the garlands.

REGINE: Yes, ma'am.

MRS ALVING *makes sure that* REGINE *has gone, then closes the door.*

MANDERS: You're sure he can't hear anything in there?

MRS ALVING: Not with the door closed. Besides, he's going out.

MANDERS: I'm still in a daze. I've no idea how I managed to down a single morsel of that delicious food.

MRS ALVING [*in restrained agitation, walking back and forth*]: Nor me. But what's to be done?

MANDERS: Yes, what's to be done? For the life of me, I don't know. I'm completely inexperienced in these matters.

MRS ALVING: I'm convinced nothing untoward has happened yet.

MANDERS: No, heaven forbid! But it's an unseemly situation just the same.

MRS ALVING: The whole thing's a passing fancy on Osvald's part; you can be sure of that.

MANDERS: Well, as I say, I'm not very knowledgeable in these matters; but I think without a doubt –

MRS ALVING: She must leave the house. And immediately. That's as clear as day –

MANDERS: Yes, self-evidently.

MRS ALVING: But where to? It would be inexcusable if we –

MANDERS: Where to? Back home to her father, of course.

MRS ALVING: To whom, did you say?

MANDERS: To her –. Yes, but of course, Engstrand isn't –. Good Lord, Mrs Alving, how can this be possible? You really must be mistaken.

MRS ALVING: I'm sorry; I'm not the least mistaken. Johanne had to confess everything to me – and Alving couldn't deny it. So there was no alternative but to get the matter hushed up.

MANDERS: No, I suppose that was all that could be done.

MRS ALVING: The girl left our service immediately, and was given a generous sum to keep quiet for a while. The rest she arranged for herself when she got to town. She renewed an old acquaintance with Engstrand, dropped a hint, I'd imagine, about how much money she had and spun him a tale about some foreigner or other who was supposed to have anchored here with his yacht that summer. Then she and Engstrand got married post-haste. Well, you married them yourself.

MANDERS: But how am I to make sense of this – I distinctly remember when Engstrand came to arrange the wedding. He was so utterly heartbroken and berated himself so bitterly for the wanton behaviour he and his fiancée were guilty of.

MRS ALVING: Well, of course he had to take the blame on himself.

MANDERS: But how deceitful of him! And towards *me*! I'd honestly never have believed that of Jakob Engstrand. Well, I'm going to have to deal with him most seriously; that he can rely on. – And the immorality of such a match! All for the sake of money –! How large was the amount the girl had at her disposal?

MRS ALVING: It was three hundred speciedaler.[52]

MANDERS: Yes, just imagine – for a paltry three hundred spe-ciedaler, to get himself married to a fallen woman!

MRS ALVING: So what would you say about me, getting mar-ried to a fallen man?[53]

MANDERS: But mercy upon us – what are you saying? A fallen man?

MRS ALVING: You believe perhaps that Alving was purer when I walked with him to the altar than Johanne was when Eng-strand married her?

MANDERS: Yes, but they're vastly different things –

MRS ALVING: Not so different, really. There was certainly a big difference in price – a paltry three hundred speciedaler and a whole fortune.

MANDERS: But how can you compare two such dissimilar things? After all, you had consulted[54] with your heart and with your family.

MRS ALVING [not looking at him]: I thought you understood where what you call my heart had strayed at the time.

MANDERS [distant]: Had I understood any such thing, I would not have become a daily guest in your husband's house.

MRS ALVING: Well, the fact remains that I certainly did not consult with myself.

MANDERS: But with your closest relatives, then; as is pre-scribed; with your mother and both your aunts.

MRS ALVING: Yes, that's true. The three of them totted up the figures for me. Oh, it's remarkable how swiftly they con-cluded that it would be utter madness to refuse such an offer. If Mother could look up now and see what all that magnifi-cence had brought with it!

MANDERS: Nobody can be held responsible for the outcome. But the fact remains that your marriage was sealed in abso-lute compliance with the law.

MRS ALVING [at the window]: Oh yes, this business of law and order! I often think they're the cause of all the unhappi-ness in the world.

MANDERS: Mrs Alving, that's a sinful thing to say.

MRS ALVING: That's as may be; but I can't bear all these bonds and considerations any longer. I just can't! I have to work my way out to freedom.

MANDERS: What do you mean by that?

MRS ALVING [*drumming on the window frame*]: I should never have covered up Alving's lifestyle. But at the time I didn't dare do anything else – for my own sake as much as anyone's. That's how cowardly I was.

MANDERS: Cowardly?

MRS ALVING: If people had got to know anything, they'd have said: poor man, it's hardly surprising he kicks over the traces, with a wife who runs away from him.

MANDERS: And there might have been some justification in saying that.

MRS ALVING [*looking fixedly at him*]: If I was the person I should have been, I'd take Osvald aside and say: 'Listen, my boy, your father was a depraved[55] human being –'

MANDERS: Heavens above –

MRS ALVING: – and then I'd tell him everything I've told you – lock, stock and barrel.

MANDERS: Mrs Alving, I'm almost horrified at you.

MRS ALVING: Yes, I know. I know that! I'm horrified at the thought myself. [*Moves away from the window.*] That's how cowardly I am.

MANDERS: And you call it cowardice to fulfil your obvious duty and obligation? Have you forgotten that a child should love and honour his mother and father?[56]

MRS ALVING: Let's not generalize about this. Let us ask, should Osvald love and honour Chamberlain Alving?

MANDERS: Isn't there a voice in that mother's heart of yours that forbids you to shatter your son's ideals?

MRS ALVING: Yes, but what about the truth, then?

MANDERS: Yes, but what about ideals then?

MRS ALVING: Oh – ideals, ideals! If only I weren't the coward I am.

MANDERS: Don't go throwing ideals aside, Mrs Alving – that may bring a terrible vengeance. Especially now with Osvald.

Osvald doesn't seem to have many ideals, more's the pity.
But from what I can see his father stands as just such an
ideal.

MRS ALVING: You're right there.

MANDERS: And these impressions of his were awakened and
fostered in him by you yourself in your letters.

MRS ALVING: Yes; I felt bound by duty and obligation, so I lied
to my boy year in and year out. Oh, how cowardly – how
cowardly I've been!

MANDERS: You've established a beautiful illusion in your son's
mind, Mrs Alving – and you truly shouldn't undervalue that.

MRS ALVING: Hm; who knows whether that really is such a
good thing. – But any underhand goings on with Regine are
out of the question, at least. He's not going to go and make
that poor girl unhappy.

MANDERS: Good God, no, that would be dreadful!

MRS ALVING: If I knew he was serious and that it would lead
to his happiness –

MANDERS: What do you mean? Then what?

MRS ALVING: But it wouldn't; Regine isn't like that
unfortunately.

MANDERS: And so? What do you mean?

MRS ALVING: If I wasn't such an abject coward I'd say to him:
marry her, or arrange things to suit the two of you; but let's
have no deceit.

MANDERS: Merciful heavens –! You mean a legally recognized
marriage? What a monstrous –! It's unheard of –!

MRS ALVING: Unheard of, you say? Hand on heart, Pastor
Manders: don't you think there are plenty of married
couples around the country who are just as closely related?

MANDERS: I simply don't understand you.

MRS ALVING: Oh, yes you do.

MANDERS: No doubt you're thinking of the possibility that –.
Yes, unfortunately, family life isn't always as pure as it
should be. But in the circumstances you're alluding to, one
can never know for sure – not with certainty at least. But
with *this* on the other hand – to think that you, a mother,
could possibly permit –!

MRS ALVING: But I *won't*. I couldn't permit it for any price on earth; that's exactly what I'm saying.

MANDERS: No, because you're a coward, as you put it. But if you weren't such a coward –! God in heaven – what a horrifying union!

MRS ALVING: Yes, but then it's said that we're all descended from such a union. And who arranged things that way here on earth, Pastor Manders?

MANDERS: Madam, I will not debate such a question with you; you are far from being in the right state of mind. But that you dare to say it's cowardly of you –!

MRS ALVING: All right, let me tell you what I mean. I am nervous and frightened, because there's some kind of ghostlike feeling lodged inside me, which I can never be quite rid of.

MANDERS: What did you call it?

MRS ALVING: Ghostlike. When I heard Regine and Osvald in there it was as though I saw ghosts. But I almost believe we are ghosts, all of us, Pastor Manders. It's not just the things we've inherited from our fathers and mothers that return in us. It's all kinds of old dead opinions and all sorts of old dead doctrines[57] and so on. They aren't alive in us; but they are lodged in there all the same, and we can never be rid of them. I only have to pick up a newspaper and read it, and it's as though I see ghosts creeping between the lines. There must be ghosts living throughout the entire land. They must lie as thick as sand, I'd say. And we are so wretchedly frightened of the light,[58] all of us.

MANDERS: Ah – so here we see the dividends of your reading. Fine fruits indeed! Oh, these despicable, rebellious, free-thinking books!

MRS ALVING: You're wrong, dear pastor. You were the very man who provoked me into thinking; and for that I thank you.

MANDERS: Me?

MRS ALVING: Yes, when you forced me to submit to what you called my duty and obligation; when you extolled as right and proper what my whole soul rebelled against as an abomination. That was when I began to examine the stitching that held your teachings together. I only wanted to unpick a single knot, but the instant I'd loosened *that*, the whole thing fell apart. And then I realized it was machine sewn.

MANDERS [*quietly, shaken*]: And is that what was won by my life's hardest battle?

MRS ALVING: Call it rather your most miserable defeat.

MANDERS: It was the greatest victory of my life, Helene; victory over myself.

MRS ALVING: It was a crime against us both.

MANDERS: To plead with you and say: woman, go home to your lawful husband, when you came to me in despair and cried: 'Here I am, take me!' Was *that* a crime?

MRS ALVING: Yes, I think it was.

MANDERS: We two don't understand each other.

MRS ALVING: Not any more, at least.

MANDERS: Never – never even in my most secret thoughts, have I seen you as anything other than another man's wife.

MRS ALVING: Hm – I wonder?

MANDERS: Helene –!

MRS ALVING: We forget so easily who we once were.

MANDERS: Not me. I'm the same as I ever was.

MRS ALVING [*changing tack*]: Well, well – let's not talk any more about old times. Now you sit up to your eyes in boards and committees; and I go around here battling with ghosts, both on the inside and on the outside.

MANDERS: The outside ones, I can probably help you overcome. After everything I've heard from you today with such horror, my conscience cannot defend letting a vulnerable young girl remain in your house.

MRS ALVING: Don't you think it would be best if we could see her provided for? I mean – with a good marriage.

MANDERS: Indubitably. I think that would be desirable for her in all respects. Regine is of course at an age now – well, I don't really understand these things, but –

MRS ALVING: Regine matured early.

MANDERS: Yes, didn't she? I do have a vague recollection of her being noticeably well developed in the corporeal sense when I prepared her for confirmation. But in the meantime, at least, she'll have to go home; under her father's watchful eye. Ah, but of course Engstrand isn't –. That he – that *he* could conceal the truth like that from me!

There is a knock on the door leading to the hallway.

MRS ALVING: Who can *that* be? Come in!

ENGSTRAND [*in his Sunday best, standing in the doorway*]: I do beg your pardon, but –

MANDERS: Aha! Hm –

MRS ALVING: Oh, is it you, Engstrand?

ENGSTRAND: – none of the maids was around, and so I took the bold liberty of knocking –.

MRS ALVING: Well, all right. Come in. Did you want to speak to me about something?

ENGSTRAND [*comes in*]: No, ma'am, thanking you all the same. It was more the pastor I wanted a little word with.

MANDERS [*walking up and down*]: Hm; really? You want to speak to me, do you?

ENGSTRAND: Aye, I'd be awful glad if –

MANDERS [*stops in front of him*]: Well; may I ask what about?

ENGSTRAND: Well, it was this, pastor, now that we're settling up down there – thanking you kindly, ma'am. – And now that we've finished with everything; I was thinking it would be very nice and fitting, if us what's worked so sincere together all this time – I was thinking, we should end on a little prayer meeting this evening.

MANDERS: A prayer meeting? Down at the orphanage?

ENGSTRAND: Well, maybe if the pastor don't think it's fitting, then –

MANDERS: Oh, I certainly think it is, but – hm –

ENGSTRAND: I've been conducting a little prayer meeting myself down there of an evening –

MRS ALVING: Have you?

ENGSTRAND: Aye, now and then; sort of a little edification as you'd call it. But I'm just a humble, lowly man and I've not got the proper gifts, Lord knows – and so I was thinking, that since Pastor Manders happened to be out here, then –

MANDERS: Yes, but you see, Engstrand, I have a question I must put to you first. Are you in the proper state of mind for such a meeting? Do you feel your conscience to be clear and free?

ENGSTRAND: God help us, it wouldn't be wise to go talking about conscience, pastor.

MANDERS: But that's precisely what we *are* going to speak about. So, what's your answer?

ENGSTRAND: Well, conscience – that can be terrible sometimes.

MANDERS: Well, that much you admit at least. But could you tell me straight – what's the situation with regard to Regine?

MRS ALVING [*quickly*]: Pastor Manders!

MANDERS [*reassuring*]: Allow me –

ENGSTRAND: With Regine! [*Looking at* MRS ALVING] Jesus, you're really frightening me now! Nothing bad's happened to Regine, has it?

MANDERS: Let's hope not. What I mean is this – what is the situation as regards you and Regine? You call yourself her father? Yes?

ENGSTRAND [*unsure*]: Well – hm – the pastor knows all about me and Johanne, God rest her.

MANDERS: No more distortion of the truth. Your late wife informed Mrs Alving of the true situation, before she left her service.

ENGSTRAND: Well, I'll be –! She did, did she, after all?

MANDERS: You've been found out, Engstrand.

ENGSTRAND: When she'd sworn and cursed so solemnly –

MANDERS: She cursed!

ENGSTRAND: No, she just swore, but so deeply sincere.

MANDERS: And for all these years you have concealed the truth from me. Concealed it from *me*, from the very person who always put such unconditional trust in you.

ENGSTRAND: Aye, I'm afraid I probably have.

MANDERS: Have I deserved this of you, Engstrand? Haven't I always been ready to stretch a helping hand out to you in word and deed as far as was in my power? Answer! Haven't I?

ENGSTRAND: Aye, things wouldn't have looked too bright for me on many an occasion, if I hadn't had Pastor Manders.

MANDERS: And this is how you repay me. Have me enter false-hoods in the Parish Register and then for years on end withhold information from me that you owed both to myself and to the truth. Your conduct has been entirely inexcusable, Engstrand; and from now on it is over between us.

ENGSTRAND [*with a sigh*]: Aye, I suppose it is. I understand.

MANDERS: Yes, for how could you possibly justify yourself?

ENGSTRAND: But then should she have gone and done herself more damage by talking about it? If the pastor was to imagine now that he was in the same plight as our dearly beloved Johanne –

MANDERS: Me?

ENGSTRAND: Jesus, I don't mean exactly the *same*. I mean, what if the pastor had something to be ashamed of in the eyes of the world, as they says. We menfolk shouldn't condemn a poor woman too severe, pastor.

MANDERS: And neither do I. It is to you I am directing my accusations.

ENGSTRAND: May I be permitted to put a tiny little question to the pastor?

MANDERS: Very well, ask.

ENGSTRAND: In't it right and proper for a man to raise the fallen?

MANDERS: Yes, of course.

ENGSTRAND: And in't a man bound to keep his word of honour?

MANDERS: Yes, he certainly is; but –

ENGSTRAND: Back then, when Johanne got herself into trouble with that Englishman – or perhaps it was an American or Russian, as they call 'em – well, then she came into town. Poor thing, she'd spurned me once or twice in the past; 'cos she only had eyes for what was handsome, she did; and I had this defect with my leg, of course. Well, the pastor will remember: I'd ventured myself to go into a dance hall, where seafaring sailors was carrying on all drunk and intoxicated, as they says. And when I tried exhorting them to wander new paths –

MRS ALVING [*at the window*]: Hm –

MANDERS: I know, Engstrand; those brutes threw you down the stairs. You've related that incident to me before. You carry your defect with honour.

ENGSTRAND: I don't boast about it, pastor. But what I wanted to tell you was this: that she came and confided everything to me with a wailing[59] and a gnashing of teeth.[60] I must say, pastor, it fair broke my heart to listen to it.

MANDERS: It did, did it, Engstrand? And then what?

ENGSTRAND: Well, so I says to her: that American, he's off roaming the seven seas, he is. And you, Johanne, I says, you've committed a sinfulness and you're a fallen creature. But Jakob Engstrand, I says, stands on two good legs, he does – well, that was meant more like a parable, pastor.

MANDERS: Yes, I understand; just continue.

ENGSTRAND: Well, that's when I rose her up and joined her in honest wedlock, so folks wouldn't know how wayward she'd been with foreigners.

MANDERS: All this was most commendable of you. What I simply cannot approve of is that you could bring yourself to accept money –

ENGSTRAND: Money? Me? Not a farthing!

MANDERS [to MRS ALVING, questioning]: But –?

ENGSTRAND: Oh aye – hold on – now I remember. Johanne did have a shilling or two, as a matter of fact. But I didn't want nothing to do with *that*. Fie, I says, mammon, that's the wages of sin,[61] that is; this loathsome gold – or bank-notes or whatever it was – we'll throw it back in the American's face, I says. But he'd gone off and vanished over the stormy seas, pastor.

MANDERS: Was he now, my good Engstrand?

ENGSTRAND: Indeed, he was. So Johanne and I agreed that the money should go to the upbringing of the child, and *that's* how it was; and I can account and vouch for every single shilling.

MANDERS: But this changes things quite significantly.

ENGSTRAND: Well, that's how it was, reverend pastor. And I think I can dare to say I've been a good father to Regine – as far as my strength allowed at least – for I am a frail man, alas.

MANDERS: Now, now, my dear Engstrand –

ENGSTRAND: But I think I can say I brought up the child and lived lovingly with my Johanne, God rest her, and kept discipline in the home, as scripture demands. But it wouldn't occur to me to go to Pastor Manders boasting and priding myself on how I, I too for once, had done a good deed here in this world. No, when something like that happens to Jakob Engstrand he keeps mum about it. But sadly it don't happen too often, I'd say. And when I come to Pastor Manders, I've more than enough with talking about what's wicked and frail. 'Cos I'll say, as I just said – conscience can be an ugly thing, now and then.

MANDERS: Give me your hand, Jakob Engstrand.

ENGSTRAND: Oh, goodness, pastor –

MANDERS: Come on, no false modesty. [*Shakes his hand.*] There!

ENGSTRAND: And if I might most humbly dare to beg forgiveness of the pastor –

MANDERS: You? No, on the contrary; I'm the one who should be asking your forgiveness –

ENGSTRAND: Oh Lord, no.

MANDERS: Yes, most certainly. And I do so with all my heart. Forgive me for misjudging you like this. And if I could show you some sign or other of my sincere regret and goodwill towards you –

ENGSTRAND: Would you, pastor?

MANDERS: With the greatest of pleasure –

ENGSTRAND: 'Cos, as it happens there's an opportunity for that now. With the money I've been blessed to put aside out here, I'm thinking of setting up a kind of sailors' home down in town.

MRS ALVING: *You?*

ENGSTRAND: Aye, it would be a kind of refuge you might say. The temptations of this world are manifold for the sailor who wanders on dry land. But in this home of mine, he could feel like he was under a father's watchful eye, I thought.

MANDERS: What do you say to that, Mrs Alving?

ENGSTRAND: It's not too much I have to offer, Lord knows; but if I could just get a charitable helping hand, then –

MANDERS: Yes, yes, we'll have to weigh the matter up carefully. Your venture appeals to me hugely. But go on ahead now and prepare everything and get the candles lit, to make it a bit festive. And we'll have an edifying moment together, my dear Engstrand; because I do believe now that you're in the right frame of mind.

ENGSTRAND: I feel I am, aye. Goodbye, then, Mrs Alving, and thank you for everything; and take good care of Regine for me. [*Wiping a tear from his eye*] My dearest Johanne's little girl – hm, it's strange – but it's as though she'd grown attached to the roots of my heart. Aye, that she has.

He bows and goes out through the hall.

MANDERS: Well, Mrs Alving, now what do you have to say about the man! *That* was quite a different explanation we got there.

MRS ALVING: Yes, it certainly was.

MANDERS: You see how terribly cautious one has to be in condemning a fellow human being. But what an intense joy it is to discover that one's been mistaken. What do *you* say?

MRS ALVING: I say you are, and always will be, a big child, Manders.

MANDERS: Me?

MRS ALVING [*placing both her hands on his shoulders*]: And I say that I'd like to fling both my arms around your neck.

MANDERS [*withdrawing quickly*]: No, no, Lord bless you – such impulses –

MRS ALVING [*with a smile*]: Oh, you mustn't be frightened of me.

MANDERS [*near the table*]: You have such an exaggerated way of expressing yourself sometimes. Now then, let me gather up these documents and put them in my case. [*Does as he says.*] There we go. Well, goodbye for now. Keep your eyes about you when Osvald comes back. I'll look in on you later.

He takes his hat and goes out through the hall door.

MRS ALVING [*sighs, looks out of the window for a moment, tidies the room a little and goes to the dining room but stops*

in the doorway with a stifled cry]: Osvald, are you still sitting at the table!

OSVALD [*from the dining room*]: I'm just finishing my cigar.

MRS ALVING: I thought you'd taken a little walk up the road.

OSVALD: In this weather?

A glass clinks. MRS ALVING *lets the door stand open and
sits with her knitting on the sofa by the window.*

OSVALD [*from inside*]: Wasn't that Pastor Manders leaving
just now?

MRS ALVING: Yes. He went down to the orphanage.

OSVALD: Hm.

The glass and carafe clink again.

MRS ALVING [*with a worried glance*]: Osvald dear, you should
be careful with that liqueur. It's strong.

OSVALD: It keeps the damp out.

MRS ALVING: Wouldn't you rather come in here and sit
with me?

OSVALD: I'm not allowed to smoke in there.

MRS ALVING: You know you can smoke cigars.

OSVALD: All right, I'm coming, then. Just a tiny little drop
more. – There.

*He comes into the living room with a cigar and closes the
door after him.*

Brief silence.

OSVALD: Where's the pastor gone?

MRS ALVING: I just told you; he went down to the orphanage.

OSVALD: Oh yes, that's right.

MRS ALVING: You shouldn't sit at the table so long, Osvald.

OSVALD [*holding his cigar behind his back*]: But I find it so
pleasant, Mother. [*Pats and caresses her.*] Imagine how it
feels – to be back home, to sit at my mother's very own table,
in my mother's dining room, and to eat my mother's delicious food.

MRS ALVING: My darling, darling boy!

OSVALD [*somewhat impatient, paces up and down, smoking*]:
How else should I occupy myself here? I can't get anything
done –

MRS ALVING: Can't you?

OSVALD: In this dull weather? Without a glimmer of sun all day? [*Crosses the room.*] Oh, this inability to work –

MRS ALVING: Perhaps it wasn't so wise of you to come home.

OSVALD: Yes, Mother; I had to come.

MRS ALVING: Well, I'd sacrifice the pleasure of having you here with me ten times over, rather than see you –

OSVALD [*stopping by the table*]: But tell me, Mother – is it really such a pleasure for you to have me home?

MRS ALVING: A pleasure to have you home?

OSVALD [*folding up a newspaper*]: It seems to me it would almost be the same to you whether I existed or not.

MRS ALVING: And you have the heart to say that to your mother, Osvald?

OSVALD: But you've been able to live perfectly well without me before.

MRS ALVING: Yes, I have lived without you – that's true.

Silence. The evening is slowly drawing in. OSVALD *paces around. He has put his cigar down.*

OSVALD [*stops by* MRS ALVING]: Mother, may I sit next to you on the sofa?

MRS ALVING [*making room for him*]: Yes, do, my dear boy.

OSVALD [*sitting down*]: I have to tell you something now, Mother.

MRS ALVING [*anxiously*]: All right!

OSVALD [*staring straight ahead*]: Because I can't bear it any longer.

MRS ALVING: Bear what? What's the matter?

OSVALD [*as before*]: I couldn't bring myself to write to you about it; and ever since I got home –

MRS ALVING [*gripping him by the arm*]: Osvald, what *is* all this?

OSVALD: I tried both yesterday and today to drive these thoughts away – to free myself of them. But I can't.

MRS ALVING [*gets up*]: Speak out plainly now, Osvald!

OSVALD [*pulls her down on the sofa again*]: Just sit there, and I'll try to tell you. – I've been complaining a lot of being tired from the journey –

MRS ALVING: Well, yes! And?

OSVALD: But that's not what's wrong with me, this is no ordinary tiredness –

MRS ALVING [*wants to jump up*]: You're not ill, are you Osvald?

OSVALD [*drags her back down yet again*]: Sit down, Mother. Just calm down. I'm not exactly ill either; not what one would normally call ill. [*Brings his hands to his head.*] Mother, I'm spiritually broken – wrecked – I can never work again!

> He buries his head in her lap and sobs, with his hands in front of his face.

MRS ALVING [*pale and trembling*]: Osvald! Look at me! No, no, this isn't true.

OSVALD [*looking up in despair*]: Never able to work again! Never – never! To be like a dead man alive. Mother, can you think of anything so awful?

MRS ALVING: My poor boy. How did this awful thing happen to you?

OSVALD [*sitting up again*]: That's just what I can't comprehend. I've never lived a riotous life. Not in any respect. You mustn't think that of me, Mother. I've never done that.

MRS ALVING: No, I am sure you haven't, Osvald.

OSVALD: And yet this thing happens to me! This appalling disaster!

MRS ALVING: Oh, but it'll pass, my dear, sweet boy. It's nothing but over-exertion. Trust me on that.

OSVALD [*heavily*]: I thought that at first too; but that's not how it is.

MRS ALVING: Tell me from beginning to end.

OSVALD: Yes, I shall.

MRS ALVING: When did you first notice it?

OSVALD: It was soon after I'd been at home last, and arrived back in Paris. I started getting these violent pains in my head – mostly at the back of my head, I think. It was as though a tight iron band had been screwed around my neck and up.

MRS ALVING: And then?

OSVALD: At first I didn't think it was anything other than the usual headaches I suffered from so badly when I was growing up.

MRS ALVING: Yes, yes –

OSVALD: But that wasn't it; I soon realized that. I couldn't work any longer. I wanted to start on a big new painting; but it was as though my talents had failed me; all my strength was somehow paralysed; I couldn't focus on any firm ideas; the world swam before me – racing round. Oh, it was a dreadful state to be in. I sent for a doctor in the end – and from him I got my answer.

MRS ALVING: How do you mean?

OSVALD: He was one of the top doctors down there. First I had to describe to him what I was feeling; and then he started asking me a whole lot of questions that I couldn't see the relevance of; I couldn't comprehend what the man was driving at –

MRS ALVING: Well?

OSVALD: Then he finally said it: right from your very birth something in you has been worm-eaten – he used exactly that expression, 'vermoulu'.[62]

MRS ALVING [tense]: What did he mean by that?

OSVALD: I didn't understand it either, and I asked him for a more detailed explanation. And then the old cynic said – [Clenches his fist.] Oh –!

MRS ALVING: What did he say?

OSVALD: He said: the sins of the fathers are visited upon the children.[63]

MRS ALVING [rises slowly]: The sins of the fathers –!

OSVALD: I nearly punched him in the face –

MRS ALVING: The sins of the fathers –

OSVALD [smiles grimly]: Yes, what do you think? Naturally I assured him that such a thing was out of the question. But do you think he gave up even then? No, he held on to his notion; and it was only when I brought out your letters and translated all the passages that were about Father –

MRS ALVING: What then –?

OSVALD: Well, then, of course he had to admit that he was on the wrong track; and so I learned the truth. The inconceivable truth! That I ought to have abstained from those youthful years spent in light-hearted, blessed happiness with my companions. It had been too much for my strength. I have myself to blame!

MRS ALVING: Osvald! Oh no; don't think that!

OSVALD: There was no other possible explanation, he said. *That's* the dreadful thing. An incurable wreck for the rest of my life – due to my own folly! Everything I wanted to accomplish here in the world – not to dare think about it – not to be *able* to think about it. Oh, if only I could just live over again – undo everything I've done!

He throws himself face down on to the sofa.

MRS ALVING wrings her hands and walks back and forth, silently struggling with herself.

OSVALD [*after a while, he looks up and props himself up on his elbow*]: If it had been something inherited at least – something I couldn't have helped. But this! To have thrown away in such a shameful, thoughtless, frivolous way one's own happiness, one's own health, everything in the world – one's future, one's life –!

MRS ALVING: No, no, my dear, darling boy; this is impossible! [*Bending over him*] Your situation isn't as desperate as you think.

OSVALD: Oh, you don't know –. [*Leaps up.*] And then, Mother, that I should cause you all this sorrow! Many's the time I've practically wished and hoped that you didn't really care so much about me.

MRS ALVING: I, Osvald; my only boy! The only thing I have in this world; the only thing I care about.

OSVALD [*grasps both her hands and kisses them*]: Yes, yes, of course, I know that. When I'm at home, of course, I see it. And that's one of the hardest things for me. – But now at least you know. And we shan't talk about it any more today. I can't cope with thinking about it for too long at a time. [*Pacing*] Get me something to drink, Mother!

MRS ALVING: Drink? What do you want to drink now?

OSVALD: Oh, anything. You've got some cold punch in the house.

MRS ALVING: Yes, but Osvald my dear –!

OSVALD: Don't make it difficult, Mother. Please! I *must* have something to wash down all these nagging thoughts. [*Walks into the conservatory.*] Oh, how – how dark it is here!

    MRS ALVING *rings a bell cord to the right.*

OSVALD: And this interminable rain! Week after week it can go on; whole months. Never to get a glimmer of sun! On all my visits home, I can't remember ever seeing the sun shine.

MRS ALVING: Osvald – you're thinking about leaving me!

OSVALD: Hm – [*Drawing a heavy breath*] I'm not thinking about anything. *Can't* think about anything! [*In a low voice*] But I probably won't.

REGINE [*from the dining room*]: Did you ring, ma'am?

MRS ALVING: Yes, let's have the lamp in here.

REGINE: At once, ma'am. It's already lit. [*Goes out.*]

MRS ALVING [*goes over to* OSVALD]: Osvald, don't hold back with me.

OSVALD: I'm not, Mother. [*Goes over to the table.*] I feel I've told you a great deal.

    REGINE *brings the lamp in and puts it on the table.*

MRS ALVING: Listen, Regine, perhaps you could fetch us a half bottle of champagne.

REGINE: Yes, ma'am. [*Goes out again.*]

OSVALD [*strokes his mother's head*]: That's more like it. I knew my mother wouldn't let her boy go thirsty.

MRS ALVING: My poor, dear Osvald; how could I possibly refuse you anything now?

OSVALD [*eagerly*]:[64] Is that *really* true, Mother? Do you mean that?

MRS ALVING: In what way? What do you mean?

OSVALD: That you couldn't refuse me anything?

MRS ALVING: But my dear Osvald –

OSVALD: Shh!

REGINE [*brings in a tray with a half-bottle of champagne and two glasses, which she puts on the table*]: Shall I open –?

OSVALD: No thank you. I'll do it.

    REGINE *goes out again.*

MRS ALVING [*sits at the table*]: What was it you meant – that I shouldn't refuse you?

OSVALD [busy opening the bottle]: First a glass – or two.
    The cork pops; he fills one glass and is about to fill the
    other.
MRS ALVING [holding her hand over it]: Thank you – not
    for me.
OSVALD: Well, for me then!
    He empties his glass, refills it, and empties it again; then
    he sits at the table.
MRS ALVING [expectant]: Well?
OSVALD [without looking at her]: Tell me – I thought you and
    Pastor Manders looked strangely – hm, subdued at the
    supper table.
MRS ALVING: You noticed?
OSVALD: Yes. Hm – [After a brief pause] Tell me – what do
    you think of Regine?
MRS ALVING: What do I think?
OSVALD: Yes, isn't she splendid?
MRS ALVING: Osvald dear, you don't know her as well as I do –
OSVALD: So?
MRS ALVING: I'm afraid Regine remained at home too long. I
    should have brought her here earlier.
OSVALD: Yes, but isn't she splendid to look at, Mother? [Fills
    his glass.]
MRS ALVING: Regine has many serious flaws –
OSVALD: Oh, what does that matter?
    He drinks again.
MRS ALVING: But I am fond of her nonetheless; and I am
    responsible for her. I wouldn't want anything to happen to
    her for all the world.
OSVALD [jumps to his feet]: Mother, Regine is my only
    salvation!
MRS ALVING [gets up]: What do you mean?
OSVALD: I can't bear this mental torment on my own here.
MRS ALVING: Don't you have your mother to bear it with you?
OSVALD: Yes, that was what I thought; and that's why I came
    home to you. But it won't work. I can see it; it won't work.
    Life will be unbearable for me out here!
MRS ALVING: Osvald!

OSVALD: I must live differently, Mother. Which is why I must leave you. I shan't have you seeing it.

MRS ALVING: My poor, unhappy boy! Oh but Osvald, while you're as ill as you are now –

OSVALD: If it was just the illness alone, I'd probably stay with you, Mother. You're the best friend I have in the world.

MRS ALVING: Yes, that's right, Osvald; I am, aren't I!

OSVALD [*wandering restlessly about*]: But it's the agony, the gnawing, the regret – and then this terrible anguish. Oh – this deathly anguish.

MRS ALVING [*following him*]: Anguish? What anguish? What do you mean?

OSVALD: Oh, you mustn't ask me more. I don't know. I can't describe it for you.

MRS ALVING *goes over to the right and pulls the bell rope.*

OSVALD: What do you want?

MRS ALVING: I want my boy to be happy, that's what. He shan't go around here brooding. [*To* REGINE, *who appears in the doorway*] More champagne. A whole bottle.

REGINE *goes.*

OSVALD: Mother!

MRS ALVING: Don't you think we know how to live out here on the estate too?

OSVALD: Isn't she splendid to look at? Look how she's built! So strong and healthy.

MRS ALVING [*sits at the table*]: Sit down, Osvald, and let's talk calmly together.

OSVALD [*sitting*]: You probably don't know this, Mother, but I've done Regine a wrong that I must make good.

MRS ALVING: You!

OSVALD: Or a little foolishness – whatever you want to call it. Very innocent, by the way. When I was last home –

MRS ALVING: Yes?

OSVALD: – she often asked me about Paris, so I'd tell her a bit about things down there. Then I remember one day I found myself saying: wouldn't you like to come down there yourself?

MRS ALVING: And?

OSVALD: I saw her turn bright red, and then she said: yes, I'd really like that. All right, I answered, I'm sure that can be arranged – or something of the sort.

MRS ALVING: And?

OSVALD: Naturally I'd forgotten the whole thing. But when I asked her the day before yesterday whether she was pleased I was staying at home for so long –

MRS ALVING: Yes?

OSVALD: – she looked at me really oddly, and then asked: but what's going to happen about my trip to Paris?

MRS ALVING: Her trip!

OSVALD: And then I got it out of her that she'd taken the whole thing seriously, that she'd gone around here thinking about me the whole time, and that she'd even tried to learn French –

MRS ALVING: So that's why –

OSVALD: Mother – when I saw that splendid, beautiful, healthy young girl standing before me – I'd never of course noticed her much before – but when she stood there, as if with open arms ready to receive me –

MRS ALVING: Osvald!

OSVALD: – then I realized that it was in her my salvation lay; because I saw the joy of life in her.

MRS ALVING [surprised]: The joy of life –? Can there be salvation in that?

REGINE [entering from the dining room with a bottle of champagne]: I'm sorry I took so long; but I had to go down to the cellar – [Puts the bottle on the table.]

OSVALD: And fetch another glass.

REGINE [looks at him in surprise]: Ma'am's glass is there, Mr Alving.

OSVALD: Yes, but get one for yourself, Regine.

REGINE gives a start and flashes a shy, sidelong glance in MRS ALVING's direction.

OSVALD: Well?

REGINE [quietly and hesitantly]: Is that with Ma'am's permission –?

MRS ALVING: Fetch the glass, Regine.

REGINE *goes out into the dining room.*

OSVALD [*watches her as she goes*]: Have you noticed how she walks? So bold, so unabashed.

MRS ALVING: This isn't happening, Osvald!

OSVALD: The matter is decided. Surely you can see that. There's no use objecting.

    REGINE *comes in with an empty glass, which she keeps in her hand.*

OSVALD: Sit down, Regine.

    REGINE *gives* MRS ALVING *a questioning look.*

MRS ALVING: Sit down.

    REGINE *sits on a chair near the dining-room door, still holding the empty glass.*

MRS ALVING: Osvald – what were you saying about the joy of life?

OSVALD: Yes, the joy of life, Mother – no one knows much about that here at home. I never feel it here.

MRS ALVING: Not when you're with me?

OSVALD: Not when I'm home. But you don't understand that.

MRS ALVING: Yes, yes, I think I almost do understand – now.

OSVALD: That – and the joy of work. Well, they're one and the same thing really. But none of you know anything about that either.

MRS ALVING: You're probably right. Tell me more, Osvald.

OSVALD: Well, it's just that I think people here are taught to believe that work is a curse and punishment for their sins, that life's something miserable, something we'd do best to get out of, sooner rather than later.

MRS ALVING: A vale of tears, yes. And we certainly succeed in making it so.

OSVALD: And that's precisely what people refuse to accept out there. Nobody really believes in those teachings any more. Out there you can feel a kind of blessed elation at just being in the world. Mother, have you noticed that everything I've painted has been about the joy of life? Always, always about the joy of life? With light and sunshine[65] and Sunday in the air – and radiant, happy faces. That's why I'm afraid of staying here at home with you.

MRS ALVING: Afraid? What is it you're afraid of here with me?

OSVALD: I'm afraid that everything that's finest in me might turn to ugliness here.

MRS ALVING [*fixes her gaze on him*]: You really believe *that* would happen?

OSVALD: I know it for certain. Live the same life here at home as out there, and still it wouldn't be the same life.

MRS ALVING [*having listened intently, gets up with big, thoughtful eyes*]: Now I see how it all fits together.

OSVALD: What do you see?

MRS ALVING: Now I see it for the first time. And now I can speak.

OSVALD [*gets up*]: Mother, I don't understand.

REGINE [*getting up too*]: Perhaps I should go?

MRS ALVING: No, stay here. Now I can speak. Now, my boy, you shall know everything. And then you can choose. Osvald! Regine!

OSVALD: Quiet! It's the pastor.

MANDERS [*comes in through the hall door*]: Well, we've had a most heart-warming moment down there.

OSVALD: So have we.

MANDERS: Engstrand must be helped with this sailors' home. Regine must move in with him and help him out –

REGINE: No, thank you, pastor.

MANDERS [*only just noticing her*]: What –? Here – and with a glass in your hand?

REGINE [*putting the glass down quickly*]: *Pardonnez moi –!*

OSVALD: Regine will be moving, but with me, Pastor Manders.

MANDERS: Moving? With you!

OSVALD: Yes, as my wife – if she so demands.

MANDERS: Mercy on us –!

REGINE: It's none of my doing, pastor.

OSVALD: Or she'll stay here, if I stay.

REGINE [*involuntarily*]: Here?

MANDERS: I am utterly mortified by you, Mrs Alving.

MRS ALVING: Neither thing will happen; because I can speak out now.

MANDERS: No, but you won't, surely! No, no, no!

MRS ALVING: Oh yes, I both can and will. And no ideals will be destroyed in so doing.

OSVALD: Mother, what's being hidden from me here?

REGINE [*listening*]: Ma'am! Listen! There are people scream-ing outside.

She goes into the conservatory and looks out.

OSVALD [*going towards the window on the left*]: What's going on? Where's that light coming from?

REGINE [*shouts*]: The orphanage is on fire!

MRS ALVING [*going towards the window*]: On fire!

MANDERS: On fire? Impossible. I was only just down there.

OSVALD: Where's my hat? Oh, never mind –. Father's orphan-age! [*Runs out through the garden door.*]

MRS ALVING: My shawl, Regine! The whole place is alight!

MANDERS: Terrible! Mrs Alving, *there* blazes the judgement on this house of disorder.

MRS ALVING: Yes, I'm sure. Come on, Regine.

MRS ALVING *and* REGINE *hurry out through the hallway.*

MANDERS [*clasping his hands*]: And not insured! [*Follows them out.*]

ACT THREE

The room as before. All the doors are open. The lamp is still burning on the table. It is dark outside apart from a faint glow to the left in the background.

MRS ALVING, *with a large shawl over her head, is standing in the conservatory, looking out.* REGINE, *also wearing a shawl, stands slightly behind her.*

MRS ALVING: Everything's burned. Right to the ground.

REGINE: It's still burning in the cellar.

MRS ALVING: Why doesn't Osvald come up? There's nothing to be saved.

REGINE: Shall I maybe go down to him with his hat?

MRS ALVING: He doesn't even have his hat?

REGINE [*pointing to the hall*]: No, it's hanging there.

MRS ALVING: Let it hang there. Surely he must be coming up soon. I'll go and look for him myself.

She goes out through the garden door.

MANDERS [*coming in from the hall*]: Isn't Mrs Alving here?

REGINE: She just went down into the garden.

MANDERS: This is the most horrendous night I've ever experienced.

REGINE: Yes, a dreadful accident, isn't it, pastor?

MANDERS: Oh, don't talk about it! I barely dare think about it.

REGINE: But how can it have happened –?

MANDERS: Don't ask me, Miss Engstrand! How would *I* know that? Perhaps *you're* also –? Isn't it enough that your father –?

REGINE: What about him?

MANDERS: Oh, he's put my head in a complete spin.

ENGSTRAND [*comes in from the hall*]: Pastor –!

MANDERS [*turning round with a look of terror*]: Are you after me here too?

ENGSTRAND: Yes, I've got to bleedin' well –! Oh, Lord forgive me! But this is all so terrible, pastor!

MANDERS [*pacing up and down*]: Alas it is, alas!

REGINE: What's going on?

ENGSTRAND: Oh, it all started with this here prayer meeting, see. [*Quietly*] We've got the old goat now, my child! [*Loudly*] And to think that *I* should be to blame for Pastor Manders' being to blame for such a thing!

MANDERS: But I assure you, Engstrand –

ENGSTRAND: But there weren't nobody but the pastor carrying on with the candles down there.

MANDERS [*halts*]: Yes, so you insist. But I honestly can't recall having a candle in my hand.

ENGSTRAND: And there's me, what distinctly *saw* the pastor take the candle, snuff it out with his fingers and throw the stub right there into the shavings.

MANDERS: And you saw me do that?

ENGSTRAND: Aye, saw it plain.

MANDERS: I just cannot comprehend it. It's not my habit to put candles out with my fingers.

ENGSTRAND: Aye, and awful careless it looked. But can it really be so bad, pastor?

MANDERS [*pacing back and forth uneasily*]: Oh, don't ask!

ENGSTRAND [*walks with him*]: And the pastor hasn't insured it either?

MANDERS [*still pacing*]: No, no, no. You heard what I said.

ENGSTRAND [*following him about*]: Not insured! And then to go right over and set fire to the whole lot. Jesus, Jesus, what a disaster!

MANDERS [*wiping the sweat from his forehead*]: Yes, you may well say that, Engstrand.

ENGSTRAND: And to think such a thing should happen to a charitable institution, what was to be of benefit to both

town and country, as they says. I don't suppose the magazines will go too gentle on the pastor.

MANDERS: No, that's just what I keep thinking. That's almost
the worst thing about all this. All those hateful attacks and
accusations –! Oh, it's too frightful to contemplate!

MRS ALVING [*comes in from the garden*]: Nothing will induce
him to come away from the embers.

MANDERS: Ah, there you are, Mrs Alving.

MRS ALVING: Well, you got out of giving your speech, Pastor
Manders.

MANDERS: Oh, I would so gladly have –

MRS ALVING [*in a low voice*]: It was best it went as it did. That
orphanage would not have brought any blessing with it.

MANDERS: You think not?

MRS ALVING: Do *you* think so?

MANDERS: But it was a terrible misfortune all the same.

MRS ALVING: Let's keep this short and sweet, talk it over as
a business matter. – Are you waiting for Pastor Manders,
Engstrand?

ENGSTRAND [*in the doorway to the hall*]: Aye, that I am.

MRS ALVING: Then do sit down, for now.

ENGSTRAND: Thank you, I'm all right standing.

MRS ALVING [*to* PASTOR MANDERS]: You'll be leaving on the
steamboat presumably?

MANDERS: Yes, it leaves in an hour.

MRS ALVING: Please, be so good as to take all the papers back
with you. I don't want to hear another word about this
matter. I've got other things to think about now –

MANDERS: Mrs Alving –

MRS ALVING: I'll send you the power of attorney later, for you
to arrange everything as you wish.

MANDERS: I'll take that upon myself most gladly. Unfortunately the original terms of the bequest must be completely
altered now.

MRS ALVING: That stands to reason.

MANDERS: Yes, my initial thoughts are that I'll arrange for
the Solvik estate to be transferred to the parish.[66] The
arable land cannot, of course, be said to be entirely without

value. It'll always come in useful for something. And as for the interest from the capital in the savings bank, perhaps I could best use it to support some venture that might be seen to be of benefit to the town.

MRS ALVING: Just as you wish. The matter's of complete indifference to me now.

ENGSTRAND: Don't forget my sailors' home, pastor!

MANDERS: Yes, certainly, now you mention it. Although it'll need careful evaluation.

ENGSTRAND: To hell with evaluating –. Lord, forgive me!

MANDERS [with a sigh]: And then, unfortunately, I don't know how much longer I shall be dealing with these matters. Whether public opinion might not force me to step down. That, of course, is wholly dependent on the outcome of the fire investigation.

MRS ALVING: What are you saying?

MANDERS: And the outcome cannot possibly be guessed at beforehand.

ENGSTRAND [coming closer to him]: Oh aye, but it can. For here before you stands I, Jakob Engstrand in person.

MANDERS: Yes, but –?

ENGSTRAND [lowering his voice]: And Jakob Engstrand in't the man to desert a worthy benefactor in his hour of need, as they says.

MANDERS: Yes, but my dear man – how –?

ENGSTRAND: Jakob Engstrand is like as to an angel of deliverance, pastor!

MANDERS: No, no, I honestly couldn't accept such a thing.

ENGSTRAND: Oh, I reckon what will be, will be. I know someone what's taken the blame upon himself for others once before.

MANDERS: Jakob! [Shaking his hand.] You are a rare character. Well, you shall be helped too, with your sailors' refuge; on that you can depend.

ENGSTRAND wants to thank him but cannot from sheer emotion.

MANDERS [puts his travel bag over his shoulder]: Let's be off. The two of us will travel together.

ENGSTRAND [*by the dining-room door, quietly to* REGINE]:
Follow me, girl. You'll live in a gold-feathered nest.[67]

REGINE [*tosses her head*]: Merci!

She goes out into the hall and fetches the PASTOR's *travelling clothes.*

MANDERS: I wish you well, Mrs Alving! And may a spirit of
orderliness and lawfulness soon enter this dwelling.

MRS ALVING: Farewell, Manders!

She walks towards the conservatory, where she sees
OSVALD *coming through the garden door.*

ENGSTRAND [*as he and* REGINE *help the* PASTOR *on with his*
coat]: Goodbye, my child. And if you're ever in trouble, you
know where to find Jakob Engstrand. [*Quietly*] Little Harbour
Street, eh –! [*To* MRS ALVING *and* OSVALD] And the house for
those wayfaring sailors, it'll be called 'Chamberlain Alving's
Home', it will. And if I get to run it according to *my* designs, I
dare promise it'll be worthy of the chamberlain, God rest him.

MANDERS [*at the door*]: Hm – hm! Come along, my dear Engstrand. Goodbye; goodbye!

He and ENGSTRAND *go out through the hall.*

OSVALD [*going over to the table*]: What sort of house was he
talking about?

MRS ALVING: Oh, it's some kind of refuge that he and Pastor
Manders want to set up.

OSVALD: It'll burn just like this one.

MRS ALVING: What makes you say that?

OSVALD: Everything will burn. There'll be nothing left as a
reminder of Father. And I'm burning up here too.

REGINE *looks at him, taken aback.*

MRS ALVING: Osvald! You shouldn't have stayed down there
so long, my poor boy.

OSVALD [*sits down at the table*]: I think perhaps you're right.

MRS ALVING: Let me dry your face, Osvald; you're quite wet.
[*She dries his face with her handkerchief*]

OSVALD [*stares expressionlessly ahead of him*]: Thank you,
Mother.

MRS ALVING: Aren't you tired, Osvald? Do you want to sleep
perhaps?

OSVALD [*afraid*]: Sleep – no, no! I never sleep; I only pretend. [*Gloomily*] That will come soon enough.

MRS ALVING [*looks worriedly at him*]: I think you must be ill after all, my darling boy.

REGINE [*tense*]: Is Mr Alving ill?

OSVALD [*impatiently*]: And close all the doors! This deathly anguish –

MRS ALVING: Close them, Regine.

REGINE *shuts the doors and stands by the hall door.* MRS ALVING *takes her shawl off;* REGINE *does likewise.*

MRS ALVING [*draws a chair close to* OSVALD's, *and sits by him*]: There. Let me sit beside you now –

OSVALD: Yes do. And Regine must stay here too. Regine must always be near me. You'll reach out that helping hand to me, Regine. Won't you?

REGINE: I don't understand –

MRS ALVING: Helping hand?

OSVALD: Yes – when it's called for.

MRS ALVING: Osvald, don't you have your mother here to reach out a hand to you?

OSVALD: You? [*Smiling*] No, mother, that helping hand you will never give me. [*Laughing sadly*] You! Ha-ha! [*Looks at her seriously.*] Mind you, there could hardly be anyone more appropriate. [*Suddenly angry*] Why are you so formal with me,[68] Regine? Why can't you call me Osvald?

REGINE [*quietly*]: I don't think ma'am would like it.

MRS ALVING: Very soon you will be allowed to. So come here and sit down with us, you too.

REGINE *sits quietly and hesitantly on the other side of the table.*

MRS ALVING: And now, my poor tormented boy, now I shall lift the burdens from your mind –

OSVALD: You, Mother?

MRS ALVING: – everything you've spoken of, guilt and regret and self-reproach –

OSVALD: And you think you can do that?

MRS ALVING: Yes, now I can, Osvald. You were talking earlier about the joy of life; and it was as though a new light

was shed over everything that's happened in my entire
life.

OSVALD [*shakes his head*]: I don't understand.

MRS ALVING: You should have known your father when he
was a young lieutenant. *He* was certainly filled with the joy
of life!

OSVALD: Yes, I know.

MRS ALVING: It was like a sunny Sunday[69] just looking at him.
And such incredible energy and vitality he had!

OSVALD: And –?

MRS ALVING: And then this joyous child, because he *was* like
a child back then – had to while away his time here, in a
middling-sized town that had no real joy to offer, only diver-
sions. He was stuck here without any vocation in life, with
nothing but a civil service appointment.[70] With no glimmer
of any work which he could throw himself into with all his
soul – he had nothing but paperwork. Without one single
friend capable of feeling what the joy of life might be; only
layabouts and drinking companions –

OSVALD: Mother –!

MRS ALVING: Then what had to happen happened.

OSVALD: What had to happen?

MRS ALVING: You said yourself earlier this evening, how
things would be for you if you stayed at home.

OSVALD: Are you trying to say that Father –?

MRS ALVING: Your poor father could never find any outlet for
this excessive joy of life inside him. And I didn't bring any
Sunday sunshine into his home either.

OSVALD: Not even you?

MRS ALVING: They had taught me about duties and the like,
things I've gone around believing in for so long. It always
seemed to come down to duty – *my* duties and *his* duties
and –. I'm afraid I made this home unbearable for your poor
father, Osvald.

OSVALD: Why didn't you ever write about any of this to me?

MRS ALVING: I've never seen it before in terms that meant I
could touch on it with you – his son.

OSVALD: So how did you see it then?

MRS ALVING [*slowly*]: I saw only one thing; that your father was a broken man before you were born.

OSVALD [*quietly*]: Ah –!

He gets up and goes over to the window.

MRS ALVING: And day in and day out I thought about this one thing; that Regine actually belonged here in this house – as much as my own son.

OSVALD [*turning suddenly*]: Regine –?

REGINE [*leaps up and asks quietly*]: Me –?

MRS ALVING: Yes, now you know it, both of you.

OSVALD: Regine!

REGINE [*to herself*]: So Mother was that sort.

MRS ALVING: Your mother was good in many ways, Regine.

REGINE: Yes, but she was still that sort. Well, I've thought as much sometimes, but –. Well, Mrs Alving, may I have permission to leave at once?

MRS ALVING: Do you really want that, Regine?

REGINE: Yes, indeed I do.

MRS ALVING: You're naturally free to do as you wish, but –

OSVALD [*moves towards* REGINE]: Leave now? But this is where you belong.

REGINE: *Merci*, Mr Alving – well, I suppose I can say Osvald now.[71] But it really wasn't in *that* way I'd thought it.

MRS ALVING: Regine, I haven't been open with you –

REGINE: No, shame to say, you haven't. If I'd known Osvald was sickly –. And now that there can't ever be anything serious between us –. No, I really can't be staying out here in the country wearing myself out on invalids.

OSVALD: Not even for somebody who's so close to you?

REGINE: Not likely. A poor girl has to take advantage of her youth; otherwise she might end up with nothing[72] before she knows it. And *I* have the joy of life in me too, ma'am!

MRS ALVING: Yes, unfortunately; but just don't throw yourself away, Regine.

REGINE: Oh, whatever will be will be. If Osvald takes after his father, I probably take after my mother, I reckon. – May I ask, ma'am, if Pastor Manders knows all this about me?

MRS ALVING: Pastor Manders knows everything.

REGINE [*busies herself with her shawl*]: Right, then I'd better make sure to get on that steamboat as quick as I can. Pastor Manders is so nice, so easy to deal with, and I certainly think I've as much right to a bit of that money as him – that vile carpenter.

MRS ALVING: Indeed you have, Regine.

REGINE [*staring straight at* MRS ALVING]: Madam might have done better to raise me as a gentleman's daughter; that would have suited me better. [*Tossing her head*] But hell – makes no difference! [*With a bitter glance at the unopened bottle*] I might get to drink champagne with gentlefolk yet.

MRS ALVING: And if you ever need a home, Regine, then come to me.

REGINE: No thank you, ma'am. I'm sure Pastor Manders will look after me. And if things go really wrong, then I know a house where I do belong.

MRS ALVING: Where?

REGINE: Chamberlain Alving's Home.

MRS ALVING: Regine – I see it now – you're going to your ruin!

REGINE: Pah! *Adieu.*

   She curtseys and goes out through the hall.

OSVALD [*looking out of the window*]: Has she gone?

MRS ALVING: Yes.

OSVALD [*mumbles to himself*]: I think it was wrong, all this.

MRS ALVING [*goes behind him and lays her hands on his shoulders*]: Osvald, my dearest boy – has it shaken you badly?

OSVALD [*turns to face her*]: All this about Father you mean?

MRS ALVING: Yes, about your unhappy father. I'm frightened it might have affected you badly.

OSVALD: How can you think that? It came as a huge surprise, of course; but it doesn't basically make any difference.

MRS ALVING [*pulls her hands away*]: No difference! That your father was desperately unhappy!

OSVALD: Of course I can feel sympathy for *him*, as for any other person, but –

MRS ALVING: Nothing more? For your own father!

OSVALD [*impatiently*]: Oh Father – Father! I've never known anything about Father. The only thing I remember about him is that he made me throw up once.

MRS ALVING: That's a dreadful thought! Shouldn't a child feel love for his father even then?

OSVALD: When a child has nothing to thank his father for? Has never known him? Are you really holding so tight to that old superstition, when you're so enlightened otherwise?

MRS ALVING: And for you it's just a superstition –?

OSVALD: Yes, you must surely see that, Mother. It's one of those opinions put in circulation in the world, and then –

MRS ALVING [*shaken*]: Ghosts!

OSVALD [*walking across the floor*]: Yes, you may well call them ghosts.

MRS ALVING [*agitated*]: Osvald – so you don't love me either!

OSVALD: I know you at least –

MRS ALVING: Yes, you know me; but that's all!

OSVALD: And I know how fond you are of me; and I have to be grateful for that. And you can be so tremendously helpful to me, now that I'm ill.

MRS ALVING: Yes, I can, can't I, Osvald? Oh, I could almost bless the illness that drove you home to me. Because I can see that now, I don't *have* you – I must *win* you.

OSVALD [*impatiently*]: Yes, yes; these are just so many empty phrases. You've got to remember that I'm a sick man, Mother. I can't concern myself much with others; I've enough to do thinking about myself.

MRS ALVING [*in a soft voice*]: I'll be patient and undemanding.

OSVALD: And cheerful too, Mother!

MRS ALVING: Yes, my dearest boy, you're quite right. [*Walks over to him.*] Have I taken away all the regret and self-reproach now?

OSVALD: Yes, you have. But who'll remove this anguish?

MRS ALVING: Anguish?

OSVALD [*walks across the floor*]: Regine would have done it, without hesitation.

MRS ALVING: I don't understand. What is all this about anguish – and Regine?

OSVALD: Is it very late in the night, Mother?

MRS ALVING: It's almost morning. [*Looking out into the conservatory*] Dawn's beginning to break over the mountaintops. And it's going to be a clear day, Osvald! Soon you'll see the sun.

OSVALD: I look forward to that. Oh, there may be many things for me to be joyful about and live for –

MRS ALVING: I should think so!

OSVALD: Even if perhaps I can't work, then –

MRS ALVING: Oh, you'll soon be able to work again now, my dearest boy. Now you no longer have all those nagging, oppressive thoughts to brood over.

OSVALD: Yes, it was good that you managed to lift all those illusions from me. And now that I've come through that – [*Sits on the sofa.*] We're going to talk now, Mother –

MRS ALVING: Yes, let's.

She pushes an armchair towards the sofa and sits close to him.

OSVALD: – and the sun will rise as we do so. And then you will know. And then I'll no longer have this anguish.

MRS ALVING: What will I know?

OSVALD [*without listening to her*]: Mother, didn't you say earlier this evening that there wasn't a thing in the world that you wouldn't do for me if I asked?

MRS ALVING: Yes, I did say that!

OSVALD: And you stand by that, Mother?

MRS ALVING: You can depend on it, my darling only boy! I live for nothing else, just for you alone.

OSVALD: Yes, all right, let me tell you –. Listen, Mother, you have a strong powerful mind, I know you do. Now, you're going to sit very calmly as you listen to this.

MRS ALVING: But what terrible thing is it –?

OSVALD: You're not to scream. You hear? Do you promise me? We'll sit and talk very calmly about this. Do you promise me, Mother?

MRS ALVING: Yes, yes, I promise; just tell me!

OSVALD: Well, the fact is that my being tired – and my inability to think about work – that's not the illness itself –

MRS ALVING: What is the illness then?

OSVALD: The disease that I've inherited,[73] it – [*points to his forehead and adds very quietly*] it's lodged in here.[74]

MRS ALVING [*almost speechless*]: Osvald! No – no!

OSVALD: Don't scream. I can't bear it. Oh, yes, it sits lurking in here. And it can break loose at any moment, any hour.

MRS ALVING: Oh, what horror –!

OSVALD: Stay calm now. That's the way things are –

MRS ALVING [*leaps to her feet*]: This isn't true, Osvald! It's not possible! It can't be!

OSVALD: I had *one* attack down there.[75] It soon passed. But when I got to know what a state I'd been in, that was when the anguish came raging over me, hounding me; and so I came home to you as quickly as I could.

MRS ALVING: So that's the anguish –!

OSVALD: Yes, because this thing is so indescribably hideous, you see. If only it had been some ordinary mortal illness –. Because I'm not afraid of dying; although, of course, I'd like to live as long as possible.

MRS ALVING: Yes, yes, Osvald, you must!

OSVALD: But this is so dreadfully hideous! Like being turned back into a baby again; having to be fed, having to be –. Oh – it can't be described!

MRS ALVING: A child has its mother to nurse it.

OSVALD [*leaps up*]: No, never; that's exactly what I don't want! I can't bear the idea that I might live like that for years on end – getting old and grey. And then you might die and leave me. [*Sits down in* MRS ALVING's *chair.*] Because it wouldn't necessarily prove fatal straight away, the doctor said. He called it a kind of softening of the brain – or something similar. [*Smiles tiredly.*] I think that phrase sounds so lovely. I'll always think of cherry-coloured, velvety drapes – something that's delicate to stroke.

MRS ALVING [*screams*]: Osvald!

OSVALD [*leaps up again and walks across the room*]: And now you have taken Regine from me! If only I had her! She'd have given me that helping hand, I'm sure.

MRS ALVING [*goes over to him*]: What do you mean, my darling boy? Could there possibly be any kind of helping hand I wouldn't want to give you?

OSVALD: When I got over my attack in Paris, my doctor told me that when it comes again – and it will come again – there will be no more hope.

MRS ALVING: How could he be so heartless as to say –

OSVALD: I forced him to it. I told him I had arrangements to make –. [*Smiles slyly.*] And I had too. [*Takes a little box from his breast pocket.*] Mother, you see this?

MRS ALVING: What is it?

OSVALD: Morphine powder.

MRS ALVING [*looks at him in shock*]: Osvald – my boy?

OSVALD: I've managed to save up twelve capsules –.

MRS ALVING [*snatching at it*]: Give me the box, Osvald!

OSVALD: Not yet, Mother.

> *He hides the box away in his pocket again.*

MRS ALVING: I am not going to survive this!

OSVALD: It must be survived. If I'd had Regine here now, I would have told her how things were with me – and asked her for that last helping hand. She would have helped me; I'm certain of it.

MRS ALVING: Never!

OSVALD: As soon as this dreadful thing had overtaken me, and she saw me lying there as helpless as a little baby, incurable, lost, hopeless – beyond salvation –

MRS ALVING: Regine would never have done this!

OSVALD: Regine would have done it. Regine was so admirably light-hearted. And she'd soon get bored of looking after an invalid like me.

MRS ALVING: Then thank goodness Regine's not here!

OSVALD: So, now you must give me that helping hand, Mother.

MRS ALVING [*screams loudly*]: Me!

OSVALD: Who more appropriate than you?

MRS ALVING: Me? Your mother!

OSVALD: That's precisely why.

MRS ALVING: Me, who gave you life!

OSVALD: I didn't ask you for life. And what kind of life is it you've given me? I don't want it! You'll take it back!

MRS ALVING: Help! Help!

She runs out into the hall.

OSVALD [*chasing after her*]: Don't leave me! Where are you going?

MRS ALVING [*in the hall*]: To fetch the doctor for you, Osvald! Let me get out!

OSVALD [*in the hall*]: You're not getting out of here. And nobody's coming in.

A key is turned.

MRS ALVING [*comes back in*]: Osvald! Osvald – my child!

OSVALD [*following her*]: Do you have a mother's heart – when you can watch me suffering this unspeakable anguish!

MRS ALVING [*after a moment's silence, says in a controlled voice*]: Here is my hand on it.

OSVALD: Will you –?

MRS ALVING: If it is necessary. But it won't *be* necessary. No, never, it's impossible!

OSVALD: Well, let's hope so. And let's live together as long as we can. Thank you, Mother.

He sits in the armchair that MRS ALVING *has moved over to the sofa. Day is breaking; the lamp is still burning on the table.*

MRS ALVING [*approaches him cautiously*]: Do you feel calm now?

OSVALD: Yes.

MRS ALVING [*leaning over him*]: This has all been a terrible figment of your imagination, Osvald. All of it a figment. All this turmoil has been too much for you. But now you'll be able to rest. At home with your own mother, my blessed boy. Whatever you point at will be yours, just as when you were a little child. – You see. Now the attack is over. You see how easily it went! Oh, I knew it. – And do you see, Osvald, what a beautiful day we're going to have? Bright sunshine! Now you can really get to see your home.

She goes over to the table and puts out the lamp. Sunrise. The glacier and peaks in the background are bathed in gleaming morning light.

OSVALD [*sits in the armchair with his back towards the land-scape, without moving; suddenly he says*]: Mother, give me the sun.

MRS ALVING [*by the table, looks at him, puzzled*]: What did you say?

OSVALD [*repeats dully and tonelessly*]: The sun. The sun.

MRS ALVING [*goes across to him*]: Osvald, how are you feeling?

  OSVALD *seems to shrink in his chair; all his muscles go limp; his face is expressionless; his eyes stare vacantly.*

MRS ALVING [*trembling with fear*]: What is this? [*Screams loudly*] Osvald! What's the matter with you? [*She gets on her knees and shakes him.*] Osvald! Osvald! Look at me! Don't you know me?

OSVALD [*toneless as before*]: The sun. – The sun.

MRS ALVING [*jumps to her feet in despair, tears at her hair with both hands and screams*]: This is unbearable! [*Whispers as though paralysed*] This is unbearable! Never! [*Abruptly*] Where does he keep them? [*Searching his chest urgently*] Here! [*Shrinks back a step or two and screams*] No; no; no! – Yes! – No; no!

  She stands a few steps away from him with her hands twisted in her hair and stares at him in speechless horror.

OSVALD [*sits motionless as before and says*]: The sun. – The sun.

AN ENEMY OF THE PEOPLE[1]

THE PEOPLE[1]

A Play[2] in Five Acts

CHARACTERS

DOCTOR TOMAS STOCKMANN,
the spa's medical officer[3]
MRS[4] STOCKMANN, *his wife*
PETRA, *their daughter, a teacher*[5]
EILIF[6] and MORTEN, *their sons,*
aged thirteen and ten
PETER STOCKMANN, *the doctor's elder brother,*
mayor of the town and local police chief,[7]
chairman of the spa's board, etc.
MORTEN KIIL, *a master tanner,*
Mrs Stockmann's guardian
HOVSTAD, *editor of* The People's Messenger[8]
BILLING, *assistant on* The People's Messenger
HORSTER, *a ship's captain*
ASLAKSEN, *a printer*
PEOPLE AT A PUBLIC MEETING,
MEN OF VARIOUS CLASSES AND OCCUPATIONS,[9]
A FEW WOMEN, AND A GROUP OF SCHOOLBOYS

The action takes place in a coastal
town in southern Norway.

ACT ONE

Evening in the doctor's living room; it is modestly but pleas-antly furnished. In the right-hand wall there are two doors; the door further back leads out to the hall, the nearer one leads into the doctor's study. In the facing wall, opposite the hall door, is a door leading to the other rooms occupied by the family. In the middle of this wall is the wood-burner, and closer to the foreground a couch with a mirror over it, and an oval table with a table covering[10] in front of it. On the table is a lit lamp with a lampshade. An open door in the background leads to the dining room. Inside, a dining table laid out for an evening meal, also with a lamp on it.

BILLING *is sitting at the dining table with a napkin under his chin.* MRS STOCKMANN *is standing by the table, handing him a plate with a large slice of roast beef on it. The other places at the table are abandoned, and the table is in disarray, as at the end of a meal.*

MRS STOCKMANN: Well, when you come an hour late, Mr Billing,[11] you have to make do with cold food.

BILLING [*eating*]: It's marvellous – absolutely perfect.

MRS STOCKMANN: You know how precise Stockmann is about keeping to his meal times –

BILLING: It doesn't bother me in the least. I almost think it tastes better when I can sit and eat like this alone and undisturbed.

MRS STOCKMANN: Well, as long as you're enjoying it –. [*Turns to the hall door, listening*] I expect that'll be Mr Hovstad.

BILLING: Yes, perhaps.

The MAYOR *comes in. He is wearing an overcoat and his official hat and carries a stick.*

THE MAYOR: A very good evening, Katrine.

MRS STOCKMANN [*coming into the living room*]: Well I never – so it's you? Good evening. How nice of you to come up and see us!

THE MAYOR: I was just passing, so – [*Glances towards the dining room.*] Ah, but you're entertaining, it seems.

MRS STOCKMANN [*a little embarrassed*]: No, absolutely not; it's just a chance visit. [*Hurriedly*] Wouldn't you like to go in and have a bite too?

THE MAYOR: Me! No, thank you. Heavens above, hot food in the evening; not with *my* digestion.

MRS STOCKMANN: Oh, but just for once –.

THE MAYOR: No, no, bless you; I'll stick to my tea and buttered bread. It's healthier in the long run – and rather more economical too.

MRS STOCKMANN [*smiling*]: You really mustn't go thinking that Tomas and I are complete spendthrifts.

THE MAYOR: Not you, sister-in-law; that couldn't be further from my mind. [*Points towards the* DOCTOR's *study*] He isn't home perhaps?

MRS STOCKMANN: No, he's gone for a little walk after supper – he and the boys.

THE MAYOR: Goodness me, can that be healthy? [*Listens.*] Ah, that's probably him.

MRS STOCKMANN: No, that's unlikely. [*A knock at the door*] Come in!

MR HOVSTAD *enters from the hall.*

MRS STOCKMANN: Well, well, if it isn't Mr Hovstad –!

HOVSTAD: Yes, I do apologize; I was held up over at the printshop. Good evening, Mr Mayor.

THE MAYOR [*greets him rather stiffly*]: Mr Hovstad. Editor. Come on business, I take it?

HOVSTAD: In part. It's something that might go in the newspaper.

THE MAYOR: That I can believe. My brother seems, from what I hear, to be an extremely prolific contributor to *The People's Messenger.*

HOVSTAD: Yes, he allows himself to write in *The People's Messenger* when he has a home truth to offer about this or that.

MRS STOCKMANN [*to* HOVSTAD]: But, wouldn't you like to –? [*Points towards the dining room.*]

THE MAYOR: Well, good Lord, I don't blame him in the least for writing for the readership among whom he might expect to find most sympathy. Besides, I've no personal reason, of course, to harbour any ill-will towards your newspaper, Mr Hovstad.

HOVSTAD: No, quite right.

THE MAYOR: All in all, a marvellous spirit of tolerance reigns in our town; an excellent sense of public spirit.[12] And that comes from our having a great common venture to rally around – a venture that's of equal concern to every right-minded citizen –

HOVSTAD: The Spa Institute, yes.

THE MAYOR: Precisely. We have our great, new, magnificent Spa Institute. You mark my words! The Spa will prove to be this town's most precious asset, Mr Hovstad. Without a doubt!

MRS STOCKMANN: That's precisely what Tomas says.

THE MAYOR: What a remarkable upturn this town has had in just the last couple of years! There's a good flow of money between people; life and activity. Property and land values are rising with each day.

HOVSTAD: And unemployment's falling.

THE MAYOR: That too, yes. The burden of the poor rates[13] on the propertied classes has been reduced most pleasingly and will be still further, so long as we get a really good summer this year; a substantial volume of visitors – a good number of invalids to spread the institute's reputation.

HOVSTAD: And there's every prospect of that, I hear.

THE MAYOR: The signs are very promising. Inquiries are coming in every day about apartments and the like.

HOVSTAD: Well, the doctor's article will come at the perfect time then.

THE MAYOR: Written something new, has he?

HOVSTAD: This is something he wrote last winter; a recommendation for the Spa – a report on the beneficial health-giving conditions of our town. But at the time I put the article aside.

THE MAYOR: Aha, some snag with it, I expect?

HOVSTAD: No, not at all; but I thought it was better to wait until now in the spring; after all, it's now that people start to plan ahead and think about their summer vacations –

THE MAYOR: Quite right, absolutely right, Mr Hovstad.

MRS STOCKMANN: Yes, Tomas is tireless when it comes to the Spa.

THE MAYOR: Well, he is, of course, employed by the Spa.

HOVSTAD: Yes, and, of course, *he* was also the one to create it at the start.

THE MAYOR: Oh, he was, was he? Really? Yes, I do hear occasionally that certain people are of that opinion. But I rather thought that *I* had a modest part in this enterprise too.

MRS STOCKMANN: Yes, Tomas always says that.

HOVSTAD: Yes, who's denying that, Mr Mayor, sir? You set the matter in motion and turned it into a practical reality; we all know that. I just meant the idea came from the doctor at the start.

THE MAYOR: Yes, ideas are certainly something my brother's had plenty of in his time – unfortunately. But when something's to be put into action, it demands an altogether different kind of man, Mr Hovstad. And I really did think that in this house at least –

MRS STOCKMANN: But, my dear brother-in-law –

HOVSTAD: But, Mr Mayor, how can you –?

MRS STOCKMANN: Go on in now and get something inside you, Mr Hovstad; I'm sure my husband will be here soon.

HOVSTAD: Thank you, just a bite perhaps. [*Goes into the dining room.*]

THE MAYOR [*lowering his voice a little*]: It's incredible how these people who descend from peasants can never rid themselves of that ingrained lack of tact.

MRS STOCKMANN: But is it worth troubling yourself over? Can't you and Tomas share the credit as brothers?

THE MAYOR: Yes, you'd have thought so; but it doesn't appear that everybody is content to share.

MRS STOCKMANN: Oh, what nonsense! You and Tomas get along marvellously. [*Listens.*] There, I think he's coming.

She goes out and opens the hall door.

DR STOCKMANN [*laughing and talking outside*]: Look, I've another guest for you, Katrine. Isn't that splendid? Do come in, Captain Horster; hang your coat there on the peg. Ah, but you don't wear an overcoat, do you? Just imagine, Katrine. I grabbed him in the street; he practically refused to come up with me!

CAPTAIN HORSTER *comes inside and greets* MRS STOCKMANN.

DR STOCKMANN [*in the doorway*]: In you go, boys. They're ravenous again, Katrine –! Come here, Captain Horster; you really must have a taste of this roast beef – [*He ushers* HORSTER *into the dining room.*]

EILIF *and* MORTEN *go in too.*

MRS STOCKMANN: But, Tomas, don't you see –

DR STOCKMANN [*turning in the doorway*]: Oh, it's you, Peter! [*Goes over and reaches out to shake the* MAYOR*'s hand.*] Well, that's splendid.

THE MAYOR: Unfortunately, I'll have to go in a moment –

DR STOCKMANN: Oh, rubbish! The toddy will be on the table soon. You're not forgetting the toddy, are you, Katrine?

MRS STOCKMANN: Certainly not; the water's already on the boil.

She goes into the dining room.

THE MAYOR: Toddy too –!

DR STOCKMANN: Yes, just sling yourself down, and let's enjoy ourselves.

THE MAYOR: No thank you; I don't partake of toddy parties.

DR STOCKMANN: But this is hardly a party.

THE MAYOR: Well, I think –. [*Looks towards the dining room.*] It's remarkable how much food they can put away.

DR STOCKMANN [*rubbing his hands*]: Yes, isn't it a joy to see young people eating? Always an appetite, eh! That's as it should be. Got to have food! For strength! They're the ones who will dig about in the fermenting stuff of the future, Peter.

THE MAYOR: May I ask what's to be 'dug about in' here, as you put it?

DR STOCKMANN: You'll have to ask the youngsters about that – when the time comes. *We* don't see it ourselves. Naturally. Two old fogeys like us –

THE MAYOR: Well, really! But it's a very peculiar turn of phrase –

DR STOCKMANN: Oh, you mustn't be too pedantic with me, Peter. It's just that I feel such intense happiness and joy, let me tell you. I feel so indescribably content with all this budding, bursting life around me. They really are magnificent times we're living in! It's as though a whole new world were springing up around us.

THE MAYOR: You think so, do you?

DR STOCKMANN: Yes, you can't see it as well as I can naturally. You've lived with this around you every day of your life; and then your impression of it is dimmed. But I, after having to sit up north[14] in my far-flung little corner all those years, barely ever seeing an outsider with a stimulating word to say to me – for me, it's as though I'd moved into the centre of a thronging metropolis –

THE MAYOR: Hm, a metropolis –!

DR STOCKMANN: Yes, I know things are on a smaller scale here than in many other places. But there's life here – so much promise, an infinite number of things to work and to fight for; and *that's* the main thing. [*Calls*] Katrine, hasn't the postman been?

MRS STOCKMANN [*from the dining room*]: No, nobody's been.

DR STOCKMANN: And a decent income too, Peter – that's something you learn to value when, as we have, you've lived on the edge of starvation –

THE MAYOR: But, good Lord –

DR STOCKMANN: Oh yes, things were often pretty tight for us up there, you can be sure. And now, to be able to live like a lord! Today, for example, we had roast beef for lunch; yes, and we had some left for supper too. Won't you take a slice? Or can't I at least show it to you? Come here –

THE MAYOR: No, no – really –!

DR STOCKMANN: Well, come over here then. You see this? We've got a table cover.

THE MAYOR: Yes, I noticed that.

DR STOCKMANN: And we've got a lampshade too. You see? Katrine's scrimped for all this! And it makes the living room so cosy. Don't you think? Just stand here – no, no, no; not there. Right there, yes! Just look how the light gathers downwards –. I really do think it looks elegant. Don't you?

THE MAYOR: Yes, when one can allow oneself such a luxury –

DR STOCKMANN: Oh yes, I think I can allow myself that now. Katrine says I earn almost as much as we spend.

THE MAYOR: Almost, yes –!

DR STOCKMANN: But a man of science ought to live in a little style. I'm sure an ordinary district governor[15] spends far more than I do in a year.

THE MAYOR: I daresay! A district governor, a top senior official –[16]

DR STOCKMANN: All right, your average merchant, then! A man like that spends many times more –

THE MAYOR: Well, that's to be expected.

DR STOCKMANN: Anyway, Peter, I certainly don't squander money to no purpose. But I really don't think I can deny myself the heart-warming pleasure of seeing people in my home. I need it, you see. After sitting shut out of things for so long – for me it's one of life's necessities to be together with bold, enterprising young people, liberal-minded people, full of purpose – and that's what they are, all those men sitting in there, enjoying their food. I wish you knew Hovstad a little –.

THE MAYOR: Ah, yes, Hovstad, that's right; he told me he wants to print another article of yours.

DR STOCKMANN: An article of mine?

THE MAYOR: Yes, about the Spa. An article you wrote this winter.

DR STOCKMANN: Oh that, yes! – No, but I don't want that going in just yet.

THE MAYOR: You don't? But I'd have thought *now* would have been the perfect moment.

DR STOCKMANN: Yes, you may be right; under ordinary circumstances – [*Walking across the room*]

THE MAYOR [*watching him*]: But what could possibly be extraordinary about the circumstances now?

DR STOCKMANN [*stops still*]: Well, Peter, I honestly can't tell you for the moment; at least not this evening. There may be a great many things that are extraordinary about the circumstances; or then again absolutely nothing. It may be that it's just a figment of my imagination.

THE MAYOR: I must admit this all sounds extremely mysterious. Is there something going on? Something I'm to be kept out of? I'd have thought that I, as chairman of the Spa's board –

DR STOCKMANN: And I would have thought that I – well, let's not tear each other's hair out over this, Peter.

THE MAYOR: Good Lord! I'm not in the habit of tearing people's hair out, as you put it. But I must demand, most categorically, that any proposals be put forward and decided upon in a businesslike manner, through the legally constituted authorities. I cannot allow illicit paths or back doors to be used here.

DR STOCKMANN: When have *I* ever used illicit paths or back doors?

THE MAYOR: You have an ingrained tendency to take your own path, at least; and in a well-ordered society that's almost as inadmissible. The individual[17] must be ready to comply with the community[18] as a whole, or more precisely, with the authorities whose job it is to watch over the welfare of that community.

DR STOCKMANN: That may be. But what the hell has that got to do with me?

THE MAYOR: Well that, my good Tomas, is what you never seem willing to learn. But watch out; you'll pay for it some time – sooner or later. Now I've said it. Goodbye.

DR STOCKMANN: But are you stark raving mad? You're on completely the wrong track –

THE MAYOR: I don't tend to be. And incidentally, I object to being – [*Calls into the dining room*] Goodbye, sister-in-law. Goodbye, gentlemen. [*Goes out.*]

MRS STOCKMANN [*comes into the living room*]: Did he leave?

DR STOCKMANN: Yes, and in an absolute fury.

MRS STOCKMANN: But, Tomas dear, what have you done to him this time?

DR STOCKMANN: Not a thing. He can't possibly expect me to give him a full account before the time comes.

MRS STOCKMANN: What would you give him an account of?

DR STOCKMANN: Hm! Leave that to me, Katrine. – But it's strange the postman hasn't been.

> HOVSTAD, BILLING *and* HORSTER *have got up from the table and come into the living room.* EILIF *and* MORTEN *come a little later.*

BILLING [*stretching his arms*]: Ah, after a meal like that, God strike me dead, you feel like a new man.

HOVSTAD: The mayor wasn't in the best of moods this evening.

DR STOCKMANN: It's his stomach; he has a poor digestion.

HOVSTAD: Doubtless it was the two of us from *The Messenger* that he couldn't stomach.

MRS STOCKMANN: I thought you were getting on with him rather well.

HOVSTAD: Yes; but it's really no more than a kind of armistice.

BILLING: *There* you have it. That word sums up the situation perfectly!

DR STOCKMANN: We mustn't forget Peter's a solitary man, poor chap. He hasn't the comforts of a home to enjoy; just work and more work. And all that damned weak tea he pours down his throat! Now then, pull a few chairs up to the table, boys. Katrine, isn't that toddy coming?

MRS STOCKMANN [*going into the dining room*]: I'm bringing it now.

DR STOCKMANN: And sit on the couch next to me, Captain Horster. A rare visitor like yourself –. There now, take your places, my friends.

They sit at the table. MRS STOCKMANN *brings a tray with the toddy heater,[19] glasses, decanters and other items.*

MRS STOCKMANN: Here you go! Here's some arrack,[20] and this is rum, and there's the cognac. Help yourselves, everyone.

DR STOCKMANN [*taking a glass*]: We shall indeed. [*Mixing a toddy*] And now for the cigars. Eilif, you seem to know where the box is. And you, Morten, can get my pipe. [*The two* BOYS *go into the room on the right*] I have a suspicion Eilif pinches a cigar now and then! – but I pretend not to notice. [*Calls out*] And my smoking-cap[21] too, Morten. Katrine, why don't you tell him where I left it. Ah, he's got it.

The BOYS *bring him what he has asked for.*

DR STOCKMANN: Help yourselves, my friends. I stick to my pipe, of course; this pipe has been with me on many a stormy walk up in Nordland. [*They clink glasses.*] Cheers! Well, it's certainly a good deal better to be sitting here safe and snug.

MRS STOCKMANN [*who sits knitting*]: Do you sail soon, Captain Horster?

HORSTER: I expect to be ready sometime next week.

MRS STOCKMANN: And then you'll be off to America?

HORSTER: That's the plan.

BILLING: But then you won't be able to take part in the council elections.

HORSTER: Is there going to be another election?

BILLING: Didn't you know?

HORSTER: No, I don't involve myself in all that.

BILLING: But surely you take an interest in public affairs?

HORSTER: No, I don't know much about them.

BILLING: Still, we all have to vote at least.

HORSTER: Even those who understand nothing?

BILLING: Understand? What do you mean? Society is like a ship; everyone must come together at the helm.

HORSTER: That might be all right on land; but it would come to no good on a ship.

HOVSTAD: It's astonishing how little most sailors care about the country's affairs.

BILLING: Quite extraordinary.

DR STOCKMANN: Seafarers are like migratory birds; they feel equally at home in the south or the north. But that's why the rest of us must be all the more active, Mr Hovstad. Will there be anything of public interest in *The Messenger* tomorrow?

HOVSTAD: Not about local affairs. But the day after tomorrow I was thinking of including your article –

DR STOCKMANN: Ah, hell, the article! No, listen, you'll have to wait with that.

HOVSTAD: Oh? We've got plenty of space right now, and I thought now was the perfect time –

DR STOCKMANN: Yes, yes, you may be right; but you'll have to wait anyway. I'll explain later –

PETRA, *wearing a hat and cloak and with a bundle of exercise books under her arm, comes in from the hall.*

PETRA: Good evening.

DR STOCKMANN: Hello, Petra; are you back?

Mutual greetings; PETRA *takes off her things and puts them down on a chair by the door.*

PETRA: So you've all been sitting here enjoying yourselves, while I've been out slaving!

DR STOCKMANN: Well, come and enjoy yourself too!

BILLING: Shall I mix you a little drink?

PETRA [*coming to the table*]: Thanks, I'd rather do it myself; you always make it too strong. Oh, by the way, Father – I've got a letter for you. [*Goes to the chair on which she put her outdoor clothes.*]

DR STOCKMANN: A letter! From whom?

PETRA [*looking in her coat pocket*]: I got it from the postman just as I was leaving –

DR STOCKMANN [*getting up and going over to her*]: And you haven't given it to me until now!

PETRA: I really didn't have the time to run up again. Here, there it is!

DR STOCKMANN [*grabbing the letter*]: Let me see, let me see, my child! [*Looks at the envelope.*] Yes, as I thought –!

MRS STOCKMANN: Is *that* what you've been waiting for, Tomas?

DR STOCKMANN: It is indeed; I must go in immediately and –. Where can I find a candle, Katrine? I presume there isn't a lamp in my room!

MRS STOCKMANN: Oh yes, the lamp's already lit on your desk.

DR STOCKMANN: Good, good. Excuse me for a moment – [*Goes into his study to the right.*]

PETRA: What on earth can it be, Mother?

MRS STOCKMANN: I don't know; he's been asking about the postman constantly these last few days.

BILLING: Some out-of-town patient, I take it –

PETRA: Poor Father; he'll have more than he can cope with soon. [*Mixes a glass for herself.*] Ah, I'm going to enjoy this!

HOVSTAD: Have you been teaching at the evening school again?

PETRA [*sipping from her glass*]: Two hours.

BILLING: And four hours earlier today at the college –

PETRA [*sits at the table*]: Five.

MRS STOCKMANN: And you have essays to mark tonight, I see.

PETRA: A whole heap, yes.

HORSTER: You seem to have rather a lot to cope with yourself.

PETRA: Yes; but that's a good thing. It makes you so wonderfully tired afterwards.

BILLING: And you like that?

PETRA: Yes, because then you sleep so well.

MORTEN: You must be ever so sinful, Petra.

PETRA: Sinful?

MORTEN: Yes, if you work that much. Mr Rørlund says work is a punishment for our sins.

EILIF: Pff, you're so stupid, believing in stuff like that!

MRS STOCKMANN: Now, now, Eilif!

BILLING [*laughing*]: No, but that's brilliant!

HOVSTAD: So you wouldn't want to work that much, Morten?

MORTEN: No, I would not.

HOVSTAD: What do you want to be, then?

MORTEN: I want to be a Viking.

EILIF: But then you'd have to be a pagan.

MORTEN: Well, then I could *become* a pagan.

BILLING: I'm with you there, Morten! That's exactly what I say.

MRS STOCKMANN [*signals to him*]: Really now, Mr Billing, I'm sure you don't.

BILLING: Oh yes, God strike me dead –! I *am* a pagan and proud of it. Just wait and see, we'll all be pagans soon.

MORTEN: And *then* can we do exactly what we want?

BILLING: Yes, Morten, you see –

MRS STOCKMANN: You'll go to your room now, boys; I'm sure you've both got homework to do for tomorrow.

EILIF: Can't *I* stay just a bit longer –

MRS STOCKMANN: You too, off you go, both of you.

The BOYS *say good night and go into the room on the left.*

HOVSTAD: Do you really think it can harm the boys to hear that sort of thing?

MRS STOCKMANN: I don't know; but I don't approve of it.

PETRA: Yes but, Mother, I believe that's very wrong of you.

MRS STOCKMANN: Quite possibly, but I don't approve of it; not here at home.

PETRA: There's so much dishonesty both in the home and in school. In the home there's a rule of silence, and in school we have to stand up and lie to the children.

HORSTER: You have to lie?

PETRA: Yes, don't you think we're obliged to teach a great many things we don't believe in ourselves?

BILLING: Yes, that's all too true, I'm sure.

PETRA: If only I had the funds, I'd start a school of my own, and there things would be very different.

BILLING: Oh, funds –

HORSTER: Well, if you're considering doing that, Miss Stockmann, you're welcome to have premises at my place. My father's big old house, God rest him, stands almost empty; there's an enormous dining room downstairs –

PETRA [*laughing*]: Ah, thank you; but I doubt anything will ever come of it.

HOVSTAD: No, I think Miss Petra's more likely to come over to us journalists. By the way, have you had time to take a little look at that English story[22] you promised to translate for us?

PETRA: No, not yet; but you'll get it in good time.

DR STOCKMANN *comes in from his room with the open letter in his hand.*

DR STOCKMANN [*waving the letter*]: Well, this news will get the town talking, believe me!

BILLING: News?

MRS STOCKMANN: What kind of news?

DR STOCKMANN: A huge discovery, Katrine.

HOVSTAD: Oh?

MRS STOCKMANN: That you've made?

DR STOCKMANN: Yes, *me*. [*Walks back and forth*] Now let them come and say, as always, that it's all some fanciful notion and the ideas of a madman! But they'll think twice all right! Haha, they'll think twice, I'm sure!

PETRA: But, Father, tell us what it is then.

DR STOCKMANN: Yes, yes, just give me time, and I'll tell you all everything. If only Peter were here now! Well, it just goes to show, how we human beings go around passing judgement like the blindest of moles –

HOVSTAD: What do you mean, doctor?

DR STOCKMANN [*stops by the table*]: Isn't it the commonly held opinion that our town is a healthy place?

HOVSTAD: Yes, that goes without saying.

DR STOCKMANN: An exceedingly healthy place, moreover – a place that deserves the warmest recommendation to our fellow beings, both sick and healthy –

MRS STOCKMANN: Yes, but, Tomas dear –

DR STOCKMANN: And recommended and lauded it we have. I've written and written in *The People's Messenger* and in pamphlets –

HOVSTAD: Yes. And?

DR STOCKMANN: This Spa Institute, which has been described
    as the town's artery, the town's nerve-centre, and – and the
    devil knows what –

BILLING: 'The beating heart of our town' I allowed myself
    once in a festive moment to –

DR STOCKMANN: Yes, that too. But do you know what it is in
    reality, this great, splendid, lauded Spa Institute, that has
    cost so much money – do you know what it is?

HOVSTAD: No, what is it?

MRS STOCKMANN: Well? What is it?

DR STOCKMANN: The entire Spa is a cesspit!

PETRA: The Spa, Father?

MRS STOCKMANN [*at the same time*]: Our Spa?

HOVSTAD [*likewise*]: But, doctor –

BILLING: Unbelievable!

DR STOCKMANN: The whole Spa is a whited, poisoned sepul-
    chre, I tell you. A health hazard of the greatest magnitude.
    All that foul sludge up there in Mølledalen[23] – all that stuff
    that smells so vile – it's infecting the water in the feed pipes
    that lead to the well-house; and that same damned poison-
    ous mess is oozing down to the beach too –

HORSTER: Where the sea baths are?

DR STOCKMANN: Precisely.

HOVSTAD: What makes you so certain of all this, doctor?

DR STOCKMANN: I've investigated the matter scrupulously.
    Oh, I've suspected something of the sort for a long time.
    Last year there were some curious cases of illness here
    among the Spa's guests – cases of typhoid and gastric illness –

MRS STOCKMANN: Yes, there were indeed.

DR STOCKMANN: Back then we thought the visitors had
    brought these infections with them; but later – this winter – I
    began to think otherwise; so I set about investigating the
    water, as best I could.

MRS STOCKMANN: So *that's* what you've been so busy with?

DR STOCKMANN: Indeed, you might well say I've been busy,
    Katrine. But I didn't have the necessary scientific equipment
    here, so I sent samples of the drinking water and the

seawater to the University to get an accurate analysis done by a chemist.

HOVSTAD: And now you've got it?

DR STOCKMANN [*displaying the letter*]: I have it here! It's proven that there's decayed organic matter in the water – infusoria in vast quantities. It's seriously harmful to the health whether taken internally or externally.

MRS STOCKMANN: It's a mercy then that you followed it up in time.

DR STOCKMANN: Yes, you can say that again.

HOVSTAD: And what do you intend to do now, doctor?

DR STOCKMANN: Get the situation put right, naturally.

HOVSTAD: So that's possible?

DR STOCKMANN: It has to be possible. Otherwise the whole Spa is unusable – ruined. But there's no need for alarm. I'm very clear about what needs doing.

MRS STOCKMANN: But, Tomas, my sweet, how could you keep all this such a secret?

DR STOCKMANN: Oh, I should have rushed about town talking about it, perhaps, before I had complete certainty? No, thank you; I'm not that mad.

PETRA: Yes, but at home with us –

DR STOCKMANN: Not with a living soul. But tomorrow you can run up to the old 'Badger' –

MRS STOCKMANN: Tomas, really –!

DR STOCKMANN: Yes, all right, all right, grandfather, then. Well, the old boy will have something to wonder at now; he thinks I'm cracked in the head, of course. Oh yes, and there are others who think the same, I've noticed. But now they'll see, these goodly folk – now they'll see –! [*Walks about, rubbing his hands*] There'll be such a to-do in town, Katrine! You've no idea. All the water pipes must be relaid.

HOVSTAD [*getting up*]: All the water pipes –?

DR STOCKMANN: Yes, of course. The intake is too low; it'll have to be moved a lot higher up.

PETRA: So you were right after all.

DR STOCKMANN: Yes, you remember, Petra? I wrote opposing them when they were to start building. But back then nobody wanted to listen to me. Well, now I'll launch a broadside at them, believe me – yes, because I've written a report for the Spa's board; it's been sitting here ready for a whole week; I've just been waiting for this. [*Shows the letter.*] And now it'll go off this instant. [*Goes into his room and comes back with some papers.*] Look! Four closely written pages! And the letter needs to be enclosed. A newspaper, Katrine! Get me something as wrapping. Good; there now; give it to – to – [*stamps his foot*] oh, what the hell's her name again? Anyway, give it to the maid; tell her to take it down to the mayor right away.

    MRS STOCKMANN *goes out through the dining room with the packet.*

PETRA: What do you think Uncle Peter will say, Father?

DR STOCKMANN: What should he say? Surely he can't be anything but pleased at such a vital truth coming to light.

HOVSTAD: May I put a small notice about your discovery in *The People's Messenger*?

DR STOCKMANN: Yes, I'd be most grateful.

HOVSTAD: It is, of course, desirable that the public be informed sooner rather than later.

DR STOCKMANN: It most certainly is.

MRS STOCKMANN [*coming back*]: She's just gone with it.

BILLING: Well, God strike me dead, you'll be the town's number one man, doctor!

DR STOCKMANN [*walking contentedly about*]: Oh, nonsense; basically I've done no more than my duty. I've been a lucky treasure hunter; nothing more; although –

BILLING: Hovstad, don't you think the town should have a parade for Dr Stockmann?

HOVSTAD: I'd certainly back that.

BILLING: And I'll talk to Aslaksen about it.

DR STOCKMANN: No, dear friends, forget such silliness; I won't hear of any such celebrations. And if the Spa's board should get ideas about awarding me a salary increase, I won't accept it. I tell you, Katrine – I won't accept it.

MRS STOCKMANN: No, Tomas, quite right.

PETRA [*lifting her glass*]: Cheers, Father!

HOVSTAD and BILLING: Cheers, Doctor! Your health!

HORSTER [*clinks glasses with* DR STOCKMANN]: Here's hoping this brings you nothing but happiness.

DR STOCKMANN: Thank you, thank you, my dearest friends! I'm so absolutely thrilled – Oh, what a joy it is to know that one has made a worthy contribution to one's home town and one's fellow citizens. Hurrah, Katrine!

> *He puts both arms round her neck and swirls her round. She squeals and protests. Laughter, clapping and cheering for the* DOCTOR. *The* BOYS *poke their heads round the door.*

ACT TWO

The doctor's living room. The door into the dining room is closed. Late morning.

MRS STOCKMANN [*comes in from the dining room with a sealed letter in her hand, goes to the right-hand door nearest to the front and peeps in*]: Are you home, Tomas?

DR STOCKMANN [*from within his room*]: Yes, I've just got back. [*Comes in.*] What is it?

MRS STOCKMANN: A letter from your brother. [*Hands it to him.*]

DR STOCKMANN: Aha, let's see! [*Opens the letter and reads*] 'The manuscript you submitted is hereby returned –' [*Reads on in a murmur*] Hmm –

MRS STOCKMANN: And then what does he say?

DR STOCKMANN [*putting the papers in his pocket*]: Well, he just writes that he'll come up himself around midday.

MRS STOCKMANN: You really must remember to stay at home then.

DR STOCKMANN: Yes, that's no problem; I've finished my morning visits.

MRS STOCKMANN: I'm very curious to know how he takes it.

DR STOCKMANN: You'll see, he won't exactly be pleased it was me, and not him, who made the discovery.

MRS STOCKMANN: Yes quite, so that worries *you* too?

DR STOCKMANN: Well, deep down he'll be pleased, you can be sure. But, still – Peter's so damned afraid that anyone else might accomplish something for the good of the town.

MRS STOCKMANN: But, you know what, Tomas – then you ought to be kind and share the honour with him. Couldn't it be presented as if he was the one who's put you on the right track –?

DR STOCKMANN: Yes, I've no objection to that. As long as I get the matter put right –

Old MORTEN KIIL *puts his head in the hall door.*

MORTEN KIIL [*looks around inquisitively, laughs to himself and asks slyly*]: Is it – is it true?

MRS STOCKMANN [*moving towards him*]: Father! – It's you!

DR STOCKMANN: Well, I never, Father-in-law – good morning, good morning!

MRS STOCKMANN: Oh, but do come in.

MORTEN KIIL: I shall, if it's true; otherwise I'll go again.

DR STOCKMANN: If what is true?

MORTEN KIIL: This madness about the water system. Is it true?

DR STOCKMANN: Yes, it certainly is true. But how did *you* come to hear about *that*?

MORTEN KIIL [*coming in*]: Petra paid me a flying visit on her way to the school –

DR STOCKMANN: Oh, really?

MORTEN KIIL: Uh-huh; and then she tells me –. I thought she was just trying to make a fool of me; but then that's not like Petra.

DR STOCKMANN: No, how could you even think it!

MORTEN KIIL: Oh, you can't trust anybody; you can be made into a fool before you know it. So it really is true, then?

DR STOCKMANN: Yes, it certainly is. Sit yourself down, Father-in-law. [*Urges him to sit on the sofa.*] And isn't it an absolute blessing for the town –

MORTEN KIIL [*suppressing his laughter*]: A blessing for the town?

DR STOCKMANN: Yes, that I made this discovery in time –

MORTEN KIIL [*still laughing*]: Indeed, indeed! – But I'd never have thought you'd play such monkey tricks on your own flesh-and-blood brother!

DR STOCKMANN: Monkey tricks!

MRS STOCKMANN: But, Father dear –

MORTEN KIIL [*resting his hands and chin on the handle of his stick and winking at the* DOCTOR *roguishly*]: How did it go now? Wasn't it something to do with some creatures that had got into the water-pipes?

DR STOCKMANN: That's right, infusoria –

MORTEN KIIL: And a whole lot of these creatures had got in, Petra said. A staggering number.

DR STOCKMANN: Well yes; there might be hundreds of thousands of them.

MORTEN KIIL: But nobody can see them – wasn't that it?

DR STOCKMANN: That's right; you can't see them.

MORTEN KIIL [*with quiet chuckling laughter*]: Well, the devil take me,[24] if this isn't the best I've heard from you yet.

DR STOCKMANN: How do you mean?

MORTEN KIIL: But you'll never ever get the mayor to believe such a thing.

DR STOCKMANN: Well, we'll have to see about that.

MORTEN KIIL: Do you think he could be that mad?

DR STOCKMANN: I'm hoping the whole town will be that mad.

MORTEN KIIL: The whole town! Yes, that's not impossible, damn it. But they've got it coming; it'll serve them right. They think they're so much cleverer than us oldies. Hounded me[25] out of the council,[26] they did. Yes, I say that, because they voted me out like a dog. But now they'll get their come-uppance. You just press on with those monkey tricks, Stockmann!

DR STOCKMANN: But, Father-in-law –

MORTEN KIIL: All monkey tricks, I say! [*Gets up.*] If you manage to make the mayor and his friends run around with red faces, I'll give a hundred kroner to the poor right away!

DR STOCKMANN: Well, that's most kind of you.

MORTEN KIIL: Yes, I've not got a lot to spare, let me tell you; but if you pull this off I'll donate fifty kroner[27] to the poor at Christmas.

MR HOVSTAD *comes in from the hall.*

HOVSTAD: Good morning! [*Stops.*] Oh, apologies –

DR STOCKMANN: No, come in; come in.

MORTEN KIIL [*chuckling again*]: Him! Is he in on this too?

HOVSTAD: What do you mean?

DR STOCKMANN: Well yes, he certainly is.

MORTEN KIIL: I should have guessed! It's going to appear in the papers. Oh, you're a fine one, you are, Stockmann! But you just keep plotting; I'll be off now.

DR STOCKMANN: No, stay a bit, Father-in-law.

MORTEN KIIL: No, I'll be off now. And just think up every monkey trick you can; you damn well[28] won't have done it for naught!

   He leaves; MRS STOCKMANN *follows him out.*

DR STOCKMANN [*laughing*]: Imagine, Hovstad – the old man doesn't believe a word about this thing with the water supply.

HOVSTAD: Oh, was *that* what –?

DR STOCKMANN: Yes, that's what we were discussing. And perhaps that's what you've come about too?

HOVSTAD: Yes, it is. Have you got a moment, doctor?

DR STOCKMANN: As long as you want, my friend.

HOVSTAD: Have you heard anything from the mayor?

DR STOCKMANN: Not yet. He's coming over later.

HOVSTAD: I've thought a lot about this matter since yesterday evening.

DR STOCKMANN: And?

HOVSTAD: For you, as a doctor and man of science, this water system business is an isolated matter. I mean, it wouldn't occur to you that it's linked up with many other things.

DR STOCKMANN: Oh, in what way –? Let's sit down, my friend. – No, there, on the sofa.

   MR HOVSTAD *sits down on the sofa,* DR STOCKMANN *in an armchair on the other side of the table.*

DR STOCKMANN: Now? You were saying –?

HOVSTAD: You said yesterday that the polluted water came from impurities in the soil.

DR STOCKMANN: Yes, it comes, without a doubt, from that toxic swamp up in Mølledalen.

HOVSTAD: Forgive me, doctor, but I believe it comes from a quite different swamp.

DR STOCKMANN: What sort of swamp?

HOVSTAD: The swamp in which our entire municipal life stands rotting.

DR STOCKMANN: Oh, but damn it, Mr Hovstad, what kind of talk is this?

HOVSTAD: All the town's affairs have shifted bit by bit into the hands of a bunch of bureaucrats —[29]

DR STOCKMANN: Oh come now, they're not all bureaucrats.

HOVSTAD: No, but those that aren't bureaucrats, they're the hangers-on and the friends of bureaucrats; it's the rich, those with old established names in the town; they're the ones who govern over us and control us.

DR STOCKMANN: Yes, but these people have expertise and insight.

HOVSTAD: Did they show expertise and insight when they laid the water pipes where they are now?

DR STOCKMANN: No, *that* was clearly a huge folly on their part. But that'll be put right now.

HOVSTAD: You think it will happen that smoothly?

DR STOCKMANN: Smoothly or not – it'll happen all the same.

HOVSTAD: Yes, provided the press gets involved.

DR STOCKMANN: That won't be necessary, my friend, I'm sure my brother –

HOVSTAD: Excuse me, doctor, but I'm telling you that I intend to take this matter up.

DR STOCKMANN: In the newspaper?

HOVSTAD: Yes. When I took over *The People's Messenger*, my objective was to blow apart this ring of stubborn old bigots who sit on all the power.

DR STOCKMANN: But you've told me yourself how that ended; you almost ruined the paper with it.

HOVSTAD: Yes, back then we had to beat a retreat, that's true. Because there was a danger that the Spa Institute wouldn't happen, if these men fell. But now it's in place, and these fine gentlemen can be dispensed with.

DR STOCKMANN: Dispensed with, perhaps; but we still owe them a huge debt of gratitude.

HOVSTAD: Yes, and that'll be acknowledged with all due accord. But a journalist of the people like myself can't let an opportunity like this slip away from him. The myth of the infallibility of those who govern us must be shaken. Such notions must be eradicated, like any other superstition.

DR STOCKMANN: I agree wholeheartedly, Mr Hovstad; if it's a superstition, then away with it!

HOVSTAD: The mayor's your brother, of course, so I'd be reluctant to touch him. But I'm sure you believe, as I, that truth comes before any other consideration.

DR STOCKMANN: Well, yes, that goes without saying. – [*Bursting out*] But –! But –!

HOVSTAD: You mustn't think ill of me. I'm no more self-interested or power-hungry than most people.

DR STOCKMANN: My dear friend – who'd think such a thing?

HOVSTAD: I come from humble stock, as you know; and I've had enough opportunity to see what's most needed in the lower rungs of society. And that is to partake in the running of our public affairs, doctor. *That's* what develops people's faculties, knowledge and self-respect –

DR STOCKMANN: I understand that absolutely –

HOVSTAD: Yes – and I believe a journalist carries a heavy burden of responsibility when he wastes an opportune moment for the emancipation of the many – of the little people, the downtrodden. I'm quite aware – in higher circles they'll call it agitation or the like; but they must say as they please. As long as my conscience is clear, then –

DR STOCKMANN: Quite so! Quite so, my dear Mr Hovstad. But still – damn it all –! [*A knock is heard at the door.*] Come in!

> ASLAKSEN *the printer appears at the hall door. He is poorly but respectably dressed, in black, with a slightly crumpled white neckerchief; he wears gloves and holds a top hat in his hand.*

ASLAKSEN [*bows*]: Forgive me, doctor, sir, for being so bold –

DR STOCKMANN [*getting up*]: Well, look here – if it isn't Aslaksen!

ASLAKSEN: It is indeed, doctor.

HOVSTAD [*standing up*]: Is it me you're after, Aslaksen?

ASLAKSEN: No, it isn't; I didn't know we'd meet here. No, it was the doctor himself actually –

DR STOCKMANN: Well, how can I be of service?

ASLAKSEN: Is it true, as Billing told me, that the doctor's thinking of procuring a better water system for us?

DR STOCKMANN: Yes, for the Spa Institute.

ASLAKSEN: Indeed, I understand. Well, then I've come to say that I'll do everything in my power to support you in that.

HOVSTAD [*to the* DOCTOR]: You see!

DR STOCKMANN: That's most kind of you, but –

ASLAKSEN: Because it might just come in useful to have us small tradesmen behind you. We do after all form a kind of solid majority[30] in this town – when we really *want* to, that is. And it's always good to have the majority with you, doctor.

DR STOCKMANN: That's undeniable; but I just can't see there'd be the necessity for any special measures here. I think that such a plain, straightforward matter –

ASLAKSEN: Well, it might be useful nonetheless; I know the local authorities well; those in power aren't too willing to go along with proposals from others. Which is why I don't think it would be out of place if we were to demonstrate a little.

HOVSTAD: Absolutely, yes.

DR STOCKMANN: Demonstrate, you say? I see, and how exactly would you demonstrate?

ASLAKSEN: With great temperance naturally, doctor; I always strive for temperance; after all, temperance is the principal virtue of a citizen[31] – in *my* opinion at least.

DR STOCKMANN: And that's something you're known for too, Mr Aslaksen.

ASLAKSEN: Indeed, I think I dare say so. And this matter of the water supply; it's extremely important to us small tradesmen. The Spa shows signs of turning into something of a little goldmine for this town. It's the Spa that we'll all rely on to make a living, we homeowners more than anyone. So naturally we're very keen to back the institute all we can.

And since I happen to be the head of the Homeowners' Association –[32]

DR STOCKMANN: Yes –?

ASLAKSEN: – and, moreover, an agent for the Temperance Society[33] – the doctor knows presumably that I work for the cause of temperance?

DR STOCKMANN: Yes, it hardly needs saying.

ASLAKSEN: Well – then it's not difficult to understand that I come in contact with a lot of people. And being known as a prudent and law-abiding citizen, as you said yourself, doctor, I have a certain influence in the town – a sort of modicum of power – if I may say.

DR STOCKMANN: I'm well aware of that, Mr Aslaksen.

ASLAKSEN: Quite – that's why it would be a simple matter for me to get a petition together, if it comes to the crunch.

DR STOCKMANN: A petition, you say?

ASLAKSEN: Yes, a kind of petition of thanks from the citizens of this town for your bringing this important public matter forward. It goes without saying it would have to be composed with the proper temperance, so it doesn't upset the authorities, nor, I might add, anyone else in a position of power. And as long as we're careful about *that*, then nobody could take us in bad faith, surely?

HOVSTAD: But even if they didn't much like it –

ASLAKSEN: No, no, no! No disrespect towards the authorities, Mr Hovstad. No opposition against people with whom our lives are so closely bound. I've had enough of that in my day, and no good ever comes of it. But no man can be denied his prudent and frank expression of opinion as a citizen.[34]

DR STOCKMANN [*shakes his hand*]: I can't tell you, dear Mr Aslaksen, what an absolute joy it is to find all this support among my fellow citizens. I'm so glad – so glad! Listen; how about a little glass of sherry?

ASLAKSEN: No, thank you; I never touch spirits.

DR STOCKMANN: A glass of beer then; what do you say?

ASLAKSEN: No, thank you, not that either, doctor. I don't touch anything so early in the day. But I'll be off into town now to talk with some of the homeowners and prepare the mood.

DR STOCKMANN: Well, that's most kind of you, Mr Aslaksen; though I find it impossible to get it into my head that such measures should be necessary; I feel this matter should take care of itself.

ASLAKSEN: The authorities do make heavy work of things, doctor. Though, Lord knows, I'm not saying that to blame them –

HOVSTAD: We'll kick them into action in the paper tomorrow, Aslaksen.

ASLAKSEN: Yes, but not too violently, Mr Hovstad. Proceed with temperance, or you won't shift them; you can take my word for it; my experiences are garnered in the school of life. – Well now, I shall bid the doctor farewell. You know now that we small tradesmen, at least, stand behind you like a wall. You have the solid majority on your side, doctor.

DR STOCKMANN: Thank you for that, my dear Mr Aslaksen. [*Gives him his hand.*] Goodbye!

ASLAKSEN: Are you coming down to the printshop, Mr Hovstad?

HOVSTAD: I'll come on later; I've still got a little more to do.

ASLAKSEN: Right you are.

Nods and goes out; DR STOCKMANN *follows him into the hall.*

HOVSTAD [*as the* DOCTOR *comes in again*]: So what do you say to that, doctor? Don't you think it's time to air this place out and shake up all this inertia and half-heartedness and cowardice?

DR STOCKMANN: Are you referring to Aslaksen?

HOVSTAD: Yes, I am. He's one of those in the swamp, however good a man he might be in other respects. And that's how most of them are here; they dither and waver from side to side; with so much care and caution they never dare to take a decisive step.

DR STOCKMANN: Yes, but Aslaksen was really so genuinely well-meaning, I thought.

HOVSTAD: There's one thing I value more; and that's to stand as a solid, self-assured man.

DR STOCKMANN: I'm in absolute agreement with you there.

HOVSTAD: Which is why I mean to grab this opportunity now, and see if I can't perhaps manage to get these well-meaning types to act like men. The worship of authority *must* be eradicated in this town. This grossly inexcusable error with the water system must be made apparent to every voting citizen.

DR STOCKMANN: Very well; if you think it's for the common good, so be it; but not before I've spoken to my brother.

HOVSTAD: I'll draft an editorial piece in the meantime anyway. And if the mayor doesn't want to take the matter up –

DR STOCKMANN: But how can you think that possible?

HOVSTAD: Oh, it's a possibility. And *then* –?

DR STOCKMANN: Well, then I promise you – listen; then you can publish my report – put the whole thing in.

HOVSTAD: I can? Is that a promise?

DR STOCKMANN [*handing him the manuscript*]: Here it is; take it with you; it can't do any harm for you to read it through; and then you can give it back to me afterwards.

HOVSTAD: Good, good; I certainly shall. And now, goodbye, doctor.

DR STOCKMANN: Goodbye. You'll see it'll all go as smoothly as anything, Mr Hovstad – so smoothly.

HOVSTAD: Hm! – We'll see. [*Nods and goes out through the hall.*]

DR STOCKMANN [*goes over to the dining room and looks in*]: Katrine –! Oh, you're back home, Petra?

PETRA [*coming in*]: Yes, I've just got back from the school.

MRS STOCKMANN [*coming in*]: Hasn't he been here yet?

DR STOCKMANN: Peter? No. But I've had a long talk with Hovstad. He's rather taken by the discovery I've made. Yes, it's of much wider scope than I thought initially, you see. And he's put his newspaper at my disposal, should that be necessary.

MRS STOCKMANN: But do you think that'll be necessary?

DR STOCKMANN: Not a bit. But it gives you a sense of pride, nonetheless, to know you have the liberal-minded, independent press on your side. Yes, and imagine – I've had a visit from the head of the Homeowners' Association too!

MRS STOCKMANN: Oh? And what did he want?

DR STOCKMANN: To support me too. They'll all support me if it comes to the crunch, Katrine – you know what I've got behind me?

MRS STOCKMANN: Behind you? No, what have you got behind you?

DR STOCKMANN: The solid majority.

MRS STOCKMANN: Really? That's a good thing for you, is it, Tomas?

DR STOCKMANN: Yes, I'd have thought so, very good! [*Walks up and down rubbing his hands*] By God, it's gratifying to stand like this in brotherly union with one's fellow citizens!

PETRA: And to do something so good and useful, Father!

DR STOCKMANN: Yes, and what's more, for one's own home-town, Petra!

MRS STOCKMANN: That was the doorbell.

DR STOCKMANN: That must be him – [*There is a knock at the door.*] Come in!

THE MAYOR [*comes in from the hall*]: Good morning.

DR STOCKMANN: Good to see you, Peter!

MRS STOCKMANN: Good morning, Brother-in-law. How are things?

THE MAYOR: So-so, thank you. [*To* DR STOCKMANN] Yesterday, after office hours, I received a report from you pertaining to the condition of the water at the Spa Institute.

DR STOCKMANN: Yes. Have you read it?

THE MAYOR: Yes, I have.

DR STOCKMANN: And what do you say on the matter?

THE MAYOR [*with a sidelong glance*]: Hm! –

MRS STOCKMANN: Come on, Petra.

She and PETRA *go into the room on the left.*

THE MAYOR [*after a pause*]: Was it necessary to carry out all these investigations behind my back?

DR STOCKMANN: Yes, so long as I didn't have absolute certainty –

THE MAYOR: And you feel you have that now?

DR STOCKMANN: Yes, you must surely be persuaded of that yourself.

THE MAYOR: Is it your intention to present this paper to the Spa's board by way of an official document?

DR STOCKMANN: Well, yes. Something must be done about the matter; and fast.

THE MAYOR: You use, as always, very strident language in your report. Among other things, you say that what we offer the visitors to our Spa is some form of permanent poisoning.

DR STOCKMANN: But, Peter, can it be characterized otherwise? Just imagine – water that's poisonous if used either internally or externally! And that by unfortunate sick people who turn to us in good faith, and who pay us exorbitant amounts to regain their health!

THE MAYOR: And your deductions take you to the conclusion that we must build a sewer that can drain this purportedly foul sludge from Mølledalen, and that the water pipe must be relaid.

DR STOCKMANN: Well, do you know of any other solution? I don't.

THE MAYOR: I visited the regional engineer[35] this morning on some pretext. And I brought up – half in jest – these proposals as something that we ought perhaps to consider at some time in the future.

DR STOCKMANN: Some time in the future!

THE MAYOR: He smiled at my seeming extravagance – naturally. Have you taken the trouble to consider what these suggested changes would cost? According to the information I received, the expenses would probably run up to several hundred thousand kroner.

DR STOCKMANN: Would it be that expensive?

THE MAYOR: Yes; and here's the worst. The work would require a period of at least two years.

DR STOCKMANN: Two years, you say? Two whole years?

THE MAYOR: At least. And what will we do with the Spa in the meantime? Shall we close it? Yes, we'd be forced to. Or you think perhaps that people will come to us once the rumour's out that the water might be a health hazard?

DR STOCKMANN: But, Peter, that's what it *is*.

THE MAYOR: And all this now – just now when the institute is taking off. Our neighbouring towns also satisfy certain criteria that could make them potential spa resorts. Don't you think they'd immediately swing into action to draw the entire stream of visitors to themselves? Yes, without a doubt. And we'd be left standing; we'd probably have to close down the whole costly institute, and then you'd have ruined your native town.

DR STOCKMANN: I – ruined –!

THE MAYOR: It's solely thanks to the Spa that the town has any future worth mentioning. You must realize that as well as I.

DR STOCKMANN: But then what do you think should be done?

THE MAYOR: I've been unable to persuade myself from your report that this situation with the water at the Spa is as alarming as you claim.

DR STOCKMANN: If anything, it's worse, Peter! Or at least it will be in the summer when the warm weather comes.

THE MAYOR: As I said, I think you're exaggerating hugely. A good doctor has to have a proper understanding of procedure – he has to know how to counteract any harmful effects and to remedy them, if they make themselves visibly apparent.

DR STOCKMANN: And so –? What then –?

THE MAYOR: The existing water supply at the Spa is a reality and must clearly be dealt with as such. But it's reasonable to assume that the committee may, in its own time, be per-suaded to consider whether, within acceptable bounds of pecuniary sacrifice, it might perhaps be possible to introduce certain improvements.

DR STOCKMANN: And you think I'd go along with anything so devious?

THE MAYOR: Devious?

DR STOCKMANN: Yes, it would be devious – a fraud, a lie, a downright crime against the public, against the whole community!

THE MAYOR: I have, as I've said, been unable to persuade myself that there is any actual imminent danger.

DR STOCKMANN: Oh yes, you have! Anything else is impos-sible. The truth and accuracy of my report is blindingly obvious, I know it! And you understand it perfectly, Peter;

but you just don't want to accept it. It was you who got it pushed through so the Spa and water system were placed where they are now; and it's *that* – it's that damned blunder that you don't want admit to. Pah! – Don't you think I see through you?

THE MAYOR: And even if that was so? If I guard my reputation with a certain anxiety, it's for the benefit of the town. Without moral authority I cannot guide or direct affairs in the way I deem most advantageous for the greater good. For this – and for a variety of other reasons – it is of paramount importance to me that your report is not presented to the committee. It must be withheld for the common good. I will then bring the issue up for discussion later, and we will do our best discreetly. But nothing – not a single word must reach the public domain about this disastrous matter.

DR STOCKMANN: Well, that can't be prevented now, my dear Peter.

THE MAYOR: It must and shall be prevented.

DR STOCKMANN: It's not possible, I tell you; there are far too many people who know about it.

THE MAYOR: Know about it! Who? It surely can't be those gentlemen at *The People's Messenger* who –?

DR STOCKMANN: Oh yes, them as well. The independent, liberal-minded press will, I think, ensure that the committee does its duty.

THE MAYOR [*after a short pause*]: You are an inordinately imprudent man, Tomas. Haven't you considered the consequences that this might carry with it for you?

DR STOCKMANN: Consequences? Consequences for me?

THE MAYOR: For you and yours, yes.

DR STOCKMANN: What the hell is *that* supposed to mean?

THE MAYOR: I believe that I have, throughout my life, proved an obliging and helpful brother to you.

DR STOCKMANN: Yes, you have; and I thank you for it.

THE MAYOR: No need. I've also been forced to it to some degree – for my own sake. It was always my hope that I could keep you tolerably in check, by helping to improve your financial position.

DR STOCKMANN: You what? So it was just for your own sake –!

THE MAYOR: To some degree, I say. It's awkward for a civil servant when his nearest relative goes about compromising himself time after time.

DR STOCKMANN: And that's what you think I do?

THE MAYOR: Yes, I'm afraid you do, without knowing it. You have a restless, argumentative, rebellious disposition. And then there's your unfortunate compulsion to write on every possible and impossible topic. No sooner do you get some idea than you have to write a newspaper article or an entire pamphlet about it.

DR STOCKMANN: Yes, but isn't it every man's duty as a citizen of this country to share it with the general public, when he seizes upon a new idea?

THE MAYOR: Oh, the general public has no need whatsoever for new ideas. The public is best served by the good, old, accepted ideas it already has.

DR STOCKMANN: And you can say that straight out?

THE MAYOR: Well, I have to talk straight with you some time. So far I've sought to avoid it, since I know how short-tempered you are; but now I must tell you the truth, Tomas. You have no idea how much damage you do to yourself with your hot-headedness. You complain about the authorities, yes, about the government even – running them down; claiming that you've been pushed aside, persecuted. But can you expect otherwise – a man as difficult as you?

DR STOCKMANN: What, now I'm difficult too, am I?

THE MAYOR: Yes, Tomas, you are an extremely difficult man to work with. I've experienced that for myself. You set yourself above all other considerations; you seem to forget that it's to me you owe your position here as medical officer to the Spa –

DR STOCKMANN: I was the perfect man for the job! I and nobody else! I was the first to see that the town could become a flourishing spa town; and back then I was the only one who saw that. I stood alone fighting for the idea for years; and I wrote and wrote –

THE MAYOR: Undeniably. But the time still wasn't ripe; well, that was hardly something you could judge from that back-water of yours. But when the appropriate moment came, then I – and the others – took the matter into our hands –

DR STOCKMANN: Yes, and then you botched my whole wonderful plan. Oh yes, it's plain now what clever chaps you were!

THE MAYOR: In my opinion all that's plain is that you're spoiling for another fight. You want to finish your superiors off – it's an old habit with you. You can't bear anyone in authority over you; you look askance at anyone who occupies a superior official position; you consider him a personal enemy – and immediately one weapon of attack is as good as the next. But now I've made you aware of the interests that are at stake for the whole town – and consequently for myself too. And therefore I am telling you, Tomas, I am inexorable in the demand that I now intend to present you with.

DR STOCKMANN: What kind of demand?

THE MAYOR: Since you've been loose-tongued enough to discuss this ticklish affair with outsiders, despite the fact it ought to have remained a boardroom secret,[36] the matter can't, of course, be hushed up. Rumours of all sorts will be spread far and wide, and the ill-disposed among us will feed these rumours with all kinds of additions. It will be essential, therefore, that you counter such rumours publicly.

DR STOCKMANN: Me! How? I don't understand.

THE MAYOR: It is expected that you will, after renewed investigations, come to the conclusion that this issue is nowhere near as dangerous or as alarming as you'd initially imagined.

DR STOCKMANN: Aha – you expect that!

THE MAYOR: Furthermore, it is expected that you foster and publicly express confidence in the board that it will thoroughly and conscientiously carry out whatever's necessary to alleviate any possible defects.

DR STOCKMANN: Yes, but the board will never be able to do that, so long as it carries on cheating and patching things up! I'm telling you, Peter; and that is my full and firm conviction –!

THE MAYOR: As an employee you have no right to foster any independent convictions.

DR STOCKMANN [*taken aback*]: No right to –?

THE MAYOR: As an employee, I'm saying. As a private person – Lord above, that's quite another matter. But as a subordinate public servant at the Spa, you do not have the right to express any convictions that run contrary to those of your superiors.

DR STOCKMANN: This is going too far! That I, as a doctor, a man of science, should not be permitted to –!

THE MAYOR: The issue being discussed here is not purely scientific; it's a combined issue; it is both a technical and financial issue.

DR STOCKMANN: It can be whatever the hell it wants! I want the freedom to express myself on every possible issue in the world.

THE MAYOR: Go ahead! But just not about the Spa. – We forbid you.

DR STOCKMANN [*shouting*]: We forbid –! We! You and those –

THE MAYOR: *I* forbid it – *I*, your most senior superior. And when I forbid you something, you had better obey.

DR STOCKMANN [*controlling himself*]: Peter – if you weren't my brother –

PETRA [*throwing open the door*]: Father, you're not to stand for this!

MRS STOCKMANN [*after her*]: Petra, Petra!

THE MAYOR: Oh, been eavesdropping, have we?

MRS STOCKMANN: Sounds travel so easily here; we couldn't help –

PETRA: No, you're right, I *was* listening.

THE MAYOR: Well, actually I'm pleased –

DR STOCKMANN [*moving closer*]: You spoke to me about 'to forbid' and 'to obey' –?

THE MAYOR: You've forced me to speak in that tone.

DR STOCKMANN: And I'm to make a public statement eating my own words?

THE MAYOR: We consider it an unavoidable necessity that you make a public statement of the kind I have demanded.

DR STOCKMANN: And if I don't – obey?

THE MAYOR: Then we shall issue a statement ourselves to re-assure the public.

DR STOCKMANN: Very well; but then I'll write opposing you. I shan't budge; I'll prove that *I* am right, and that you are wrong. And then what will you all do?

THE MAYOR: Then I shall be unable to prevent your dismissal.

DR STOCKMANN: What –?

PETRA: Father – dismissal!

MRS STOCKMANN: Dismissal!

THE MAYOR: Dismissal as medical officer. I shall see myself obliged to apply for your immediate discharge, to remove you from any involvement in the Spa's affairs.

DR STOCKMANN: And the board would dare do that!

THE MAYOR: You're the one playing dare here.

PETRA: Uncle, that's a shocking thing to do to a man like Father!

MRS STOCKMANN: Will you just be quiet, Petra!

THE MAYOR [*looks at* PETRA]: Aha, so we're already engaging in public debates, are we? Yes, naturally. [*To* MRS STOCK-MANN] Sister-in-law, you seem to be the most reasonable one in this house. Exercise whatever influence you might have over your husband; get him to realize what this will bring with it both for his family –

DR STOCKMANN: My family is of no concern to anybody but me!

THE MAYOR: – both for his family, I say, and for the town he lives in.

DR STOCKMANN: I'm the one who wants what's best for the town! I want to expose the faults that must sooner or later come to light. Oh yes, it'll be plain that I love my native town.

THE MAYOR: You, when in blind obstinacy you go about cutting off the town's primary source of sustenance?

DR STOCKMANN: That source is poisoned, man! Are you mad? We live here by peddling foul sludge and putrefaction! The whole of our flowering municipal life is sucking its sustenance from a lie!

THE MAYOR: Fantasies – or worse. The man who flings such offensive insinuations at his own hometown has to be society's enemy.

DR STOCKMANN [*moves towards him*]: And you dare –!

MRS STOCKMANN [*throwing herself between them*]: Tomas!

PETRA [*grasps her father by the arm*]: Calm down, Father!

THE MAYOR: I won't be subjected to violence. You've been warned now. Just remember what you owe your family. Goodbye.

He leaves.

DR STOCKMANN [*walking up and down*]: And I have to tolerate such treatment! In my own house, Katrine! What do you say to that!

MRS STOCKMANN: Yes, it is shameful, Tomas –

PETRA: I could kill Uncle!

DR STOCKMANN: It's my own fault. I should have put my claws out long ago! – shown my teeth! – bitten back! – And to call me an enemy of society! Me! By God, I shan't take that lying down.

MRS STOCKMANN: But, Tomas my sweet, your brother has all the power on his side.

DR STOCKMANN: Yes, but I have right on mine, Katrine!

MRS STOCKMANN: Right? What use is it to have right on your side when you have no power?

PETRA: But, Mother, really! – How can you talk like that?

DR STOCKMANN: So, you're saying it's no use in a free society to have right on your side? You're hilarious, Katrine. And besides – haven't I got the liberal-minded, independent press before me – and the solid majority behind me? That's power enough, I'd have thought!

MRS STOCKMANN: But, good heavens, Tomas, you're surely not thinking of –?

DR STOCKMANN: What aren't I thinking of?

MRS STOCKMANN: – of standing up against your brother, I mean.

DR STOCKMANN: What the devil else would you want me to do, if not stand by what's right and true?

PETRA: Yes, that's what I'd ask too.

MRS STOCKMANN: But it won't be of any use; when they won't, they won't.

DR STOCKMANN: Hoho, Katrine, just give it time, and you'll see how I'll drive this war through.

MRS STOCKMANN: Yes, you might just drive your dismissal through – that's what.

DR STOCKMANN: Then at least I'll have done my duty towards the public – to society. Yes, I – who've been called an enemy of society!

MRS STOCKMANN: But towards your family, Tomas? Towards us here at home? Do you think *that* is doing your duty towards the people you're meant to provide for?

PETRA: Oh, don't always think about us first, Mother.

MRS STOCKMANN: Yes, it's easy for *you* to talk; if it comes to the crunch you can stand on your own feet. – But remember the boys, Tomas; and consider yourself a bit too, and me –

DR STOCKMANN: But I think you're quite mad, Katrine! If I fell to my knees like a miserable coward before Peter and his damned clique – would I ever have another moment's happiness in my life again?

MRS STOCKMANN: Well, that I don't know; but God preserve us from the happiness we'll all have if you continue to defy him. Then you'll find yourself back without bread on the table, without any regular income. I think all of us have had enough of that in the past; remember, Tomas; think about what that means.

DR STOCKMANN [*his body contorts and he clenches his fists*]: And this is what these office lackeys can bring down on a free and honest man! Isn't that dreadful, Katrine?

MRS STOCKMANN: Yes, you've been treated abominably, that's quite true. But, good heavens, there's so much injustice in this world that one has to bow to. – Here are the boys, Tomas! Look at them! What's to become of them? Oh, no, no, you wouldn't have the heart –.

EILIF *and* MORTEN, *carrying their schoolbooks, have meanwhile come in.*

DR STOCKMANN: The boys –! [*Suddenly recovers himself.*] No, not even if the entire world crashed down, would I bow my neck under that yoke. [*Walks towards his room.*]

MRS STOCKMANN [*following him*]: Tomas – what are you going to do?

DR STOCKMANN [*by the door*]: I'm going to earn the right to look my sons in the eye when they're full-grown free men. [*Goes in.*]

MRS STOCKMANN [*bursting into tears*]: Dear God, help and preserve us all!

PETRA: Father's a good man! He's not giving in.

    The BOYS *ask in surprise what is going on;* PETRA *signals to them to be quiet.*

ACT THREE

The editorial office of The People's Messenger. *In the background, to the left, is the entrance door; to the right in the same wall is a door with glass panels, through which the printshop can be seen. In the wall to the right is another door. In the middle of the room is a large table covered with papers, newspapers and books. In the foreground, to the left, a window, in front of which stands a desk and a high chair. There are a couple of armchairs by the table, and other chairs standing along the wall. The room is gloomy and unappealing; the furniture is old, the armchairs are stained and torn. In the printshop a couple of typesetters are seen at work, and further away a hand-press is in operation.*

MR HOVSTAD *is sitting at the desk, writing. A moment later* BILLING *comes in from the right with* DR STOCKMANN's *manuscript in his hand.*

BILLING: Well, I never –!

HOVSTAD [*whilst writing*]: Have you read it all?

BILLING [*putting the manuscript on the desk*]: Yes, I most certainly have.

HOVSTAD: The doctor's very sharp, don't you think?

BILLING: Sharp? He's crushing, God strike me dead, he is. Every word falls with such weight – how shall I say – like the blow of a sledgehammer.

HOVSTAD: Yes, but remember these people don't fall at the first blow.

BILLING: True; but then we'll go on striking – blow after blow, until the whole feudal elite come tumbling down. When I sat in there reading this, it was as though I glimpsed the revolution coming from afar.

HOVSTAD [*turning round*]: Shhh! – Just don't say that so Aslaksen hears.

BILLING [*lowering his voice*]: Aslaksen is a chicken, a wimp; not a jot of manly courage in him. But you'll get your way this time, surely. Eh? The doctor's article will go in, won't it?

HOVSTAD: Yes, as long as the mayor doesn't decide to give in –

BILLING: That would be damned annoying.

HOVSTAD: Well, fortunately we can turn the situation to our advantage whatever happens. If the mayor doesn't go along with the doctor's suggestion, he'll have all the small tradesmen at his throat – the entire Homeowners' Association and the others. And if he does go along with it, he'll fall out with a whole bunch of the Spa's big shareholders, who've been his strongest backers till now –

BILLING: Yes, that's right; because they'll probably have to dish out a big pile of money –

HOVSTAD: Yes, you can bet on it. And then the ring will be broken, you see, and then day in and day out we'll make it evident in the paper to the public that the mayor is incompetent in one thing after another, and that all the positions of trust in the town, the whole municipal council, ought to be handed over to liberal-minded people.

BILLING: Yes, God strike me dead, that's perfect! I see it – I see it; we're standing right near the very beginning of a revolution!

There is a knock at the door.

HOVSTAD: Shhh! [*Calls out*] Come in!

DR STOCKMANN *comes in through the door to the left in the background.* MR HOVSTAD *moves towards him.*

HOVSTAD: Ah, it's the doctor! Well?

DR STOCKMANN: Print away, Mr Hovstad!

HOVSTAD: So it's come to that?

BILLING: Hurrah!

DR STOCKMANN: Print away, I say. Yes, it has indeed come to that. But now they'll get what they've asked for. Now it'll be war here in town, Mr Billing!

BILLING: War to the knife[37] I hope! And knife to the throat, doctor!

DR STOCKMANN: The report is only a start. My head is already full of sketches for some four or five other articles. Where have you put Aslaksen?

BILLING [*calls into the printshop*]: Aslaksen, come in here for a moment!

HOVSTAD: Four or five more articles, you say? About the same issue?

DR STOCKMANN: No – far from it, my friend. No, they'll be about entirely different things. But it all stems from the water system and the sewers. One thing drags the next with it, you understand. It's like when you start tearing away at an old house – just the same.

BILLING: God strike me dead, that's so true; you never feel you're finished until you've torn down the whole rickety building.

ASLAKSEN [*coming from the printshop*]: Torn down? The doctor's not thinking of tearing down the Spa house, surely?

HOVSTAD: Far from it; don't you worry.

DR STOCKMANN: No, it was something quite different. So, Mr Hovstad, what do you say to my report?

HOVSTAD: I think it's an absolute masterpiece –

DR STOCKMANN: Yes, isn't it –? Well, I'm glad to hear it, glad to hear it.

HOVSTAD: It's so clear and to the point; you don't need to be an expert at all to see how everything connects. I dare say you'll get every enlightened man on your side.

ASLAKSEN: And all the prudent ones, I hope?

BILLING: Prudent and imprudent – practically the whole town, I think.

ASLAKSEN: Well, then I dare say we can print it.

DR STOCKMANN: Yes, I should think so!

HOVSTAD: It'll go in early tomorrow.

DR STOCKMANN: Yes, damn it all, not a single day must be wasted. Listen, Mr Aslaksen, I wanted to ask *this* of you: that you take personal charge of the manuscript.

ASLAKSEN: I suppose I can do that.

DR STOCKMANN: Look after it as if it was gold! No misprints; every word is crucial. And I'll pop in again later; perhaps I could do a bit of proof-reading. I can't say how eager I am to see it in print – hurled forth –

BILLING: Hurled – yes, like lightning!

DR STOCKMANN: – offered up for the judgement of my competent fellow citizens. Oh, you can't imagine what I've been subjected to today. People have threatened me with one thing and another: they've wanted to rob me of my most obvious human rights –[38]

BILLING: What! Your human rights!

DR STOCKMANN: – they have tried to degrade me, tried to turn me into a lily-livered coward, demanded that I put personal interest before my most deeply held, most sacred convictions –

BILLING: God strike me dead, if that isn't just too gross.

HOVSTAD: Well, you can expect anything from that quarter.

DR STOCKMANN: But they won't get far with me; they'll get it in black and white. Every single day now I'll drop anchor, so to speak, in *The People's Messenger* and bombard them with one explosive article after another –

ASLAKSEN: Yes, but listen now –

BILLING: Hurrah; there'll be war, there'll be war!

DR STOCKMANN: – I shall strike them to the ground, I shall crush them, raze their fortifications before the eyes of our entire right-thinking public! That's what I'll do!

ASLAKSEN: But temperately, doctor, please; fire with temperance –

BILLING: No; no! Don't spare the dynamite![39]

DR STOCKMANN [*carrying on regardless*]: Because this is no longer just about the water system and sewers, you see. The whole of society must be cleansed, disinfected –

BILLING: Ah, a timely word indeed!

DR STOCKMANN: All these old bunglers must be swept away, you understand. And in every possible domain! Endless vistas have opened before me today. It's not all quite clear to me yet; but I'm sure I shall work it out. Energetic, young standard-bearers, that's what we need to go out in search of now, my friends; we must have new commanders at all our foreposts.

BILLING: Hear, hear!

DR STOCKMANN: And as long as we stick together it will go very smoothly, very smoothly. This transformation will run off the stocks like a ship. Don't you think?

HOVSTAD: I, for my part, believe that we have every prospect now of placing the municipal leadership where it rightfully belongs.

ASLAKSEN: And as long as we proceed temperately, I can't imagine it would be too risky.

DR STOCKMANN: Who the hell cares whether it's risky or not! What I'm doing, I'm doing in the name of truth and for the sake of my conscience.

HOVSTAD: You're a man worthy of support, doctor, sir.

ASLAKSEN: Yes, nobody could deny it, the doctor is a true friend to this town; a real friend of the community.

BILLING: Dr Stockmann is, God strike me dead, a friend of the people, Aslaksen!

ASLAKSEN: I expect the Homeowners' Association will soon use those very words.

DR STOCKMANN [moved, he grasps their hands]: Thank you, thank you, my dear loyal friends – it's so heartening to hear this; my distinguished brother called me something very different. Well, he'll get that back with interest, by God! But now I must be off to visit some poor devil –. I'll come back, as I said. Take very good care of the manuscript, Aslaksen – and, for heaven's sake, don't take out any exclamation marks! Add a couple rather! Splendid, splendid; goodbye for now – goodbye!

Farewells are exchanged as he is accompanied to the door and leaves.

HOVSTAD: He can be an invaluable asset to us.

ASLAKSEN: Yes, as long as he keeps to this business with the Spa Institute. But if he goes further, it would be inadvisable to join company with him.

HOVSTAD: Hm – well that all depends –

BILLING: You're always so damned fearful, Aslaksen!

ASLAKSEN: Fearful? Yes, when it comes to local men of power, then I am fearful, Mr Billing; that's something I've learned in the school of experience, let me tell you. But set me up in big politics, against the government itself, and then see if I'm fearful.

BILLING: No, you're not, no; but that's exactly what makes you so inconsistent.

ASLAKSEN: I am a man of conscience, that's the thing. If you let loose on the government, then you don't do the community any harm at least; because those men aren't troubled by it, you see – they'll stand as secure as ever. But the *local* authorities, *they* can be ousted, and then you can end up with incompetence at the helm, resulting in irreparable harm to homeowners and others.

HOVSTAD: But the education of the people[40] through self-governance – don't you consider *that*?

ASLAKSEN: When a man's got interests that need protecting, he can't think about everything, Mr Hovstad.

HOVSTAD: Then pray God I never get any interests.

BILLING: Hear – hear!

ASLAKSEN [*smiles*]: Hmm! [*Points to the desk.*] That editor's stool was occupied by District Governor Stensgård before you.

BILLING [*spits*]: Pah! That turncoat.

HOVSTAD: I'm no weathercock – and never will be.

ASLAKSEN: A politician should never forswear anything, Mr Hovstad. And you, Mr Billing, I think you should also take a reef or two in your sails these days; after all, you're applying for the post of secretary at the magistrate's[41] office.

BILLING: I –!

HOVSTAD: *You*, Billing?

BILLING: Yes, but – you must realize, dammit, that I'm just doing it to annoy those venerable old fools.

ASLAKSEN: Well, it's none of my business. But when I'm accused of cowardice and inconsistency in my opinions, then I'd like to have it stressed: Aslaksen's political past is open to anybody and everybody. I've undergone no other change, than to grow more temperate, you see. My heart is still with the people; but I don't deny that my head is somewhat inclined towards the authorities – the local ones, at least.

He goes into the printshop.

BILLING: Shouldn't we try to get rid of him, Hovstad?

HOVSTAD: Do you know anybody else who'd be prepared to give us paper and printing on credit?

BILLING: It's a damned shame that we don't have the necessary capital.

HOVSTAD [*sitting down at his desk*]: Yes, if only we had *that*, then –

BILLING: Suppose you approach Dr Stockmann?

HOVSTAD [*leafing through papers*]: Oh, what use would that be? He owns nothing.

BILLING: No, but he's got a good man in the wings, old Morten Kiil – 'the Badger', as they call him.

HOVSTAD [*writing*]: Are you that certain *he* owns anything?

BILLING: Yes, God strike me dead, he most certainly does! And some of it is sure to come to the Stockmann family. He's bound to be thinking about making provision – for the children at least.

HOVSTAD [*half turning*]: Are you building on *that*?

BILLING: Building? I'm not building on anything.

HOVSTAD: You'd be right not to. And as for that position at the magistrate's, you oughtn't to build on that either; because I can assure you – you won't get it.

BILLING: You think I don't know that already? But that's exactly what's so dear to me, *not* to get it. A rebuttal like that fires your fighting spirit. It gives you a kind of supply of fresh bile, and that can certainly be needed in a dull backwater like this, where hardly anything really rousing ever happens.

HOVSTAD [*who is writing*]: Right, yes.

BILLING: Anyway – they'll be hearing from me soon! – I'll go in now and write that appeal to the Homeowners' Association.

He goes into the room on the right.

HOVSTAD [*sitting at his desk, biting on his pen and speaking slowly*]: Hmm – right, yes. [*A knock is heard.*] Come in!

PETRA *comes in through the left-hand door in the background.*

HOVSTAD [*getting up*]: Oh, it's you? What are you doing *here*?

PETRA: I'm sorry but –

HOVSTAD [*pulling an armchair up*]: Won't you sit down?

PETRA: No, thank you; I won't be staying.

HOVSTAD: It's something from your father perhaps –?

PETRA: No, from me. [*Takes a book out of her coat pocket.*] Here's your English story.

HOVSTAD: Why are you giving it back?

PETRA: I'm sorry, but I don't want to translate it.

HOVSTAD: But you promised me –

PETRA: Well, I hadn't read it then. And you obviously haven't read it either?

HOVSTAD: No; as you know, I don't understand English; but –

PETRA: Quite; which is why I wanted to tell you that you must look for something different. [*Puts the book on the table.*] This really can't be used in *The People's Messenger*.

HOVSTAD: Why not?

PETRA: Because it's completely at odds with your own opinions.

HOVSTAD: Well, that's not necessarily –

PETRA: You don't seem to understand. It's about how a super-natural power [42] looks after the so-called good people in the world and ensures that everything turns out for the best for them in the end – and how the so-called bad people get their punishment.

HOVSTAD: Yes, but that's perfect. That's just the sort of thing people want.

PETRA: And you want to be the person to give them this sort of thing? You don't believe a word of it yourself. You know very well that isn't how things are in reality.

HOVSTAD: Indeed, you're perfectly right; but an editor can't always act as he'd prefer. He often has to bow to people's opinion on less important issues. After all, politics is the chief priority in life – for a newspaper at least; and if I want to carry people with me on matters of emancipation and progress, then I can't frighten them off. When they find a moral tale like this lower down on the pages, they're more

willing to go along with what's printed above – they feel
somehow safer.

PETRA: Goodness! You surely aren't so deceitful as to set traps
for your readers; you're not some sort of spider!

HOVSTAD [*smiling*]: Thank you for having such faith in me.
But, you're right, it was in fact only Billing's line of thought,
not mine.

PETRA: Billing's!

HOVSTAD: Well; he said something of the sort recently at
least. And it's actually Billing who's so anxious to get the
story in; I don't know the book myself, as I said.

PETRA: But how can Billing, with his emancipated views –?

HOVSTAD: Oh, Billing is a man of many parts. He's even
applied for the position of secretary to the magistrate's
office, so I hear.

PETRA: I don't believe it, Mr Hovstad. How could he bring
himself to do such a thing?

HOVSTAD: Well, you'll have to ask him that.

PETRA: I'd never have thought that of Billing.

HOVSTAD [*looks at her more intently*]: Really? Do you find it
so surprising?

PETRA: Yes. Or, then again, perhaps not. Oh, I don't know –

HOVSTAD: Us hacks aren't of much worth, Miss.

PETRA: You really mean that?

HOVSTAD: Now and then it's what I think.

PETRA: Well yes, perhaps in the usual day-to-day wrangling,
that I can understand. But now, when you've taken on such
an important cause –

HOVSTAD: This thing with your father, you mean?

PETRA: Precisely, yes. Right now, I imagine you must feel you're
a man of greater worth than most.

HOVSTAD: Yes, I do feel something of the sort today.

PETRA: Yes, you must, surely? Oh, it's a splendid vocation
you've chosen. Blazing a trail for neglected truths and for
new, courageous points of view –. The very fact of standing
up and speaking out fearlessly on behalf of a wronged man –

HOVSTAD: Especially when that wronged man – hm! – I don't
rightly know how to –

PETRA: When he's so deeply principled and honest, you mean?

HOVSTAD [*more quietly*]: Especially when he's your father, I meant.

PETRA [*taken aback*]: What? –

HOVSTAD: Yes, Petra – Miss Petra.

PETRA: Is *that* what comes first and foremost for you? Not the cause itself? Not the truth; not my father's heartfelt caring and generosity?

HOVSTAD: Well yes – yes, obviously, that too.

PETRA: No, thank you; you've given yourself away now, Mr Hovstad; and I will never believe you about anything ever again.

HOVSTAD: Can you take it so amiss if it's mainly for your sake –?

PETRA: What I'm angry with you for is that you haven't been honest with Father. You've talked to him as though the truth and the community's well-being were uppermost in your mind. You've made fools of both Father and me; you're not the man you made yourself out to be. And for that, I shall never forgive you – never!

HOVSTAD: You oughtn't to say that so harshly, Miss Petra; least of all now.

PETRA: Why not now, as well as any time?

HOVSTAD: Because your father can't manage without my help.

PETRA [*looking down at him*]: So you're that sort of man? Shame on you!

HOVSTAD: No, no; really I'm not. It just came over me kind of unawares; you mustn't think that of me.

PETRA: I know what to think. Goodbye.

ASLAKSEN [*coming from the printshop urgently and with an air of secrecy*]: Christ Almighty, Mr Hovstad! – [*Sees* PETRA.] Oops, didn't mean that –

PETRA: There's the book; you'd better give it to somebody else. [*Goes towards the exit.*]

HOVSTAD [*following her*]: But, Miss Stockmann –

PETRA: Goodbye.

   She leaves.

ASLAKSEN: Mr Hovstad, listen!

HOVSTAD: All right, all right; what is it now?

ASLAKSEN: The mayor's out in the printshop.

HOVSTAD: The mayor, you say?

ASLAKSEN: Yes, he wants to speak to you. He came in by the back door – didn't want to be seen, you understand.

HOVSTAD: What could it be about? No, wait – I'll go myself –
  He goes to the door of the printshop, opens it, greets the MAYOR *and invites him in.*

HOVSTAD: Keep watch, Aslaksen, so nobody –

ASLAKSEN: Understood –
  He goes out into the printshop.

THE MAYOR: Didn't expect to see me here, did you, Mr Hovstad?

HOVSTAD: No, I didn't actually.

THE MAYOR [*looking round*]: You've made it very comfortable for yourself in here; very nice.

HOVSTAD: Oh –

THE MAYOR: And here I come without a by-your-leave making demands on your time!

HOVSTAD: Not at all, Mr Mayor; at your service. But let me relieve you of your – [*Takes the* MAYOR's *hat and stick and puts them on a chair.*] And wouldn't your honour[43] like to sit down?

THE MAYOR [*sits at the table*]: Thank you.
  HOVSTAD *sits at the table too.*

THE MAYOR: Something most – most vexing has happened to me today, Mr Hovstad.

HOVSTAD: Oh? Well, of course; with the numerous duties the mayor has, then –

THE MAYOR: The cause today is the medical officer.

HOVSTAD: Oh? The doctor?

THE MAYOR: He's written some sort of report to the Spa's board, concerning a number of supposed defects with the Spa.

HOVSTAD: No, really?

THE MAYOR: Yes – hasn't he told you? I thought he said –

HOVSTAD: Ah, that's true, he did mention something –

ASLAKSEN [*coming from the printshop*]: I should probably take the manuscript –

HOVSTAD [*annoyed*]: Hm! It's there on the desk.

ASLAKSEN [*finds it*]: Good.

THE MAYOR: But look, that's *it* there –

ASLAKSEN: Yes, this is the doctor's article, Mr Mayor.

HOVSTAD: Oh, is *that* what you're talking about?

THE MAYOR: The very thing. What do you think of it?

HOVSTAD: Well, I'm no expert, of course, and I've only glanced through it.

THE MAYOR: But you're allowing it to go to print?

HOVSTAD: I can't very well refuse a man writing under his own name –

ASLAKSEN: I have no say in the paper, Mr Mayor –

THE MAYOR: Of course not.

ASLAKSEN: I just print what's put in my hands.

THE MAYOR: Quite so.

ASLAKSEN: So if you'll excuse – [*Heads towards the printshop.*]

THE MAYOR: No, wait a moment, Mr Aslaksen. With your permission, Mr Hovstad –

HOVSTAD: Of course, Mr Mayor –

THE MAYOR: You are a prudent and thoughtful man, Mr Aslaksen.

ASLAKSEN: I'm delighted the mayor thinks so.

THE MAYOR: And a man with a wide circle of influence.

ASLAKSEN: Well, mainly amongst modest folk, of course.

THE MAYOR: Modest taxpayers are the richest in number – here as elsewhere.

ASLAKSEN: They are indeed.

THE MAYOR: And I have no doubt that you know what the general mood is among them. Isn't that so?

ASLAKSEN: I'd like to think so, yes, Mr Mayor.

THE MAYOR: Well – seeing as there's such a praiseworthy willingness for sacrifice amongst the town's less affluent citizens, then –

ASLAKSEN: How do you mean?

HOVSTAD: Sacrifice?

THE MAYOR: It's a splendid sign of public spirit, a truly splendid sign. I might almost have said that I hadn't expected it. But then, of course, you know the public mood better than I.

ASLAKSEN: Yes but, Mr Mayor –

THE MAYOR: And it'll be no mean sacrifice that the town will have to make.

HOVSTAD: The town?

ASLAKSEN: But I don't understand –. It's the Spa –!

THE MAYOR: According to a provisional estimate, the alterations that the Spa's medical officer deems desirable will run to a couple of hundred thousand kroner.

ASLAKSEN: Yes, that's a lot of money; but –

THE MAYOR: Naturally, it'll be necessary for us take out a municipal loan.[44]

HOVSTAD [rising]: Surely the idea can't be that the town –?

ASLAKSEN: Would it come out of the town's funds? Out of the meagre pockets of our small tradesmen?

THE MAYOR: Well, my honourable Mr Aslaksen, where else would the funds come from?

ASLAKSEN: That's something the gentlemen who own the Spa must see to.

THE MAYOR: The Spa owners see no way of stretching themselves more than they have already.

ASLAKSEN: Is that certain, Mr Mayor?

THE MAYOR: I've assured myself of it. So if people really want these extensive alterations, the town will have to pay for them itself.

ASLAKSEN: But, Christ Almighty – beg pardon! – but this is quite a different matter, isn't it, Mr Hovstad!

HOVSTAD: Yes, it certainly is.

THE MAYOR: The most disastrous thing is that we'll be forced to close the Spa for a couple of years.

HOVSTAD: Close? Close it completely!

ASLAKSEN: For two years!

THE MAYOR: Yes, that's how long the work will take – at least.

ASLAKSEN: But, Christ Almighty, we'll never hold out, Mr Mayor! How are we homeowners to earn a living in the meantime?

THE MAYOR: That, I'm afraid, is extremely difficult to answer, Mr Aslaksen. But what would you have us do? Do you think we'll get a single visitor here if we encourage them in some fantasy about our water being putrid, that we're living on pestilent soil, that the entire town –

ASLAKSEN: And the whole thing's just a fantasy?

THE MAYOR: I haven't, with the best will in the world, been able to convince myself otherwise.

ASLAKSEN: But then it really is downright indefensible of Dr Stockmann – well, excuse me, Your Honour, but –

THE MAYOR: You are merely expressing a lamentable truth, Mr Aslaksen. My brother has unfortunately always been a reckless man.

ASLAKSEN: And still you want to support him in such a thing, Mr Hovstad!

HOVSTAD: But who could have thought –?

THE MAYOR: I have composed a concise statement outlining the relevant facts, as they ought to be interpreted from an objective standpoint, indicating how any potential defects might be remedied in a manner proportionate to the Spa's funds.

HOVSTAD: Have you got this article with you, Mr Mayor?

THE MAYOR [*fumbling in his pocket*]: Yes; I brought it just in case you –

ASLAKSEN [*quickly*]: Christ Almighty, there he is!

THE MAYOR: Who? My brother?

HOVSTAD: Where – where!

ASLAKSEN: He's coming through the printshop.

THE MAYOR: Disastrous! I don't want to bump into him here, and I still had a few matters to discuss with you.

HOVSTAD [*pointing to the door on the right*]: Go in there for now.

THE MAYOR: But –?

HOVSTAD: You'll find Billing in there, that's all.

ASLAKSEN: Quick, quick, Mr Mayor – he's coming.

THE MAYOR: Yes, yes; but get him on his way again quickly.

He goes out through the right-hand door, which ASLAK-SEN *opens for him, and then shuts after him.*

HOVSTAD: Look busy, Aslaksen.

He sits down and writes. ASLAKSEN *starts to rummage among a heap of newspapers on a chair to the right.*

DR STOCKMANN [*coming in from the printshop*]: Here I am again. [*Puts down his hat and stick.*]

HOVSTAD [*writing*]: Already, doctor? Do hurry up with that thing we talked about, Aslaksen. Time's very tight for us today.

DR STOCKMANN [*to* ASLAKSEN]: No proofs to be had yet, I hear.

ASLAKSEN [*without turning round*]: No, how could the doctor think that?

DR STOCKMANN: No, of course; but I'm impatient, as you'll understand. I shan't rest or relax until I see it in print.

HOVSTAD: Hmm; it'll probably be a good while yet. Don't you think, Aslaksen?

ASLAKSEN: Yes, I'm afraid it might be.

DR STOCKMANN: All right, my friends; then I'll come back later; I'm happy to come back twice if needs be. Such an important cause – the welfare of the whole town – this really is no time to be idle. [*He is about to leave but stops and comes back.*] But, listen – there's one other thing I need to discuss with you.

HOVSTAD: Sorry; but couldn't we do it another time –?

DR STOCKMANN: I can tell you in two words. You see, it's just that – when people read my article in the paper tomorrow and get to know that I've spent the whole winter quietly working away for the good of the town –

HOVSTAD: Yes but, doctor –

DR STOCKMANN: I know what you're going to say. You don't think it was any more than my damned duty – a citizen's plain duty. Of course; I know that as well as you. But my fellow townsfolk, you see –. Good Lord, these dear people, they think so highly of me –

ASLAKSEN: Yes, our citizens have indeed thought most highly of you until today, doctor.

DR STOCKMANN: Yes, and that's why I'm worried they'll – well, what I wanted to say was: when this reaches them – especially the poorer classes – like a rallying cry for them to take the town's affairs into their own hands in future –

HOVSTAD [*getting up*]: Ahem, doctor, I won't hide it from you –

DR STOCKMANN: Aha – I knew there was something brewing! But I won't hear of it. If people are busy preparing anything of the sort –

HOVSTAD: Preparing what?

DR STOCKMANN: Well, something or other – a parade, or a banquet, or a subscription list[45] for a token of honour – or whatever else, then you must promise me solemnly and faithfully to put a stop to it. And you too, Mr Aslaksen; you hear me!

HOVSTAD: I'm sorry, doctor, we may as well tell you sooner rather than later, the truth is –

MRS STOCKMANN, *wearing a hat and coat, enters through the left-hand door in the background.*

MRS STOCKMANN [*sees the* DOCTOR]: Aha, just as I guessed!

HOVSTAD [*moving towards her*]: Goodness, you here too, Mrs Stockmann?

DR STOCKMANN: What the hell do *you* want here, Katrine?

MRS STOCKMANN: I'm sure you know very well what I want.

HOVSTAD: Won't you sit down? Or perhaps –

MRS STOCKMANN: No, thank you; don't trouble yourself. And you mustn't take offence at my coming to fetch my husband; I'm the mother of three children, let me tell you.

DR STOCKMANN: Oh, come, come; we do all know that.

MRS STOCKMANN: Well, it really doesn't seem that you're thinking much about your wife and children today; or you wouldn't behave like this, plunging us all into misfortune.

DR STOCKMANN: But you're utterly mad, Katrine! Should a man with a wife and children not be allowed to proclaim the truth – not be allowed to be a valuable and active citizen – not be allowed to serve the town in which he lives!

MRS STOCKMANN: Everything in moderation, Tomas.

ASLAKSEN: That's just what I say. Temperance in all things.

MRS STOCKMANN: Which is why you're doing us a wicked disservice, Mr Hovstad, when you lure my husband away from house and home and fool him into doing all this.

HOVSTAD: I am certainly not fooling anybody into –

DR STOCKMANN: Fooling! You think *I* am allowing myself to be fooled!

MRS STOCKMANN: Yes, you are indeed. I know you're the cleverest man in town; but you're awfully easy to fool, Tomas. [*To* HOVSTAD] And just think, he'll lose his position at the Spa if you print what he's written –

ASLAKSEN: What!

HOVSTAD: Yes, but you know what, doctor –

DR STOCKMANN [*laughing*]: Ha-ha, just let them try –! No, my dear – they'll think twice. Because I've got the solid majority behind me, you see!

MRS STOCKMANN: Yes, that's what so unfortunate, to have something that awful behind you.

DR STOCKMANN: What twaddle, Katrine – go home and look after your house and leave me to look after society. How can you be so apprehensive when I'm so confident and happy? [*Walks up and down, rubbing his hands*] The truth and the people will win this battle, you can swear on it! Oh, I see the whole liberal-minded band of citizens rallying in one victorious army –! [*Stops beside a chair.*] What – what the hell is *that*?

ASLAKSEN [*looks at the chair*]: Whoops!

HOVSTAD [*likewise*]: Hmm –!

DR STOCKMANN: If it isn't Mr Authority's top end!

He picks up the MAYOR's *hat delicately between his fingertips and holds it up in the air.*

MRS STOCKMANN: The mayor's hat!

DR STOCKMANN: And here's his swagger stick[46] too. How in the devil's name –?

HOVSTAD: Well, you see –

DR STOCKMANN: Ah, I understand! He's been here to talk you round. Ha-ha! He came to the right man there! And then he spotted me in the printshop –. [*Bursts out laughing.*] Did he run, Mr Aslaksen?

ASLAKSEN [*quickly*]: He ran all right, doctor.

DR STOCKMANN: Ran, leaving his stick and –. Oh, rubbish! Peter doesn't run from anything. But where the hell have you hidden him? Ah! – in there, of course. Now you'll see, Katrine!

MRS STOCKMANN: Tomas – I am begging you –!

ASLAKSEN: Careful, doctor.

DR STOCKMANN has put the MAYOR'*s hat on his head and picked up his stick; he goes over and flings the door open, bringing his hand up to the brim of the hat in a salute.*

The MAYOR *comes in, red with rage.* BILLING *comes behind him.*

THE MAYOR: What's the meaning of this riotous behaviour?

DR STOCKMANN: Some respect, please, my good Peter. I'm the one with the authority in this town now.

He strolls up and down.

MRS STOCKMANN [*almost in tears*]: No, but Tomas, please!

THE MAYOR [*following him about*]: Give me my hat and stick!

DR STOCKMANN [*as before*]: If you're the chief of police, I'm chief citizen of this whole town, don't you know!

THE MAYOR: Take that hat off, I tell you. Remember it's a regulation uniform hat!

DR STOCKMANN: Pff; you think the lion[47] that's been aroused in our people will let itself be frightened by regulation hats? Yes, because we're going to make a revolution in town tomorrow, I'll have you know. You threatened to depose me; but now I shall depose you – depose you from all your offices of trust –. You don't think I can? Oh yes; I have the victorious forces of society with me. Hovstad and Billing will thunder in *The People's Messenger*, and Aslaksen will march forth at the head of the entire Homeowners' Association –

ASLAKSEN: No, doctor, I won't.

DR STOCKMANN: But of course you will –

THE MAYOR: Aha! Mr Hovstad may, however, decide to join in with this agitation?

HOVSTAD: No, Mr Mayor.

ASLAKSEN: No, Mr Hovstad isn't so mad that he'd go and ruin both himself and his newspaper for the sake of some fantasy.

DR STOCKMANN [*looking around*]: What's the meaning of this?

HOVSTAD: You've presented your case in a false light, doctor; and I am therefore unable to support it.

BILLING: No, after everything Mr Mayor was so kind as to inform me of in there –

DR STOCKMANN: False! You leave that to me. Just print my article; I'll be man enough to defend it.

HOVSTAD: I'm not printing it. I cannot and will not and dare not print it.

DR STOCKMANN: Dare not? What kind of talk is that? You're the editor; and it's the editors who rule the press, I'd have thought!

ASLAKSEN: No, it's the subscribers, doctor.

THE MAYOR: Fortunately.

ASLAKSEN: It is public opinion, the enlightened general public, the homeowners and all the others; *they* rule the newspapers.

DR STOCKMANN [*composedly*]: And I have all these forces against me?

ASLAKSEN: Yes, you have. It would mean the complete ruin of the middle class,[48] if your article was printed.

DR STOCKMANN: I see. –

THE MAYOR: My hat and stick!

    DR STOCKMANN *takes off the hat and puts it on the table along with the stick.*

THE MAYOR [*picks them both up*]: Your mayoral dignity came to an abrupt end.

DR STOCKMANN: It's not the end yet. [*To* HOVSTAD] So, it's completely impossible to get my article into *The People's Messenger*?

HOVSTAD: Quite impossible; partly out of regard for your family.

MRS STOCKMANN: Oh, you really mustn't trouble yourself over his family, Mr Hovstad.

THE MAYOR [*taking a sheet of paper from his pocket*]: It will be sufficient, for the guidance of the public, for this to appear. It is an official statement. There you are.

HOVSTAD [*taking the paper*]: Excellent; I'll see it goes in.

DR STOCKMANN: But not mine. You think you can silence me and stifle the truth! But that won't go as smoothly as you think. Mr Aslaksen, take my manuscript this instant and print it as a leaflet – I shall publish it – at my own expense. I want four hundred copies; no, I want five, six hundred.

ASLAKSEN: I daren't lend my workshop to such a thing, not if you offered me gold, doctor. I daren't out of regard for public opinion. You won't get it printed anywhere in the whole town.

DR STOCKMANN: Then give it back to me.

HOVSTAD [*giving him the manuscript*]: Here you are.

DR STOCKMANN [*fetches his hat and stick*]: This *will* come out anyway. I shall read it out at a large public meeting; all my fellow citizens will hear the voice of truth!

THE MAYOR: No association in the whole town will lend you a hall for such a purpose.

ASLAKSEN: Not a single one; I'm absolutely sure.

BILLING: No, God strike me dead if they will.

MRS STOCKMANN: That really would be too shameful! But why would they turn against you like this, to the last man?

DR STOCKMANN [*angrily*]: I'll tell you why. Because all the men in this town are nothing but old women – just like you; they only ever think about their families, not about society.

MRS STOCKMANN [*takes his arm*]: Then I'll show them an – an old woman who can act like a man – for once. Because I'm standing by you now, Tomas!

DR STOCKMANN: Well said, Katrine! And this will out, by God! If I can't get a hall to rent, then I'll hire a drummer to walk through the town with me, and I shall read it out at every street corner.

THE MAYOR: You can't be that mad!

DR STOCKMANN: Oh yes, I am!

ASLAKSEN: You won't get a single man in the whole town to come with you.

BILLING: No, God strike me dead if you do!

MRS STOCKMANN: Just don't give in, Tomas. I'll ask the boys to go with you.

DR STOCKMANN: That's a brilliant idea!

MRS STOCKMANN: Morten will be happy to; and Eilif, he'll come as well, I'm sure.

DR STOCKMANN: Yes, and Petra, of course! And you too, Katrine!

MRS STOCKMANN: No, no, not me; but I'll stand at the window and watch you; I will do that.

DR STOCKMANN [*puts his arms round her and kisses her*]: Thank you! Thank you! Well, my good sirs, now we'll fight this out! I want to see if lily-livered cowardice has the power to muzzle the patriot who wants to cleanse society.

> *He and his wife leave through the left-hand door in the background.*

THE MAYOR [*shaking his head slowly*]: Now he's driven *her* mad too.

ACT FOUR

A very large old-fashioned room in Captain Horster's house. An open set of folding doors in the background lead to an ante-room. In the left-hand wall are three windows; a plat-form has been placed in the middle of the opposite wall; on this is a small table with two candles, a bell, and a water carafe and glass. The rest of the room is lit by lamps between the windows. In the foreground to the left, there is a table with a candle on it, and a chair. On the right-hand side, to the front, is a door, and next to it some chairs.

A large crowd of TOWNSPEOPLE *of every status.[49] A* FEW WOMEN *and* SCHOOLBOYS *can be seen among them. More and more people are gradually streaming in from the back, filling the hall.*

FIRST CITIZEN [*to* ANOTHER MAN *he bumps into*]: So you're here again tonight, Lamstad?
THE MAN SPOKEN TO [SECOND CITIZEN]: I'm at all the pub-lic meetings, I am.
A MAN NEXT TO HIM [THIRD CITIZEN]: You've brought your whistle, yes?
SECOND CITIZEN: 'Course I have. Haven't you?
THIRD CITIZEN: 'Course! And Skipper Evensen said he'd bring a whacking great big horn, he did.
SECOND CITIZEN: He's great, Evensen!
     Laughter among the group.
FOURTH CITIZEN [*joining them*]: Here, tell me, what's going on here tonight?

SECOND CITIZEN: It's Dr Stockmann; wants to deliver a speech against the mayor.

FOURTH CITIZEN: But the mayor's his brother.

FIRST CITIZEN: Makes no difference; Dr Stockmann's not one to be scared.

THIRD CITIZEN: But he's in the wrong, of course; it was in *The Messenger*.

SECOND CITIZEN: Yes, he must be in the wrong this time; seeing as they didn't want to lend him a hall down at the Homeowners' Association or the Club.[50]

FIRST CITIZEN: Wasn't even given use of the Spa hall.

SECOND CITIZEN: Well, you can understand why.

A MAN [*in a different group*]: Whose side should we take in this business, eh?

ANOTHER MAN [*also in this group*]: Just watch Aslaksen, and do whatever *he* does.

BILLING [*with a folder under his arm, pushes his way through the crowd*]: Excuse me, gentlemen! Can I come through perhaps? I'm reporting for *The People's Messenger*. Thank you very much!

He sits down at the table to the left.

A WORKER: Who's that there?

ANOTHER WORKER: You must know *him* surely? It's that Billing chap who works on Aslaksen's paper.

HORSTER *guides* MRS STOCKMANN *and* PETRA *in through the door on the right in the foreground.* EILIF *and* MORTEN *follow them.*

HORSTER: This is where I thought the family could sit; it's easy to slip out from here, if anything happens.

MRS STOCKMANN: Do you think there'll be a disturbance then?

HORSTER: You never can tell – with so many people –. But sit yourself down and don't worry.

MRS STOCKMANN [*sits down*]: It was so kind of you to offer Stockmann the hall.

HORSTER: Well, when nobody else would, then –

PETRA [*who has sat down too*]: And it was courageous too, Horster.

HORSTER: Oh, I wouldn't say it took that much courage.

MR HOVSTAD and MR ASLAKSEN arrive simultaneously but make their way through the crowd separately.

ASLAKSEN [*goes over to* HORSTER]: Hasn't the doctor arrived yet?

HORSTER: He's waiting in there.

Activity by the door in the background.

HOVSTAD [*to* BILLING]: There's the mayor. You see!

BILLING: Yes, God strike me dead if he hasn't turned up after all!

The MAYOR *manoeuvres his way carefully through the crowd, greets people politely and positions himself by the wall to the left. Shortly afterwards* DR STOCKMANN *comes in through the door to the right in the background. He is dressed in black, with a formal jacket and white neckerchief. A few people clap uncertainly, are gently shushed. It goes quiet.*

DR STOCKMANN [*in a lowered voice*]: How are you, Katrine?

MRS STOCKMANN: I'm fine, thank you. [*More quietly*] Don't get worked-up now, Tomas.

DR STOCKMANN: Oh, I know how to handle myself, dear. [*Looks at his watch, climbs up on to the platform and bows.*] It's a quarter past now – so I'd like to start – [*Takes his manuscript out.*]

ASLAKSEN: A chairman should surely be elected first.

DR STOCKMANN: No, that's really not necessary.

SOME GENTLEMEN [*shouting*]: Oh, yes it is!

THE MAYOR: I'd assume too that a moderator should be elected.

DR STOCKMANN: But I've summoned this meeting to give a speech, Peter!

THE MAYOR: The medical officer's speech may lead to some divergence of opinion.

MORE VOICES [*from the crowd*]: A chairman! A moderator!

HOVSTAD: The general citizens' will seems to demand a chairman.

DR STOCKMANN [*controlled*]: Very well; let the citizens' will have its way.

ASLAKSEN: Wouldn't the mayor perhaps be willing to assume that duty?

THREE GENTLEMEN [*clapping*]: Bravo! Bravo!

THE MAYOR: For various reasons that are easy to comprehend, I must decline. But fortunately we have in our midst a man I think everybody can accept. I refer to the head of the Home-owners' Association, Mr Aslaksen.

MANY VOICES: Yes, yes! Long live Aslaksen! Hurrah for Aslaksen!

DR STOCKMANN *takes his manuscript and walks down from the platform.*

ASLAKSEN: When my fellow citizens' trust calls upon me, I'll not be unwilling –

Applause and cheering. ASLAKSEN *mounts the platform.*

BILLING [*writing*]: Right, so – 'Mr Aslaksen, book printer, elected by acclamation.'

ASLAKSEN: And now that I stand here, may I be permitted to say a few concise words? I am a modest and peaceable man, who holds by prudent temperance, and by – by temperate prudence; as is recognized by all who know me.

SEVERAL VOICES: Yes! Yes, Aslaksen!

ASLAKSEN: I have learned, in the school of life and experience, that temperance is a virtue that best befits a citizen –

THE MAYOR: Hear, hear!

ASLAKSEN: – and prudence and temperance are also that by which society is best served. I would therefore entreat the honourable citizen who has called this meeting that he strive to remain within the bounds of temperance.

A MAN [*up by the door*]: To the Temperance Society! A toast!

A VOICE: What the heck!

SEVERAL VOICES: Shh, Shh!

ASLAKSEN: No interruptions, gentlemen! – Does anybody wish to take the floor?

THE MAYOR: Mr Moderator.

ASLAKSEN: Mayor Stockmann has the floor.

THE MAYOR: In view of the close family ties that I have, as you doubtless know, with the current medical officer, I would have preferred not to speak tonight. But my relationship to the Spa Institute and my concern for the town's most vital interests compel me to propose a motion. I assume that not a single citizen here in this room would find it desirable that untrustworthy and exaggerated accounts about the sanitary conditions of our Spa and town be spread wider afield.

SEVERAL VOICES: No, no, no! Not at all! We protest!

THE MAYOR: I would therefore propose that this assembly ought not to permit the medical officer to read or to present his views on this matter.

DR STOCKMANN [*aggravated*]: Not permit –! What –!

MRS STOCKMANN [*coughing*]: Ahem! – ahem!

DR STOCKMANN [*collecting himself*]: I see, yes; not permit.

THE MAYOR: In my statement in *The People's Messenger*, I have informed the public of the principal facts, so that every fair-minded citizen may, with ease, reach his own verdict. From it, you will see that the medical officer's suggestion – apart from being a vote of no confidence against the town's leading men – ultimately means burdening the taxpaying residents of this town with the unnecessary expenditure of at least one hundred thousand kroner.

Hostility and blowing of whistles.

ASLAKSEN [*ringing his bell*]: Silence,[51] gentlemen! I beg to support the mayor's proposal. It is also *my* opinion that there's a hidden motive for the doctor's agitation. He talks about the Spa; but it's a revolution he's aiming at – he wants to put the leadership into other hands. Nobody doubts the doctor's honourable intentions; Lord no, there can be no two opinions about that. *I* am also a friend of people's self-governance, as long as it doesn't come at too high a price to the taxpayers. But *that* would be the outcome here; which is why – no, God dammit – beg pardon – but I cannot go along with Dr Stockmann this time. One can pay too high a price even for gold; that's *my* opinion.

Lively approval from all sides.

HOVSTAD: I too feel called upon to account for my position. Dr Stockmann's agitation seemed to win considerable approval to begin with, and I supported it as impartially as

I could. But then it became apparent that we'd allowed ourselves to be misled by a false representation of –

DR STOCKMANN: False –!

HOVSTAD: A less than reliable representation of the facts, then. The mayor's statement has proved that. I hope nobody in this town doubts my liberal principles; *The Messenger*'s stance on the larger political questions is well known to each of you. But I have learned from experienced and prudent men that in purely local matters a paper must proceed with a certain caution.

ASLAKSEN: In full agreement with the speaker.

HOVSTAD: And in this particular matter, it is now beyond doubt that Dr Stockmann has the general will against him. But, gentlemen, what is an editor's first and noblest obligation? Is it not to operate in accordance with his readers? Hasn't he received a kind of unspoken mandate to promote the welfare of his like-minded fellows, vigorously and tirelessly? Or am I perhaps mistaken in this?

MANY VOICES: No, no! The editor's right!

HOVSTAD: It has been a most painful struggle for me to break with a man in whose house I have lately been a frequent guest – a man who until this very day enjoyed the undivided goodwill of his fellow citizens – a man whose only – or at least major – flaw is that he consults his heart more than his head.

SOME SCATTERED VOICES: That's true! Hurrah for Dr Stockmann!

HOVSTAD: But my duty to this community demanded I break with him. And there is another concern that drives me to confront him, and, if possible, stop him on the perilous path he has embarked upon; and that is my concern for his family –

DR STOCKMANN: Keep to the water supply and sewage!

HOVSTAD: – concern for his spouse and his poor needy children.

MORTEN: Is that us, Mother?

MRS STOCKMANN: Hush!

ASLAKSEN: So, I shall put the mayor's proposal to the vote.

DR STOCKMANN: There's no need! Tonight I don't intend to speak about the swinish filth down there at the Spa House. No; you shall hear quite a different story.

THE MAYOR [*under his breath*]: What is it this time?

A DRUNKEN MAN [*up by the entrance door*]: I am a tax-payer![52] And so I have a right to an opinion too! And I am of the complete – firmly incomprehendible opinion –

A NUMBER OF VOICES: Be quiet over there!

OTHERS: He's drunk! Chuck him out!

The DRUNKEN MAN *is turned out.*

DR STOCKMANN: Do I have the floor?

ASLAKSEN [*ringing his bell*]: Dr Stockmann has the floor!

DR STOCKMANN: If anybody, even a few days ago, had dared make any such attempt at gagging me, as they have tonight – I would have defended my sacred human rights like a lion! But that doesn't matter to me now; because now I have more important things to talk about.

The crowd presses closer to him. MORTEN KIIL *comes into view among them.*

DR STOCKMANN [*continuing*]: I've thought and I've pondered a great deal these last few days – pondered over so many things that in the end they turned into an utter jumble in my head –

THE MAYOR [*coughs*]: Hm –!

DR STOCKMANN: – but then I worked it out; I saw precisely how everything connects. And that is why I'm standing here tonight. I have some great revelations to make to you, my fellow citizens! I want to report a discovery of a very different scope than the trifling matter of our water supply being poisoned and our Health Spa built on a plague-infested ground.

MANY VOICES [*shouting*]: Don't talk about the Spa! We don't want to hear it! Not that!

DR STOCKMANN: I've said I want to talk about the important discovery I've made over the last few days – the discovery that our spiritual wells are poisoned, and that our entire civic community rests on a plague-infested ground of lies.

ASTONISHED VOICES [*hushed*]: What's that he's saying?

THE MAYOR: Such an insinuation –!

ASLAKSEN [*with his hand on the bell*]: The speaker is urged to be temperate.

DR STOCKMANN: I have loved my native town as much as any man can love the home of his younger years. I wasn't old when I left here, and distance, longing and memories somehow cast an increased glow over the town and its people.

Some clapping and shouts of support are heard.

DR STOCKMANN: There I sat for many years in that frightful backwater far in the north. When I met some of the people who live dotted here and there among the screes, I often thought that those poor, decrepit creatures might have been better served if they'd got a vet up there rather than a man like me.

Murmuring in the hall.

BILLING [*puts his pen down*]: Well, God strike me dead if I've ever heard –!

HOVSTAD: This is an insult to decent common folk![53]

DR STOCKMANN: Just wait a bit! – I don't think anyone can say of me that I forgot my native town up there. I sat rather like an eider[54] on its eggs; and what I hatched, well – that was the plan for the Spa Institute here.

Applause and objections.

DR STOCKMANN: And when fate at long, long last smiled down upon me and granted me the chance to come back home – yes, my fellow citizens, then I knew I had no other desire in this world. Well, yes, I had this desire, to work eagerly, untiringly and passionately for the welfare of my hometown and of the public.

THE MAYOR [*looking up in the air*]: Your method is somewhat peculiar – hm!

DR STOCKMANN: So here I was, blindly enjoying life. But yesterday morning – no, it was actually on the evening before – my spiritual eyes were opened, and the first thing I saw was the unbelievable idiocy of the authorities –

Commotion, shouts and laughter. MRS STOCKMANN *coughs energetically.*

THE MAYOR: Mr Moderator!

ASLAKSEN [*ringing*]: By the power vested in me, I –!

DR STOCKMANN: It's petty to get hung up on a word, Mr
Aslaksen! I just mean that I suddenly realized what unbelievably swinish behaviour our leading men were guilty of
down there at the Spa. I can't abide leading men at any
price! – I've had enough of those people in my time. They're
like billy-goats in a field of saplings; they wreak havoc in
every direction; they block a free man's path no matter
which way he turns – and I'd like nothing better than for us
to have them eradicated like any other vermin –.

Unease in the room.

THE MAYOR: Mr Moderator, can such remarks be allowed to
pass?

ASLAKSEN [*with his hand on his bell*]: Doctor –!

DR STOCKMANN: I can't comprehend how it has taken me
until now to see these gentlemen in their true light; particularly since I've had such a splendid specimen before my eyes
virtually every day here in town – my brother Peter – slow
off the mark and a bumbling bigot.

Laughter, commotion, blowing of whistles. MRS STOCK-
MANN *sits coughing.*

   ASLAKSEN *rings his bell forcefully.*

THE DRUNKEN MAN [*who has come back in again*]: You talking about me? Yeah, 'cos my name's Peter Sloe, all right, but
I'm bloody well not –

ANGRY VOICES: Get that drunkard out! Show him the door!

   The MAN *is thrown out again.*

THE MAYOR: Who was that man?

FIRST CITIZEN: Didn't recognize him, Mr Mayor, sir.

SECOND CITIZEN: He's not from this town.

THIRD CITIZEN: He's probably a timberman[55] from over
at – [*The rest is inaudible.*]

ASLAKSEN: The man was clearly intoxicated on stout. Carry
on, doctor; but do conduct yourself with temperance.

DR STOCKMANN: Very well, my fellow citizens; I shall make
no further pronouncements on our leaders. And if anyone
imagines, from what I've just said, that I'd like to kill these
gentlemen off tonight, then he's mistaken – seriously mistaken. I cherish the comforting conviction that these laggards,

these old men with their world of dying ideas, are taking excellent care of their own demise; there's no need for any doctor's help to hasten their mortal departure. Besides, *they* aren't the sort of people who pose the greatest danger to society; *they* aren't the most active in poisoning our spiritual wells and contaminating the ground beneath us; *they* aren't the most dangerous enemies of truth and freedom in our society.

SHOUTS FROM ALL SIDES: Who then? Who? Name them!

DR STOCKMANN: Yes, rest assured, I shall name them! Because *that* is in fact the great discovery I made yesterday. [*Raises his voice*] The most dangerous enemies to truth and freedom among us are the solid majority. Yes, that damned solid, liberal majority: there! Now you know it!

Tremendous uproar. Most people are shouting, stamping and blowing their whistles. Some of the OLDER GENTLE-MEN *among them exchange stolen glances and seem to gloat.* MRS STOCKMANN *gets up nervously.* EILIF *and* MORTEN *walk threateningly towards some* SCHOOL-BOYS *who are making a commotion.* ASLAKSEN *rings his bell and pleads for calm.* HOVSTAD *and* BILLING *both speak but are inaudible. Finally there is silence.*

ASLAKSEN: The chairman expects the speaker to withdraw his imprudent remarks.

DR STOCKMANN: Never, Mr Aslaksen! It's the majority here in our community who are robbing me of my freedom and who want to prohibit me from telling the truth.

HOVSTAD: The majority always have right on their side.

BILLING: And so does the truth; God strike me dead!

DR STOCKMANN: The majority never have right on their side, never I tell you! That's one of those lies in society against which any independent, thinking man must wage war. Who is it that constitutes the greater part of the population in a country? The intelligent people, or the stupid ones? I think we'd have to agree that stupid people make up a quite terrifying, overwhelming majority the world over. But never in all eternity, damn it all, can it be right for the stupid people to rule over the intelligent ones!

Uproar and cries.

DR STOCKMANN: Oh, yes; you can shout me down all right; but you can't argue against me. The *might* is with the many – unfortunately – but not the *right*. The right is with myself and a few other solitary individuals. The minority is always in the right.

Huge uproar again.

HOVSTAD: Haha; so Dr Stockmann's turned aristocrat since the day before yesterday!

DR STOCKMANN: I've said already that I can't be bothered to waste words on that puny, narrow-chested, short-winded bunch who lag astern. Life's beating pulse has no business with them. Rather, I am thinking of the few, those individuals among us who have embraced all the new, vigorous truths. Such men stand at the outposts, as it were, so far ahead that the solid majority has yet to catch up with them – and *there* they fight for truths that are still too newly born into the world of consciousness to have gained any majority support.

HOVSTAD: Oh right, so now the doctor's turned into a revolutionary leader!

DR STOCKMANN: Yes, I bloody well have, Mr Hovstad! I intend to start a revolution against the lie that the majority has a monopoly on the truth. What kinds of truths do the majority habitually flock around? They are truths so advanced in years, that they're on the way to being decrepit. But when a truth is that old, it's also well on the way to becoming a lie, gentlemen.

Laughter and derision.

DR STOCKMANN: Yes, all right, you don't have to believe me; but not all truths are the long-lived Methuselahs[56] people imagine. An averagely built truth lives – let's say – as a rule seventeen or eighteen, at most twenty years; rarely longer. But truths of such advanced years are always dreadfully scrawny. And yet it is only *then* that the majority adopts them and recommends them to society as wholesome spiritual food. But there's not much nutritional value in such a diet, I can assure you; and as a doctor, I should know. All these truths of the majority can be likened to last year's cured meats; they're like rancid, furry, green-salted hams. And from these comes all the moral scurvy that runs so rampant in our communities.

ASLAKSEN: It occurs to me that the honourable speaker is drifting somewhat off script.

THE MAYOR: I must concur with the moderator's opinion.

DR STOCKMANN: No, but I think you're quite mad, Peter! I'm sticking as closely to the script as I can! Since what I want to talk about here is precisely that the masses, the many, this damned solid majority – that it's these, I tell you, who are poisoning our spiritual wells and infecting the ground beneath us.

HOVSTAD: And this because our great liberal majority are prudent enough to defer to truths that are certain and approved?

DR STOCKMANN: My dearest Mr Hovstad, don't talk of certain truths! The truths that the masses, that the public, approve are the truths that the fighters at the outposts held to be certain in our grandfathers' day. Those of us fighting at the outposts today no longer recognize them; and I do not believe there is any other certain truth apart from this: that no society can live a healthy life on such old, marrowless truths.

HOVSTAD: Instead of standing there, talking up-in-the-air like that, it would be amusing to hear what these marrowless old truths are that we all live on.

Sounds of agreement from many quarters.

DR STOCKMANN: Oh, I could reel off a multitude of such abominations; but for now I'll stick to *one* approved truth, which is actually a foul lie, but which Mr Hovstad and *The Messenger* and all *The Messenger*'s supporters live by nevertheless.

HOVSTAD: And that is –?

DR STOCKMANN: It's the doctrine you've inherited from your forefathers, that you preach mindlessly far and wide – the doctrine that the common folk, the hordes, the masses, are the nation's core – that it is the very people itself – that the common man, the ignorant and uncultivated member of

society, has as much right to condemn or approve, to govern and control, as the few spiritually noble individuals.

BILLING: God strike me dead, I've never –

HOVSTAD [*shouting at the same time*]: Citizens, take note of
this!

ANGRY VOICES: Oho! Aren't we the people? Is it only noble
folk who should govern?

A WORKER: Out with that man – talking like that!

ANOTHER: Chuck him out the door!

ANOTHER [*calling out*]: Toot your horn, Evensen!

*A horn blasts out, whistles are blown, and there is a
raging uproar in the room.*

DR STOCKMANN [*when the noise has quietened a little*]: But
be reasonable now! Can't you bear to hear the voice of truth
for *once*? I certainly don't expect you all to agree with me
right away; but I'd certainly have expected Mr Hovstad to
admit I was right, when he'd gathered himself a little. Mr
Hovstad does after all claim to be a freethinker –[57]

PERPLEXED VOICES [*hushed*]: Freethinker, did he say? Is the
editor a freethinker?

HOVSTAD [*shouting*]: Prove it, Dr Stockmann! When have I
ever said that in print?

DR STOCKMANN [*chewing it over*]: No, damn it all, you're
quite right – *that* free-spoken you've never been. But I
wouldn't want to get you into trouble, Mr Hovstad. Let's
assume I'm the freethinker then. Because now I shall turn to
natural science to make it clear to each and every one of you,
that *The People's Messenger* is leading you shamefully by
the nose, when it declares that *you* – the common folk, the
masses, the crowd – make up the nation's true core. That's
just a newspaper lie! The common people are merely the
base material from which the nation must fashion true
people.

Snarls, laughter and unease in the room.

DR STOCKMANN: Yes, because isn't that the way of things in
the rest of the living world? There's a great difference, surely,
between a cultivated and uncultivated species of animal?
Just look at an ordinary farm hen. What meat value has a

stunted chicken carcase of that sort? Not a great deal! And
what kind of eggs does it lay? Any half respectable crow or
raven can lay almost as decent an egg. But take a well-bred
Spanish or Japanese hen, or a noble pheasant or turkey – yes,
then you'll see the difference all right. And now let me turn to
dogs, to whom we humans are so closely related. First, imagine
a simple common dog – I mean, the kind of vile, ragged, badly
behaved mongrel that runs around in the streets fouling the
house walls. And put one of these mongrels next to a poodle
whose pedigree goes back several generations, and who comes
from a noble house where it's been fed with good food and had
the chance to hear harmonious voices and music. Don't you
think that the poodle's cranium has developed quite differently from that of the mongrel?[58] Yes, you can be sure. It is
these cultivated poodle puppies that showmen train to do the
most amazing tricks. Things an ordinary peasant mongrel
could never learn if it stood on its head.

    Scattered commotion and joking.

A CITIZEN [*shouts*]: Are you turning us into dogs now, too?

ANOTHER CITIZEN: We're not animals, doctor!

DR STOCKMANN: Ah, but by God, we are animals, old chap!
    We are, all of us, the finest animals anyone could wish. But
    there certainly aren't many noble animals among us. Oh,
    there's a quite terrifying distance between poodle-humans
    and mongrel-humans. And the hilarious thing is that our
    editor, Mr Hovstad, agrees with me entirely, so long as we're
    talking about four-legged animals –

HOVSTAD: Well, they are what they are.

DR STOCKMANN: Quite; but as soon as I extend this law to
    those on two legs, Mr Hovstad stops short; then he no longer
    dares to believe his own beliefs, to think his own thoughts
    to their conclusion; then he turns the whole doctrine on its
    head, proclaiming in *The Messenger* that the peasant cock-
    erel and street mongrel – that *these* are the truly splendid
    specimens in the menagerie. But that's the way of it, always,
    so long as the mentality of the common man remains inside
    you, and so long as you haven't worked your way out to
    spiritual nobility.

HOVSTAD: I lay no claim to any such nobility. I descend from simple farming stock; and I'm proud that I have my roots deep among the common folk who are being insulted here.

MANY WORKERS: Hurrah for Hovstad! Hurrah! Hurrah!

DR STOCKMANN: The kind of common folk I'm talking about are not just found in the lower depths; they are creeping and crawling all around us – right up to the highest echelons of society. Just look at your own fine, dapper mayor! My brother Peter is as good a commoner as anyone who wears two shoes –

Laughter and shushing.

THE MAYOR: I object to such personal remarks.

DR STOCKMANN [*unperturbed*]: – and he's not that way because he's descended, just as I am, from some nasty old pirate from Pomerania or thereabouts – yes, because we are –

THE MAYOR: Absurd hearsay. I deny it!

DR STOCKMANN: – but he's like that because he thinks the thoughts of his superiors, and believes what his superiors believe. People who do *that* are spiritual commoners; and that's why at bottom my magnificent brother Peter is so terribly far from being noble – and consequently so far from being liberal-minded too.

THE MAYOR: Mr Moderator –!

HOVSTAD: So it's the noble folk who are the liberal people here in this country? That's interesting news!

Laughter in the crowd.

DR STOCKMANN: Indeed, that comes with my new discovery. And, what also comes with it is this: that liberal-mindedness and morality are practically the same thing. I say, therefore, that it's inexcusable when *The Messenger* promotes, day after day, the false doctrine that it's the masses, the crowd, the solid majority who can lay claim to liberal-mindedness and morality – and that vice, swinishness and spiritual depravity ooze out of high culture, like the foul sludge that's oozing into the Spa from the tanneries up there in Mølledalen!

Commotion and interruptions.

DR STOCKMANN [*unperturbed, laughs in his excitement*]: And yet this same *People's Messenger* can go on preaching

that the masses should be lifted to more elevated living conditions! But, damn it all – if *The Messenger*'s teachings were
right, then to elevate the masses would be tantamount to
toppling them straight into depravity! But fortunately, the
idea that culture corrupts is nothing more than an old,
inherited lie.[59] No, it is ignorance, poverty, ugly living conditions that do that devil's work! In a house which isn't aired
and swept each day – my wife Katrine maintains that the
floor ought to be washed too; although that's open to
debate – anyway – within two or three years in such a house,
I tell you, people lose the capacity to think or act morally.
Lack of oxygen debilitates the conscience. And there must, it
seems, be a huge dearth of oxygen in many, many houses
here in town, since the entire solid majority have so little
conscience that they want to build the town's progress on a
quagmire of lies and deceit.

ASLAKSEN: Such grave accusations shouldn't be hurled at an
entire community.

A GENTLEMAN: I suggest the moderator order the speaker to
stand down.

EAGER VOICES: Yes, yes! That's right! Make him stand down!

DR STOCKMANN [*flaring up*]: Then I shall shout the truth
from every street corner! I shall write it in the out-of-town
newspapers! The whole country will learn what's going on
here!

HOVSTAD: The doctor seems almost intent on destroying this
town.

DR STOCKMANN: Yes, I hold my native town so dear that I'd
rather destroy it than see it flourish on a lie.

ASLAKSEN: These are strong words.

   Commotion and whistles being blown. MRS STOCKMANN
   coughs to no avail; The DOCTOR *no longer hears her.*

HOVSTAD [*shouting over the din*]: A man who wishes to destroy
an entire community must be an enemy of its citizens.

DR STOCKMANN [*with growing passion*]: It's of no consequence if a lie-ridden community is destroyed. It should be
razed to the ground, I say! All those who live a lie should be

eradicated like vermin! You'll bring a plague upon the entire country in the end; you'll make it so the entire country deserves to be laid waste. And if it comes to *that*, then I say from the depths of my heart: let the entire country be laid waste, let this entire people be eradicated!

ONE MAN [*in the crowd*]: That's the talk of an enemy of the people![60]

BILLING: There sounded, God strike me dead, the voice of the people!

THE WHOLE CROWD [*shouting*]: Yes, yes, yes! He's an enemy of the people! He hates his country! He hates our whole people!

ASLAKSEN: I am, both as a citizen of this country and as a human being, deeply shaken by what I've had to listen to here. Dr Stockmann has betrayed himself in ways I'd never have dreamed possible. I must sadly concur with the opinion expressed here by our most worthy citizens; and I hold that we ought to give that opinion expression in a resolution. I propose the following: 'This meeting declares that it considers the medical officer, Dr Tomas Stockmann, an Enemy of the People.'

A storm of cheers and applause. Many people encircle the DOCTOR, *blowing their whistles at him.* MRS STOCKMANN *and* PETRA *have got up.* MORTEN *and* EILIF *are fighting the other* SCHOOLBOYS *who have also been whistling. Some adults separate them.*

DR STOCKMANN [*to the men who are whistling*]: Oh, what fools ye be – I tell you this –

ASLAKSEN [*ringing his bell*]: The doctor no longer has the floor. A formal vote needs to be taken; but, to spare any personal feelings, this should be done in writing and anonymously. Have you got some clean paper, Mr Billing?

BILLING: I've got blue paper *and* white here –

ASLAKSEN [*steps down*]: Excellent; that'll be quicker. Cut it into pieces – that's it, yes. [*To the assembly*] Blue means no; white means yes. I'll come round to collect the votes myself.

PETER STOCKMANN *leaves the room.* ASLAKSEN *and a couple of other citizens go round the hall with the slips of paper in their hats.*

A GENTLEMAN [*to* HOVSTAD]: What's come over the doctor, eh? What are we to make of all this?

HOVSTAD: Well, you know how hot-headed he is.

SECOND GENTLEMAN [*to* BILLING]: Listen, Billing, you visit the house. Have you noticed if the man drinks?

BILLING: God strike me dead if I know what to say. The toddy's always on the table when anybody comes.

THIRD GENTLEMAN: No, I just think he's a bit unhinged at times.

FIRST GENTLEMAN: Yes, I wonder if there's any hereditary madness in the family?

BILLING: Could well be, yes.

FOURTH GENTLEMAN: No, it's pure malice, that's what; revenge for something or other.

BILLING: Well, he mentioned a pay rise a day or so ago; but he didn't get it.

ALL THE GENTLEMEN [*together*]: Aha; that explains it!

THE DRUNKEN MAN [*who is in the crowd*]: I want a blue one! And a white one too!

SHOUTS: It's that drunkard again! Get him out!

MORTEN KIIL [*approaching the* DOCTOR]: So, Stockmann, do you see now what comes of such monkey tricks?

DR STOCKMANN: I've done my duty.

MORTEN KIIL: What was it you said about the tanneries in Mølledalen?

DR STOCKMANN: You heard; I said they were where all the muck came from.

MORTEN KIIL: From *my* tannery too?

DR STOCKMANN: Unfortunately, your tannery's probably the worst.

MORTEN KIIL: Are you going to get *that* printed in the newspapers?

DR STOCKMANN: I shan't brush anything under the carpet.

MORTEN KIIL: *That* may cost you dear, Stockmann. [*Goes out.*]

MR VIK[61] [*walks over to* CAPTAIN HORSTER *without greeting the* LADIES]: So, captain, you lend out your house to enemies of the people, eh?

HORSTER: I think I can do what I want with my own property, Mr Vik.

MR VIK: So, you'd have nothing against my doing the same with mine.

HORSTER: What do you mean, sir?

MR VIK: You'll hear from me tomorrow. [*Turns his back on him and goes.*]

PETRA: Wasn't that your shipowner, Captain Horster?

HORSTER: Yes, it was Mr Vik.

ASLAKSEN [*with the voting papers in his hands, climbs up on to the platform and rings the bell*]: Gentlemen, allow me to inform you of the result. By all votes to one –

A YOUNG GENTLEMAN: That was the drunkard's!

ASLAKSEN: By all votes to one intoxicated man's, this citizens' assembly declares the medical officer, Dr Tomas Stockmann, an enemy of the people. [*Shouts and noises of approval*] Long live our old and honourable community of citizens! [*More approval*] Long live our accomplished and capable mayor, who has so loyally ignored the ties of blood! [*Cheering*] The meeting is closed. [*Climbs down.*]

BILLING: Long live the moderator!

THE WHOLE CROWD: Hurrah for Aslaksen!

DR STOCKMANN: My hat and jacket, Petra! Captain, have you any room on your ship for passengers to the New World?

HORSTER: For you and yours, doctor, room will be found.

DR STOCKMANN [*as* PETRA *helps him get his jacket on*]: Good. Come on, Katrine! Come on, boys!

    He takes his wife by the arm.

MRS STOCKMANN [*quietly*]: Tomas, my sweet, let's go by the back door.

DR STOCKMANN: No back doors, Katrine. [*With raised voice*] You'll hear more from this enemy of the people before he shakes the dust from his feet![62] I'm not as meek and mild as a certain man was; I shall not say: 'I forgive you, for you know not what you do.'[63]

ASLAKSEN [*shouts*]: That is a blasphemous comparison, Dr
   Stockmann!

BILLING: That is, God strike – That's a shocking thing for a
   serious-minded man to hear.

A GRUFF VOICE: And he's threatening us too!

AGITATED VOICES: Let's break his windows! Duck him in the
   fjord!

A MAN IN THE CROWD: Blow your horn, Evensen! Toot, toot!
   Blowing of horn and whistles, wild screaming. The DOC-
   TOR *goes with his family towards the exit,* HORSTER
   clearing the way for them.

THE WHOLE CROWD [*yelling after them as they leave*]: Enemy
   of the People! Enemy of the People!

BILLING [*as he tidies his notes*]: Well, God strike me dead, I
   wouldn't want to be over at the Stockmanns' drinking toddy
   tonight!
   *The crowd presses towards the exit. The noise continues
   outside; shouts of 'Enemy of the People!' are heard from
   the street.*

ACT FIVE

Dr Stockmann's study. Bookcases and cabinets containing various medicines line the walls. In the background is a door leading to the hall; downstage left, a door leading to the living room. In the wall to the right there are two windows, in which all the panes are broken. In the middle of the room stands the doctor's desk, covered with books and papers. The room is in disorder. It is late morning.

DR STOCKMANN *in his dressing-gown, slippers and smoking cap, is bent over, raking about under one of the cabinets with an umbrella; finally he pulls out a stone.*

DR STOCKMANN [*talking through the open living-room door*]: Katrine, I've found another one.

MRS STOCKMANN [*from the living room*]: Oh, I'm sure you'll find a lot more.

DR STOCKMANN [*adds the stone to a heap of others on the table*]: I'm going to keep these stones like sacred relics. Eilif and Morten will look at them every day, and when they're grown up they'll inherit them from me. [*Rakes about under a bookcase.*] Hasn't – oh, what the hell's her name – that girl – hasn't she gone for the glazier yet?

MRS STOCKMANN [*coming in*]: Yes, but he said he wasn't sure he could come today.

DR STOCKMANN: I think you'll find he doesn't dare.

MRS STOCKMANN: No, Randine also thought he didn't dare because of the neighbours. [*Talks into the living room*]

What do you want, Randine? Oh, right. [*Goes in and comes straight back.*] There's a letter for you, Tomas.

DR STOCKMANN: Let me see that. [*Opens and reads it.*] Ah, I see.

MRS STOCKMANN: Who's it from?

DR STOCKMANN: From the landlord. He's giving us our notice.

MRS STOCKMANN: Are you serious? But he's such a decent man –

DR STOCKMANN [*looking at the letter*]: He dare not, he says, do otherwise. He does it with the greatest reluctance; but dare not do otherwise – with regard to his fellow citizens – on account of public opinion – is dependent on – dare not offend certain influential men –

MRS STOCKMANN: Well, there you see, Tomas.

DR STOCKMANN: Yes, yes, I see it all right; they're cowards in this town, the whole lot of them; not one of them dares do anything on account of all the others. [*Throws the letter on to the table.*] But it makes no odds to us now, Katrine. We're leaving for the New World now, and then –

MRS STOCKMANN: Yes, but, Tomas – this business of leaving, is it really so well advised?

DR STOCKMANN: Should I stay here, perhaps, after they've pilloried me as an enemy of the people, branded me, smashed my windows! And just look at this, Katrine; they've ripped a hole in my black trousers too.

MRS STOCKMANN: Oh, dear; and they're your best!

DR STOCKMANN: People should never wear their best trousers when they're out fighting for truth and freedom. Not that I care much about my trousers, of course; you can always patch them up for me. But it's the fact that the mob, the masses, dare to intrude on my person as though they were my equals, *that's* what I can't stomach, dammit!

MRS STOCKMANN: Yes, they've behaved appallingly towards you in this town, Tomas; but does *that* mean we have to leave the country altogether?

DR STOCKMANN: And you don't think the plebeians are just as insolent in every other town here? Oh yes, it's probably much of a muchness. Still, let the mongrels snarl – *that's* not

the worst of it; the worst is that they're slaves to party politics this whole country over. Mind you – it might not be any
better in the free West; the solid majority, and liberal public
opinion and all those other evils are rampant even *there*. But
everything's on a grander scale over there, you see; they
might kill people, but they don't torture them; they don't
squeeze a free soul in a vice, as they do here. And, as a last
resort, you can keep your distance of course. [*Paces the
floor*.] If only I knew where there was a virgin forest or a
little South Sea island to be bought cheaply –

MRS STOCKMANN: Yes, but the boys, Tomas!

DR STOCKMANN [*stopping still*]: Oh, you're strange, Katrine!
Would you prefer the boys to grow up in a society like ours?
You saw for yourself last night that half the population are
raving mad; and if the other half haven't lost their senses, it's
because they're idiots with no sense to lose.

MRS STOCKMANN: Yes but, Tomas my sweet, you do let your
tongue run away with you.

DR STOCKMANN: So! What I'm saying isn't true, perhaps?
Don't they turn every concept upside down? Don't they
take right and wrong and stir it into a hotchpotch? Don't
they call everything a lie that I know to be the truth? But
the maddest thing of all is that adult liberal people go
about in droves here, telling themselves and others that
they're free-minded.[64] Have you heard anything like it,
Katrine?

MRS STOCKMANN: Yes, yes, of course, it's completely mad,
but –

PETRA *comes in from the living room.*

MRS STOCKMANN: Are you back from school already?

PETRA: Yes; I've been given my notice.

MRS STOCKMANN: Your notice!

DR STOCKMANN: You too?

PETRA: Mrs Busk gave me my notice; so I thought it best I
leave immediately.

DR STOCKMANN: You did right, by God!

MRS STOCKMANN: Who'd have thought Mrs Busk was such
an awful woman!

PETRA: Oh, Mother, Mrs Busk isn't the least bit awful; I could clearly see how painful it was for her. But she said she didn't dare do otherwise; and so I was given notice.

DR STOCKMANN [*laughing and rubbing his hands*]: She didn't dare do otherwise either! Oh, it's delightful!

MRS STOCKMANN: Well, after those appalling scenes last night, then –

PETRA: It wasn't just *that*. Listen to this, Father!

DR STOCKMANN: What?

PETRA: Mrs Busk showed me no fewer than three letters she'd got this morning –

DR STOCKMANN: Anonymous, I presume?

PETRA: Yes.

DR STOCKMANN: Yes, they don't *dare* risk their names, Katrine!

PETRA: And in two of them it said that a man who frequents this house had talked at the Club last night about my having over-emancipated views on various subjects –

DR STOCKMANN: And you didn't deny it, I presume?

PETRA: No, you know I wouldn't. Mrs Busk has pretty emancipated views herself, when we're one to one; but now that this has come out about me, she doesn't dare keep me on.

MRS STOCKMANN: And to think – it's someone who frequents our house! That shows you what you get for your hospitality, Tomas!

DR STOCKMANN: We're not going to live in this filth any longer. Pack as quickly as you can, Katrine; let's get away from here, the sooner the better.

MRS STOCKMANN: Quiet; I think there's someone out in the hall. Go and see, Petra.

PETRA [*opens the door*]: Oh, is it you, Captain Horster? Do come in, please.

HORSTER [*coming in from the hall*]: Good morning. I felt I had to drop by and hear how things were.

DR STOCKMANN [*shaking his hand*]: Thank you – that's extremely kind of you.

MRS STOCKMANN: And thank you, Captain Horster, for helping us get back last night.

PETRA: But how did you manage to get home again?

HORSTER: Oh, somehow or other; I'm pretty strong, and those people are mostly mouth.

DR STOCKMANN: Yes, absolutely extraordinary, isn't it – the swine-like cowardice of these people? Come here and I'll show you something! Look, here are all the stones they lobbed in at us. Just look at them! There are no more than two decent-sized rocks in this entire heap, by God; the rest are nothing but little stones – pebbles. And yet they stood out there shouting and swearing that they'd beat me to a pulp; but action – action – no, you don't see much of that in this town.

HORSTER: That was probably just as well for you this time, doctor!

DR STOCKMANN: Well, of course. But it's aggravating all the same; if it ever comes to a scuffle of any serious national import, then you'll see that public opinion will be in favour of turning tail, and the solid majority will run for the hills like a flock of sheep, Captain Horster. *That*'s what's so sad; it really hurts me to think of it –. Oh, but what the hell – this is just a lot of silly nonsense. If they've called me an enemy of the people, then let me be an enemy of the people!

MRS STOCKMANN: You'll never be that, Tomas.

DR STOCKMANN: I wouldn't swear to it, Katrine. A cruel word can be like the scratch of a pin on your lungs. And that damned phrase – I can't get rid of it; it's fixed itself here under my heart; there it lies, digging away and sucking up sour juices. And no magnesia can cure it.

PETRA: Pah! – you should just laugh at them, Father,

HORSTER: I'm sure people will come to see things differently one day, doctor.

MRS STOCKMANN: Yes, Tomas, as sure as you're standing here.

DR STOCKMANN: Yes, maybe when it's too late. But good riddance to them! Let them wallow here in their muck and rue the fact they drove a patriot into exile. When do you set sail, Captain Horster?

HORSTER: Hm! – That was actually what I came to talk to you about –

DR STOCKMANN: Oh, is there some problem with the ship?

HORSTER: No; but it seems I shan't be going with it.

PETRA: You've not been given your notice?

HORSTER [*smiling*]: I most certainly have.

PETRA: You too.

MRS STOCKMANN: There, you see, Tomas!

DR STOCKMANN: And all for the sake of the truth! Oh, if I'd known anything like this –

HORSTER: Don't worry yourself on that account; I'm certain to find a job with one of the shipowners out of town.

DR STOCKMANN: And it's that merchant, isn't it, Mr Vik – a man of means, independent of everyone –! Pah, it's disgusting!

HORSTER: He's a pretty decent fellow otherwise; and he said himself he'd have liked to keep me on if only he'd dared –

DR STOCKMANN: But he didn't dare? No, of course not!

HORSTER: He said, it's not that simple when you belong to a party –

DR STOCKMANN: Well, the honourable gentleman got that right! A party is like a meat grinder; it minces everybody's heads together into a mush, so they all become mush-heads and meatheads!

MRS STOCKMANN: But Tomas, dear!

PETRA [*to* HORSTER]: If only you hadn't walked us home, things might not have gone this far.

HORSTER: I don't regret that.

PETRA [*holding her hand out to him*]: Well, thank you!

HORSTER [*to the* DOCTOR]: But what I wanted to say was that if you really do want to leave, I've thought of another solution –

DR STOCKMANN: Excellent; as long as we get away soon –

MRS STOCKMANN: Shh; wasn't that a knock?

PETRA: I think it's Uncle.

DR STOCKMANN: Aha! [*Calls out*] Come in!

MRS STOCKMANN: Tomas, my sweet, just promise me –
     The MAYOR *comes in from the hall.*

THE MAYOR [*in the doorway*]: Oh, you're busy. Well, then I'd prefer –

DR STOCKMANN: No, no; come right in.

THE MAYOR: But I wanted to speak to you in private.

MRS STOCKMANN: We'll go into the sitting room for now.

HORSTER: And I'll come back later.

DR STOCKMANN: No, no, you go in with them, Captain Horster; I need to get some further details –

HORSTER: Yes, yes, I'll wait then.

He follows MRS STOCKMANN *and* PETRA *into the living room.*

The MAYOR *says nothing but glances at the windows.*

DR STOCKMANN: You might find it a bit draughty in here today? Put your hat on.

THE MAYOR: Thank you, if I may. [*Does so.*] I think I caught a chill last night; I got cold standing there –

DR STOCKMANN: Oh, really? It seemed warm enough to me.

THE MAYOR: I regret that it wasn't in my power to prevent these nocturnal excesses.

DR STOCKMANN: Do you have anything in particular to say to me, besides that?

THE MAYOR [*takes out a large letter*]: I have this document for you from the Spa committee.

DR STOCKMANN: Am I dismissed?

THE MAYOR: Yes, with effect from today. [*Places the letter on the table.*] It pains us; but – to be frank – we didn't dare do otherwise on account of public opinion.

DR STOCKMANN [*smiling*]: Didn't dare? I've heard *that* word earlier today.

THE MAYOR: I'd ask you to see your situation clearly. You mustn't count on having any future practice whatsoever in town.

DR STOCKMANN: To hell with the practice! But what makes you so certain?

THE MAYOR: The Homeowners' Association has started a list that's being taken from house to house. Every right-minded citizen is being urged not to use you; and I guarantee not one single house owner[65] will risk refusing his signature; they simply won't *dare*.

DR STOCKMANN: Of course not; I don't doubt it. But what of it?

THE MAYOR: If I could give you any advice, it would be this – that you move away from town for a while –

DR STOCKMANN: Yes, I've been toying with the idea of leaving town.

THE MAYOR: Right. And when you've had six months or so to reflect, and can bring yourself, after mature consideration, to offer a few apologetic words acknowledging your error –

DR STOCKMANN: Then I might perhaps get my position back, you mean?

THE MAYOR: Perhaps; it's certainly not impossible.

DR STOCKMANN: Yes, but what about public opinion? The board surely wouldn't dare do that on account of public opinion.

THE MAYOR: Opinion is a very variable thing. And, to be honest, it's a matter of utmost importance to us to obtain such an admission from your hand.

DR STOCKMANN: Yes, I'm sure you're all licking your lips at the prospect! But, damn it all, don't you remember what I said about such foxy tricks!

THE MAYOR: Back then your position was rather more favourable; back then you had reason to assume you had the whole town covering your back –

DR STOCKMANN: Yes, and now I have the whole town at my throat –. [*Flaring up*] But no, not if the devil himself and his grandmother were at my throat –! Never – never, I say!

THE MAYOR: No man with family responsibilities dares behave like this. You wouldn't dare, Tomas.

DR STOCKMANN: I wouldn't dare! There's only one thing in the world a free man doesn't dare; and you know what that is?

THE MAYOR: No.

DR STOCKMANN: No, naturally; but *I* shall tell you. A free man doesn't dare foul himself like some tramp, he doesn't dare conduct himself so he has to spit in his own eye!

THE MAYOR: This all sounds mighty plausible, of course; and if some other explanation didn't lie behind your obstinacy – but clearly it does –

DR STOCKMANN: What do you mean by *that*?

THE MAYOR: You understand very well what I mean. But, as
  your brother and as a prudent man, I'd advise you not to
  build too confidently on hopes and prospects that might so
  very easily come to nothing.

DR STOCKMANN: What on earth are you getting at?

THE MAYOR: Are you really asking me to believe that you're
  ignorant of the terms of Mr Kiil's will?

DR STOCKMANN: I know that the few scraps he owns are
  going to some foundation for destitute old craftsmen. But
  what's that got to do with me?

THE MAYOR: To begin with, we're not talking about a few
  scraps here. Mr Kiil is a rather wealthy man.

DR STOCKMANN: I never had any idea –!

THE MAYOR: Hm – really? So you've no idea either, that a
  rather substantial share of his fortune will come to your
  children, and that you and your wife will enjoy the interest
  for the rest of your lives. He's not told you that?

DR STOCKMANN: No, by God, he hasn't! Quite the opposite;
  he's always ranted on about how unreasonably high his
  taxes were. But are you absolutely certain about this, Peter?

THE MAYOR: I have it from an entirely reliable source.

DR STOCKMANN: But, good Lord, then Katrine is secure – and
  the children too! I must tell her at once – [Shouts] Katrine,
  Katrine!

THE MAYOR [holds him back]: Shh, not a word yet!

MRS STOCKMANN [opening the door]: What's happening?

DR STOCKMANN: Oh, nothing, nothing; you just go back in.
  MRS STOCKMANN closes the door.

DR STOCKMANN [pacing the floor]: Secure! – Just imagine,
  they're all secure! And for life! Oh what a blessed feeling it
  is to know one is secure!

THE MAYOR: Yes, but that is precisely what you are not. Mr
  Kiil can annul his will any day or hour he wishes.

DR STOCKMANN: But he won't do that, my dear Peter. The
  Badger's much too gleeful that I've got one over you and
  your venerable pals.

THE MAYOR [gives a start and looks at him quizzically]: Aha!
  That throws a light on various things.

DR STOCKMANN: Various things?

THE MAYOR: This has clearly been a coordinated manoeuvre. These violent, reckless attacks that you have – in the name of truth – directed at the town's leaders –

DR STOCKMANN: What about them?

THE MAYOR: They were nothing other than the agreed price for that vengeful old Morten Kiil's will.

DR STOCKMANN [almost speechless]: Peter – you're the most low-down plebeian I've ever known in my life.

THE MAYOR: It's over between us. Your dismissal is irrevocable; we have a weapon against you now.

　　He leaves.

DR STOCKMANN: Curse him, curse him! [Shouts out] Katrine, the floor needs to be washed after him! Get her to bring a bucket in here – that – that – oh, devil take it – that girl who's always got soot on her nose –

MRS STOCKMANN [in the doorway to the living room]: Shh, shh, Tomas, now!

PETRA [also in the doorway]: Father, Grandfather's here, asking if he can talk to you alone.

DR STOCKMANN: Yes, of course he can. [By the door] Come in, Father-in-law.[66]

　　MORTEN KIIL *comes in.* DR STOCKMANN *shuts the door after him.*

DR STOCKMANN: So, what can I do for you? Won't you sit down?

MORTEN KIIL: Shan't sit. [Looks around.] Looks nice in here today, Stockmann.

DR STOCKMANN: Yes, don't you think?

MORTEN KIIL: Very nice, yes – and fresh air too; you've got plenty of that oxygen stuff you were talking about yesterday. You must have a splendidly good conscience today, I'd imagine.

DR STOCKMANN: I have indeed.

MORTEN KIIL: Yes, I can imagine. [Taps his chest.] But do you know what *I* have here?

DR STOCKMANN: A good conscience too, I hope.

MORTEN KIIL: Pah! No, something much better than that.

He takes a thick wallet out, opens it, and shows some papers.

DR STOCKMANN [*looking at him in astonishment*]: Shares in the Spa?

MORTEN KIIL: They weren't hard to come by today.

DR STOCKMANN: And you've been out buying –?

MORTEN KIIL: As many as I could afford.

DR STOCKMANN: But, my dear father-in-law – with the desperate situation of the Spa now –!

MORTEN KIIL: If you go about it like a sensible human being, I reckon you'll get the Spa back on its feet.

DR STOCKMANN: Well, you can see for yourself that I'm doing everything I can, but –. They're all completely mad in this town!

MORTEN KIIL: Yesterday you said that the worst of the muck came from my tannery. But if *that* was true, then my grandfather and my father before me, and myself too, have for many a long year been fouling this town, almost like three angels of death. Do you think I'm going to let that shame stick?

DR STOCKMANN: I'm afraid you're going to have to.

MORTEN KIIL: No, thank you. I shall hold on to my good name and reputation. People call me 'the Badger', I've heard say. A badger; that's a type of pig, isn't it; but they'll never get that on me. I mean to live and die a clean man.

DR STOCKMANN: And how do you intend to go about *that*?

MORTEN KIIL: *You* will cleanse me, Stockmann.

DR STOCKMANN: I!

MORTEN KIIL: Do you know where I got the money from to buy these shares? No, of course, you can't know; but I shall tell you. It's the money that Katrine and Petra and the little boys will have after I'm gone. Yes, because I've put a fair bit away after all, you see.

DR STOCKMANN [*flaring up*]: And you've gone and used Katrine's money on this!

MORTEN KIIL: Yes, that money is now invested in the Spa, all of it. And now I'm eager to see if you're that raging – barking – mad after all, Stockmann! If you go on letting creatures and such nasties come from my tannery, it'll be as if you tore wide strips of skin from Katrine, and Petra too, and the boys; and no proper husband and father does that – unless he's a madman, that is.

DR STOCKMANN [*who is pacing up and down*]: Yes, but I *am* a madman; I *am* a madman!

MORTEN KIIL: You're not that raving mad surely, when it comes to your wife and children.

DR STOCKMANN [*stops in front of him*]: Why couldn't you talk to me before you went off and bought all that rubbish?

MORTEN KIIL: What's done has more clout, I'd say.

DR STOCKMANN [*walks restlessly about*]: If only I wasn't so certain of my case –! But I'm so utterly convinced I'm right.

MORTEN KIIL [*weighing the wallet in his hand*]: Carry on with this madness, and these aren't worth much. [*Puts the wallet in his pocket.*]

DR STOCKMANN: But, damn it all, science must surely be able to find some neutralizing substance; some preventive or other –

MORTEN KIIL: You mean something to kill these creatures?

DR STOCKMANN: Yes, or render them harmless.

MORTEN KIIL: Couldn't you experiment with some rat poison?

DR STOCKMANN: Oh, nonsense! – But everybody's saying it's just a figment of the imagination. Let it be a figment then! Let them stew in it! After all, these ignorant, mean-hearted mongrels harangued me as an enemy of the people – and they were ready to tear the clothes off my back too!

MORTEN KIIL: And then all the windows they've smashed for you!

DR STOCKMANN: And then there's my duty towards my family! I must discuss this with Katrine; she has a good grasp of such things.

MORTEN KIIL: That's good; just you listen to a sensible wife's advice.

DR STOCKMANN [*advancing towards him*]: How could you be so perverse! Putting Katrine's money in the balance; putting me in this horrible, agonizing torment! When I look at you, it's like looking at the devil himself –!

MORTEN KIIL: Well, then, it's best I go. But before two o'clock, I shall want an answer. *Yes* or *no*. If it is *no*, the shares will go to the foundation – and on this very day.

DR STOCKMANN: And then what does Katrine get?

MORTEN KIIL: Not a jot.

The hall door opens. MR HOVSTAD *and* MR ASLAKSEN *come into view.*

MORTEN KIIL: Oh, look at those two!

DR STOCKMANN [*stares at them*]: What! Do *you* still have the nerve to enter my home?

HOVSTAD: Yes, we do indeed.

ASLAKSEN: We have something to talk to you about, you see.

MORTEN KIIL [*whispers*]: Yes or no – before two o'clock.

ASLAKSEN [*glancing towards* HOVSTAD]: Aha!

MORTEN KIIL *leaves.*

DR STOCKMANN: So, what do you want with me? Make it brief.

HOVSTAD: I can well understand your taking umbrage at us for the stance we took at the meeting yesterday –

DR STOCKMANN: You call that a stance? Yes, a wonderfully non-existent stance! Old-womanish, I'd call it –. To hell with you!

HOVSTAD: Call it whatever you like; we *couldn't* do otherwise.

DR STOCKMANN: You didn't *dare* do otherwise. Isn't that it?

HOVSTAD: Yes, if you like.

ASLAKSEN: But why didn't you drop a little hint in advance? Just give Mr Hovstad or myself the wink?

DR STOCKMANN: A hint? About what?

ASLAKSEN: About what was behind it all.

DR STOCKMANN: I don't understand.

ASLAKSEN [*with a conspiratorial nod*]: Oh, I think you do, Dr Stockmann.

HOVSTAD: There's no need to keep it hidden any longer.

DR STOCKMANN [*looking from one to the other alternately*]: Yes, but, in the devil's name –!

ASLAKSEN: Might I ask – isn't your father-in-law going about town buying up all the Spa's shares?

DR STOCKMANN: Yes, he's been out buying Spa shares today; but –?

ASLAKSEN: You'd have been wiser to get somebody else to do it – who wasn't quite so close to you.

HOVSTAD: And you shouldn't have acted under your own name. Nobody needed to know, after all, that the attack on the Spa came from you. You should have consulted me, Dr Stockmann.

DR STOCKMANN [*looks straight ahead; something seems to dawn on him, and he says in astonishment*]: Can this be possible? Can such things be done?

ASLAKSEN [*smiles*]: It appears they can, indeed. But they should be done discreetly, you understand.

HOVSTAD: And it's preferable to have several people in on it; the responsibility of the individual is always lessened when he has others with him.

DR STOCKMANN [*composed*]: To the point, gentlemen – what do you want?

ASLAKSEN: Mr Hovstad can perhaps best –

HOVSTAD: No, you say it, Aslaksen.

ASLAKSEN: Well, it's *this* – now that we know how all the pieces fit, we think we might dare to put *The People's Messenger* at your disposal.

DR STOCKMANN: *Now* you dare? But what about public opinion? Aren't you afraid a storm will rise against us?

HOVSTAD: We'll just have to ride the storm out.

ASLAKSEN: And the doctor will need to be quick off the mark. As soon as your attack has served its purpose –

DR STOCKMANN: As soon as my father-in-law and I have got hold of the shares cheaply, you mean –?

HOVSTAD: I presume it's mainly out of scientific concern that you feel driven to take over the baths.

DR STOCKMANN: Oh, absolutely; it was out of scientific concern that I got the old Badger to go along with all this. So now we'll patch up the water pipe a bit and dig about in the

beach a bit, without it costing the town funds half a krone.
That'll do it, don't you think? Yes?

HOVSTAD: I think so – when you have *The People's Messenger*
with you.

ASLAKSEN: In a free society the Press is a force, doctor.

DR STOCKMANN: I see; as is public opinion of course; and
you, Mr Aslaksen, I assume you'll be taking the Homeowners' Association on your conscience?

ASLAKSEN: Both the Homeowners' Association and my temperance friends. Rest assured.

DR STOCKMANN: But, gentlemen – well, I feel ashamed to ask;
but – your price –?

HOVSTAD: Ideally we'd have helped you for nothing at all,
you'll understand. But *The Messenger* is on a weak footing;
it's not doing too well; and to close the newspaper down
now, when there's so much to work for in the bigger political
arena, is something I'd be loath to do.

DR STOCKMANN: Oh, absolutely; that would indeed be an
awful blow for a friend of the people like yourself. [*Flares
up*] But I, I am an enemy of the people! [*Dashes around the
room.*] Where's my stick? Where the hell have I put my stick?

HOVSTAD: What's this?

ASLAKSEN: You're never going to –

DR STOCKMANN [*stops still*]: And if I didn't give you a single
penny from all my shares? We rich folk are close to our
money, you must remember!

HOVSTAD: And *you* must remember that this affair with the
shares can be represented in two ways!

DR STOCKMANN: Yes, you're the man for that all right; if I
don't come to the aid of *The People's Messenger*, then you'll
doubtless take a jaundiced view of the whole affair; you'll
hunt me down, I'd imagine – pursue me – try to throttle me
as a dog throttles a hare.

HOVSTAD: All according to nature's law; every animal wants
to survive.

ASLAKSEN: One has to take one's food where one can find it,
you understand.

DR STOCKMANN: Well, see if you can find something out in the gutter; [*pacing about the room*] because now we're going to bloody well see who's the strongest animal out of the three of us! [*Finds his umbrella and swings it.*] Hey, look here –!

HOVSTAD: Surely you're not going to assault us!

ASLAKSEN: Do be careful with that umbrella.

DR STOCKMANN: Out of the window with you, Mr Hovstad!

HOVSTAD [*by the hall door*]: Are you completely insane!

DR STOCKMANN: Out of the window, Mr Aslaksen! Leap to it, I say! No time like the present.

ASLAKSEN [*running round the desk*]: Temperance, doctor; I'm a fragile man; I can't take much – [*Screams*] Help, help!

    MRS STOCKMANN, PETRA *and* HORSTER *come in from the living room.*

MRS STOCKMANN: But heaven help us, Tomas! What's going on here?

DR STOCKMANN [*swinging his umbrella*]: Jump out, I say! Down into the gutter!

HOVSTAD: An assault on an innocent man! I call you to witness, Captain Horster. [*He hurries out through the hall.*]

ASLAKSEN [*confused*]: Aargh, if only I understood the local conditions –.[67] [*Slips out through the living room.*]

MRS STOCKMANN [*holding on to the* DOCTOR]: But control yourself, Tomas!

DR STOCKMANN [*throwing his umbrella down*]: Well, by God, if they didn't get away after all.

MRS STOCKMANN: But what did they want from you?

DR STOCKMANN: You'll find out later; right now I've other things to think about. [*Goes to the table and writes on a visiting-card.*] Look at this, Katrine; what does it say?

MRS STOCKMANN: Three big *Nos*; but what is this?

DR STOCKMANN: You'll find that out later too. [*Hands over the card.*] There, Petra; get that sooty girl to run up to the Badger with this as fast as she can. Hurry up!

    PETRA *goes with the card out through the hall.*

DR STOCKMANN: Well, if I've not been visited by all the devil's messengers today, then I don't know what! But now I shall sharpen my pen against them, until it's like a dagger; I shall dip it in venom and gall; I shall hurl my inkwell straight at their skulls!⁶⁸

MRS STOCKMANN: Yes, but we're leaving, Tomas.

PETRA *comes back*.

DR STOCKMANN: Well?

PETRA: Done.

DR STOCKMANN: Good. – Leaving, did you say? No, I'll be damned if we are! We're staying put, Katrine!

PETRA: We're staying!

MRS STOCKMANN: Here, in town?

DR STOCKMANN: Yes, right here; it's here the sacred battle-ground is; it's here the fight will be; it's here I shall be victorious! As soon as I've got my trousers sewn up, I'll go out into town and look for a house; we've got to have a roof over our heads for the winter after all.

HORSTER: You'll have that in my house.

DR STOCKMANN: Can I?

HORSTER: Yes, you certainly can; I've plenty of room, and I'm almost never home.

MRS STOCKMANN: Oh, how kind of you, Captain Horster!

PETRA: Thank you!

DR STOCKMANN [*shaking his hand*]: Thank you, thank you! Well, that's one worry less! So I'll begin in earnest right now, today. Oh, there's such an infinite amount here to dig about in, Katrine! But it's a good thing I've got so much time at my disposal now; yes, because listen; I've been dismissed from the Spa, you see –

MRS STOCKMANN [*sighs*]: Oh dear, I was waiting for that.

DR STOCKMANN: – and they want to take my practice away from me too. But just let them! They won't take the poor folk from me at least; those who pay nothing and who, by God, need me the most. But they'll bloody well have to listen to me, I'll preach, in season and out of season, as is written some place.

MRS STOCKMANN: But, Tomas my sweet, I think you've seen what preaching achieves.

DR STOCKMANN: You're hilarious, Katrine. Should I perhaps let myself be driven off the field by public opinion, the solid majority and other such devilry? No, thank you! What I want is so obvious and simple and totally straightforward. All I want is to bang it into those mongrels' heads that the liberals are a free man's most deceitful enemies – that these party manifestos wring the necks of every budding young truth – that this regard for rearguard ideas turns any sense of morals and fairness on its head, until it's just hideous to live here in the end. Well, don't you agree, Captain Horster, I should be able to get people to grasp *that* much?

HORSTER: Very likely; I don't really understand these things.

DR STOCKMANN: Well, look here – I'll explain! It's the big party chiefs who must be eradicated. A party chief is like a wolf, you see – a ravenous grey-foot – who needs so and so many livestock each year if he's to exist. Now just look at Hovstad and Aslaksen! How many young animals don't *they* wipe out, or maim and tear to pieces so they'll never be anything more than homeowners or subscribers to *The People's Messenger*! [*Perches on the edge of the table.*] Oh, my little Katrine, come here – look how beautifully the sun falls in here today! And how blessed I am with all this fresh spring air coming in.

MRS STOCKMANN: Yes, if we could only live on sun and spring air, Tomas.

DR STOCKMANN: Well, you'll have to scrimp and save a bit too – then everything will be fine. *That's* the least of my worries. No, what's worse is *this* – that I don't know of any man noble and free enough to dare take up my task after me.

PETRA: Oh, don't think about that, Father; you've got time. But look, the boys are already back!

EILIF *and* MORTEN *come in from the living room.*

MRS STOCKMANN: Have you been given the day off?

MORTEN: No; but we were fighting with the others at break –

EILIF: That's not true; it was the others fighting us.

MORTEN: Yes, and then Mr Rørlund said it was best we stay at home for a few days.

DR STOCKMANN [*snaps his fingers and jumps up from the table*]: I've got it! I've got it, by God! You are never going to set foot in that school again!

THE BOYS: No more school!

MRS STOCKMANN: But, Tomas –

DR STOCKMANN: Never, I say! I shall educate you myself – that is, you shan't learn a blessed thing –

MORTEN: Hooray!

DR STOCKMANN: – but I shall make you into free and noble men. – Listen, Petra, you'll have to help me with that.

PETRA: Yes, Father, you can rely on it.

DR STOCKMANN: And my school will be held in the room where they harangued me as an enemy of the people. But we must have more boys; I must have at least twelve to begin with.

MRS STOCKMANN: Well, you certainly won't find them here in town.

DR STOCKMANN: We'll see about that. [*To the* BOYS] Don't you know any street urchins – regular guttersnipes –?

MORTEN: Yes, Father, I know lots!

DR STOCKMANN: Well, that's perfect; get hold of a few specimens for me. I'll experiment with the mongrels for once; there are some outstanding brains among them now and then.

MORTEN: But what'll we do once we're free and noble men?

DR STOCKMANN: Then you'll chase every grey-foot wolf into the distant west, boys!

EILIF *looks rather doubtful;* MORTEN *jumps and cries* '*Hurrah!*'

MRS STOCKMANN: Hm, as long as it's not the wolves chasing you, Tomas.

DR STOCKMANN: Are you quite mad, Katrine? *Chase me! Now* – when I am the town's strongest man!

MRS STOCKMANN: The strongest – *now*?

DR STOCKMANN: Yes, and I'd dare go so far as to say that *now* I'm one of strongest men in the whole world.

MORTEN: Really?

DR STOCKMANN [*lowering his voice*]: Shhh! You mustn't tell anyone yet; but I've made a huge discovery.

MRS STOCKMANN: Again?

DR STOCKMANN: Of course, of course! [*Gathers them round him, and talks to them confidingly*] The fact is, you see, that the strongest man in the world is he who stands most alone.

MRS STOCKMANN [*smiling and shaking her head*]: Oh, Tomas, Tomas!

PETRA [*confidently, as she grasps his hands*]: Father!

Acknowledgements

'The strongest man in the world,' Dr Stockmann famously pronounces in *An Enemy of the People*, 'is he who stands most alone.' Those involved in this new Penguin Classics edition of Henrik Ibsen's modern prose plays have, with all due modesty, begged to disagree. This project is very much the result of a collective effort.

Many therefore deserve thanks. The project was initiated by Alexis Kirschbaum, then editor of Penguin Classics. As we moved into first draft stage it was taken over by a new Penguin editor, Jessica Harrison, who has shown patience, flexibility and good cheer all along, as well as being an admirably alert reader.

On behalf of all involved, I would like to extend a special thanks to the Norwegian Ministry of Foreign Affairs. Without their generous support it would have been impossible to stick to our original ambitions. Along the way workshops have twice been hosted by the Norwegian Embassy in London, where I would like to thank Eva Moksnes Vincent and Anne Ulset in particular, and once by the Centre for Ibsen Studies at the University of Oslo, where Frode Helland and Laila Yvonne Henriksen deserve thanks. We are also very grateful to the Faculty of Humanities at the University of Oslo for letting us base this edition on *Henrik Ibsens Skrifter* (*HIS*). It makes this the first English-language edition based on the most comprehensive critical edition of Ibsen available. The extensive critical apparatus which only became available with *HIS* has also been a most valuable resource in our work and in composing our own endnotes.

A special group of expert readers have been invaluable during the many rounds of feedback and revisions: Paul Binding, Colin Burrow, Terence Cave, Janet Garton and Toril Moi. A number of other people have participated in seminars and discussions or offered their help or advice on various points, and I would like to mention Carsten Carlsen, Bart van Es, Frode Helland, Stein Iversen, Christian Janss, Peter D. McDonald, Randi Meyer, Martin Puchner, Anne Rikter-Svendsen,

Bjørn Tysdahl, Marie Wells, Gina Winje and Marianne Wimmer, in addition, of course, to the four translators involved in the project, Deborah Dawkin, Barbara Haveland, Erik Skuggevik and Anne-Marie Stanton-Ife. Many thanks also go to my employer, The Department of Literature, Area Studies and European Languages, University of Oslo, and to the governing body of St Catherine's College, Oxford, and its master, Roger Ainsworth, for hosting me so generously as Christensen Visiting Fellow during the spring of 2013.

A particular debt of gratitude is owed to Professor Terence Cave, who has ended up acting as the main reader and my main support throughout the project. It is difficult to conceive where we would have been without his sensitive readings and stubborn commitment to the cause, the re-creation of Ibsen's storyworld. I would also like to thank Janet Garton for her special investment in this volume, and to extend my warmest thanks to my family, Norunn, Anne Magdalene and Johannes Sakarias Bru Rem, for their patience.

Transferring Ibsen into English has been an exceptionally challenging task, a work that has inspired in us all an even greater respect for this towering artist. For those of us who have acted as readers and re-readers of various versions of these translations, it has also demonstrated how exceptionally difficult the art of translation can be. Finally, I would therefore like to thank the translators, without whom these new texts would not exist, for their stubbornness, persistence and commitment, and, not least, for their competence and gift for mediation.

Tore Rem
Oslo, August 2015

Notes

PILLARS OF THE COMMUNITY

1. *Pillars of the Community*: The Norwegian word 'samfund' can mean both 'society' and 'community', but the meaning in this play is most often clearly closer to the latter. We have therefore chosen to break with the convention of calling this play *The Pillars of Society*.

2. *Consul*: A consul was a local businessman appointed to facilitate a foreign nation's trade interests. In 1877 there were around 210 such consuls in Norway.

3. *Mrs*: The term is 'fru', indicating that the woman in question is married and has a relatively high social standing (belonging to the bourgeoisie or the higher levels of the rural community). The term 'madam' was at this time used for married women from lower social strata.

4. *schoolmaster*: The title 'adjunkt' was used for teachers in the higher level of the education system, equivalent to secondary school and high school.

5. *merchant*: A merchant ('grosserer') in this respect dealt in large quantities of goods, but the term was also used for grocers more generally.

6. *uphold*: The verb ('støtte') used here echoes the plural noun 'støtter' ('pillars') in the play's title. It has often been translated as 'support', but this does not quite convey Aune's serious commitment to, and authority within, his community.

7. *Mr Chief Clerk*: By the late nineteenth century, the title 'herr' was used in connection with all higher offices and with a number of other professions of different social categories. The title did not at that time signal a social distinction.

8. *the Workers' Association*: The establishment of labour societies began in Norway in the 1860s, first with the Kristiania (now

Oslo) Labour Society. These societies were at first of a philan-
thropic bent, but had become more political by the late 1870s.

9. *larger societies and communities*: The word 'samfund' can
mean both 'society' and 'community' (cf. above). Both words
are used in the translation, depending on context.

10. *whited sepulchres*: Cf. Matthew 23:27: 'Woe unto you, scribes
and Pharisees, hypocrites! for ye are like unto whited sepulchres, which indeed appear beautiful outward, but are within
full of dead men's bones, and of all uncleanness.'

11. *tares grow in amongst the wheat here too*: Cf. Matthew
13:24–5: 'The Kingdom of Heaven is likened unto a man which
sowed good seed in his field: But while men slept, his enemy
came and sowed tares among the wheat, and went his way.'

12. *Volunteer Nurses*: Women in charge of the social work in
a Lutheran parish. In a Norwegian context, the title was
relatively new in Norway at this time, with the first institution for the training of 'diakonisser' established in Kristiania in
1868.

13. *railway business*: When Ibsen visited Norway from July to September 1874, several newspapers were running articles on the
planned railway between Kristiania and the area along what is
now the Oslo fjord. There were heated debates about whether
the line ought to run inland or along the coast.

14. *'Woman as Servant to the Community'*: Fictitious title clearly
meant to satirize the conduct literature of the period, prescrib-
ing the role of women in society.

15. *sports and more sports*: The Norwegian term 'idræt' was at
this time often seen in contrast to English 'sport', with the
former having a more utilitarian slant. Traditional Norwegian
sports included skiing, skating, shooting, sailing and rowing,
although German and Swedish gymnastics had also become
popular from the 1850s onwards.

16. *student Tønnesen*: In order to be called 'student', the person in
question would have to have passed the 'examen artium' which
qualified a student for university.

17. *Prodigal Tønnesen*: An allusion to the parable of the prodigal
son, Luke 15:11–32. The Norwegian adjective 'forlorne sønn'
means 'lost' or 'wayward', so the effect is starker here than in
the English. There are several variations on this theme later in
the play. See also *Ghosts*, note 38.

18. *held lectures in public halls*: It was quite uncommon for women
to give lectures at this time. But Aasta Hansteen (1824–1908),

an advocate for women's rights, had criticized the Church's view of women during a Scandinavian lecture tour in 1876, and Ibsen's mother-in-law, the writer Magdalene Thoresen (1819–1903), was the first woman writer in Scandinavia to give readings from her own works (1867).

19. *A Norseman's word*: When the men who had signed the Norwegian constitution in 1814 parted, they gave the promise: 'Enige og troe, indtil Dovre falder!' ('United and loyal, until (the mountain) Dovre falls!'). Here, the phrase indicates more generally that the word of a Norwegian can be trusted.

20. *council*: Norway had introduced a certain level of local administration in so-called communes (municipalities) in 1837. The most important tasks of these entities were the care of paupers and the running of elementary schools.

21. *inland route*: In contemporary debates the inland railway line was primarily supported by farmers and the forestry business and competed with the plans for a line along the coast.

22. *tracts of forest*: Timber, pulp and paper were among Norway's most important export products in the nineteenth century.

23. *family-minded*: The compound 'familjesind' literally means 'family mentality' or 'family spirit', a way of thinking dominated by a sense of loyalty and duty to the family.

24. *telegram*: The first telegraph line in Norway had been established in 1855, and this new communication network had reached the northernmost towns by 1871.

25. *circus troupe*: The word 'beriderselskab' refers more specifically to a travelling circus with horses.

26. *that woman*: The word 'fruentimmer' originally meant 'a woman's room'. By this period it was used as a humorous or pejorative reference to a woman.

27. *co-shipowner*: In the south of Norway shipping was typically organized in partnerships, and many members of the local communities of coastal towns would be part owners of ships.

28. *I'm in my fifties now*: Average age expectancy for men in Norway was forty-eight years in the 1870s, and three years more for women. Only 5 per cent of the population were over sixty-five years during the nineteenth century.

29. *the consul*: Here used as a polite form of address in the third person.

30. *great and good works*: An allusion to Ove Malling's popular patriotic work *Store og gode Handlinger av Danske, Norske og Holstenere* (1777) (*Great and Good Actions of Danes,*

Norwegians and Holsteinians), a series of portraits of exemplary historical figures in the then union of Denmark-Norway.

31. *gas pipe*: Gas was primarily used for lighting. The first Norwegian gas works was established in Kristiania in 1847.

32. *the poor school*: The 'almueskolen' of the original was a type of school for the general populace, traditionally catering for those least well off.

33. *this stuffy air*: The word 'stueluft' (literally 'living room air') is a key concept in Ibsen which comes up again in his penultimate play, *John Gabriel Borkman* (1896). 'Stueluft' stands in opposition to another, more frequently used compound, namely 'friluft' (literally: 'free air' or 'outdoors air').

34. *four hundred kroner*: A timberman working in ship construction might earn two kroner a day around this time.

35. *Mr Consul, sir*: Vigeland uses the polite form 'de' ('you') to Bernick, who is socially above him. He later addresses him as 'Mr Consul', and this therefore seems to be the solution that best captures the polite form of address.

36. *You*: Bernick and Rummel are social equals, and Rummel here uses the informal 'du'.

37. *cane*: The 'spanskrør' of the original was a long, thin cane made from palm wood, used for punishment.

38. *breakfast*: Ibsen uses the word 'frokost' in its Norwegian sense, i.e. 'breakfast', rather than what became Danish usage in the latter half of the nineteenth century, i.e. 'lunch'.

39. *absolute certainty*: The original expression is 'troen i hændene' ('faith in one's hands'), often associated with St Thomas, who doubted Christ's resurrection until he had touched His wounds. A reference to having solid evidence.

40. *My conscience burdened*: The original uses 'ubelastet' here, literally 'unladen' ('jeg må have min samvittighed ubelastet', literally 'I must have my conscience unladen'), and it is only used this once in Ibsen. It implies a conscience without load, but was used more commonly in a financial context meaning 'without debt'. It corresponds simultaneously to Bernick having a free conscience and to his concern that he will not be seen as responsible.

41. *French raid on the Kabyles*: Refers to the French actions in Algeria in the 1840s. The Kabyles are Berbers in northern Algeria.

42. *in this country ... the immigrant families*: Trade in Norway had for centuries been dominated by immigrants and their descendants. Businesspeople were often from Sweden, Germany and Denmark.

43. *dead as a citizen*: The word 'borgerlig' means both 'citizen' and 'bourgeois'. The latter sense, lost here and in the common English rendering 'middle class' in other contexts, resonates throughout the play.

44. *In two months I'll be back*: From 1870 steamships from Norway via Liverpool were the standard way of travelling to America. The total travel time was around two weeks.

45. *freights*: Around 60 per cent of all Norwegian shipping went between third countries. This trade was vulnerable to changes in the international economy and was hard hit by economic slumps in the middle of the 1870s.

46. *illuminations*: Lighting arrangements for feasts of various kinds.

47. *buck up*: The phrase 'mande dig op' literally means 'man yourself up', or 'show some courage'.

48. *You do know*: Rummel and Bernick use the formal second-person pronoun 'de' when addressing Miss Hessel. This polite mode of address was more or less compulsory in bourgeois and higher social milieux at the time.

49. *stuff*: The original has 'malm', meaning 'ore', a word that runs through Ibsen's entire oeuvre and acquires a particularly central function in *John Gabriel Borkman* (1896).

50. *Get away from me*: See Christ's response to Satan in Matthew 4:10: 'Get thee hence, Satan.'

51. *transparency*: Transparent banner or large placard, lit from behind.

52. *citizen of the state*: The term 'statsborger' refers to a person belonging not just to the local community, but the wider community of the state.

53. *true citizen*: Here a distinction is made between the public sphere and the private.

54. *book of family devotions*: A 'huspostille', a Lutheran collection of sermons for the entire year, used for daily homilies.

55. *Old friendship doesn't rust*: A Norwegian saying.

56. *life's work*: The original has the compound 'livsgerning' (literally 'life's doing' or 'life's work'), a more succinct and poetic term which refers to the totality of what one has achieved or will achieve in life. It also has associations with 'calling'.

57. *the spirit of truth, the spirit of freedom*: The concepts of truth and freedom were often activated in political rhetoric in the aftermath of the French Revolution and in connection with other revolutionary movements of the nineteenth century.

A DOLL'S HOUSE

1. *A Doll's House*: Ibsen claimed to have coined the word 'dukke-hjem', which means 'doll home' rather than 'doll's house'. It had in fact already been used in 1851 by his friend Paul Botten-Hansen, for whom it seems to have invoked an unreal and dreamy existence. The standard word was 'dukkehus'.

2. *lawyer*: Two different terms are used in the original here: 'advokat' and 'sagfører'. Helmer is the former, Krogstad the latter. An 'advokat' was at this time used for a barrister with the right to appear before the Norwegian High Court. Krogstad is a 'sagfører', a lawyer of a lower status than Helmer. He has passed the final examination in law, and has the right to appear in cases in both civil and criminal law.

3. *Mrs*: The term is 'fru', indicating that the woman in question is married and has a relatively high social standing (belonging to the bourgeoisie or the higher levels of the rural community). The term 'madam' was at this time used for married women from lower social strata.

4. *maid*: 'Stuepigen' refers to a maid with a particular responsibility for cleaning and keeping tidy the more private areas of the house, but who would also assist with receiving family guests and serving.

5. *comfortably*: The original 'hyggeligt' is a key word in what might be called a Danish and Norwegian cult of domesticity, akin to the German notion of 'Gemütlichkeit'. 'Cosy' and 'comfortable' later in this act are translations of the related words 'hyggelig', 'hygge' and 'hygget seg'.

6. *hallway*: The original has 'forstuen', the first room (after an entrance or the like) you entered in a house or an apartment, from which there was access to the other rooms.

7. *Christmas tree*: This German tradition was introduced in Norway from the middle of the nineteenth century, first in the towns and among the bourgeoisie. The tree was decorated in secret by the parents before the doors to the living room were opened on Christmas Eve.

8. *Half a krone*: In 1875 Norway changed to a decimal system in which one krone equalled 100 øre. To make it immediately clear that Nora is being very generous, for those unfamiliar with Norwegian currency, half a krone is used rather than the fifty 'øre' of the original.

9. *spending-bird*: The original has 'spillefugl', from the German 'Spielvogel', a toy bird; 'spille' means both to play and to waste.

10. *a woman thou art*: In the original the archaic form 'du est' is used to signal a humorous formality.

11. *dress material*: Servants received some of their pay in the form of goods and were often given at least one new piece of clothing for Christmas.

12. *hang the money*: Small home-made paper baskets filled with fruit, sweets and raisins were hung on the Christmas tree and harvested by the children during Christmas.

13. *miraculous*: This is the first instance of the key and recurring word 'vidunderligt' or 'det vidunderlige'. 'Vidunderligt' is a stronger expression than 'wonderful' in modern English. It is something which, according to *Ordbog over det danske sprog* (*Dictionary of the Danish Language*), appears as 'nearly supernatural or unfathomable in its grandeur, excellent qualities or "inexplicability" and which creates an overwhelming impression and thrill. It is above the everyday, the usual, the ordinary, having the character of something unreal, unearthly, fairy-tale-like in its beauty and magnitude.' In order to avoid the excessively religious connotations of 'the miracle', this translation has opted for phrases such as 'the miraculous' and 'the miraculous thing'.

14. *travelling clothes*: During the decade in which the play was written, this would often be a jacket or a paletot, a waisted overcoat. Jackets of sealskin were popular from the mid 1870s.

15. *Department*: The Norwegian word 'departementet' might also be translated as 'ministry', but Helmer's work has been with the civil service and not particularly high-powered or prestigious.

16. *Twelve hundred speciedaler*: Before Norway in 1875 introduced kroner, it had used 'speciedaler'. One speciedaler at this point equalled four kroner.

17. *little school*: Teaching was among the few socially acceptable professions for women of the upper and middle classes. Women from the middle classes might also work in shops and offices.

18. *spa*: The first Norwegian spa was opened in 1837 and was soon followed by others. These were used for treating both physical and mental illness.

19. *your circumstances*: The genitive pronoun 'eders' (plural 'your') is a more formal variant of 'deres'; this distinction is not available in English.

20. *lottery*: Denmark at this time had a state lottery. Lotteries were forbidden by law in Norway, except for charity.

21. *a wife can't borrow without her husband's consent*: Married women were formally without independent legal status and were not allowed to enter into economic transactions on their own, although this was not always adhered to in practice.

22. *solicitor's clerk*: A 'sagførerfuldmægtig' was a person with the right to do certain kinds of business for a lawyer, a subordinate but responsible and respectable position.

23. *telegram*: The first telegraph line in Norway had been established in 1855, and this new communication network had reached the northernmost towns by 1871.

24. *front door*: The word 'porten' may mean gate rather than door.

25. *Do you remember this, Mrs Helmer?*: The original has 'Husker fruen' ('Does the lady remember'). Such use of the third-person form and title communicated politeness, at times also condescension and distance.

26. *atmosphere*: The word 'dunstkreds' in the original specifically refers to air with a bad smell. It is associated with infectious matter, miasma.

27. *Christmas Day*: The most important holy day of the year. Families would traditionally keep to themselves, and not receive or go on visits.

28. *Miss Nora*: Using the first name shows a degree of intimacy, while the use of her title (which is 'fru' ('Mrs') rather than 'frøken' ('Miss') in the original) preserves some formality.

29. *got herself into trouble*: The phrase 'kommen i ulykke' refers even more explicitly to a woman who has been seduced and become pregnant outside of marriage.

30. *Consul*: A consul was a local businessman appointed to facilitate a foreign nation's trade interests. In 1877 there were 210 such consuls in Norway.

31. *Neapolitan fisher-girl*: Motif used in nineteenth-century genre painting.

32. *tarantella*: The most famous of all Italian folk dances, dating back to medieval times. The Danish author and scientist Vilhelm Bergsøe, who became Ibsen's friend during his first stay in Italy in 1864–8, described the tarantella as a popular folk tradition and noted the belief that the dancer was in a state of possession.

33. *consumption of the spine*: Rare neurological form of tertiary syphilis. In contemporary scientific belief the last phase of this degenerative illness was thought to include an attack on inner

organs, including the marrow. This might lead to paralysis, heart failure and madness. The patient might be symptom-free for long periods between the various phases of the illness.

34. *elfin-girl*: In ancient Norse tradition elves were considered dangerous creatures. Ibsen here seems to build on a Romantic view, also associated with Shakespeare, where elves are more friendly, attractive and gracious. They are generally shy, but may appear in moonlight.

35. *first-name terms*: By saying 'vi er dus' Helmer here notes a breach of etiquette. Polite society required that one would only use the intimate 'du' ('you') to people one would address by first name, generally only the close family. Two people who knew each other well might in rare cases use 'du' and first names even in more official settings. With others present, with whom the parties were not on intimate terms, it was customary to switch to the polite form 'de'.

36. *Let whatever comes come*: An allusion to two hymns in the Lutheran hymn book, one of them by Martin Luther.

37. *abominable process of destruction*: A biblical expression, 'ødelæggelsens vederstyggelighed', in the original. See, e.g., Matthew 24:15: 'When ye therefore shall see the abomination of desolation . . .'

38. *poor innocent spine*: A reference to the contemporary idea that syphilis was an inherited disease, transferable from father to son.

39. *higher up*: Etiquette required that no woman showed her legs above the ankle. For a woman to show the upper part of her stocking to a man other than her husband was a daring act.

40. *guide or instruct*: The single word 'vejlede' means both 'instruct' and 'guide'.

41. *back stairs*: These were used by the servants and for deliveries.

42. *the most terrible thing*: The original's 'det forfærdelige' (repeated in Act Three) is an instance of an adjective used with the definite article but no following noun, a stylistic possibility in Norwegian employed by Ibsen to denote a central idea, communicating a certain indeterminacy or enigmatic quality. Other instances of the same in this play include, most centrally, 'det vidunderlige' ('the miraculous thing').

43. *black cloak*: The 'domino' was originally a piece of winter clothing which only reached down over part of the chest and back, used by clerics. It was later commonly used for masquerades, by both men and women.

44. *I'd have liked to –*: A respectable woman would generally be accompanied home.

45. *past our door*: Biblical allusion. See Exodus 12:23: 'the Lord will pass over the door.'

46. *child of joy and good fortune*: The original has the poetic compound 'lykkebarn', literally 'luck child' or 'good fortune child'. Helmer later berates Nora by calling her 'Du ulyksalige', 'You unfortunate [one]'.

47. *cap of invisibility*: It was a common folk belief that the subterranean creatures could make themselves invisible by putting on a piece of clothing.

48. *borne in my arms*: Biblical allusion. See Matthew 4:6: 'He shall give his angels charge concerning thee: and in their hands they shall bear thee up, lest at any time thou dash thy foot against a stone.'

49. *Give it to me*: Helmer insists on his legal right to read his wife's letters.

50. *I'll guide and instruct you*: According to the Danish theologian Erik Pontoppidan's explanation of Luther's Small Cathecism, a married man ought to 'faithfully love, honour, direct, govern and provide for' his wife. The original repeats the word 'vejlede', cf. above, but here also uses 'råde', 'give advice'.

51. *your religion*: Here the Evangelical-Lutheran form of Christianity.

52. *he is freed according to the law from all obligations towards her*: Divorce was only possible on grounds of adultery, desertion or impotence. The 'guilty party' would lose his or her rights to common property and parental influence and would be barred from remarrying.

GHOSTS

1. *Ghosts*: The Norwegian title, 'Gengangere', literally means 'something that or someone who walks again'. There are rare examples of it being used in contemporary scientific discussions of inherited syphilis.

2. *Family Drama*: Ibsen's chosen term was not an established sub-category of drama.

3. *Mrs*: The term is 'fru', indicating that the woman in question is married and has a relatively high social standing (belonging to the bourgeoisie or the higher levels of the rural community).

The term 'madam' was at this time used for married women from lower social strata.

4. *chamberlain*: A title which could be a mere honorary title granted by a royal person, as in this case. It was not as exclusive as, for example, the title of the British Lord Chamberlain, and Mr Alving did not serve at court.

5. *in the service*: The phrase 'i huset' ('in the house') can simply mean that one is a member of the household, but can also refer to employment as a servant.

6. *the left*: Ibsen always pictures the stage from the perspective of the audience.

7. *idiot*: The original has 'menneske', literally 'person' or 'man' (in the generic sense). Here the word is used pejoratively.

8. *we are but frail*: Biblical allusion. See Romans 6:19: 'the infirmity of your flesh'. Engstrand, who has just been called 'menneske', here again uses this word (including himself and all 'mennesker' among those who are frail).

9. *steamship*: The coastal steamer afforded the easiest connection between places along the fjords and other parts of the country.

10. *damned*: The original has 'fan'', a coarse form of the more acceptable 'fanden' (the devil). Norwegian swear words are on the whole of a religious kind. It is hard to find English equivalents that are strong enough without being sexual or appearing anachronistic. See A Note on the Translation.

11. *What the hell's*: See note 10 above.

12. *Fi donc*: French interjection communicating contempt.

13. *Pied de mouton*: Literally 'sheep's foot', a cloven foot.

14. *I'll bleedin' well*: See note 10 above.

15. *God-awful*: See note 10 above.

16. *wayfaring mariners*: An example of Engstrand's tendency to mimic a higher or more archaic style, with internal inconsistencies as a result (in the original Engstrand uses the vulgar plural form of seamen, 'sjømænder' instead of the formally correct 'sjømænd').

17. *seven or eight hundred kroner*: A little above the annual salary for a labourer.

18. *bleedin'*: See note 10 above.

19. *savoir vivre*: French for the art of living, knowing how to live life to the full.

20. *three hundred speciedaler*: Before Norway in 1875 introduced kroner, it had used 'speciedaler'. One speciedaler at this point equalled four kroner.

21. *church register*: The parish registers functioned as the only public registers at this time.

22. *Miss*: The word 'jomfru' used in the original refers to a young, unmarried woman. A somewhat dated, conservative usage in the second half of the nineteenth century, when the word had for the most part been superseded by 'frøken' (Miss). 'Jomfru' means both 'maiden' and 'virgin'. In Ibsen's modern prose dramas the word only appears in one other place, when Hedvig in *The Wild Duck* (1884) describes a picture of Death and a maiden from *Harrison's History of London*.

23. *farmer*: The original 'Landman' literally means 'countryman', as opposed to 'city folk'.

24. *hallway*: The original has 'forstuen', the first room (after an entrance or the like) you entered in a house or apartment, from which there was access to the other rooms.

25. *hot chocolate*: A conventional drink among the bourgeoisie, later replaced by coffee.

26. *Is the pastor sitting comfortably?*: Use of the the third-person form of address indicates distance, as in 'would the gentleman like . . . ?'

27. *guiding hand*: A common religious phrase. An allusion to God's guidance, or to Providence more generally.

28. *intellectual trends*: The word 'åndelige' includes the meanings of both 'spiritual' and 'intellectual'.

29. *Solvik*: The name literally means 'Sunny bay'. Older farms with 'Sol' as a prefix in their name would often be found in sunny spots, on the more attractive, sunny side of the valley.

30. *estate*: Aristocracy in Norway had been formally abolished in 1821. The term 'herregården' generally referred to a large farm with a certain history of having played a significant social, economic and cultural role in the area.

31. *higher purpose*: The original has the more succinct compound 'livsopgave', literally 'life task' or 'task in life', again with a more poetic ring and connotations of a noble calling.

32. *my colleague's*: Probably a reference to an evangelical revivalist clergyman. The evangelical movement stressed individual conversion and repentance, and opposed a more rationalist, liberal theology.

33. *Divine Providence*: The demand that one trust God's guidance is clearly expressed in the Danish theologian Erik Pontoppidan's authoritative explanations of Martin Luther's Small Catechism.

34. *social burden*: The compound noun 'fattigbyrder' used here means more literally 'the burden of (taking care of) the poor'. The care of the poor had been the responsibility of local government since the Poor Law of 1845 and would make up around 30–40 per cent of total communal expenditure around this time. Taxes would be paid according to land ownership, wealth and income.

35. *cause offence*: A biblical allusion. See 1 Corinthians 10:32: 'Give none offence, neither to the Jews, nor to the Gentiles, nor to the church of God.'

36. *all manner of things to wrestle with*: The original uses the word 'anfægtelser', which means temptations or strong religious doubts, but here more specifically refers to the mental state of having to wrestle with these temptations or doubts.

37. *office*: Homes had offices where business was conducted, and this was usually the sole preserve of men; cf. Torvald Helmer's office in *A Doll's House*. Here, Mrs Alving is associated with the office, but never Chamberlain Alving.

38. *Prodigal Son*: An allusion to the parable of the prodigal son, Luke 15:11–32. The Norwegian adjective 'forlorne' means 'lost' or 'wayward', so the effect is starker here than in the English 'prodigal'. See also *Pillars of the Community*, note 17.

39. *first name*: This use of a person's first name indicates a high degree of intimacy and close acquaintance. As the older of the two, it is Manders's prerogative to suggest the mode of address. This choice communicates both his close relationship to the family (especially Mrs Alving) and his superior position.

40. *inward man*: Biblical allusion. See, e.g., Romans 7:22–3: 'For I delight in the law of God after the inward man: But I see another law in my members, warring against the law of my mind, and bringing me into captivity to the law of sin which is in my members.'

41. *private room*: The word 'kammeret' refers to a smaller, private room. Chamberlain Alving seems to have spent time alone here rather than in the office.

42. *the joys of life*: The original has the compound 'livsglad', literally 'happy in life' or 'enjoying life'. It is the first glimpse in the play of the central concern with Osvald's 'livsglæde', translated as 'joy of life', and his 'arbejdsglæden', the 'joy of work'.

43. *paternal home*: The original uses the word 'fædrenehjemmet', meaning 'home of the father', rather than the more common 'familjehjemmet', 'family home'.

44. *get married*: Women of the upper and middle classes were generally not supposed to take on paid work, but to be provided for by their husbands. Men were therefore unable to marry before they could provide for their families.

45. *unlawful relationships*: During this time, a law of 1842 forbidding cohabitation was still in force. It stated that extramarital sex could be punished with imprisonment or fines.

46. *wild marriages*: The phrase Ibsen uses here, 'såkaldte vilde ægteskaber' (literally 'so-called wild marriages'), is a reference to a relationship based on free love. Ibsen has probably borrowed the expression from the German.

47. *life of freedom*: The original has the more poetic compound 'frihedsliv', literally 'freedom life'.

48. *my husband*: In the original Mrs Alving refers to her husband by his surname, which was common practice when a wife spoke about her husband to people from outside the family circle.

49. *But a wife is not entitled to stand as judge over her husband*: See Ephesians 5:22–3: 'Wives, submit yourselves unto your own husbands, as unto the Lord. For the husband is the head of the wife, even as Christ is the head of the church: and he is the saviour of the body.'

50. *Helene*: When Pastor Manders here switches to her first name, he discloses that the two have or have had a more intimate relationship. Elsewhere, he addresses her as 'Mrs Alving'. See above, note 39.

51. *government almanac*: An annual publication containing the most important information on state institutions and affairs.

52. *three hundred speciedaler*: A very large sum for a servant. Johanne seems to have been paid around four times the standard annual salary for a servant.

53. *fallen man*: The expression 'falden mand', 'fallen man' (with reference to gender rather than the generic 'menneske'), is a neologism in Dano-Norwegian, mimicking the conventional reference to 'falden kvinde', 'fallen woman'.

54. *consulted*: A reference to the customs of engagement and marriage. See King Christian V's Norwegian Law of 1687 in which a man desiring to be married should ask the woman's parents or guardians for her hand, but with her consent.

55. *depraved*: The word 'forfaldent' literally means 'decrepit', 'ruined', 'decayed', with associations of 'fallen'.

56. *a child should love and honour his mother and father*: The Fourth Commandment. See Exodus 20:1–17.

57. *dead doctrines*: The word 'tro', translated as 'doctrines' here, also means 'faith', 'belief'.

58. *frightened of the light*: The compound word 'lysrædde' literally means 'light-fearful' or 'afraid of the light'.

59. *wailing*: The expression 'grædendes tårer' is common in the comedies of Ludvig Holberg (1684–1754). Here Engstrand adds an ungrammatical 's', displaying his working-class register.

60. *gnashing of teeth*: The expression 'tænders gnidsel' is used several times in Matthew with reference to eternal damnation.

61. *the wages of sin*: See Romans 6:23: 'For the wages of sin is death.'

62. *'vermoulu'*: 'État vermoulu' is a French expression meaning 'worm-eaten' and was at that time used of patients with syphilis.

63. *the sins of the fathers are visited upon the children*: An Old Testament notion. See Exodus 20:5: 'for I the Lord thy God am a jealous God, visiting the iniquity of the fathers upon the children unto the third and fourth generation of them that hate me.'

64. *eagerly*: The original has the compound 'livfuldt', literally 'life full' or 'full of life'.

65. *light and sunshine*: A reference to French impressionism, known in Norway from around 1870. It may possibly also allude to the group of Scandinavian painters associated with Skagen in northern Denmark in the 1870s and '80s, 'the Skagen painters'.

66. *parish*: The original's 'landsognet' was a rural district belonging to a market town, but constituting an independent commune or municipality.

67. *gold-feathered nest*: The phrase 'leve som guld i et æg' literally means 'live like gold in an egg', a twist on the Norwegian idiom 'live like the yolk in an egg', i.e., being in the best place possible.

68. *Why are you so formal with me*: Polite conventions meant that one could not use the informal 'du' without being on first-name terms with someone. Here the expression 'Hvorfor kan du ikke sige du til mig?' of the original means 'Why can't you (the informal 'du') say you (the informal 'du') to me?' By now choosing the informal 'du' in addressing her, and asking her to use the same mode of address, he is challenging the norms of the servant–master relationship.

69. *sunny Sunday*: The word is 'søndagsvejr', literally 'Sunday weather'. Cf. the note on impressionism above.

70. *civil service appointment*: A state office to which one formally had to be appointed by the king.

71. *I suppose I can say Osvald now*: Since Regine is Osvald's half-sister, and now knows it, she seems to mean that they are equals and that she is in a position where she can suggest that they change their mode of address.

72. *end up with nothing*: The expression 'stå på bar bakke' literally means to 'stand on bare ground', meaning being without the means to provide for oneself. Regine is not in command of the idiom, adding an indefinite article ('en bar bakke').

73. *inherited*: One's 'arvelod' refers to the totality of one's inheritance. Cf. also the contemporary scientific theories that considered syphilis an inheritable disease, transferable from father to son.

74. *lodged in here*: Osvald hints at the fact that the illness has now attacked his brain. This would belong to the symptoms that were associated with the tertiary and terminal phase of syphilis.

75. *I had one attack down there*: One of the leading contemporary medical authorities on syphilis, Alfred Fournier, noted that a patient who had survived a first attack would often not be able to cope with a second or third attack.

AN ENEMY OF THE PEOPLE

1. *Enemy of the People*: The word 'folkefiende' had in rare instances been used in Swedish and Danish before this, in the sense of 'enemy of democracy'. There are no recorded earlier uses of it in Norwegian. Ibsen had been characterized as an 'enemy of society' ('samfundets fiende') in a debate in the Norwegian parliament in 1882.

2. *Play*: Ibsen had long wavered between calling *An Enemy of the People* 'lystspil' (a kind of light comedy) or 'skuespil' (play), but finally decided on the latter.

3. *medical officer*: 'Badelæge', i.e. a doctor employed at a spa.

4. *Mrs*: The term 'fru' indicates that the woman in question is married and has a relatively high social standing (belonging to the bourgeoisie or the higher levels of the rural community). The term 'madam' was at this time used for married women from lower social strata.

5. *teacher*: The title, 'lærerinde', is gender specific in the original, referring to a female teacher. From the middle of the century women gradually became more accepted as teachers in state

elementary schools. It became one of the few professions available to unmarried women of the bourgeoise.

6. *Eilif*: The spelling has been changed from 'Ejlif' to 'Eilif' in order to facilitate pronunciation ('ej' is the old Dano-Norwegian way of spelling the diphthong 'ei').

7. *mayor of the town and local police chief*: The 'byfogd' (here 'mayor') was a local judge and in charge of the lowest court in the towns. In smaller towns the same person would at that time fill the roles of head of police and administrative head of the court.

8. *People's Messenger*: The name *'Folkebudet'*, literally *'The Folk Messenger'*, is reminiscent of a number of democratically inclined newspapers of the time, many of which had the prefix 'Folk'.

9. *various classes and occupations*: The terms classes ('klasser') and standing (the plural form 'stænder' meant social standing or occupational status) were roughly synonymous in nineteenth-century Norway, but the latter, somewhat more general categorization was the more frequent.

10. *table covering*: Not a table cloth for the dining table, but a heavier cloth ('bordtæppe') often richly decorated with embroidery.

11. *Mr Billing*: The title 'herr' was by this time used in connection with all higher offices and with a number of other professions of different social categories. At this time the title did not signal social distinctions.

12. *public spirit*: The original uses the word 'borgerånd', literally 'a spirit of citizenship', meaning a commitment and loyalty to the state and to society more generally.

13. *poor rates*: The overall costs for taking care of the poor went up in the 1870s, but not in terms of the share of communal expenses.

14. *up north*: The expression 'nordpå' ('in the north') refers to northern Norway, today the provinces of Nordland, Troms and Finnmark.

15. *district governor*: The 'amtmand' was the highest-ranked civil servant in the local regions, the counties. In 1866 Norway was divided into twenty counties.

16. *a top senior official*: The 'amtmand' (see previous note) and the bishop were the highest authorities in a county.

17. *the individual*: Loyalty towards authority was often motivated by the Fourth Commandment, to 'honour thy father and thy mother', and elaborated on in various Lutheran cathechisms.

18. *the community*: The original 'samfundet' means both 'society' and 'community'. See *Pillars of the Community*, note 1.

19. *toddy heater*: The word 'kogemaskine' literally means 'boiling machine'; it was a metal container which could be used for heating water.

20. *arrack*: Alcoholic beverage based on rice and palm juice, originally Indian.

21. *smoking-cap*: The 'kalot' was a form of headgear used by men, not least balding men.

22. *English story*: Newspapers would often publish serial stories at the bottom of the page, either as mere entertainment or (commonly) for their moral or didactic content. Many of these stories would be translated from English.

23. *Mølledalen*: The name literally means 'Mill Valley'.

24. *the devil take me*: The original has 'fan'', a coarse form of the more acceptable 'fanden' (the devil). Norwegian swear words are on the whole of a religious kind. It is hard to find English equivalents that are strong enough without being sexual or appearing anachronistic

25. *Hounded me*: Kiil is playing on words; 'hundsvoterte mig' literally means 'hound-voted me out', i.e. that he was voted out like a dog. The noun 'hundsvott' is a rare and strongly pejorative term, literally the genitalia of a female dog.

26. *council*: A certain local autonomy had been established in 1837, in the form of an executive committee, 'formandskabet'. The representatives were elected by those who had the right to vote in parliamentary elections; men without property and women were excluded.

27. *fifty kroner*: The monthly salary for a labourer was around fifty kroner at this time.

28. *damn well*: See note 24 above.

29. *bureaucrats*: The members of the civil service ('embedsmænd') dominated local government. The local pastor would typically often also hold the position of mayor, particularly in rural districts.

30. *solid majority*: The expression 'kompakt majoritet' is here used for the first time in Dano-Norwegian, indicating a large and unchanging majority.

31. *citizen*: The term used here is 'statsborger' (literally 'citizen of the state').

32. *Homeowners' Association*: Home ownership was the minimal requirement for the right to vote.

33. *Temperance Society*: The first Norwegian temperance society had been founded in 1845, and was followed by a number of societies for teetotallers, the first of which was established in 1859, after which the temperance movement lost support.

34. *But no man can be denied his prudent and frank expression of opinion as a citizen*: An allusion to the Norwegian Constitution's section 100, securing the freedom of expression ('frimodige ytringer').

35. *regional engineer*: With the growth in communal responsibilities from the middle of the nineteenth century, a town engineer ('stadsingeniør') would often be part of a professionalized local administration.

36. *boardroom secret*: In a couple of instances there seems to be this confusion of the responsibilities of the management and the board.

37. *war to the knife*: Originally a rallying cry ('War to the knife and knife to the hilt') related to the issue of slavery. It first seems to have appeared in the Kansas *Atchison Squatter Sovereign* (*c.* 1854).

38. *human rights*: The idea of the individual's inalienable rights had been formulated in the American Declaration of Independence in 1776 and in the French Declaration of the Rights of Man and of the Citizen in 1789. The term 'menneskerettigheder', literally 'human rights', appears anachronistic in English.

39. *dynamite*: Dynamite had been invented by the Swede Alfred Nobel in 1863.

40. *education of the people*: Probably a reference to the function of local government as a kind of education into citizenship ('borgeropdragelse').

41. *magistrate*: The state representative in the towns. This could be an individual or made up of a small board.

42. *supernatural power*: 'Styrelse' more specifically refers to a belief in Divine Providence.

43. *your honour*: The use of title 'byfogden' ('the mayor') in the original here indicates a polite address in the third person, in the place of the formal pronoun 'de' (you).

44. *municipal loan*: The rural communes were on the whole cautious about taking up mortgages in this period.

45. *subscription list*: A promise of money. The signatories committed themselves to giving a loan or providing some other form of economic transaction.

46. *swagger stick*: A short stick traditionally used by the commanding officer as a sign of status. Here used in jest to refer to the mayor's walking stick.

47. *lion*: Norway's official heraldic emblem, a lion with a crown and a battle-axe. Here a symbolic reference to the people rising up ('vågnende folkeløve' literally means 'awakening lion of the people').

48. *middle class*: The original is 'borgerskapet', meaning the 'bourgeoisie' but also 'the citizens', and a series of connected words.

49. *every status*: The original has the words 'alle stænder', cf. 'stand' versus 'klasse', note 9 above.

50. *the Club*: A number of exclusive societies ('borgerklubben', literally 'the club of the bourgeoisie' or 'of the citizens') with similar names had been founded in the late eighteenth and early nineteenth centuries. These had been losing influence from the 1840s onwards, however.

51. *Silence*: The original has 'Silentium', a Latin expression used conventionally in meetings to command silence.

52. *I am a taxpayer*: Tax liability was based on land ownership in the rural districts and on income and wealth in the towns.

53. *common folk*: 'Almue' referred both to a large crowd and, more generally, to the great masses of the people, often used in a pejorative way of speaking about the uncultivated and uneducated.

54. *eider*: A large duck found all along the Norwegian coast, but especially in the north.

55. *timberman*: 'Lasthandler' more specifically refers to a timber trader.

56. *Methuselahs*: According to Genesis 5:21–7, Methuselah is said to have died at the age of 969.

57. *freethinker*: Originally a seventeenth-century concept referring to someone whose thinking ran counter to religious orthodoxy.

58. *the poodle's cranium has developed quite differently from that of the mongrel*: Ibsen was familiar with Charles Darwin's theory of evolution. *On the Origin of Species* had first appeared in Danish translation in 1872.

59. *inherited lie*: A 'folkeløgn' (literally 'people's lie') is a lie which has been taken up by the people at large.

60. *an enemy of the people*: In Shakespeare's *Coriolanus*, which Ibsen may have drawn on here, the protagonist is sentenced 'as enemy to the people and his country' (III.iii).

61. *Mr Vik*: Ibsen's stage direction first only calls him 'a fat man'.

62. *shakes the dust from his feet*: An allusion to Christ's admonition to his disciples in Matthew 10:14: 'And whosoever shall not receive you, nor hear your words, when ye depart out of that house or city, shake off the dust of your feet.'

63. *'I forgive you, for you know not what you do'*: An allusion to Christ's words during the Crucifixion. See Luke 23:34: 'Then said Jesus, Father, forgive them; for they know not what they do.'

64. *free-minded*: In this instance the Norwegian 'frisindede' is translated literally, as 'free-minded', in order to retain the more general sense of the term. The usual translation, 'freethinking', is problematic because of its political connotations. The political party 'Det frisindede Venstre' ('The free-minded Left') was liberal. In the rest of the translation 'frisindet' has generally been translated as 'liberal' and 'liberal-minded'.

65. *house owner*: The original uses 'husfader', literally 'father of the house'.

66. *Father-in-law*: The polite address was commonly used towards the elderly, even within the family. Dr Stockmann here uses the formal 'De' (you).

67. *if only I understood the local conditions*: Aslaksen also appears in an earlier play by Ibsen, *The League of Youth* (1869), as a comic drunkard, where he has a catchphrase, 'de lokale forhold' ('the local conditions'), with the last line of that play being 'it depends on the local conditions'. The reprise of the catchphrase here is clearly intended as a comic touch for contemporary theatre-goers.

68. *I shall hurl my inkwell straight at their skulls*: An allusion to the story of Luther throwing his inkpot at the devil.

THE MASTER BUILDER AND OTHER PLAYS
HENRIK IBSEN

The Master Builder / Little Eyolf / John Gabriel Borkman / When We Dead Awaken

'I couldn't believe there was a master builder in all the world who could build such an enormously high tower. And then the fact that you were standing up there yourself, at the very top! In person! And that you weren't the slightest bit dizzy. That was the most - kind of - dizzying thought of all'

Ibsen's last four plays were sensational bestsellers, performed in theatres across Europe. These final works, exploring sexuality and death, the conflict between generations, the drive for creativity and the frailty of the body, cemented Ibsen's dramatic reputation, and continue to fuel debate today on whether they celebrate freedom and love or are instead savagely ironic studies of our shared human flaws. This new translation, the first to be based on the latest critical edition of Ibsen's works, offers the best version available in English.

A new translation by Barbara Haveland and Anne-Marie Stanton-Ife
With an introduction by Toril Moi
General Editor Tore Rem